Still Waters

FORTHCOMING IN THE SANDHAMN MURDERS SERIES

Closed Circles

VIVECA STEN

STILL WATERS

TRANSLATED BY MARLAINE DELARGY

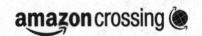

amazon crossing

This is a work of fiction. Names, characters, organizations, places, events, and incidents are either products of the author's imagination or are used fictitiously.

Previously published as *I de lugnaste vatten* by Forum in Sweden in 2008. Translated from Swedish by Marlaine Delargy. First published in English by AmazonCrossing in 2015.

Published by AmazonCrossing, Seattle

www.apub.com

ISBN-13: 9781503945708

ISBN-10: 1503945707

Cover design by Kimberly Glyder

Printed in the United States of America

For my brave mother

Prologue

Everything was completely still and peaceful as only winter can be, when the archipelago belongs to those who live there, and the raucous summer visitors have not yet taken over the islands.

The water was dark and shining, the cold of winter lying heavily on the surface. Odd patches of snow rested on the rocks. A few mergansers stood out like dots against the sky, and the sun was low on the horizon.

"Help me," he yelled. "Help me, for God's sake!"

Someone threw a tangle of rope out to him, and he rushed to loop it around his body in the ice-cold water.

"Pull me up," he said, panting as he grasped the side of the boat with fingers that had already begun to stiffen from the cold.

When the anchor attached to the rope was thrown over the rail, he seemed more confused than anything, as if he didn't understand that its weight would soon drag him to the bottom.

That he only had a few seconds left to live before his body followed the heavy lump of iron.

His hand breaking the surface of the water, tangled in the abandoned fishing net, was the last visible thing. The waters closed over it with an almost imperceptible sigh.

Then there was only the sound of the engine, as the boat turned to make its way back to the harbor.

MONDAY,
THE FIRST WEEK

Chapter 1

"Here, Pixie! Come here!"

The man gazed irritably at the dachshund as she ran down the beach; she had been cooped up on the boat for several days. He really should have kept her on the leash. Dogs were not allowed to run loose in the summer on Sandhamn, a small island in the Stockholm archipelago, but he didn't have the heart to observe the rule when the little dog was so happy to run free.

Besides, there was hardly anybody in sight so early in the morning. Those living in the few houses along the shoreline had hardly woken up. The only sound came from the screaming gulls. The air was fresh and clear, the overnight rain had given everything a newly washed feel, and the sun was already warm, promising another glorious day.

The sand was tightly packed and pleasant to walk on. The low-growing pines gave way to ryegrass and wormwood, mixed with clusters of yellow flowers. Tangled heaps of seaweed had washed up at the water's edge, and over toward Falkenskär a single yacht could be seen traveling east.

Where had that damn dog gone?

He followed her barking. Pixie was yapping, her little tail wagging from side to side. She was standing by a rock sniffing at something, but he couldn't see what it was. He went over to have a look, noticing an unpleasant smell. As he got closer it turned into a sour, suffocating miasma.

On the ground lay something that looked like a bundle of old rags.

He bent down to shoo the dog away and realized it was an old fishing net full of seaweed. Suddenly he understood what he was seeing.

The fishing net ended in two bare feet, both of which were missing several toes. Only bones protruded from what was left of the shriveled, greenish skin.

Before he could stop himself, his stomach turned inside out. A surge of pink vomit poured out and splashed his shoes.

When he was able to stand upright again, he used a little seawater to sluice out his mouth. Then he got out his cell phone and called the police.

Chapter 2

Inspector Thomas Andreasson was really looking forward to his vacation—four weeks in his summer cottage on the island of Harö in the Stockholm archipelago. Morning dips in the sea. Paddling his kayak. Barbecues. Trips to Sandhamn to visit his godson.

Thomas liked to take his vacations late in the year; the water was warmer, and the weather was usually better. But right now, just after midsummer, it was difficult not to long for an escape from the city, to be out among the islands.

Ever since he had started working with the violent crime unit in Nacka Municipality the previous year, he'd had his hands full. There was an enormous amount to learn, despite the fact that he had been on the police force for fourteen years, the last eight with the maritime police.

During that time, he had sailed most of the boats used by the maritime police, from the CB90 to Skerfe boats and RIBs. He knew the archipelago like the back of his hand. He knew exactly where the unmarked reefs were and which shallows were particularly dangerous at low tide.

As a maritime police officer he had seen a great deal and heard many fantastic explanations as to why certain individuals sailed their boats as they did, especially when it came to owners who'd had too much to drink.

He'd handled everything from stolen boats and vandalism to lost foreigners and runaway teenagers. The local population used to complain that people were fishing illegally in private waters. There wasn't much the maritime police could do about that, other than turn a blind eye when the owner of the waters took the intruders' nets and kept them as compensation.

On the whole he had been very happy with his job, and if it hadn't been for the fact that little Emily was on the way, he would have probably never considered applying for a post in the city.

Afterward, when it had all been for nothing, he hadn't had the strength to move. He had barely managed to live through each day.

But life on the police force in Nacka was intense and fast-paced, and he found himself surprisingly at home, even if he sometimes—particularly during the summer—found himself longing for the freedom of island life.

Margit Grankvist, his colleague and a considerably more experienced officer, peeked her head into the office and interrupted his thoughts.

"Thomas, come and see the old man with me. They've found a body on Sandhamn."

Thomas looked up.

The old man was the head of criminal investigation in Nacka, Detective Chief Inspector Göran Persson. He shared the prime minister's name, a fact he didn't appreciate in the slightest. He was quick to point out that his political views did not correspond with those of the prime minister. He was not, however, prepared to expound on those views. He had a somewhat portly figure, similar to that of the prime minister, and displayed a distinct lack of enthusiasm for all the comparisons.

He was an old-school officer, a man of few words, but he created a good atmosphere and was valued by his colleagues. He was conscientious and knowledgeable, and had a great deal of experience.

When Thomas walked into Persson's office, Margit was already sitting there with her ever-present cup of coffee. The department's coffeemaker produced a liquid that was positively toxic. How Margit could knock it back in such quantities was a mystery. Thomas had switched to drinking tea for the first time in his life because of it.

"The dead body of a male has been found on the northwest beach on Sandhamn," said Persson. "Evidently the body is in bad shape; it's been in the water for quite some time."

Margit made a note on her pad before looking up. "Who found it?"

"Some poor sailor. Apparently he's really shaken up. It wasn't a pretty sight. He contacted us about an hour ago, just before seven this morning. He was out walking his dog when he stumbled across the body."

"Any suspicion of murder?" asked Thomas, taking out his own notebook. "Any signs of abuse or violence?"

"Too early to say. Apparently the body was entangled in some kind of fishing net. Anyway, the maritime police are on their way to investigate, and they've organized transport to bring the body in."

Persson looked at Thomas. "I seem to remember. Do you still have that house on Harö? That's next to Sandhamn, isn't it?"

Thomas nodded. "It takes about ten to fifteen minutes to travel between the islands."

"Excellent. Local knowledge. I'd like you to go over to Sandhamn and take a look, maybe say hello to your old colleagues."

A cunning smile played on the DCI's lips.

"Is there any indication we should be opening a murder investigation?" asked Thomas, glancing at his boss.

"For the time being it's being treated as an unexplained death. If it turns into a murder investigation, Margit will lead it, but for now I think you can take care of it."

"Suits me," said Margit. "I'm up to here with all the reports that have to be in before my vacation. You carry on!" She nodded for emphasis. It was obvious that the countdown to the holidays had begun. Just a few more days of paperwork, then freedom beckoned in the form of a rented cottage on the west coast and four weeks with her family.

Persson looked at the clock. "I've been in touch with the police helicopter. They're still in town, so they can pick you and the technicians up in twenty minutes. You just need to get to the helipad at Slussen. You can get a lift back with the maritime police. Or take the Waxholmsbolaget ferry," he said with a grin.

"Fine by me," said Thomas. "You're welcome to talk me into a helicopter ride any day."

Persson got to his feet, indicating the briefing was over. "That's settled, then. Come and see me when you get back so I can get a status report." He stopped in the doorway, scratching his chin. "Play things down a bit out there, Thomas. It's the height of tourist season. We don't want a load of hysterical visitors and journalists getting ideas. You know what the tabloids are like. They'd love to swap their tired old summer standby of sex tips for speculation about a murder in the archipelago."

Margit gave Thomas an encouraging smile.

"You'll do a great job. Give me a call if you have any questions. And remember not to come to any conclusions until forensics have had their say."

Thomas pulled on the leather jacket he always wore, irrespective of the weather.

"Do you think the helicopter could drop me off on Harö when we're done?" he asked in passing on his way out.

"Of course. If the official government plane could fly Thomas Bodström to Greece for his summer holiday, I'm sure the Stockholm Police can fly Thomas Andreasson out to his summer cottage."

The *DCI* grinned at his own wit.

Margit shook her head but couldn't help smiling. "Talk later. Say hello to the islands for me."

She waved good-bye.

Chapter 3

"Hello."

Nora Linde automatically answered her cell phone before realizing it was the phone alarm sounding, not the phone ringing. Nora stretched. She turned over and looked at her husband lying in bed next to her.

Henrik was breathing peacefully, like a child. Nora envied his ability to sleep undisturbed through absolutely anything. The only thing that woke him was his hospital pager—when it went off, he was wide awake in a second.

He still looked almost the same as when they'd gotten married nearly ten years ago. Dark-brown hair, muscular abs and biceps from years of competitive sailing, sensitive doctor's hands with long, beautiful fingers. Nora didn't begrudge Henrik his stylish profile with its elegant, almost classical Greek nose. On the other hand, she thought it was wasted on a man. At least that's what she used to say to cheer herself up, because her own nose was far too short and stubby for her taste. A few strands of gray were visible in Henrik's dark hair, a reminder that he had recently turned thirty-seven, just as she had.

Her cell phone buzzed again.

Nora sighed. Getting up at a quarter to eight Monday through Friday wasn't her idea of a vacation, but if you had children on an island like Sandhamn, those children attended swimming lessons at the times available.

With a yawn she pulled on her robe and walked into the children's room. Simon, who was six, was lying with his bottom in the air and his head buried deep in the pillow. It was hard to believe he could actually breathe in that position.

Adam, who had just turned ten, had kicked off the covers and was sprawled diagonally across the bed. His white-blond hair was damp with sweat, curling slightly at the back of his neck.

Both were fast asleep.

Simon's swimming lesson began at nine o'clock, Adam's at ten thirty, so she just had time to get home with Simon and make sure Adam had some breakfast before he set off on his bike.

Perfect timing, in other words.

In spite of everything, she would probably miss the contact with the other mothers and fathers when Simon was also old enough to cycle there on his own. It was pleasant, sitting by the edge of the pool chatting as the children practiced their strokes.

She had attended swimming lessons as a child with many of the parents, so she knew most of them. At that time there had been no question of using a heated pool and warming up in the sauna afterward. They had shivered their way into the water at Fläskberget, the beach on the north side of the island where the swimming school had been until the pool area was built.

She could still remember how incredibly cold it was. But she had gained her swimming badges in water with a temperature of sixty-one degrees; those badges were still around somewhere. Presumably at her parents' house, just a few hundred yards away.

Nora went into the bathroom to get ready. As she brushed her teeth, she sleepily examined her reflection in the mirror. Tousled reddish-blond hair cut into a bob. Snub nose. Gray eyes. A body shaped by plenty of exercise; some might even call it boyish.

She was quite happy with her appearance, for the most part. Above all she liked her long, shapely legs, the result of many years of jogging. She found it so easy to think while she jogged. Her breasts weren't exactly something to shout about, particularly after two children, but then again, you could get push-up bras these days. That helped a bit.

As she showered she thought about all the things that had changed on Sandhamn since she'd been a child attending those swimming lessons. As the summer population had increased, so had the traffic to the island. Now the tourists could take a half-hour flight over the archipelago, and there was a helicopter service flying hungry diners out to the Sailors Restaurant. The conference center, situated in the Royal Swedish Sailing Society's former clubhouse, built in 1897 in the National Romantic style, was open year-round. It was also possible to hire kayaks and old-fashioned bikes to travel around the island.

The beautiful people loved coming out to Sandhamn, hobnobbing whenever there was a regatta or an international yacht race. The Gucci quota had shot up by several hundred percent, as Henrik would remark with some amusement as the big jetty in front of the clubhouse filled up with elegant women in expensive clothes and middle-aged men who carried both their rotundity and their bulging wallets with an air of authority and assurance.

Some of the residents complained about the increased traffic and the number of tourists on the island, but the majority, who depended on the employment opportunities they provided for their survival, had a positive attitude toward the development.

The contrast between the summer months, however, with two to three thousand more people staying on the island and a hundred thousand day visitors, and the winter, with its hundred and twenty residents, could not have been greater.

***

Despite the fact that Thomas had spent every summer of his life in the Stockholm archipelago, he still found it remarkably stunning in the clear morning air.

Traveling to Sandhamn by helicopter was an unexpected privilege. The view from the wide windscreen was unparalleled. The contours of the islands, strewn across the glittering water, were razor-sharp.

They had flown over Nacka and out toward Fågelbrolandet. Once they had left Grinda behind them and reached the outer islands, the character of the landscape changed. The gentler green of the inner archipelago, with its leafy trees and open meadows, changed to rocky islands with low-growing, windblown pine trees and bare expanses of rock.

When they were level with Runmarö, the characteristic view of Sandhamn opened out in front of them—a closely packed collection of red- and buff-colored houses, just where the sound between Sandhamn and Telegrafholmen began.

Thomas never tired of that first sight of the familiar outline of the little community out on the edge of the archipelago. It had existed as a post for customs and pilot boats ever since the end of the sixteenth century, through Russian devastation, bitter winters, the arrival of steamboats, and the isolation of the war years. It was still a vibrant community.

Thomas squinted through his sunglasses and looked down.

Motorboats and yachts were tied to the wooden jetties, and behind them he could just see the old pilot tower rising up from the highest point on the island. White buoys bobbed out beyond the landing stages, with green-and-red markers showing the way for both commercial traffic and leisure sailors. It was early in the morning, but the channel was already full of white sails on their way out to sea.

After only a minute or so they were over Sandhamn. The pilot rounded the elaborate eighteenth-century customhouse, and the helicopter landing stage beside it quickly came into view. With a precise maneuver he put the helicopter down in the center of the marked rectangle, just a few yards away from the wharf.

"I can wait half an hour or so, then I need to leave," said the pilot, looking at Thomas.

Thomas looked at his watch and thought for a moment. "We shouldn't be finished that quickly. You might as well go. We'll get back somehow." He turned to the two technicians, who had lifted their black bags out onto the helipad. "OK, let's go. We're heading for the west beach, north of Koberget. The maritime police are already there. No vehicles are allowed on the island, so we've got a nice brisk walk ahead of us."

Chapter 4

As Nora cycled through the harbor area with Simon on the luggage rack, she noticed a police helicopter on the landing pad. On the far side of Ångbåtsbryggan on Nacka Strand, a large police launch had moored in the spot reserved for the doctor's boat. A policeman wearing the distinctive uniform of the maritime police was standing on the deck. It was unusual to see so many police officers this early in the morning.

Something must have happened.

Nora cycled past the row of small shops, where you could buy your fill of sailing clothes, chandlery, and sail-making items, and carried on past the back of the clubhouse. She turned into the harbor and cycled along the narrow track that ran parallel with the minigolf course up to the enclosed pool area. After parking the bike behind the ice cream kiosk, she lifted Simon and set him down. She held on to him with one hand and carried the bag with his swimming gear in the other, ducked underneath the sign that said "Closed," and went into the swimming school.

In one corner, some of the parents were talking as the children ran around waiting for the swimming lesson to begin. Nora put the bag down on a lounge chair and went over to the group.

"Has something happened?"

"Didn't you see the police helicopter?" said one of the mothers. "They've found a dead body—it washed ashore on the west beach."

Nora gasped. "A dead body?"

"Yes, tangled in a fishing net, can you imagine? Apparently it was just below the Åkermarks' house." She pointed over toward one of the mothers, whose son attended swimming lessons at the same time as Simon. "They've sealed off the entire beach down there. Lotta barely got through on her way here with Oscar."

"Was it an accident?" Nora asked.

"No idea. The police wouldn't say much when she asked them. But it sounds gruesome, doesn't it?"

"Is it somebody from the island? Could it have been somebody who was out fishing and just fell in?" Nora looked at the rest of the group.

One of the fathers spoke. "I don't think anybody knows. I don't suppose it was very easy to see. But Lotta was pretty shaken up when she got here."

Nora sat down on a bench by the edge of the pool. In the water, Simon was hanging on to an orange float as he struggled to kick his legs properly. She tried to shake off the horrible feeling without success.

Despite herself, she could see the image of a person gasping for air as he became more and more entangled in a net that was slowly dragging him down.

The western part of the island was unnaturally quiet. No morning breeze disturbed the surface of the water. Even the gulls had given up their usual screaming.

Down on the beach, the maritime police had already sealed off the area where the body lay. A few curious onlookers were standing behind the police tape in a silent huddle, watching.

Thomas greeted his colleagues and walked over to the bundle on the ground.

It wasn't a pretty sight.

The torn fishing net had been shifted slightly to one side, revealing the remains of something that appeared to be the body of a man. It was still wearing the remains of a sweater and tattered pants. It looked as if something had been gnawing at one ear; only flakes of skin remained.

A looped rope was wrapped around the body, just under the arms, looking somewhat worse for wear. It appeared to be an ordinary rope, the kind used to tie up small boats. Strands of green seaweed that had dried in the sun were still hanging from the rope.

The stench in the hot sunshine was almost unbearable, and Thomas turned away as it wafted up.

Some things a person never got used to.

He quelled the impulse to vomit and walked around the body to look at it from the other side. It was difficult to draw any conclusions about the man's appearance. Clumps of dark hair clung to the skull, but it wasn't really possible to make out what he had looked like. The face was swollen, the skin suffused with water. The body was blue and spongy; it looked as if it were made of wet clay.

As far as Thomas could judge, the man had been medium height, somewhere between five six and five nine. It didn't look as if he'd been married; the ring finger on his left hand was still there, and there was nothing on it. Then again, a ring could have easily slipped off in the water.

The forensic technicians had opened their cases and were examining the scene. A middle-aged man was sitting on a rock a little way off. He was leaning back against a tree trunk, his eyes closed. Beside him stood a dachshund, snuffling anxiously. It was the dog owner who had made the gruesome discovery earlier and called the police.

The poor guy must have been waiting there for several hours, thought Thomas, as he went over to introduce himself.

"Did you find the body?"

The man nodded.

"I'll need to talk to you. I'm just going to sort something out here, then we can have a chat. Can you stay a little while? I know you've been here for quite some time, and I really appreciate that you've waited for us."

The man nodded again. He looked as if he didn't feel well. Beneath the suntan he was pale, his face almost green. There was an unpleasant smell coming from his shoes.

His morning hadn't gotten off to a particularly good start, Thomas thought before he went back to have a few words with the technicians.

"Thomas, have you come to visit?" Nora smiled when she saw Thomas, one of her oldest and closest friends, outside Westerberg's grocery store on her way back from swimming. Her bike skidded to a halt on the gravel, and she lifted Simon.

"Look who's here, Simon. Give your godfather a big hug."

She had to stretch up so Simon could reach. Although she was above average height, it was nothing compared with Thomas at six foot four. On top of that he was well built, his shoulders broad from years of handball training. He looked just like the archetypal policeman, big and reassuring, with blond hair and blue eyes.

"They ought to use you on recruitment posters for the training academy," she used to tease him.

Thomas's parents lived on the neighboring island of Harö, and ever since they had attended the Friends of Sandhamn sailing camp together when they were nine, Nora and Thomas had been the best of friends.

Every summer they had picked up the threads from the previous year, and despite their parents' conviction that there was romance in the air, they had remained just good friends, nothing more.

The first time Nora got so drunk she threw up, it was Thomas who had cleaned her up and got her home without her parents knowing. At least they'd never mentioned it. When the great teenage love of his life had dumped him, Nora had done her best to console him and let him go on and on about it. They had spent a whole night sitting on the rocks as he poured his heart out.

When they were fourteen they had spent a whole summer studying for their confirmation with the priest in the chapel on Sandhamn, and both of them had done every available summer job on the island: worked in the ice cream kiosk, helped out at the bakery and at the sailing club, ran the till at Westerberg's shop. They had also danced in the Sailors Restaurant, until, hot and sweaty, they ended the evening with a nighttime dip in the sea below Dansberget as the sun was rising.

When Henrik first showed an interest in Nora by inviting her to the medical students' ball, she had called Thomas to tell him. She had been deeply attracted to Henrik, whose spontaneous charm had hit her with full force. As usual, Thomas had listened as she fell in love and prattled on.

Thomas had always wanted to join the police, just as Nora had always wanted to study law. She used to joke that when she became minister for justice, she would make him the chief of police of Sweden.

When Adam was born, Nora knew Thomas was the obvious choice for a godparent, but Henrik wanted to choose his best friend and his wife. When Simon came along, Nora insisted that Thomas be his godfather. Thomas was the kind of person they could rely on if anything happened to her or Henrik.

"I'm here to work," Thomas said with a serious expression. "Did you hear that a dead body has been found on the other side of the island?"

Nora nodded. "It sounds dreadful. I was just at the swimming school with Simon, and that was the only topic of conversation. What happened?" She looked anxiously at Thomas.

"I've no idea at this stage. All we know is that it's a man's body, and it was entangled in an old fishing net. It looked pretty bad, so it must have been in the water for quite some time."

Nora shuddered in the warm sunshine. "Terrible. But it must have been an accident, surely? I can't believe anybody could be murdered here on Sandhamn."

"We'll see. The pathologist will have to examine the body before we can draw any conclusions. The man who found it couldn't tell us much."

"He must have been shocked."

"Yeah, I feel sorry for him. Nobody expects to find a corpse when they're out on their morning walk," said Thomas with a grimace.

Nora lifted Simon back onto the bike. "Can you come over when you're finished? I'm sure you've earned a cup of coffee," she said.

Thomas smiled. "Sounds like a good idea. I'll try."

CHAPTER 5

Nora cycled home deep in thought. She wondered if the man who had died had been a resident or a total stranger. If he lived on Sandhamn, then she should have heard that someone was missing. The island was small enough for most people to keep an eye on each other. The social network was strong. But she hadn't heard a thing.

As she lifted Simon down and parked the bike by the fence, she saw her next-door neighbor, Signe Brand, watering her roses. The most glorious roses covered the south-facing wall of Signe's house, pink interspersed with red. The rose bushes were several decades old, their stems as thick as a wrist.

Signe, or Auntie Signe as Nora called her when she was little, lived in the Brand house, one of the most beautiful houses on the island, right in the middle of Kvarnberget, just by the inlet to Sandhamn. When the old windmill that had stood on Kvarnberget was moved in the 1860s, Signe's grandfather, the master pilot Carl Wilhelm Brand, saw an opportunity to make use of the land. After many years he built a truly imposing house right at the top of the hill.

Although the fashion at the time was to build houses close together in the village in order to protect each other from the wind, the master pilot built his house so that it stood alone in solitary majesty. It was the first thing visitors saw when the steamboat docked in Sandhamn, a landmark for all those who came to the island.

The master pilot had skimped on nothing when the house was being built. He used only the finest material. The National Romantic style was fully embraced, with narrow roof projections, wide decorative bargeboards, and gently curving lines in the attic and bay windows. Inside were lavish tiled stoves, specially ordered from the porcelain factory in Gustavsberg, and a huge claw-foot bathtub in what was an unusually modern bathroom for the time. There was even an indoor toilet, which provoked great surprise among the neighbors, who were used to the inconvenience of the outhouse.

Some of them had shaken their heads, muttering something about fancy city ways, but the master pilot had taken no notice. "I'll shit where I like," he had roared when the gossip reached him.

Signe had bought herself a television after resisting for many years, but that was the only thing that didn't fit in with the style of the house. Everything was so beautifully preserved it was barely noticeable that a hundred years had passed since the house was furnished.

These days, Signe lived alone in the house with her dog, a Labrador named Kajsa. From time to time she complained about the cost of everything, but each time some fresh outsider tried to tempt her with an amazing offer for what had to be one of Sandhamn's most beautiful buildings, she snorted and sent them packing.

"This is where I was born, and this is where I'm going to die," she would say without a shred of sentimentality. "No rich kid from Stockholm is moving in here."

Signe loved the house she had inherited, and Nora could understand why. When she was little, Signe had been like an extra grandmother, and Nora felt just as much at home in her house as in her parents'.

"Did you hear about what happened?" she asked Signe.

"No, what?" Signe said, putting down the watering can. She straightened up and came over to the fence.

"Somebody drowned—they found a body over on the west beach. The police are out in force."

Signe looked at her in surprise.

"You can imagine how wound up the parents at the swimming school were," Nora said.

"Somebody's dead, is that what you said?"

"Yes. I bumped into Thomas down by Westerberg's. He's here to investigate the death."

"Do they know who it is? Did you recognize the body?"

"I wasn't there. Thomas said it was a man, and the body was in a really bad state. Apparently it's been in the water for several months."

"So Thomas is here on police business. To think he's so grown up," said Signe.

"So am I. He's only a year older than me," Nora said with a grin.

"It's still hard to grasp. Time goes so quickly." Signe looked sad. "I can hardly believe you've got children of your own. It seems like just yesterday you were as small as Adam and Simon."

Nora smiled, said good-bye, and went inside. She loved her house, which she had inherited several years earlier from her grandmother. It wasn't all that big, but it was charming and had held up really well, considering it was built in 1915. On the ground floor there was a large kitchen and a big room that served as a TV room and playroom as well as a sitting room for the adults.

A small tiled stove with a delicate flower pattern had been preserved over the years. In the winter it warmed the whole ground floor. Since there were power outages occasionally in the archipelago, it was a useful asset.

Upstairs there were two bedrooms, one for her and Henrik and one for the boys. When they'd moved in they had treated the house to a complete and much-needed renovation of the kitchen and bathroom.

Nothing too over the top, just enough to make it functional and inviting.

The best thing about the house, however, was the sunny, old-fashioned greenhouse; she had filled the windowsills with Mårbacka pelargoniums. From there, it was possible—with a little bit of effort—to catch a glimpse of the sea to the west. The main thing visible, however, was Signe's house, rising up on the hill and making Nora's place look like a little hut by comparison.

"Hi, we're home," Nora shouted up the stairs to Henrik, but the house was silent. She had been nursing a faint hope that he might have gotten Adam up while she was out with Simon, but obviously they were still asleep. Despite the fact that Henrik was used to going without sleep for many hours when he was on duty at the hospital, he had no problem making up for it when they were on vacation.

With a sigh she started up the stairs.

"Boo!"

Nora jumped as Adam leaped out from behind the bathroom door.

"Were you scared?" He was beaming. "Daddy's still asleep. But I made my bed."

Nora gave him a hug. She could feel his ribs under his T-shirt. Where had her chubby baby gone, and where had this skinny little creature come from?

"Come on, you need something to eat before your swimming lesson."

She took him by the hand and went down to the kitchen. As she got out the fresh rolls she'd bought on the way home, Adam set the table.

"Don't forget your insulin, Mom," he reminded her.

Nora smiled and tried to sneak an extra hug. He was a typical big brother, responsible and caring. Since he'd been old enough to understand how important it was for a type 1 diabetic like her to take her insulin before every meal, he had made it his job to remind her.

Whenever she was a little careless, particularly when they weren't at home and were eating snacks, he got terribly anxious and told her off.

She opened the fridge and took out the pen-like device she used to inject herself with insulin. With an exaggerated gesture she held it up and showed it to Adam.

"There we are, General! Mission accomplished!"

With practiced hands she fitted the ampule to the syringe and injected the insulin into her stomach just below the navel. To her relief it appeared that neither Simon nor Adam showed any sign of developing diabetes, but it was impossible to be completely certain until they were fully grown.

She could hear Simon running in to Henrik and doing his best to wake him up by jumping up and down on the bed, which was fine by her. If she took Simon early in the morning, Henrik could at least make sure Adam got off to his lesson. And besides, Thomas was coming for coffee.

Chapter 6

The police station on Sandhamn shared its accommodation with the post office. It was a buff-colored building that looked like a typical vacation home, situated just below the old sandpit, known as Gropen, or the Hollow.

Inside was a modern office with a dozen workstations and a meeting room. About fifteen people worked there, mainly women, and they dealt with most things, from violent crime and robbery to stolen cell phones and bicycles. The station opened early in the morning and didn't close until ten o'clock at night.

As the station was linked to the police intranet, it was no problem for Thomas to use one of the terminals to write up and send his report on the dead man. There wasn't much to say, apart from the fact that they had found a body, cause of death unknown.

While he was there, he took a look at the register of missing persons.

In the district of Stockholm, two men had been reported missing. One was retired, aged seventy-four, with dementia. The report had come in two days ago.

He's probably lost in some clearing in the forest, poor guy, thought Thomas. If they didn't find him soon, he'd die of exhaustion and dehydration. It wasn't particularly unusual.

The other was a man in his fifties, Krister Berggren, who worked in an off-license that was part of the state-owned alcohol monopoly, Systembolaget, commonly known as Systemet. His employer had contacted the police at the beginning of April when he'd failed to turn up for work for ten days. He hadn't been seen since Easter weekend, the last week in March. Krister Berggren was of medium height, had dark-blond hair, and had worked at Systemet since 1971, immediately after leaving school, if Thomas's calculation was correct.

Thomas took out his cell phone and called Carina, the DCI's surprisingly pretty daughter, who worked as an administrative assistant with the police in Nacka as experience for her application to the police training academy.

"Hi, Carina, it's Thomas. Can you get in touch with the pathologists and tell them the body that's coming in might be a match for one Krister Berggren from Bandhagen, who's been missing for a few months?" Thomas gave her Berggren's ID number and address. "And you might as well find out who we'll need to contact if it is a match. If we're lucky, they might find a driver's license or ID card on him when they do the preliminary exam."

He looked back at the description of Krister Berggren on the screen. Through the window he could hear the laughter of a group of children cycling past. Another reminder that it was summer, and he'd soon be able to take off to Harö, the only place he'd found a sense of calm since Emily died. He suddenly felt a powerful longing to be sitting alone in peace on the jetty.

"It would be nice if we could solve the case this quickly and easily," he said to Carina. "It's nearly vacation time, after all."

Thursday, the First Week

CHAPTER 7

When Thomas walked into Nacka station on Thursday morning, Carina was ready and waiting. She pushed over the report that had just arrived, stamped with the pathology department logo.

"This just came in. The dead man on Sandhamn was Krister Berggren, as you thought. His wallet was in his pocket, and it was possible to make out the text on his driver's license, even though it had been in the water for so long."

As Thomas read through the report, Carina studied him. Ever since she'd started at Nacka she had been stealing glances at him. There was something about him that attracted her, but she couldn't quite put her finger on it.

He had thick blond hair, cut very short, and she had the feeling it would grow wild if it weren't tamed. There was something outdoorsy about him; it was obvious he liked to spend time in the fresh air. Around his eyes there was a mass of tiny lines, from years of squinting into the sun. He was fit and tall. She was quite a bit shorter than Thomas.

He was reputed to be an excellent policeman, sympathetic and fair. An honorable man who was good to work with. His likeable personality made him a popular member of the team, despite the fact that he kept a good deal of distance. He didn't allow anyone to get too close.

According to what Carina had heard, he had lost a child about a year ago. After that, there had been no hope for his marriage, and it had ended in divorce. There had been talk in the office about the little girl who had died of sudden infant death syndrome, but nobody knew the details.

For a long time he had been very depressed, but lately his spirits had begun to rise. At least if you believed the office gossip.

She hadn't been with anyone special recently, just dated a little. Boys her own age who bored her. Thomas—who was approaching forty—was completely different. He didn't just look good; he was a grown man, not an immature boy. On top of that, there was something about Thomas that struck a chord with Carina, although she couldn't really explain it. Perhaps it was that sense of sorrow just beneath the surface. Or the fact that he didn't really seem to notice her, which merely served to increase her interest.

She knew she didn't look too bad; she was small and neat and had a dimple in her left cheek that people often mentioned. She usually had all the approval she needed from guys, but Thomas treated her just like everyone else, in spite of the little hints she dropped.

Carina had begun to find herself errands that took her into Thomas's office. Sometimes she would treat him to a Danish pastry or a piece of cake to go with his morning coffee. She tried to make sure she was sitting close to him when they had a briefing and made every effort to attract his attention. But so far it hadn't made a bit of difference.

She lingered in the doorway as Thomas studied the report. Her eyes rested on his hand, holding the papers. She thought he had such beautiful fingers, long and slender with attractively shaped nails. From time to time she wondered what it would feel like to be touched by those fingers. Before she fell asleep she would fantasize about his hands, caressing her. How it would feel to lie close by his side, skin on skin.

Completely oblivious to Carina's thoughts, Thomas was absorbed in the report. It was written in cold, clinical language, with no emotional nuances revealing anything about the man in the descriptions. Short, clipped phrases efficiently summarized the results.

Death by drowning. Water in the lungs. Injuries to the body sustained during the time spent in the sea, as far as they could judge. Several fingers and toes missing. No trace of chemical substances or alcohol in the blood. The old fishing net was made of the same cotton fiber as Swedish fishing nets usually were. The loop of rope around the upper body had been ordinary rope. It appeared that something had been attached to the rope; the end was frayed, and traces of iron indicated that it had been in contact with a metal object.

Nothing in the report indicated that death had been caused by another person.

Suicide or an accident, in that case.

The only strange thing was the rope around the body. Thomas considered this. Why would someone have a rope around his body if he'd drowned accidentally? Had Krister Berggren tried to get out of the water after falling in? Or, if he'd committed suicide, had he made a bungled attempt to hang himself, then regretted it and jumped in instead? In which case, wouldn't he have removed the rope? Why just push it down his body? Perhaps that kind of question was unimportant given a person's state of mind just before a suicide attempt.

The fishing net could be explained away as a simple mishap. The body could have drifted into someone's net and gotten entangled in it. The loop of rope was more difficult to understand. On the other hand, his years as a police officer had taught him that certain things cannot be explained. It didn't necessarily mean anything.

If the rope hadn't been there, the death would have been written off as either an accident or suicide right away, but it was chafing Thomas's thoughts like a tiny stone in his shoe.

He decided to go over to Krister Berggren's flat. There might be a suicide note or some other information to help explain things.

Krister Berggren had lived on the far side of Bandhagen, a suburb just south of Stockholm.

Thomas parked his car, an eight-year-old Volvo 945, by the curb and looked around. The buildings were typical of the 1950s, made of buff-colored brick, four stories, and no lift. Row after row of blocks of flats met his gaze. There were a few cars parked on the street. An elderly man in a cap was making his way with the help of a walker.

Thomas opened the outer door and walked into the entrance hall. The tenants' names were listed on a board to the right. Krister Berggren had lived two floors up. Thomas walked quickly up the stairs. On each floor there were three doors made of pale-brown wood, which had become scratched over the years. The walls were painted in a nondescript shade of beige gray.

Beneath the nameplate that said "K. Berggren" was a piece of paper with *No Junk Mail* written on it in pencil. Despite this, someone had tried to shove a huge bundle of advertisements through the letterbox.

The locksmith had arrived a few minutes earlier; when he opened the door for Thomas, a stale smell immediately surged toward them in a mixture of old food and enclosed air.

Thomas started with the kitchen. On the dish rack stood several empty wine bottles and a dried-up loaf of bread. There were dirty plates in the sink. He opened the old fridge, and the stench of sour milk hit him. Moldy cheese and ham lay next to it. It was obvious nobody had been there for months.

There were no surprises in the living room. A black leather sofa, dreary sea-grass carpet that had clearly been there for some time. On the glass table, various rings left by glasses and bottles bore witness to a predilection for alcohol, coupled with a lack of interest in taking care of the furniture. A few dead potted plants stood on the windowsill. It was obvious that Krister Berggren had lived alone for many years; there was no sign that a woman had shared his life.

The bookcase was crammed with DVDs. Thomas noticed an entire shelf filled with Clint Eastwood films. A few books—some looked as if they might have been inherited, because they had old-fashioned, worn leather spines with gold lettering. On one wall hung a poster showing Formula One cars at the starting grid.

On the table were a pile of assorted catalogs, one copy of *Motor Sport*, and a TV listings magazine. There was also a brochure for the ferry company Silja Line in the pile. Thomas picked it up and looked at it more closely. Perhaps Krister Berggren had simply fallen overboard from a ferry to Finland. All the big shipping companies passed the western point of Sandhamn at around nine each evening.

He went into the bedroom and looked around. The quilt was pulled over the bed, but there were dirty clothes lying around. An old copy of the evening paper *Aftonbladet* was on the nightstand. Thomas picked it up and looked at the date: March 27. Could that be the last time Krister was at home? It matched the best-before date on the carton of sour milk in the fridge.

On a bureau stood a black-and-white photograph of a girl with a 1950s hairstyle, wearing a twinset. Thomas picked it up and turned it over. *Cecilia—1957*, it said in ornate handwriting. The girl was pretty in an old-fashioned way. Pale lipstick, beautiful eyes gazing far into the distance. She had a neat, clean air about her. Presumably she was Krister's mother. According to the records, she had died at the beginning of the year.

Thomas carried on looking for a suicide note or anything else that might explain the death but found nothing. He went back into the hall and flicked through the pile of mail. Mostly advertisements, a few envelopes that looked like bills. A postcard with a picture of a white beach on the front, and the name *Kos* covering half the card.

Call me so we can talk! Love, Kicki, it said on the back.

Thomas wondered if Kicki was Kicki Berggren, Krister's cousin, who was the only living relative they had managed to track down. He had tried to call her earlier on her home number and her cell phone but had only gotten voice mail in both cases.

A quick glance in the bathroom revealed nothing.

The toilet seat had been left up, just as you would expect from a man living on his own. A few dried-up splashes of yellow urine showed up against the white porcelain.

Thomas took a final walk around the flat. He didn't really know what he'd been expecting. If not a note, then at least something that might show that Krister Berggren had tried to take his own life one cold day in March.

Unless it had been an accident, after all.

Tuesday, the Second Week

Chapter 8

With a sigh, Kicki Berggren punched in the entry code to the apartment block in Bandhagen.

Home at last.

She had been longing for her own bed and the comfort of her apartment. *Home sweet home,* she thought with an expression of relief on her face. How true that was.

When her old school friend Agneta had talked Kicki into going with her to Kos to work as a waitress in a Swedish-owned restaurant, it had sounded like paradise. A paid vacation in the Greek islands, room and board, and a wage, which was admittedly low but would no doubt be supplemented by generous tips. That was the way Agneta had described it, at any rate. Sunshine and heat instead of darkness and slush.

It had sounded too good to be true. And indeed it had been.

Kicki Berggren had quickly come down to earth with a bump. After three months of drunken customers, all too frequently Swedes who ordered cheap food and more ouzo than they could handle, she was sick to death of her Greek paradise. She just wanted to get back to her normal life as a single girl working as a croupier for Sweden's leading casino operator. She couldn't wait to be back at her table dealing blackjack in the noisy atmosphere.

She unlocked the front door and carried her bags inside.

The apartment smelled stuffy; it was obvious she hadn't been home for a while. She left her bags in the hallway and went straight into the kitchen, where she lit a cigarette and sat down at the table. The unpacking could wait until tomorrow. She opened a bottle of ouzo she had brought with her and poured herself a glass. It wasn't too bad, she thought, with a couple ice cubes. She wondered whether she should check her e-mail but decided that could wait, too. She had gone to an Internet café on Kos from time to time, so it wasn't exactly urgent.

She picked up the phone and dialed a code to listen to her messages. She doubted there would be any. Most of her friends knew she was away, but her cell phone had died last week, so nobody had been able to get ahold of her for a while, and maybe they had tried her landline.

The first few messages were the usual telemarketing calls. Would she like some financial advice? Fat chance. What use would that be? Her meager earnings didn't stretch far enough as it was.

The last message was something of a shock.

"My name is Thomas Andreasson," she heard a deep voice say. "I'm calling from the Criminal Investigations Division in Nacka. I would like to ask you some questions about your cousin, Krister Berggren, and I'd appreciate it if you could contact me as soon as possible." He gave a number and hung up.

Kicki stubbed out her cigarette.

Why were the police calling her to ask about Krister? She tried his number, but there was no answer. Krister had never bothered to install an answering machine, so the phone rang until Kicki hung up.

She tried the number the police officer had left. She got through to an operator, who informed her that Thomas Andreasson would be available at eight o'clock the following morning.

Kicki lit another cigarette and leaned back in her chair. Flakes of ash drifted down onto the pale-blue rug, but she didn't care.

What could have happened to Krister?

They'd had a terrible fight after his mother's funeral, and since then she had neither spoken to him nor heard anything from him for several months. At first she thought the fact that she had gone off to Kos served him right, but when he didn't call and didn't reply to her texts, she'd gotten really annoyed. She had even sent a postcard asking him to call her, but there had been no response.

Fuck you, then, she had thought. He could trudge around back home in the slush while she enjoyed the Greek sunshine. God, men could be so miserable. They were like kids.

And yet she really wanted to talk to him.

There was only she and Krister left now. He was the closest thing she had to a brother. Even though his one-track mind and his lack of ambition irritated her, he was still family and could be good company. Sometimes he was the only company she had.

Neither of them had children or a long-term partner. There had been many occasions when they had emptied yet another bottle of wine that he had "happened" to have with him from his work at Systemet, and she had wondered whether they would end up sitting there like this when they were retired. Lonely losers who hadn't managed to get their act together. Old and bitter, passing their time complaining about everything.

That was why she had hardly been able to believe it when the chance of a new life had suddenly come along. For the first time they had the opportunity to do something different, to live a proper life, far away from his work at the store and her smoky evenings in the casino. The chance for a serious amount of money for both of them.

But Krister hadn't had the courage. Kicki just didn't understand it. It would have been so simple; she knew exactly what needed to be done, what needed to be said.

After all, he had proof. Written proof.

They had been sitting in his living room; Krister had been lolling on the sofa gazing at her, his eyelids heavy. His shirt was grubby, with several buttons undone. He pushed back his hair, which was in dire need of a wash, and shook his head.

"You and your ideas. You know it would never work." He topped off his glass of wine. "Want some?" He waved the bottle in her direction.

She looked at him and sighed. "No, I don't want any more wine. I want you to listen to what I'm saying." She lit yet another cigarette, feeling furious. She took a deep drag and stared at him. This place was so depressing. A typical bachelor pad. "You could at least listen," she tried again.

But he had refused to take her suggestion seriously and had dodged the issue every time she'd brought it up. She had even dragged his mother into the argument, insisting that Cecilia would have wanted him to do it. She had gone over it time and time again.

In the end she had lost her temper. "OK, you carry on sitting here, you fucking idiot," she had yelled at him. "This is your chance for a decent life, and you don't even have the guts to try!" She looked at him with utter contempt, seething with rage. "You're such a fucking coward! You'll end up sitting here in this dump until they carry you out in a box!"

With that she had stormed out, and two days later she left for Kos without speaking to him again.

And now she was regretting it.

Things hadn't been easy for Krister. His maternal grandparents had broken off all contact with his mother when she had gotten pregnant at eighteen. She had brought him up on her own and had provided for them both by working at Systemet. Being a single parent in the mid-1950s was no picnic, and Krister probably hadn't been the easiest of children. When he left school with no qualifications, she had fixed him up with a job at Systemet, and he'd never left.

He had never met his father nor his maternal grandparents. They had died without ever having seen him, embittered by the scandal to the very end.

Kicki's father had done his best to help his sister as much as he could, but he hadn't exactly been well off either. When both of Kicki's parents died in a car accident at the end of the nineties, Cecilia had tried to support Kicki, but she hadn't been able to offer much in the way of consolation.

Just a few years later, Cecilia had begun to have difficulty holding the bottles when she was working the checkout counter. It was as if her left thumb simply gave way. She started to drop bottles, and the manager was always on her back. She was in a constant state of anxiety and blamed the fact that she was close to retirement. A lifetime in the service of Systemet with all the heavy lifting involved had taken its toll.

Eventually her coworkers had persuaded her to visit the company's medical center. After a series of tests she was given a diagnosis by the doctors—she was suffering from amyotrophic lateral sclerosis, a progressive and incurable motor neuron disease that slowly paralyzes nerve after nerve, muscle after muscle. When the paralysis reaches the lungs, the patient dies.

In Cecilia's case, it was no more than a year between the diagnosis and her funeral. She simply gave up. She lay down and waited for death, slowly stiffening in the fetal position and shrinking right in front of them. She had neither the strength nor the will left to fight.

Krister had found it very difficult to deal with his mother's condition. He couldn't cope with watching her fade away. He would put off visiting her in the nursing home for as long as possible and refused to talk about Cecilia's illness. He seemed to think that everything would be all right if he just pretended that nothing was wrong.

After the funeral he had gotten so drunk that Kicki had been afraid of what he might do. He had sat at home sniveling and weeping with a bottle in each hand. After a while he had fallen asleep fully dressed on the sofa, his face red and puffy with the alcohol. It was as if he had only just grasped the fact that his mother was dead.

Kicki poured herself another glass of ouzo. Her hand was shaking as she put down the bottle; her unease over Krister was gnawing away in the pit of her stomach. She must call Thomas Andreasson first thing in the morning and find out what he wanted.

Wednesday, the second week

Chapter 9

Thomas spotted Kicki Berggren even before he reached the bottom of the stairs behind the reception desk in Nacka station.

She was wearing a white denim jacket adorned with sparkling studs. Faded jeans, a tight pink top, and high-heeled sandals completed the picture. From behind, she looked like a young girl; she had a slender figure and boyish hips. When she turned around he could see that she was a middle-aged woman, closer to fifty than forty. The blond hair was too long to be flattering. She certainly wasn't a natural blonde; the dark roots gave that away. A fine network of lines above her upper lip revealed her to be a habitual smoker. She was very tan, almost mahogany.

He wondered how she had managed to acquire a tan like that in the Swedish summer. He also noticed that she was fiddling nervously with a denim purse. It was obvious she was dying to light up, but the sign on the wall was very clear: "No Smoking."

Thomas walked up to her and held out his hand. "Good morning, I'm Thomas Andreasson. Thank you for coming in so quickly. I understand you've been away?"

"I've been in Greece," Kicki said. She gave the impression of being ill at ease, presumably because she was wondering why he wanted to speak to her.

Thomas showed her to his office.

"Coffee?" He poured two cups; coffee was a good icebreaker. "I'm afraid it doesn't taste particularly good, but it's all we've got. Please sit down." He pointed to the chair opposite his desk.

Kicki sat down and crossed her legs, her shoe dangling from one foot as if it might fall off at any moment.

"Can I smoke in here?" she asked, more in hope than expectation. She had already opened her purse and dug out a pack of cigarettes and a lighter before she asked the question.

"I'm sorry, but you're not allowed to smoke anywhere inside the building. I hope you can manage for a little while longer?"

Kicki nodded and closed her purse. Thomas could see the anxiety in her eyes.

"What did you want to talk to me about?" she asked. "My cell phone broke about a week ago, and I just got home and heard your message and realized something had happened. I've tried to call Krister lots of times, but he doesn't answer. It's nothing serious, is it? What's he done?"

The questions came tumbling out in one long breath.

Thomas took his time. This was the most difficult aspect of his job—how to tell a person that someone she cares about is dead. He decided to start with a question instead.

"Are you and your cousin close?"

Kicki nodded. "He's my only relative. His mother was my aunt. We see each other all the time; that's the way it's been ever since we were kids. He's only a year younger than me. We usually spend Christmas together, just the two of us."

Thomas took a deep breath. "I'm very sorry to tell you this, but your cousin is dead. His body was found on the island of Sandhamn in the Stockholm archipelago a week ago. He drowned and washed ashore."

Kicki's purse landed on the floor. Her mouth opened, but she was silent for a few seconds.

"He's dead?"

"I'm afraid so."

Her eyes filled with tears. Thomas passed her a box of tissues; she took one and blew her nose.

"Would you like a glass of water?" he asked.

Kicki shook her head. She bent down and picked up her purse. She placed it on her knee and clutched it with both hands. Her mouth was trembling as she stared at Thomas, tension running throughout her body.

"We think he died in the early spring. When did you last speak to him?"

"I haven't spoken to him since March. I've been away for three months, working in a Swedish restaurant on Kos."

"Was there any particular reason you went there?"

"I went with a friend who worked there before. I got back last night and heard your voice mail. I called back as soon as I could."

"How often did you usually speak to one another?" Thomas asked, offering the box of tissues once more.

Kicki squirmed uncomfortably. "It varied." She looked down, studying her bright-pink nails.

"But you were in regular contact?"

"Absolutely. We don't have any other family."

As Kicki described Krister's upbringing by his single mother, Thomas came to the conclusion that there didn't appear to be anything in Krister's background to explain why he should have ended up on Sandhamn.

"Do you have any idea why he might have been in the archipelago?" he asked. "Is there anyone he might have been visiting out there?"

Thomas looked at Kicki, but she continued staring at the floor.

Before she had time to say anything, Thomas went on. "Do you know if he ever traveled on the ferry to Finland? Was that something he did in his spare time?"

Kicki started nibbling on one of her fake nails. It was obvious she was desperate for a cigarette; she was plucking at her jacket with the other hand and seemed to be silently cursing the smoking ban inside the station.

"Yes, sometimes. Why?"

"We're wondering if he might have fallen overboard off one of the ferries. They pass by just off Sandhamn every evening. That might explain why his body washed ashore on the island."

"Krister wasn't a good swimmer. He wasn't particularly fond of water. But he did sometimes go over on the ferry, especially if there was a special deal. We went to Mariehamn together a couple years ago."

Thomas made a quick note about Krister's capabilities as a swimmer, then decided to try a different track.

"What about alcohol? Did he drink much, in your opinion?"

Kicki nodded, chewing her nail with even greater intensity. The tissues Thomas had given her were reduced to a pile of shreds. One by one they drifted onto the floor by the leg of her chair. It looked like something a baby bird might have left behind.

"He drank a bit. I mean, he worked at Systemet, so it wasn't difficult for him to bring home whatever he wanted. Besides, he didn't have much in the way of hobbies, or friends for that matter. He was perfectly happy in his own company, as long as he had something to drink and a decent show on TV."

Thomas scratched the back of his neck and gave the matter some thought. If Krister had been drunk, he might have gone outside for a breath of fresh air and tumbled into the water. That kind of thing happened far more often than people thought, but understandably the ferry companies preferred to keep it quiet.

"Is there any reason to think he could have jumped overboard? Deliberately taken his own life?" He thought about the rope looped around the body and gazed at Kicki. His words lingered in the air. It wasn't an easy question, but it had to be asked. If her cousin had been suicidal, it could explain a number of things.

Kicki Berggren opened her mouth to say something, but she changed her mind and slumped down in her seat. Her mascara had run; she took another tissue from the box and wiped her eyes as best she could.

Thomas looked at her. "Was there something you wanted to say?"

"His mother died in February. He took it really bad. Even though he wasn't prepared to visit her very often when she was ill, he was really upset afterward. He started drinking big-time."

"To the extent that perhaps he no longer wanted to live?"

Kicki lowered her eyes. "I find it difficult to believe that he would jump off a ferry. He's never talked about killing himself, in spite of the fact that he thought he'd had a lot of bad luck in his life. He used to say he'd never had a fair chance."

Her eyes filled with tears once more, and she shredded yet another tissue.

Thomas felt sorry for her; it was evident that she'd had no idea why he'd wanted to speak to her. "It could have been an accident, of course. I just wanted to know whether you thought he might have been suicidal. It's by no means certain that he killed himself. It might well have been an unfortunate combination of alcohol and circumstance."

Thomas ended the conversation by asking Kicki to call him if she thought of anything she wanted him to know. When she had gone, he made notes on the interview and placed a printout in the file.

***

Kicki walked out of the building with her head spinning. She had been so angry with Krister, but now she understood. She hadn't been able to bring herself to tell the detective why they hadn't been in touch for the last few months. She just couldn't tell him about the argument they'd had the last time they'd met. She was so ashamed of her outburst that she didn't know what to do with herself. Her harsh words had been Krister's last memory of her. Why had things turned out this way?

She stopped and took her cigarettes out of her purse. At last. As the nicotine spread through her body she began to wonder if there might be a connection in spite of everything. Had Krister decided to act on her idea after all? Without saying anything to her?

But surely that couldn't be possible. He would never have dared to do something like that alone, especially not while she was still away. Or would he?

She took another drag on the much-needed cigarette.

He must have gone on a weekend trip to Helsinki and had too much to drink. She could just picture him. Too many cheap drinks at the bar, his face growing more and more flushed as the evening went on. No doubt he had staggered out on deck to get some fresh air, drunk and overheated, and had lost his balance, just as Thomas Andreasson had said.

A pure accident.

Kicki's eyes filled with tears once more.

Poor Krister. A messy life, a messy death.

Just like his mother.

CHAPTER 10

"I thought we might barbecue some pork steaks tonight. What do you think?"

Nora looked at her husband, who was sitting on the garden seat splicing a rope. Repairing frayed ropes was almost a forgotten skill. A kind of bobbin lace–making for men. Perhaps it wasn't an occupation one would normally associate with a radiography consultant at Danderyd Hospital, but it was something Henrik enjoyed doing on those few occasions when he had time to sit quietly in the garden. He was completely focused on the task at hand.

Nora took the opportunity to nip a few wilting leaves off the pelargoniums on the gateposts as she waited for a reply.

Which didn't come.

"Henrik," she said again, feeling a surge of irritation. "You could at least give me an answer. Can we barbecue tonight?"

Henrik looked up from the rope in his hand and gazed at her. "What did you say?"

"A barbecue. Pork steaks. Tonight. It would help if we could decide what we're going to eat before the shops close."

Henrik suddenly looked guilty. "I said I'd go for a beer with the guys."

Nora sighed. Henrik would be involved in a yacht race the entire following week. The European Championship was to form part of the Sandhamn regatta, the annual competitive sailing week when the Royal Swedish Yacht Club arranged races for different types of boats.

Henrik sailed as helmsman on a Class 6, a one-design class boat with a crew of four to six. It was a class with long-standing traditions and Olympic status. Fantastic old mahogany boats kept in perfect condition by their owners still took part, but of course the new boats, like Henrik's, were made of modern material enhanced by technological advances.

His father had also sailed a Class 6 and had won the Swedish Championship several times along with a former chairman of the Royal Swedish Yacht Club, so sailing was a high priority for the Linde family.

As far as Nora was concerned, this meant that she was more or less a sailing widow for the entire week of the Sandhamn regatta.

This evening was one of the last opportunities for the whole family to have dinner together before the competition got under way. Tomorrow they were expecting guests, and then it would be time for Henrik to join the crew.

She suppressed her frustration and forced herself to adopt a pleasant tone. "Wouldn't it be nice to have dinner with the children this evening, just the family?"

"But I've promised the guys. And we need to talk tactics before the competition."

He put down the rope and looked at her apologetically. "Come on, it's not the end of the world. You know how things are."

Nora decided to drop it. There was no point in starting an argument over a dinner. "It's OK. I'll sort something out for myself and the boys." She turned to fetch a watering can. The sun had been shining on the plants all day, and the soil in the pots was bone dry.

"By the way," Henrik called after her, "my mother called. They'd like to come over on Monday to watch the racing, if that's OK. I said they were welcome, obviously."

Nora's heart sank. A visit from Henrik's parents was a full-time job. They expected to be provided with a delicious home-cooked lunch and to be entertained all day. With Henrik racing, she would have to look after them and keep an eye on the boys at the same time. And she would have to give the house a thorough cleaning before they arrived.

She had once tried to explain to her mother-in-law that she just didn't have time to keep everything in perfect order. She had been informed that if she just got herself a nice little Polish girl, everything would be fine.

"In my day, finding decent help was never a problem," her mother-in-law had said, waving her well-manicured hands. "I just don't understand mothers today who insist on doing everything themselves. Imagine how practical it would be if you had a nanny to take care of the children. You need to learn how to relax, my dear."

Henrik's parents had spent their entire working lives in the diplomatic corps, since Henrik's father had worked for the foreign office until his retirement. They had lived in various embassies all over the world, where all the household chores were taken care of by others.

It had left its mark.

The first time Henrik's father, Harald Linde, had met Thomas, he had looked him up and down. Then he had raised one eyebrow and said, in a supercilious tone, "Do I know your father?"

Even though Harald had come across as unbearably superior, Thomas had simply smiled at him and held out his hand. "I shouldn't think so," he had replied. "Unless of course you used to work at Vårby School; he taught math there."

Nora had quickly explained that Thomas was one of her best friends from childhood, and then she had discreetly attempted to change the subject. She secretly thought that Henrik's father was pompous, but she could hardly say that to Henrik.

However, her father-in-law was marginally better than his wife, who was a rail-thin woman in her seventies whose greatest pleasure was to be seen at social events.

Monica Linde was a pretentious snob who took every opportunity to prattle on about the latest exclusive dinner party she had attended or the prominent figure she had recently met. She dominated every conversation, never giving anyone else a chance to speak.

How Henrik's father had put up with her all these years was a mystery to Nora. And to everyone else. Nora's own mother simply smiled whenever Monica was mentioned; she would murmur something about how everyone was different and that it was important to look for the best in people.

Monica Linde also adored her only son and regularly reminded Nora of what a coup she had pulled off in capturing Henrik.

The fact that the reverse might be true had never occurred to Monica.

Nora had long since given up any attempt to get closer to her mother-in-law. These days, she maintained a polite but cool relationship, which worked perfectly well for all concerned. They ate Sunday lunch together at regular intervals or met up to celebrate holidays. The rest of the time Nora kept out of Monica's way as much as she could.

Fortunately, Nora's parents could almost always be relied on to pitch in with great enthusiasm when she needed some help with the boys. Without them, she and Henrik would never have managed. But every time the boys saw their paternal grandparents, they were chastised by Monica because they were not sufficiently polite or well brought up.

The idea of spending all of Monday tap-dancing for her in-laws made her groan.

"Wouldn't it be better if they came over one day when you're home?" she said. "Then they could spend some time with you, too."

She looked hopefully at her husband.

"But they want to watch the sailing."

Henrik just didn't get it. He was blind and deaf to any hint that his mother might not be the best mother-in-law in the world.

Nora gave in.

Thursday,
the second week

CHAPTER 11

As was often the case, Kicki Berggren was sitting at the computer. She had bought it secondhand on an auction website, and although it was a few years old, it worked perfectly. Kicki enjoyed being online. She could spend hours on Facebook and Twitter at night; it helped her relax when she came home from the casino.

Even if she was sometimes so tired that she could hardly stand up, she rarely felt sleepy when she finally got home after a long shift at the blackjack table. Her brain, which had been on high alert in order to keep the cards running all evening, couldn't be fooled into relaxing right away, so she would sit down at the computer to wind down. Sometimes she would check out celebrity websites, just so she could dream about a life full of possibilities.

She went to the website for Waxholmsbolaget, the ferry company. She clicked on the "Boat Schedule" link and selected Sandhamn as the destination, bringing up the timetable.

On Fridays there was a boat every two hours. You could catch a bus from Slussen out to Stavsnäs at ten after eleven; the next boat arrived in Sandhamn just after one. She could be there in a couple of hours.

She started thinking about the letter again. It had been on her mind all week. The knowledge that was the key to the future.

Would she really have the courage to make use of it?

With Krister gone, she was the only one left, and this was her only chance. And she was certain the law was on her side.

As she lit another cigarette, she made a decision. She would go to Sandhamn the following day. She didn't have to go back to work until after the weekend, so if she went over there tomorrow, she could stay until Sunday if she liked. That should give her enough time.

Friday, the second week

Chapter 12

The ferry was nearly bursting. It was the height of the summer season, and the tourists had completely taken over. Families carrying packs of Wet-Naps, retirees with their picnic baskets, people heading to their summer cottages with one load after another.

Kicki had never seen so many IKEA bags. It seemed as if the entire population of the archipelago had decided to move all their possessions in the big blue bags. In the luggage area, potted plants shared space with overfilled sacks from the discount food store, bicycles, and strollers.

With some difficulty she managed to find a seat out on deck. There was a slight breeze, but compared with the oppressive heat inside, it was sheer paradise. She flopped down with a sigh and lit a cigarette. She gazed out over Stavsnäs, the central point for traffic serving the southern islands. The white boats were lined up by the dock. Over by the gas station, a long line snaked toward the kiosk selling hot dogs and ice cream. Her stomach growled, and she wished she had bought something to eat.

In her peripheral vision she noticed yet another packed red bus pulling in at the stop; the passengers hurried toward the boats as soon as they got off.

To think that there were so many people heading for the archipelago at the same time!

When the boat docked at Sandhamn, it took forever for people to disembark. Slowly the line of passengers edged onto the deck and down the gangplank. Kicki handed over her ticket and hesitantly stepped ashore among the local residents who were meeting friends and relatives off the boat.

In one corner of the pier, a truck was busy moving cases of food and alcohol piled high on top of one another. There were people everywhere, and beyond the jetty the harbor was busy with yachts and motorboats. Countless children raced around clutching ice cream cones. The whole island seemed to be buzzing with life.

Kicki went over to the bulletin board at the back of the pier and stood there for a moment to get her bearings. She realized the harbor was lovely now that she had time to look at it properly. Directly in front of her was a long two-story building painted Falu red, with a clothes shop on the left-hand side. The sign on the awning said "Sommarboden—Everything You Need for Sunny Summer Days!"

To the left she saw the promenade, leading to the Royal Swedish Yacht Club's clubhouse. She had read about it in one of the gossip magazines; they had held a huge ball there after some sailing competition. It had been attended by the king and queen, she seemed to remember, and Princess Victoria, too.

Between the pier and the clubhouse she could see rows of boats of all types and sizes packed close together. To the right, the harbor curved in a semicircle, lined with shops and restaurants. The far end was dominated by a large yellow building that proclaimed it was the Sandhamn Inn; various signs indicated that it offered a bar, a restaurant, takeout, and outdoor seating.

Kicki decided to find somewhere to stay the night. She went over to the kiosk to buy cigarettes. As the girl handed over the pack of Princes,

Kicki asked where she might find a room that wasn't too expensive. She didn't want to pay a ridiculous amount for only one night.

"The Mission House," the blond teenager said. "They're a bed-and-breakfast. It's OK. And the breakfast is great. Otherwise it's really hard to find somewhere that doesn't cost a fortune. The Seglarhotell costs the same as hotels in the middle of Stockholm. Although it's really nice, of course."

Kicki smiled at the girl, who leaned out and pointed toward the grocery store Kicki had noticed earlier.

"It's about five hundred yards; it'll only take you five minutes to get there," she said.

Kicki picked up her bag and set off. Her sandals were immediately covered. There was sand and gravel everywhere on this island.

Chapter 13

"Get a move on, Henrik!" Nora yelled up the stairs. "They'll be here soon, and we haven't even scrubbed the potatoes yet!"

It was Friday evening, and they had invited two local couples to dinner, along with Thomas. Nora had wondered whether to invite a single female as well, but somehow it didn't feel right. Since Thomas and his wife, Pernilla, had divorced during the winter, unable to find their way back to each other after the loss of their daughter, Thomas hadn't so much as looked at another woman, let alone attempted a new relationship.

Nora shuddered as she thought about Thomas and little Emily. It had been dreadful. One minute they had a wonderful three-month-old girl; the next minute she was gone.

Emily had passed away in her sleep.

When Pernilla woke up in the morning, her breasts were sore because she hadn't fed the baby during the night. The child had been lying there cold and lifeless in the Moses basket by her side. Both parents had been devastated, but it was worse for Pernilla because she felt so guilty.

"I was so tired," she had sobbed. "I slept right through instead of taking care of her. If I'd woken up, she might still be alive. A good mother would have sensed something was wrong."

In the end, her self-reproach and guilt had broken the marriage. Thomas sought solace in his work, but Pernilla was unable to find any comfort. The separation had been inevitable.

Nora had tried to provide support as best she could, but it was impossible to get through to Thomas. He became silent, introverted. He withdrew to Harö and cut himself off.

It wasn't until the beginning of the summer that Nora began to feel she was getting back the old Thomas, her childhood friend with his tousled blond hair. But now she could see fine lines around the corners of his eyes, and his hair was peppered with gray. There was a shadow in his eyes that hadn't been there before.

"What do you want me to do?"

Henrik had crept up behind her. Nora turned and smiled. He was in a good mood; this was going to be a great evening. She pushed aside thoughts of her in-laws, who were due to arrive on Monday.

"Well, you could boil the potatoes, smoke the perch, pick some salad leaves, and make some vanilla sauce to go with the rhubarb crumble. Is that OK?" She gave him a quick peck on the cheek and handed him the bag of potatoes and a brush. "Oh, and if you could repaint the roof and build a fence before our guests arrive, that would be great!"

Henrik laughed. He was a very sociable person and enjoyed having guests. Nobody could mingle at a cocktail party like Henrik. When they had first met, Nora had been impressed by this aspect of his character; she was much less outgoing. Henrik was always ready to accept an invitation or invite friends over on the spur of the moment. As the only child of a diplomat, he was comfortable participating in a wide range of events and switching on the charm.

Nora, who preferred cozy evenings at home, had gradually begun to protest. She didn't mind the odd guest, but sometimes it was nice just to be alone as a family, particularly when the children were small and she was worn out from feeding them and getting up during the night; all she wanted to do was curl up on the sofa in front of the TV.

But Henrik had often insisted. *What could be nicer than spending time with friends,* he used to say. We can invite a few people. Just one or two. Come on. It's no big deal.

That made Nora feel dull and boring, a real party pooper. There was no point in discussing it with him; he just wouldn't listen. So she usually tried to make an effort in order to keep the peace, and she generally enjoyed the company in the end.

Tonight he was in fine form.

"I might not manage that, but if I pour you a glass of wine before I start, perhaps you'll forgive me if I only get through half?" he said, winking at Nora.

He opened the fridge and took out a bottle of Chardonnay. He poured two glasses and handed one to Nora, then found a bowl and a cutting board, ready to start on the potatoes.

Meanwhile, Nora set the table. They had decided to eat in the garden in order to enjoy the fine evening. She would be serving a mustard sauce along with the perch fillets, together with home-baked rustic baguettes with an herb butter. She had picked some rhubarb earlier and had made an old-fashioned crumble, using her grandmother's recipe.

It was going to be a lovely dinner.

By the time Kicki found her way back to the Mission House, she was still shaken. Her body was aching with tension, as if she had run a marathon.

She tried to stop thinking about the icy voice that had asked her whether she had really thought about what she was demanding. And what the consequences might be.

Kicki clamped her lips together. She had decided she wasn't going to let herself be scared off.

If life had been kinder to her, she might not have been standing here, but she had learned a long time ago that there was no point in crying over spilled milk. She loathed the helplessness that came with a lack of money. She despised the fact that she always had to smile and make herself available every evening in the casino, never making a fuss about the drunken clients who were only too happy to paw her with their sweaty hands. She yearned for something else, for another life with different opportunities.

A life that was so close right now that she could almost taste it.

She had only asked for what she was entitled to. Nothing more, nothing less. She knew what she knew, and tomorrow she would go back, and they would reach an agreement. This wasn't over, not by any means.

She took an angry drag on her cigarette. She'd had to use three matches to light it. She wasn't allowed to smoke in her room, but she couldn't care less. With a resolute expression she tried to push away the image of herself she had seen reflected in the eyes of the person who was gazing at her.

A middle-aged woman whose jeans were too tight and whose hair was too long; the color could no longer hide the strands of gray. A woman who was trying to look thirty-five, when in reality she was almost fifteen years older.

Everything reminded her of the fact that she was one of the oldest in her profession, a croupier who could be the mother of the girls at the roulette table. Colleagues who made it very clear that this was something they intended to do for only a few years. You couldn't waste any more of your life on drunken bastards who gambled away more money than they dared tell their wives about.

She'd had no problem finding her way to the Mission House, which was just past the yellow Sandhamn Värdshus. It had taken five minutes, perhaps even less. Just as the girl in the kiosk had said.

The manager made it very clear that she was lucky to get a room without having booked in advance. A last-minute cancellation freed one of the five rooms, so all she had to do was check in.

Kicki was given the key and went up to the room, which was on the second floor. It was tastefully decorated in an old-fashioned style, with lace curtains. She unpacked the few things she had brought with her, then lay down on the bed to try to gather her thoughts. She had repeatedly gone over what she was going to say. Even though she had decided to take the step, she was nervous and anxious about what was to come.

When she was ready to leave she asked the manager for directions, but she was new to the island and couldn't help. Kicki wasn't worried; she was bound to find the place. The island wasn't that big.

But it wasn't as easy as she'd expected. Eventually a teenage girl outside the bakery told her which way to go; by then it was already three o'clock.

She knocked on the door, and after a long time, when she was at the point of walking away, it opened. She gave her name and was admitted to the house. It was obvious that she was neither welcome nor expected.

After she explained her errand, there was complete silence. The owner of the house stared at her coldly for a long time before eventually looking away. The gray eyes gave no hint of a reaction to her demand. Instead, silence closed over the room like a lid; the atmosphere became oppressive, suffocating.

Kicki swallowed a couple of times and licked her lips. For a moment she wondered if she had gone too far. The unfamiliar environment was making her uncomfortable. The decor was definitely not to her taste; it was like being a visitor in another world.

Then she thought about her cousin.

"Krister's dead, and I want my share!"

She kept her eyes fixed firmly forward, determined not to sound nervous or to show her unease. She clenched one fist so tightly that the nails cut into her skin; the pain made her blink, but she tried not to let it show.

Her host suddenly stood up. The movement was so unexpected that Kicki gave a start.

"There's no need for us to fall out over this. Let me get you something to drink, then we can have a chat."

Kicki was left alone in the living room. She could hear the sound of cupboard doors opening in the kitchen, the clink of cups and saucers being placed on a tray. She glanced around the room, which was next door to a spacious dining room containing a huge table. She counted a dozen chairs around the table, with four more standing against the walls. The sea view was fantastic. You could almost touch the water.

When she looked up, she was faced once more with that searching expression in those gray eyes.

"Tea?"

She was offered a cup filled to the brim.

Chapter 14

The sight that met Thomas's gaze in the bathroom mirror was a weary, exhausted man. It definitely didn't look like someone who was due to join the Linde family soon for a pleasant evening.

He had come out to Harö just after six. He was due at Nora's in an hour, but before that he needed to shave and shower.

Thomas's house was on one side of northern Harö. His parents had bought the place back in the fifties, long before owning a cottage in the archipelago became so popular. A few years ago they had given their two sons each a part of the land.

There had been an old barn on Thomas's section. It was pretty dilapidated, but it was in a beautiful location right by the water, with a huge weeping birch beside it. Pernilla and Thomas took on the barn and put a lot of time and effort into transforming it into a proper summer home. A home that was perfect for a family.

By the time they had finished, the old barn had become a wonderful house with big windows and an open-plan interior. They had built a large loft bedroom to make full use of the high ceiling. From the front door, a narrow gravel path led down to the jetty, which they had extended so there was room to sit on summer evenings.

The house swallowed up all their spare time and money, but the result was exactly what they were hoping for.

Then they split up.

They had hardly even managed one whole summer there before they went their separate ways.

Since the property had belonged to Thomas's parents, the decision was obvious. Pernilla kept the apartment in town, and Thomas kept Harö. It was neat and tidy and entirely logical.

And heartbreaking.

After the divorce he had found a two-room apartment in Gustavsberg. It was practical and functional and only twenty minutes away from work, but it wasn't a home. If anywhere, it was only on Harö that he felt at home these days.

He got his razor and shaving cream out of the medicine cabinet and ran hot water in the sink.

He hadn't the slightest desire to get in the boat and head over to Sandhamn. But Nora had invited him weeks ago, and he didn't want to disappoint her. Especially on such short notice.

"Come on, Thomas," she had said to him. "It'll do you good to get out and about. You can't just work or bury yourself on Harö. You need to start seeing people again."

She was right, of course. But it was so difficult.

He sank down on the toilet seat with the razor in his hand. Sometimes he felt as if he didn't have the strength to take one more step.

The last fifteen months had been the worst of his life. He wouldn't wish them on his worst enemy. Nights plagued by bad dreams about Emily and his inability to save her life. Days when he could hardly bring himself to go into work because he was afraid of breaking down in front of his colleagues. The gradual disintegration of his marriage, which he had been powerless to prevent.

Since the divorce had been finalized six months ago, he had avoided social gatherings. There had been no need for the company of others, just a deep desire to be left alone and in peace.

He had devoted almost all his waking hours to work. He had no idea how many late nights he had stayed at the station. But there was something restful about the dark corridors when everyone else had gone home. The emptiness appealed to him. He enjoyed sitting at his desk in silence.

Work had been his lifeline.

Without his colleagues, he doubted whether he would have made it. Getting up every morning had been a real struggle, yet he had taken on as much work as he possibly could. Volunteered for just about everything. Sat there for hours dealing with tasks that weren't part of his job.

As if every fresh case he solved helped him to rebuild his life, little by little.

Gradually it had begun to hurt less, but the pain was replaced by weariness. It overwhelmed him. Thomas was so exhausted he didn't know what to do with himself. He could cope with the days, but by the evening he was spent.

He had slept more during the past six months than in his entire life. All he wanted to do at night was to go to bed and sink into oblivion, escape from his life. It was as if he couldn't get enough unconsciousness.

It wasn't until the light began to return in April that he started to regain some of his old energy. He was able to rest in those long, light, late spring evenings. To his surprise he found he was breathing more easily.

But the distance between the professional police officer who conscientiously did his job and the private individual who merely wanted to be left in peace had not diminished.

He sat there in the bathroom trying to gather his strength. The dinner party would be starting soon. He stood up and applied the shaving cream to his face. With a determined smile at his reflection, he began to scrape the razor firmly down his cheek.

Kicki Berggren looked around the harbor, which was now half in shadow. The unpleasant taste of the tea she had been given lingered in her mouth. She hadn't even been offered a cup of coffee—just that revolting tea.

She had tried to rest in her room for a while, but she had been far too wound up, and after an hour she gave up. She picked up her jacket and walked down to the harbor; she needed something to drink. Something strong. And something to eat would be good. She crept down the stairs to avoid the manager, who was a bit of a busybody. She couldn't deal with her chatter now; she had enough to think about.

The Divers Bar looked nice, but when she got closer she could see that all the seats outside were occupied by younger people. Girls in low-cut tops and oversize shades were sitting there with boys who had greasy, slicked-back hair and red shorts. Rosé wine was obviously cool at the moment; there was a big silver wine cooler on every table, labeled "Think pink, drink pink."

Her own opinion of rosé was based on her experiences of Mateus Rosé, which had been the drink of choice in every backyard when she was in high school. It hadn't tasted good then, and it was unlikely that it would taste good now. And she'd had more than enough of spoiled, drunk teenagers on Kos. She didn't need that here.

She looked around for an alternative.

Sandhamn Värdshus, at the far end of the harbor, looked considerably more inviting. She headed for the area marked "Bar."

When she opened the door it seemed quite gloomy, but then her eyes adjusted to the subdued lighting, and she could see that she was in a large room with dark wood paneling on the walls and a cozy atmosphere.

A young man with long blond hair in a ponytail was standing behind the bar, taking an order. The long tables were occupied by a handful of people with half-empty glasses in front of them. The place was almost empty, but then a dark bar probably wasn't the first place the tourists in their summery clothes would go on a lovely evening like this.

Through the window she could see a line of people patiently waiting for a table outside, but sitting indoors suited her perfectly. She needed to be alone for a while, and she wanted something to eat so she could get rid of the disgusting taste in her mouth.

A blackboard on the wall listed the daily specials. Everything looked appealing, and she settled on bubble and squeak with a beer.

She carried her glass over to a corner table far from the bar. She took off her jacket and placed it on the chair next to her, then dug a comb and mirror out of her purse. She dragged the comb through her long hair, then tucked it in the breast pocket of her jacket. Without thinking, she took out her cigarettes, then remembered that people were no longer allowed to smoke indoors in Sweden.

From the corner of her eye she saw a man walk in and order a beer at the bar. He picked up his glass and made his way over to her part of the room.

She automatically smiled at him. Years of welcoming strangers to the tables in the casino evoked the upward curve of her lips without a second's hesitation.

The man looked pretty good, around forty. Slim build, faded blue T-shirt and jeans, sneakers. His hair needed cutting, but at least it looked clean.

Suddenly she felt the need for some company. As their eyes met she moistened her lips and opened her mouth.

"You're welcome to sit here," she said, pointing to the chair opposite her. She smiled as he sat down.

"Do you live here?" she asked.

He looked up from his beer and nodded. "Mmm, I've got a house on the island."

"A summer cottage?"

"No, I live here all the time. I was born on Sandhamn. I've lived here all my life," he said, raising the glass to his mouth.

Kicki edged a little closer. "I'm Kicki."

"Jonny." He held out his hand for a second, then changed his mind and nodded instead.

"What do you do?" Kicki asked.

"This and that. I'm a carpenter, but I do a bit of painting as well. I do all kinds of jobs for the summer visitors."

He took a swig of his beer and wiped his mouth with the back of his hand. As he put the glass down some of the liquid spilled over onto the table, but it didn't seem to bother him.

"What kind of things do you paint?" Kicki was interested. She needed a diversion for a little while, and she was curious about life on the island.

"All kinds of things. Mostly nature." He gave an embarrassed laugh, then took a pencil out of his back pocket and reached for a napkin that was lying on the table. With rapid strokes he drew Kicki in profile. It was no more than a few lines, yet the likeness was striking. He had managed to capture both her features and her expression in seconds.

He pushed the drawing over to her.

"There you go."

"Impressive," Kicki said. "Do you do this all the time?"

"Not exactly. I spend most of my time doing carpentry in the summer. There's always something that needs fixing, and when people are on vacation, they don't want to do it themselves. They also pay well—cash, of course, but that's fine. Nobody needs to bother with a receipt, do they?" He underlined his words with a wry smile.

A blond waitress arrived with Kicki's food. She put the plate down on the table and handed over a knife and fork wrapped in a napkin. The food looked delicious, with a fried egg on the side and a generous serving of beetroot. The waitress picked up Kicki's glass with a practiced movement and smiled at them.

"Can I get you anything else?"

Kicki looked at her companion. He seemed nice. A bit shy, but interesting. There was something puppyish about him, which appealed to her.

She leaned forward, pushing back a strand of hair as she winked at him. "How about buying me a beer? Then you can tell me what people get up to on Sandhamn on a Friday night in the middle of summer. This is my first visit."

CHAPTER 15

This was what Nora called a perfect Sandhamn evening.

From the gardens, all around they could hear the sound of their neighbors also enjoying dinner outside. In the distance, Dinah Washington was singing "Mad about the Boy." The air was so still that the buzzing of the bees was clearly audible, and the swallows were flying high—a sure sign of continuing high pressure. It was almost nine o'clock, but the air was still warm. The perch fillets had been delicious, and everyone was enjoying themselves.

As dessert was served, the conversation turned to the dead man on the shore.

"How's the investigation going?" Henrik asked.

"Well," Thomas said, "there are no signs of foul play. An accident, probably. He might have fallen overboard from one of the ferries to Finland; I mean, they do pass here every night." He took some rhubarb crumble before he went on. "He was a lonely person. No immediate family, no parents still alive, no friends as far as we can tell. The only relative he had was a cousin, a woman he seemed to be fairly close to. But he had a pretty tragic life, so to speak." As he uttered the words, he regretted them. The parallel with his own life was all too clear. No family, no children; he was approaching forty and lived in a two-room apartment just like the dead man. Who was he to call Krister Berggren's life tragic?

"What makes you think he died of natural causes?" Henrik asked as he passed around the pitcher of vanilla sauce.

The question brought Thomas back to reality. He pulled himself together with some difficulty. "There's nothing to suggest anything else. He drowned. The only strange thing is that he had a rope around his waist. But that doesn't necessarily mean anything; sometimes there just isn't an explanation."

"A rope?"

"Yes, a kind of loop that had been passed over the body. It looked like ordinary rope. We haven't been able to trace it because there was nothing unusual about it."

"Was there any reason for him to take his own life?" Henrik asked.

Thomas shook his head. "I don't think so. We haven't found a suicide note. But it's hard to say for certain."

"Do you know any more about the fishing net?" Nora asked.

"No, nothing. There was a long net needle woven through one corner, but that doesn't tell us much. Besides, the body probably drifted into the net after the man died. It's hardly surprising; so many people lay their nets around the islands."

Henrik leaned forward, clearly interested. He swallowed his food as quickly as he could and went on. "What did it say on the needle?"

"There were just two letters: *GA*. Hard to draw any conclusions from that."

Nora tried to think. "Do we know anyone with those initials?"

Thomas shrugged. "I don't know if it's all that important. I mean, the net could belong to just about anyone who fishes in this part of the archipelago. Most indications still suggest that we're looking at an accident."

"What does that mean?" Nora asked.

"The case will be closed. There are no suspicious circumstances, so we'll wrap up the investigation."

"So will you get to take a vacation?" Nora asked as she poured the last of the wine.

Thomas nodded. "Very soon, I'm happy to say. I just have to finish this off next week, then I'll be heading straight for Harö."

"Are your parents there?"

"Of course. They went over at the end of April. Since they retired I think they spend more time on the island than in town." Thomas's face lit up at the thought of his parents. "They keep nagging me to take my vacation earlier, but I enjoy being there as the high season comes to an end. I'll be there when it suits me."

He raised his glass to Nora in a gesture of appreciation.

"Thank you for a wonderful dinner."

SATURDAY,
THE SECOND WEEK

CHAPTER 16

The evening had been a success, Nora thought as she made coffee. They had all been in good form and seemed to have enjoyed themselves. They had sat outside until midnight without feeling cold.

Since it was Saturday, they had a blessed reprieve from swimming lessons. They had even managed to sleep in, as much as possible with a lively six-year-old in the family.

"Come on, boys," she called to Adam and Simon, who were playing in the garden. "Let's go down to the jetty to surprise Daddy."

Henrik had gone down to sort out the fishing nets, a task that could take quite some time, so a cup of coffee would no doubt be appreciated.

She and the boys had spent almost fifteen minutes in line to buy cakes. It seemed as if half the population of Stockholm had decided to head out to the islands to make the most of this beautiful summer's day.

On the other hand, it was no great sacrifice to stand chatting in line outside the picturesque bakery, where white wrought-iron chairs and tables were set out for those customers who wanted to enjoy their purchases right away.

Henrik was very busy down by the water. Tall poles with hooks at the top lined both sides of the jetty. The nets were hung from these hooks, then poles were used to remove any seaweed—an ancient method that was still in use throughout the archipelago.

Henrik had finished cleaning approximately half of the nets, and the seaweed he had removed lay in small piles at his feet. He had taken off his shirt and was wearing only his shorts, but still the sweat was pouring down his back.

Adam dashed over to help out. Henrik would often take him along to lay the nets and would let him steer the boat a bit. Adam loved going with his dad, and Henrik was happy to spend time with him.

Where the jetty joined the land there was a small area that belonged to Henrik and Nora's house. It wasn't very big, but there was just enough room for a bench, two chairs, and a table, so they could sit by the water.

The family's boat was moored there. It was a small launch with an outboard motor and went by the name *Snurran*. It was just three yards long and had served them well for many years. It was exactly the right size to go off and find the perfect spot to swim or sunbathe or pick someone up if they were stranded in Stavsnäs after the last ferry had gone.

"Coffee time," Nora shouted to Henrik.

She sat down at the table and began to set out coffee cups and cakes. For the boys there was juice in colorful plastic mugs. Her thoughts turned to the call she had received the previous day. Her cell phone had rung while she was sitting by the pool, waiting for Simon's swimming lesson to end. The human resources director from the bank wanted to speak to her. The latest reorganization within the company meant that operations had now been divided into four regions: north, south, central, and west. Each region was now to be allocated its own legal adviser, who would answer to the regional board. Would Nora be interested in the post for the southern region? It would be based in Malmö, so she would have to be prepared to move, but she would receive a significant raise. In addition, it would be a major step up the career ladder within the bank.

Nora had felt both flattered and curious. It sounded like an exciting opportunity. It also meant that she would have a new boss, which would be a welcome change. She enjoyed her work, but she was truly sick of her current boss, who in her opinion was definitely not up to the job. He had been promoted to lead the central legal team at the bank at an unusually young age, when his predecessor had unexpectedly moved to a competitor. Ragnar Wallsten was a nonchalant, supercilious individual who liked to bad-mouth his colleagues within the organization—always behind their backs, of course.

While Nora and her fellow lawyers worked hard, he sat there with his door closed, reading financial journals. Since his office had glass walls, it wasn't difficult to see what he was up to. Nora had heard that he had married into a very well-known family within the world of finance, which might explain his inferiority complex but was no excuse for his dreadful leadership skills. How someone like Wallsten could have been appointed to such an elevated position within a major bank was a mystery, and it was incomprehensible that no one had realized how incompetent he was.

Therefore, the thought of marching into Ragnar Wallsten's office and telling him that she had secured a terrific promotion within the bank that meant he no longer had any jurisdiction over her was extremely tempting.

The HR director had told Nora that Sandelin & Partners, an independent recruitment company, would be interviewing all the candidates for the job. If she were interested, they would contact her to make arrangements.

She wondered how she was going to tell Henrik. The idea of relocating to Malmö was not going to be high on his wish list. On the other hand, she had completed her time as a clerk in Visby because that was where his hospital placement happened to be. She had also taken the full allotment of maternity leave when the boys were born, while Henrik completed his specialist training. She felt it was her turn now.

She was woken abruptly from her daydreams by Simon, who was throwing wet seaweed at her legs.

"Stop it," she said. "It's freezing!"

Simon's whole face seemed to be laughing as he bent down to pick up more seaweed. Nora held up both hands in a gesture of surrender.

"I give up—you win," she said. Simon was poised for the next onslaught.

Suddenly she heard the sound of an engine, rapidly getting louder. She shaded her eyes with her hand; it looked like Thomas's aluminum boat, a Buster. As it came closer, she could see Thomas standing behind the wheel. He swung the boat around in a wide arc, then slowed down and docked at the end of the jetty.

"Hi," said Henrik, holding out his hand. "Have you come to say thank you for last night already?"

"You're just in time for coffee," Nora said. "Sit down, and I'll fetch another cup."

"Sorry, I can't." Thomas didn't look happy. "I just wondered if I could leave the boat here for a few hours. The marina is full, and the police and medical launches are already moored at the emergency landing stage."

Nora looked at him more closely. His eyes reflected the seriousness of the situation. "What's happened?"

"Another body has been found. I'm on my way over to see what's going on."

Nora went cold all over. "Where?"

"At the Mission House. The maid found it when she went in to clean the room. Apparently the body was a real mess. Is it OK if I leave the boat here for the time being? I don't really know when I'll be able to pick it up."

"Of course. You can always tie up here, you know that."

Henrik and Nora's eyes met. Almost as one they turned and looked at the children, who were playing by the shoreline. Nora couldn't believe it. Two deaths on Sandhamn within a week. On her summer island. It seemed unreal. As a rule she didn't even bother locking the front door when she left the house.

She was seized by a sudden impulse to put her arms around her boys and never let go.

Where would this all end?

Chapter 17

Thomas walked quickly through the alleyways toward the Mission House. It was at the bottom of the hill below the chapel, next to the school. It was about a quarter mile from Nora's. If there had been no other buildings in the way, you would have been able to see the Mission House from her kitchen window.

When the evangelical movement swept through the archipelago at the end of the nineteenth century, people had gathered in this building, which resembled a church. It had been the first religious edifice on Sandhamn; the islanders' applications for a church of their own had been turned down time and time again, ever since the eighteenth century. At most the congregation had consisted of fourteen or possibly fifteen enthusiastic members.

For a few years now the Mission House had served as a bed-and-breakfast and conference center as part of the main Sandhamn Hotel. The large chapel had taken on the role of breakfast room and was occasionally used for special functions. It was a beautiful building, simple yet stylish. A building that bore the marks of times long gone.

And now there was a dead body upstairs.

Thomas nodded briefly to one of the uniformed officers he recognized, then opened the gate in the white-painted fence which enclosed the corner plot. A number of tables and garden chairs sat at the bottom of the steps. Tubs containing blue-and-yellow pansies brought color to the sandy garden, which like the rest of Sandhamn consisted of nothing more than a few feeble tufts of grass.

The main door was open, and Thomas quickly ran up the steps and into the hallway.

From the big room he could hear sobs and agitated voices. He was confronted by the sight of a near-hysterical woman sitting on a chair in one corner. Next to her stood an older woman who was trying to calm her down, in spite of the fact that she, too, was crying. There was another police officer in the room. When Thomas walked in, they all looked up.

"Anna's the one who found the body." The older woman pointed dramatically at the sobbing woman on the chair. "When she went in to clean number four."

Thomas went over to the cleaner, who was rocking back and forth and wringing her hands. It was obvious that she had been crying for some considerable time; her eyes were red and swollen. He wondered how he was going to question her; it would be impossible to get any sense out of her unless she calmed down.

He turned to the other woman, who gave the impression of being more composed.

"Thomas Andreasson, Nacka police. Do you work here?"

The woman nodded as she continued to pat the other woman on the back.

"My name's Krystyna. I'm the manager." The strong Eastern European accent came through before her voice broke. Her lower lip trembled, but she took a deep breath and went on in a slightly shrill tone. "It's the worst thing I've ever seen in my life. Dreadful! How can something like this happen here?" She turned away, her hand covering her mouth.

Thomas took out his notebook and a pen. The cleaner's sobs subsided a little and became a low mumbling.

"Could you tell me when the body was discovered?" he asked the manager.

She turned back to face him and glanced at the clock on the wall of the bright room. "We called the police immediately," she said, almost in tears again. "It can't have been more than thirty or forty minutes ago. Anna had knocked on the door several times so she could go in and clean, but there was no answer, and room four was the only one left to do."

"Was the door locked?" Thomas asked the woman in the chair.

She nodded. "Yes," she whispered. "I had to use my own key."

"Do you have any other guests at the moment?"

The manager nodded. "We're full, but there's no one in at the moment. They're all staying for the weekend. They'll be back this evening."

She was wearing a brightly colored striped apron. It looked as if she had been in the middle of making bread, because her arms and apron were covered in flour. Through a half-open door with a heavy, old-fashioned handle at the far end of the room, Thomas could just see the kitchen.

He decided to go upstairs and take a look around before continuing to question either of the women. Might as well get it out of the way. He turned to his colleague, who appeared to be in his thirties. "Could you show me the way to the room?"

The officer led the way up the stairs; the bedrooms were located along a narrow corridor. The door to number four was ajar.

As he walked in he saw the back of a person who was curled up and unnaturally still. There was an unpleasant, sweetish smell in the air—the smell of blood and death that had not yet turned into a stench.

Thomas looked around. The room was decorated in an old-fashioned, romantic style, with pine-clad walls and lace curtains. There was a small vase of flowers on the chest of drawers and a gold-framed painting of a sailboat on the wall.

The sun poured in through the window.

The contrast between the B&B and the dead woman on the bed could not have been starker.

He went over to the body and noticed that there was a large swelling above the right temple; the skin was heavily discolored with blue-and-red lines. There was a small amount of dried blood above the ear and in her hair. He moved around the bed to look closer at the face.

Suddenly he realized who it was.

Kicki Berggren, Krister Berggren's cousin, was lying dead in front of him.

He bent down. Her unseeing eyes stared up at him. She wore only a pair of red panties. Her slack breasts rested on the mattress. The covers had been pushed aside, and her clothes were strewn around the room. There was no sign that anyone else had stayed or even been in the room.

In a denim purse on the floor he found a wallet containing a driver's license, which confirmed the woman's identity as Kicki Berggren. He quickly took out his cell phone and called the station.

"It's Thomas. I've looked at the body, and forensics has to give this top priority. We also need to reconsider Krister Berggren's death. The victim is his cousin, and she was badly beaten."

It was midday by the time the investigative team arrived at the Mission House. In the meantime, the area had been cordoned off. Thomas had obtained a list of all the other guests from Krystyna and had even managed to conduct brief interviews with some of them. None had had anything significant to tell him.

The manager had been less than happy when she was informed that the whole building was now regarded as a crime scene and would be subject to a thorough examination. She was not allowed to touch anything, and the room where Kicki Berggren had been found was definitely not to be cleaned.

Since then, the day had passed at breakneck speed. The investigative team had done their best to secure as much biological evidence as possible. Since the door had been locked with the body inside and there were no signs of a struggle inside the room, there were many questions. Among other things, this could mean that Kicki Berggren had been murdered elsewhere, but Thomas always tried not to draw hasty conclusions.

He had spoken to the officer in charge of the local station and arranged to set up a temporary office there. It was obvious they needed a base on Sandhamn at this point. The investigation had moved into a completely different phase.

Chapter 18

Fuck, fuck, fuck, thought Jonny Almhult. The persistent knocking on his front door just wouldn't stop. His head felt like a brick, and he could have used his tongue to sand down his mother's skiff.

He was lying on his bed wearing the same clothes from yesterday. Lifting his head from the pillow was agony. He had no idea what time it was. He barely even knew where he was.

As he reached out and fumbled for the alarm clock, he knocked over a half-full bottle of beer. The yellowish-brown liquid poured out onto the floor and was quickly absorbed by the rug. He swore again and flopped back on the pillow.

The knocking continued.

"OK, OK. I'm coming." The words came out as a croak.

"Jonny, Jonny." His mother's voice penetrated as far as the bedroom. "Are you there, Jonny?"

"Calm down, Mom. I'm coming."

With a groan he sat up, got to his feet unsteadily, and staggered to the door. When he opened it, he was met by his mother's searching gaze. Unable to stop himself, he ran a hand over his stubble, feeling embarrassed.

"Why didn't you open the door? I've been knocking forever!"

Before Jonny had time to respond, she went on. "Do you have any idea what time it is? It's past two! I don't know how you can sleep at a time like this. The whole island is in an uproar!"

Jonny stared at her. He didn't know what she was talking about. He just wanted to go back to bed.

Ellen Almhult went on, extremely agitated. "Haven't you heard? They found another body. A woman, in the Mission House."

Jonny swallowed. If only his head hadn't been pounding like this. He leaned on the doorframe to stop himself from swaying and felt the sweat trickling down the back of his neck.

"What did she look like?" His voice was rough and hoarse.

"I had a word with Krystyna, that new woman who took over last spring. She didn't know what to do with herself."

Jonny grabbed his mother's arm with unexpected strength. "I asked you what she looked like."

"Calm down. There's no need to behave like that. She was nearly fifty; she turned up yesterday afternoon, according to Krystyna. Long blond hair. I suppose she looked like most people."

Jonny groaned inwardly. *Oh God.*

"Listen, Mom, I'm not feeling too good. I need to go back to bed."

"You're just like your father." Ellen's disapproval was clear as she compressed her lips into a thin line.

Jonny knew that expression well. He had seen it ever since he was a little boy, every time he or his father did something she didn't like. His father had spent his entire life living in the shadow of her disappointment. A disappointment Jonny couldn't handle right now.

"I'll speak to you later," he said.

"I just don't understand you," Ellen said. "Not at all."

"Please, Mom. I just need to be left in peace for a while."

"Alcohol will be the death of you, you know." She pointed a finger at him. He saw her lips begin to move and braced himself for the stream of words that he knew was bound to come.

Suddenly he couldn't bear it any longer. "I asked you to leave. I'll talk to you later."

He practically pushed her out and closed the door.

Jonny slumped to the floor. He could smell and taste his own breath. Rancid, stale beer. Too many cigarettes. The clump of fear stuck in his throat. His tongue felt like a swollen mass in his mouth. He needed a drink to calm him down and help him gather his thoughts.

He went into the kitchen, opened the fridge, and took out a beer. Standing by the sink, he knocked back the whole can and then grimaced as he dropped it in the trash. He tried hard to remember last night. The images were vague and unclear.

He had met that woman in the bar. They'd had a few beers together after he'd sat down at her table. After a while, he asked if she wanted to come back with him for a couple of drinks. They picked up their jackets and paid. The sun had gone down, but it wasn't really dark outside.

They went back to his place, which was no more than ten minutes' walk from the bar. He opened the front door and let her in. She looked around and said something about his plants. He fetched a couple beers from the kitchen, and they sat down on the sofa in the TV room. She lit a cigarette and asked if he wanted one.

She chain-smoked, complaining that she had a pain in her stomach. She moaned so much his ears had practically started bleeding.

Both of them got pretty drunk.

After a while he moved closer to her on the sofa and realized that she understood him.

If only she had listened to him, everything would have been fine. It would have been so easy to do what he wanted. So damn easy.

Chapter 19

Could there be a better way to spend a beautiful Saturday evening in the middle of summer than sitting in a meeting in a police station that was closed for the weekend? Thomas wondered.

He stared at his notes and came to the conclusion that the weekend was probably a lost cause. While the crime scene was being examined, he had called Margit to inform her of the latest developments. She hadn't appreciated the news.

DCI Persson had decided they should meet at seven o'clock on Saturday evening. That had given Thomas enough time to finish on Sandhamn and get back to the mainland. He was now sitting at one end of the conference table. Margit was on his right, with Carina next to her. Two younger officers, Kalle Lidwall and Erik Blom, had also had to give up their weekend.

Persson summarized the situation. "OK, so we have one victim who appears to have died as a result of a violent blow to the head. She is the cousin of the dead man whose body washed up on Sandhamn a couple of weeks ago. We still can't be sure, but there is nothing to indicate that Krister Berggren was intending to take his own life. Nor have we found anything to suggest that he was deliberately killed. It will be a few days before we know the exact cause of Kicki Berggren's death; the pathologists have promised to do their best, but they're short-staffed right now."

"Do the cousins have any connection to Sandhamn?" Margit asked. "Was it somewhere they used to go in the summer?"

It was obvious that she needed a vacation. She looked tired, and so far the summer sun hadn't made much of an impression on her face. She exuded an aura of impatience, as if she didn't really care about the fact that they had two unexplained deaths to investigate. All she wanted was for everything to be sorted out quickly, so she could begin her much-longed-for annual leave.

Thomas ran his hand through his short hair. "Not as far as I know. At the moment there's no clear link between Krister and Kicki Berggren and Sandhamn. But it's a bit of a coincidence for two cousins to be found dead on the same island within such a short period. We need to go through every possible connection. We'll see what we find in Kicki Berggren's apartment. Nothing we know about Krister Berggren links him to the island."

Persson cleared his throat. "We have one murder investigation on our hands at any rate. Margit, you're leading this one. Thomas, you're supporting Margit. Erik and Kalle will provide additional resources; Carina, help out wherever needed."

Carina turned to Thomas. "You only have to say the word, you know that." She pushed back her hair with a coquettish gesture. She was the only person in the room who was smiling.

Margit sighed; her expression was grim. "I'm supposed to be starting my vacation on Monday—have you forgotten that? We've rented a house on the west coast."

"Margit, we have two deaths and at least one is almost certainly murder."

Margit was on the warpath. She rarely gave in right away. Now she was fighting for her vacation as if it were a matter of life and death, rather than four weeks in July in a country where the temperature reached seventy degrees at best in the summer.

"And I also have a husband and two teenage daughters who I am responsible for. Have you ever heard the expression 'work-life balance'? I need this vacation. I've worked damn hard all year, you know that."

She stared at Persson, waving her pen around. He stared back, equally determined.

"May I make a suggestion?" Thomas said.

Persson and Margit paused their battle of wills and looked at him.

"If Margit would make herself available by phone, I could at least start on the investigation. If things take a turn for the worse, she can always get in the car and drive up, can't she? I know Sandhamn very well, and I can easily postpone my vacation for a week or two if necessary."

Margit raised her eyebrows at Persson, who sighed before responding.

"When I joined the police there was none of this garbage about work-life balance. You worked until the case was solved—that was all there was to it." He pondered for a moment, then capitulated in the face of the light of battle shining in Margit's eyes. "Very well. Margit, you can go, but you have to come back should it become necessary. And the final responsibility is yours. Until then, you and Thomas can talk by phone."

Margit looked relieved. "Of course. Thomas, you can call me anytime. I'll give you my husband's cell phone number as well, just to be on the safe side. Come to my office, and we'll go over what needs to be done." She gave him a grateful wink as she gathered up her papers and got to her feet. "This will work out perfectly," she said. The comment was clearly addressed to Persson as she turned and left the room.

***

By the time Margit and Thomas had finished drawing up their plans for the next stage of the investigation, it was late on Saturday night.

Kalle and Erik would travel over to Sandhamn the following morning to start their inquiries; Thomas would join them later in the day. During the evening they had gone through all the material on the cousins. Carina had checked every possible record on the computer to complete the picture.

Since more than 80 percent of all murders or attempted murders in Sweden were perpetrated by someone the victim already knew, they needed to get a picture of both cousins' lives and work situations, methodically going through the people around them, listing those the police would need to contact. It was like doing a jigsaw puzzle, hoping a picture of someone with a possible motive would gradually emerge.

As soon as the weekend was over they would also request all their relevant financial information. It was surprising how much you could find out by studying the ways in which people used their credit cards.

On Sandhamn, the investigation would focus on mapping Kicki Berggren's last twenty-four hours: what time she had arrived on the island, where she had gone, whether she had been seen with anyone else.

They had to find out everything they could about the people she had met during her stay. They would also contact the ferry company and the taxi firm that picked up passengers from the boat. A member of the crew might remember when she had traveled or know where she had gone. Every witness statement, however insignificant it might appear, could contribute to solving the case.

But first Thomas wanted to visit Kicki's apartment.

A home was like a silent witness to the owner's life. You could find out a great deal about a person's character, the way she lived, her friends and enemies. Perhaps he would find something that would reveal a connection between Kicki and Sandhamn.

Thomas also needed a better photograph of Kicki than her passport photo, which looked nothing like her. Door-to-door inquiries would start on Sandhamn as soon as possible, and a good likeness was essential.

After some thought, Thomas asked Carina to go with him to the apartment. In a case like this it could be useful to have a woman involved. She would see things he might miss. He was the first to admit that he wasn't exactly an expert on women.

That was one of the points Pernilla had made painfully clear to him during their last argument before the separation. He had walked into the bathroom to find Pernilla standing there holding a little nappy. It had been left behind when they were clearing away Emily's things.

"It wasn't *my* fault," she had said. Her eyes looked wild, as if she hated him at that moment.

And perhaps she did.

Thomas was thunderstruck. "I never said it was your fault," he eventually said.

She looked at him wearily, a small muscle twitching at the corner of her mouth. "For six months you haven't said a single unnecessary word to me. You don't even touch me anymore. When you do look at me, which is rare, I can see the accusation in your eyes. Do you think I don't know what's going on inside your head?" The tears began to fall, and she wiped them away. "It wasn't my fault," she repeated. "I wasn't responsible for what happened."

The chasm between them was too deep to be bridged with words, and in any case Thomas had no words at his disposal. He had never been the kind of person who was comfortable talking about his feelings, and now his emotions were in lockdown. Even the idea of trying was impossible.

He understood that Pernilla desperately needed reassurance, to know that he didn't blame her. But every time he opened his mouth to tell her, the words stuck in his throat.

Deep down, he was convinced that someone must have been responsible for Emily's death. Every time he saw her little body in his mind's eye, he was consumed by the need to blame someone. And if it wasn't Pernilla's fault, then whose fault was it?

The gnawing doubt just wouldn't go away. He couldn't stop wondering what would have happened if Pernilla had woken up that night. She was breastfeeding, after all. Shouldn't she have known instinctively that something was wrong? A part of him was aware that there was no logic to his reasoning, but he couldn't get the thought out of his mind. Why had she slept on as her child died beside her?

That was the last time they talked about Emily. A few weeks later he had moved out. The divorce had gone through quickly.

Thomas got to his feet abruptly, running his hand over his forehead as if to erase the memories. What was the point of brooding about the past? He had gone over those final hours of Emily's life so many times, and every time it was just as painful. He had to make a fresh start.

With a sigh he went over to the window and stretched to shake off the stiffness in his back. Through the window he could see one of the police launches setting off from the jetty at Nacka Strand. He caught himself wishing he were standing there at the wheel, with nothing to think about except patrolling the islands.

Then he looked away. He had a murder to investigate.

SUNDAY,

THE THIRD WEEK

Chapter 20

When Thomas went out to Sandhamn on Sunday, he had a photograph of Kicki Berggren with him. They had found it in her apartment early that morning. It was the only useful thing he and Carina had found so far.

Kicki had lived close to her cousin, in a similar residential block in Bandhagen. Her three-room apartment wasn't large, but it was well planned and considerably more homely than Krister's. It consisted of a bedroom, a living room, and a small dining room.

One corner of the living room was occupied by the computer and TV; there was also a sofa and a coffee table with piles of celebrity magazines all over the place. Thomas recognized pictures of everyone from the royal family to the Beckhams. The bookcase was from IKEA; he had the same one, but in a different color. Just like Krister's apartment, it was filled with magazines and DVDs, although there were a few books on the top shelf.

It was obvious that Kicki Berggren had been away. Her suitcase was still in the hallway, and a film of dust covered the furniture.

Thomas opened her computer to see if there was anything that might help them, but her e-mails mostly involved chats with girlfriends and the usual Internet jokes. He recognized several of those from his own inbox.

A number of websites were listed as favorites. Thomas flicked through them and noticed that she had recently visited the Waxholmsbolaget homepage, presumably to find a timetable for the ferries to Sandhamn.

None of the other pages provided clues as to the reason for her visit to the island. There were no saved documents or other information that might help them. There was nothing whatsoever on Kicki Berggren's computer that could shed any light on the matter.

Why did she go over there? Thomas wondered as he perched on the edge of her bed. The duvet cover was pale green with a pile of matching cushions in the middle of the bed. There was an ashtray containing a stubbed-out cigarette on the bedside table.

When Kicki had come to the police station, she hadn't said anything about the possibility of visiting Sandhamn, and yet she had gone there two days later. So there must have been some reason that she hadn't mentioned to him—possibly someone she had decided to visit? But why hadn't she told him? Had she already known what lay behind Krister's death?

Carina went through her clothes, most of which came from H&M and KappAhl. A number of black skirts and white blouses tied in with her profession as a croupier. The bathroom contained neatly arranged jars of moisturizers and other beauty products. An overflowing laundry basket on top of the washing machine had obviously been left for later. The bathroom cabinet contained a pack of condoms, along with painkillers and lozenges.

There was also a plethora of assorted brands of nasal drops; Carina wondered if it was the poor air quality in the casino that caused problems. She didn't know much about the life of a croupier but assumed it wasn't the healthiest working environment. Thomas had no idea.

After a while Carina called Thomas over and showed him a box she had found inside a closet.

"Look at this."

Thomas bent down; the box was full of photographs, many in black and white. He went through them at random. "Do you know who this is?" He held up a photo of a young woman.

"No."

"Krister Berggren's mother—Kicki's aunt."

Carina took the photograph and studied it carefully. "She's so beautiful. She looks like a 1950s film star!" She held up a wedding photo. "I suppose this must be Kicki's parents. The groom looks as if he's related to the girl in the other picture, doesn't he?"

Thomas leaned over to see. The groom seemed less than comfortable in his formal suit, but the bride looked happy and in love. She had a typical fifties hairstyle: neat curls and lots of hair spray. Her dress was simple but lovely, and she was holding a small bouquet of roses.

Thomas took the box into the kitchen and looked through the photographs. Many showed both Kicki and Krister at different ages, from childhood to adulthood. Neither of them had aged particularly well. The pictures of Krister as a little boy revealed a sullen child, usually peering at the camera from beneath his bangs. He rarely looked cheerful.

Kicki had been quite a pretty teenager, with long dark hair in a ponytail and only slightly too much makeup. But the pictures taken in recent years showed a woman who didn't seem happy. Her cheeks sagged, and instead of laughter lines around her eyes she had developed deep creases by the sides of her nose.

She seemed to have lived a single life for a long time; neither her e-mails nor her apartment suggested any long-term relationship. The freezer was well stocked with Weight Watchers meals for one, and the kitchen was less than well equipped.

A typical single person's household in the city, where more than 60 percent of the population lived alone and had no family.

Just like Thomas.

He saw himself with Pernilla, back in the days when they were happy and still married. When they were expecting Emily, full of anticipation and plans for the future. He hadn't imagined that just a few years later he would be approaching forty and divorced, while all his friends were fully occupied building their families. Or that he would be making regular visits to a small gravestone marking an even smaller grave and wondering what he had done wrong.

And who was to blame.

Once again, and for the umpteenth time, he reminded himself that he had to move on, to put the past behind him. He just didn't know how to go about it.

Carina gently touched his arm, concern in her eyes. "Come on, let's go. We're done here."

As soon as Thomas met up with Kalle and Erik on Sandhamn, they provided him with a brief update, and the three of them then divided up the necessary tasks.

While Erik continued knocking on doors, Thomas and Kalle visited all the shops and restaurants, starting at the north end of the island and working toward the Yacht Club. When they reached Värdshuset, the landlord shook his head. He couldn't say whether Kicki Berggren had been in the bar or not. Both the bartender and the waitress who had been working on Friday evening were temporary staff who only worked weekends. They wouldn't be back on the island until the next Friday. Thomas took their numbers but realized he would have to go and see them in order to show them the photograph of the dead woman. With a bit of luck they would be in Stockholm and could meet him at the police station.

He and Kalle carried on talking to staff in the shops and bars in the harbor area. Thomas counted a total of eleven establishments where you could buy or eat something. Not bad for a little island way out in the archipelago.

Just as they were leaving the Yacht Club's restaurant it struck him that there was one more place: the old hotel by the harbor that had been renovated a few years ago and reopened under the name the Sands Hotel.

He turned to Kalle. "Listen, we've missed the Sands; we need to go back and talk to them."

Kalle bent down and emptied his shoes for at least the tenth time. "How much sand is there on this island?" he said. "Is there no end to it? I thought the Stockholm archipelago was made up of rocks and pine trees. This is a clone of the Sahara."

"Stop whining; you could be stuck in a boiling hot police station, and instead you get to enjoy the beautiful archipelago," Thomas said.

"Easy for you to say; you've spent every summer running up and down the sand dunes."

Thomas ignored the comment and set off toward the hotel. "We'll have coffee when we get there."

To be on the safe side, they both had a Danish pastry as well, and then it was time to make a start on the door-to-door inquiries. The routine was always the same. Ring the bell, introduce themselves, show the photo of Kicki Berggren, ask the same question over and over.

By the time they had visited some thirty houses, Thomas was beginning to lose heart. Nobody recognized Kicki Berggren. It was as if she had never set foot on Sandhamn. A lot of people weren't home, which was hardly surprising on a beautiful summer day, but that just made the task all the more time-consuming since they had to make a note of the houses they would have to revisit.

Thomas realized this would take the entire following day. He wished he could call for backup, but the depressing truth was that everyone was on vacation. The moral of the story: try to avoid falling ill or getting yourself murdered in July, he thought. There are no hospital beds and no police officers. All those who could possibly take their annual leave had disappeared. With the possible exception of the press.

Persson had sent a message to say that they would be holding a press conference on Monday. The district commissioner was showing a vested interest in the case and would be attending. The newspapers were desperate for information; the combination of an idyllic locale and a summer murder was irresistible.

The media had also discovered the connection between the two people who had died. There was wild speculation about what was behind the "Killing of the Cousins on Sandhamn," as they referred to the case. The fact that it still wasn't clear whether Krister Berggren had died of natural causes was obviously irrelevant.

It wasn't difficult to spot the journalists on the island. When they weren't hanging around outside the Mission House, which was still cordoned off, they were swarming all over the village. Soon there wouldn't be a single person who hadn't been interviewed and expressed his or her views on the case.

CHAPTER 21

Jonny Almhult wanted to throw up. Sour bile surged up his throat and into his mouth. He broke out in a cold sweat on his forehead and the back of his neck. For a moment he could barely stay on his feet. He swallowed hard and grabbed ahold of the doorframe to keep his balance.

When the police had knocked on his door to ask whether he'd had any contact with Kicki Berggren, he had only just managed to hold himself together. He was already half-drunk, and it was only two thirty on Sunday afternoon. Since his mother woke him up on Saturday and told him a woman's body had been found at the Mission House, he had been drinking nonstop. He didn't dare be sober.

He had been spending all his time lying on the sofa in the living room, the thoughts going around and around in his head. From time to time he dozed off. When he woke up he suppressed the fear with more booze.

Occasionally he got a whiff of his body odor. It wasn't very nice.

Anxiously he wondered whether the cop had been able to tell that he was lying through his teeth. He had shown Jonny a photograph of the woman from the bar and asked whether he had seen her before.

Jonny had been adamant. He had never set eyes on her. He had crossed his arms so the cop wouldn't be able to see that his hands were shaking.

He had felt like the fact that she had been in his apartment was written all over his face. But the cop had merely apologized for disturbing him and wished him a nice day.

He could take his fucking nice day and shove it.

Jonny staggered back to the living room and flopped down on the sofa. He reached for the lukewarm can of beer on the table. What should he do if the cop came back? Stick to his story? Make something up?

No doubt Inger, who had served them in the bar, had already been busy gossiping about the fact that he had been sitting with that woman.

So unnecessary.

He had only wanted to have a chat with her. Nothing else. And then things had gotten out of hand. Because she didn't get it. Stupid cow.

How the hell could she go and die like that?

He went over what had happened yet again. They had been sitting on the sofa when she had started acting out. He'd had to do something. He'd had no choice.

He hadn't hit her very hard. Definitely not. Just a little slap to make her understand. He wasn't the violent type.

He knocked back the last of the beer and dropped the can on the floor with a metallic clang, and it rolled under the sofa. Why hadn't she done as she was told from the start?

And now he'd ended up in the middle of a nightmare.

He swallowed several times. He couldn't stay here. It was only a matter of time before the police realized they needed to question him. He had no intention of being caught. It wasn't his damn fault. He had never meant to kill her. That hadn't been the plan.

Without wasting any more time, he made his decision. He would head for the city. He threw a pair of jeans and a few T-shirts into a bag. He was pretty sure there was a direct ferry at three. If he got a move on, he should be able to catch it.

In the kitchen he grabbed a carton of milk and chugged it. He saw two cans of beer sitting in the fridge. Might as well take those with him. He swallowed a painkiller with the last of the milk and left the apartment.

He wondered whether he should leave a note for his mother but decided it would be simpler to call her later if he felt like it.

Jonny hurried down to the pier as quickly as he could. The *Cinderella* was waiting there, packed with tourists who had spent the day on the island and were heading home. Strollers and backpacks were everywhere. He suppressed the urge to run. *Nice and calm,* he thought. *Don't draw attention to yourself.*

The rapid walk had left him out of breath, but he made an effort to breathe quietly so no one would look at him. Keeping his head down, he boarded the boat and found a seat toward the stern. He pulled his hood down over his forehead and pretended to be asleep.

When he finally heard the three short toots indicating that the boat was departing, a sense of relief flooded his body. Then he had to rush to the toilet to throw up. Some of the vomit splashed on the floor, but he didn't care. He just about managed to clean himself up.

He spent the rest of the trip sitting in his corner, making sure he didn't make eye contact. He was desperate for a hit of snuff but didn't dare go down to the cafeteria to buy a tin. He nodded off from time to time, but it was a superficial, uneasy sleep that brought him no rest. Only a reminder that his body wanted nothing more than to drift away to a world where the events of the past few days had never happened.

The captain of the *Cinderella* steered toward Stockholm with a practiced hand. After the narrow passage through Stegesund, where the old traders' houses had been recently renovated, they reached Vaxholm, where a number of passengers disembarked. The boat then rounded southern Lidingö, with a brief stop at Gåshaga, before the familiar buildings of inner-city Stockholm appeared.

From his place at the stern of the quarterdeck Jonny watched as they sailed between Djurgården and Nacka Strand before finally docking at Strandvägen.

He picked up his bag and rummaged in his pocket for his ticket, which he handed over as he went ashore.

Now where should he go?

Chapter 22

The placards outside the newspaper kiosk sent shivers down Nora's spine.

"Sex Killing on Sandhamn—Naked Woman Found Dead," they said in thick black letters.

Usually the placards were advertising articles on how to improve your tan or get a flatter stomach for those bikini days, but this afternoon there was only room for sensational headlines. The evening tabloids had quickly translated the body of a dead woman into sex attacks in paradise, ecstatic at having found something to fill their summer editions, which under normal circumstances were seriously lacking in news. This story was an absolute gift for an editor who was on the ball and wanted to boost his sales figures.

Nora wondered whether she should refrain from buying the evening papers, but she just couldn't help herself. She almost felt ashamed as she picked up both.

She walked home with the papers under her arm, then made herself a cup of tea and went to sit in the garden. She picked a few mint leaves and dropped them into her cup; she liked the taste with the hot tea.

She could hear the boys laughing in Signe's garden. They were good at begging for a glass of Signe's black currant juice and homemade buns, and she always obliged when they scampered over, their expressions like that of a pleading cocker spaniel. Signe also baked incomparable jam tarts, which the boys loved, especially Adam.

However hard Nora tried, she just couldn't bake as well as Signe. Perhaps you had to be born before the war, she had thought with a sigh the last time her efforts hadn't found favor with Adam.

"It's not that they don't taste nice," he had said, gazing at her with those blue eyes, "it's just that they're not as nice as Auntie Signe's. But I still love you, Mommy," he had said with a wet kiss.

Picking up her cup, she opened the first newspaper and began to read. Two double-page spreads were devoted to the murder. There was an article about the unfortunate cleaner who had found the body and an almost frenzied interview that went into minute detail. The appearance of the half-naked body when it was discovered was greedily described, along with the reaction of the cleaner. They had also included speculation by the manager on the victim's life and why she had come to Sandhamn.

They had dug out an old photograph from Kicki Berggren's driver's license, in which she stared straight into the camera with a stiff expression and a dated hairstyle. Nora wondered why everyone looked so terrible in driver's license photos.

There was also a fact box giving information about the increase in violent crimes of a sexual nature in Sweden and information on attacks that had taken place in other parts of the country in recent months. The newspaper hinted that the police were unable to guarantee the safety of women. A politician had been interviewed and made authoritative statements about the importance of women being able to feel safe everywhere, particularly in the summer.

Nora was astonished by the description of Sandhamn. There was no way this could be the place where she had spent every summer since she was a child. Suddenly her beloved island had morphed into a locale for danger, for violence against women.

The second newspaper concentrated on the link to the Royal Swedish Yacht Club and all the famous sailing competitions that took place around Sandhamn.

"King Celebrates at Murder Scene," the headline screamed. A picture of His Majesty on board a boat in front of the Yacht Club restaurant dominated an entire page. The article gave a detailed account of various regattas with royal connections, before eventually moving on to a description of the crime itself.

Many of the Yacht Club's board members were well-known public figures; the newspaper had somehow managed to obtain a meaningless comment from several of them. They all expressed serious concern about what had happened.

All men, of course.

Nora sat there with the newspaper open in front of her. She thought about the connection between the deaths of Kicki Berggren and her cousin. Why would someone kill the two of them, and why on Sandhamn? She remembered the net needle Thomas had mentioned; it had been marked with the initials *GA*.

On an impulse she went into the kitchen and found the Sandhamn telephone book; it was produced by the Friends of Sandhamn and distributed only to its members. She started to go through the last names beginning with *A*. There were approximately thirty, and she carefully checked each one to see if anyone had a first name beginning with *G*. Then she did the same with those whose last names began with *G*. There were slightly fewer of these, and she searched for people whose first names began with *A*.

After a while she had a list of people whose initials were either *GA* or *AG*: a total of fifty-four people had a last name involving *G* or *A*.

She looked at the list. She knew many of them, or at least she knew of them. Sandhamn wasn't that big. As soon as she saw Thomas again, she would give him the list. He probably hadn't realized there was a special phone book that only covered Sandhamn.

Nora went back to the papers and their speculations. She was so absorbed in one of the articles that she didn't hear Henrik's footsteps when he came back from his run. She gave a start as he sat down opposite her.

"Are you reading that garbage?"

"I couldn't help it. It's so awful." She held out one of the papers so he could look. "It's like reading about a different world."

Henrik leaned forward and studied the articles. He shook his head. His T-shirt was striped with sweat, and his dark hair was damp. He wiped his forehead with the towel draped around his neck, then he pulled off his T-shirt and hung it over the white fence to dry.

"I ran past the Mission House. The whole place is cordoned off with blue-and-white police tape. They've closed it down until further notice. Not the best timing in the middle of the tourist season. On the other hand, perhaps we won't get so many tourists if this continues. I imagine people will decide to go somewhere else. I mean, what would you do if you didn't already live here?"

Henrik carried on flipping through one of the papers. He whistled when he recognized several of the board members from the Yacht Club.

"The Divers is full of reporters, by the way. Cameras everywhere you turn. Perfect for anyone who wants to get their face on TV."

He got up and turned to go inside for a shower. Nora stopped him. She had been thinking about the phone call from the bank all day and wondering when to mention it to him. She really wanted to know what he thought; hopefully he would be happy for her, in spite of everything.

"Hang on. I've got something to tell you."

Nora told him about her conversation with the HR director and the post they had discussed.

"It sounds exciting, doesn't it? Imagine working in Malmö! And the terms sound great."

Henrik looked at her with total incomprehension. The towel was still around his neck, catching the drops of sweat trickling down from his forehead. "But we can't move to Malmö," he said. "I mean, I work in Stockholm."

Nora smiled. "Yes, but you can get another job in Malmö," she said. "There are lots of good hospitals in the Öresund area. Besides, it's a terrific opportunity for me."

"But our life is here. Surely you can't be thinking of uprooting the entire family?"

He moved toward the house. She recognized the furrow in his brow. It always appeared when he was annoyed.

"We can talk about this later. I need a shower. The competition starts tomorrow, so I'm going down to the harbor to go over a few things with the crew."

Nora felt terribly disappointed. And upset. She had thought he would sit down and talk things over with her—instead he had simply walked away.

They had lived in Visby for several years because of his job. At the time there had been no question of anything other than finding a solution that worked for both of them. Now she had been offered her dream job, and he didn't even seem to want to discuss it.

It wasn't fair.

CHAPTER 23

The teenage couple was fully occupied with exploring each other's bodies. They had slipped away behind the lifeboats on the boat deck, and the boy's hand had found its way beneath the girl's white top. Her hands were caressing his back, and a subdued giggle was the only thing that gave away their presence.

The sea air was making the girl's nut-brown hair curl; it was cut in a modern style that framed her tanned face. She was still perspiring after energetically dancing at the club.

"Slow down, Robin," she said into his hair. "What if someone comes?"

The pink cocktails she had downed during the course of the evening were beginning to make her feel tipsy. She swayed slightly, and the words didn't come out all that clearly.

The boy didn't seem to have heard what she said. His hand continued to feel for her breast as he planted a series of little kisses on her throat.

The girl twisted out of his grasp and moved over to the rail.

"Slow down, I said. We've got all evening. Come and look at the view."

He tried to put his arms around her again, but she slipped away.

"Look, Sandhamn. One of my classmates lives there. I went to stay with her last year. There's lots going on there in the summer, but they did ask for ID to get into the club, even though there were tons of people in there who were obviously underage. Weird!"

The boy wasn't interested in talking, but the girl carried on gazing toward the shore.

"I wonder if you can see Ebba's house from the ship. It was in a fantastic spot by the water, right by the beach. Perfect for the summer."

The boy pulled her close to kiss her again. His hands gently caressed the area around her navel, which was exposed by her cropped top, which didn't even pretend to cover her stomach. His hands continued their journey upward once more, toward those soft, tempting breasts.

She saw the body falling down the port side of the ship just as his lips approached hers. At first, the sound of the engines prevented her from hearing anything.

The sound of the scream came when the body had already passed them.

"Robin," she said, struggling to breathe. "Did you see that? Someone fell overboard!" Her eyes were wide open, and tears of shock began to glisten. "Someone just fell into the water. We need to report it!"

The boy looked at her, his expression doubtful. "To who? Are you sure it was a person?"

She stared at him, worried. "We have to report it to someone," she said. "Anyone. They have to stop the ship and search for him!" She grabbed his hand. "Come on!"

He refused to move. Disbelief was written all over his face. Instead he attempted to pull her close again, trying to kiss her. "Forget it," he said. "You're imagining things. I'm sure it was nothing."

She pulled away. "What if someone pushed him? What if we've just witnessed a murder?"

He ignored her protests. "It was probably a bird. Anyway, it's too late to do anything now."

His hands stroked her warm skin with even greater enthusiasm. He pressed his throbbing groin against her thigh.

"Come on," he breathed in her ear. "Relax."

She struggled halfheartedly for a few seconds more, then her body softened. She turned her mouth to meet his and forgot all about the person who had fallen overboard.

Monday,

the third week

Chapter 24

The boat from Stockholm was a few minutes late. It should have arrived at eleven o'clock, but there was no sign of it yet. The pier was packed with people in shorts and thin tops. Some had brought carts to transport luggage.

"When will Grandma and Grandpa be here?" Simon asked for the third time.

"Any minute now, sweetheart. As soon as the boat gets in."

"I want ice cream," Adam said, looking over at the kiosk where a long, snaking line had formed.

Nora shook her head. "Not now. We'll be having lunch as soon as Grandma and Grandpa arrive. You'll spoil your appetite if you have ice cream now."

"But I want ice cream. Please, Mom."

Simon joined in. "Me, too. Please. Please, please, please!" He looked at her, his hands joined in prayer.

Nora gazed out across the sound. No sign of the *Cinderella*. She wasn't often delayed, but when it did happen, it was usually by quite some time. Nora gave in. It would take a while for everyone to disembark anyway.

"OK. But only a small one each. OK?"

Her voice was firm as she took out her wallet and gave Adam a fifty-kronor note.

"Don't spend more than fifteen kronor. I'll wait here for you."

She sat down on a bench next to the bulletin board displaying timetables and looked around. The harbor was full of life. The truck from the Yacht Club restaurant was busy loading goods that had arrived on the morning boat. One of the island's craftsmen puttered by on his platform moped, every inch crammed with sacks.

The fruit-and-vegetable stall had opened outside Westerberg's grocery store. The tempting array of sun-ripened tomatoes and other vegetables lying side by side with melons and nectarines reminded Nora of a market in the south of France. At one side of the stall an elderly lady was practically standing on her head in the potato bin, skillfully picking out the smallest and finest new potatoes. She held them up one by one, carefully examining them in the sunlight before setting them in her bag. The girl behind the register rolled her eyes, but the customer ignored her.

A little girl waiting for her mother to finish shopping was gazing at the boxes of raspberries and strawberries packed closely together.

Idyllic, thought Nora. *If it weren't for the fact that people were being murdered on this island.*

Just as the *Cinderella* docked at the landing stage, the boys came back clutching their ice cream.

Nora's mother-in-law was elegantly dressed as usual, in white shorts and matching wedge-heeled espadrilles. She was wearing a white straw hat and looked as if she were going out for lunch on the Riviera rather than visiting her grandchildren in the archipelago. Nora's father-in-law trailed behind, carrying their suitcase.

When Monica saw Nora, she put on an artificial smile. Then she spotted the boys.

"Darlings!" she shouted so loudly that everyone in the vicinity turned around. "Grandma's sweethearts! My little angels!"

She took a step back and contemplated the ice cream with a critical expression. "Why are you eating ice cream now? I thought we were having lunch shortly? You'll spoil your appetites. Did Mommy say you could have those?"

Nora suppressed a sigh and went over to greet her mother-in-law.

Monica kissed her on both cheeks in the French manner. *What the hell is wrong with a good old Swedish hug?* Nora thought. She greeted her father-in-law more warmly and offered to take the suitcase.

Lunch was waiting at home: gravlax with new potatoes. Dessert was a bought almond tart; she couldn't be bothered to spend all morning preparing a meal for guests who had invited themselves. There was no point in making an effort anyway—her mother-in-law would simply tell one of her countless stories about all the dinner parties she had given in various embassies, where everything had been homemade by Monica herself in spite of the fact that she was catering for dozens of guests.

As a diversionary tactic, Nora had invited Signe to lunch. Not even Monica dared to tackle Signe. Those gentle eyes turned to ice-cold steel at the least attempt. Signe couldn't bear anyone showing off. And she knew exactly why she had been invited; there had been no need for Nora to explain.

Monica looked at her daughter-in-law with curiosity shining in her eyes. She tucked a bony arm through Nora's.

"I want to know all about these dreadful murders. What's happening on this island? During all the years I've been coming here, I've never heard of anyone so much as hurting a fly. Is it some foreigner? I'm sure it is. We all know what they're like."

Nora never got used to the way Monica scattered her prejudices around as if it were the most natural thing in the world. Patiently, she tried to explain that she didn't really know much more than what was in the newspapers. Which Monica had no doubt read from cover to cover.

But Monica wasn't about to give up that easily. "That stylish friend of yours with the police . . . Torben. I'm sure he knows what's going on?"

"Thomas," Nora corrected her.

Monica carried on regardless. "He must be well informed. Do you think there might be some big gang behind it all? You are locking the doors at night, I presume?"

She looked at Simon and Adam, who were busy finishing their ice cream. Adam's shirt was already stained with chocolate. Nora swallowed her annoyance and decided she'd change his clothes when they got home.

"Is it a good idea to have the boys here when the police haven't cleared up these murders?" Monica went on. "You need to put the children's safety first, Nora."

Without waiting for a response, she adjusted her hat and embarked on a long story about a break-in at a good friend's house down in Båstad, which the police had failed to solve.

The point of the story was unclear, and Nora was merely required to nod from time to time. It seemed like a small price to pay to avoid an argument.

Chapter 25

After almost ten hours of door-to-door inquiries, Thomas came by on Monday evening to see how Nora was doing.

He had decided to stay on the island and spend the night at the local station, which meant he could take the first boat back to Stockholm on Tuesday morning, when the whole team would gather for a meeting.

He opened the door as he knocked and walked straight into the kitchen without waiting for an answer. Nora was busy making dinner.

She greeted him with a wan smile.

Nora and the boys had just waved her in-laws off from the jetty. Henrik wasn't expected back until later. Thomas was welcome to stay and eat with them as long as he was prepared to listen to a tirade about her mother-in-law. She handed him a cold beer and poured herself a glass of wine. He sat down at the kitchen table as Nora ranted about Monica.

When she had calmed down, she fetched a piece of paper with a long list of names on it. She sat down beside Thomas and explained what she had done.

"I've made you a list. I went through the Sandhamn phone book yesterday and looked for subscribers with the initials *G* and *A*—the initials that were on that net needle, the one you didn't think you'd be able to identify. There are fifty-four people on the list, but only three who have both initials."

Thomas smiled. "Nora Linde, master detective?"

Nora glared at him. "I'm only trying to help."

"I'm joking. I need all the help I can get. Margit's off on a vacation to the west coast, so she's running the investigation by remote control. Most of the people I need to talk to have already left, and Kalle and Erik have their hands full trying to track down witnesses."

"I think the problem will be locating them," Nora said, taking a sip of her wine. "There are no addresses on the island that can be linked to the names."

Thomas put his hands behind his head and gave the matter some thought. Nora's list was a good idea. He should have thought of it himself, instead of just dismissing the net needle. Especially now that he had a murder investigation on his hands. The question was how to find the people Nora had identified.

The buildings on Sandhamn were mainly in the village itself, and in Trouville on the southeastern side of the island, where most of the summer cottages lay. But there were also a considerable number of houses dotted around the rest of the island, so you could find residential properties just about anywhere, with no designated street names. There were also plenty of unnamed alleyways and historical indicators such as Mangelbacken or Adolf Square, places that were often named after someone who had lived or worked in a particular place. If you put it all together, it added up to a distinct lack of specific addresses. They could call the numbers on the list but would lose the ability to show the photograph of Kicki.

Thomas finished off his beer. He needed some sustenance before he gave the problem further thought.

***

A few hours later they were sitting in the garden drinking coffee. They had eaten fresh pasta mixed with grated Parmesan, halved cherry tomatoes, and basil. Homemade focaccia with black olives had tasted deliciously fresh after five minutes in the microwave, and the bottle of Rioja had gone down well.

The boys had fallen asleep right after dinner. Long, sunny days and lots of swimming caught up with them in the evenings. Although they had insisted they weren't the least bit sleepy, they had dropped off in seconds. The fact that their grandmother had been at them all day might well have contributed to their exhaustion, too.

Thomas had read them a long bedtime story. Adam had been quick to point out that it was only Simon who needed a story. He himself was ten years old and perfectly capable of reading his own story. However, that hadn't stopped him from listening with great interest.

Since Emily died, Thomas had spent more time than ever with Simon, who was very fond of his godfather. He seemed to understand that Thomas was deeply affected by grief, even if he never talked about it.

"Have you heard from Pernilla lately?" Nora asked tentatively.

"Not much. I got a postcard from Halmstad midsummer, but that's the only sign of life I've had from her in months."

"Do you miss her?"

Thomas rested his chin on one hand, his eyes fixed on some distant point. It was a little while before he answered. "I miss the life we had together. The company, the feeling that we were a couple. Little things like knowing someone cares if you're home late from work. Sometimes I feel as if I might as well move in to the police station." He lifted his cup halfway to his mouth, and a shadow passed across his face. "After all, nobody would even notice if I didn't come home. Maybe I should get a dog."

"Do you often think about what happened?" Nora couldn't stop the tears springing to her eyes. She had taken Emily's death almost as hard as Thomas. The thought of finding your little girl cold and dead beside you when you woke was unbearable.

She swallowed quickly and drank some of her wine to prevent the tears from falling.

Thomas didn't appear to have noticed anything. He carried on talking, almost to himself. "Sometimes I wonder what Emily would look like if she were alive today. I can still see her as a baby, but she'd be a little girl now, walking and talking." He shook his head. "Emily was never meant to grow up." His voice thickened slightly. He took a sip of his coffee, then another. "I envy you when I see your boys. They're terrific. Simon's great."

Nora placed a consoling hand over his. "You'll get another chance to have a family of your own. Trust me, you're a real catch. You're bound to meet someone new and have children."

Thomas gave a wry smile, then shrugged. "At the moment it doesn't seem all that important. I'm happy with my own company. I get by. And you and your family have been a great support for me, just so you know. I really do appreciate it."

"You're always welcome here," Nora said, topping off their glasses with the last of the wine. "So how's the investigation going?"

"No luck so far," Thomas said. "It seems so strange. Two people turning up dead within a few weeks. It's as if one of those English detective TV series has suddenly become a reality. The only thing missing is an English inspector with a pipe." Thomas laughed but quickly became serious again. "We don't actually know if both of them were murdered. Kicki Berggren was killed by another person, but the only thing we know about her cousin is that he drowned. We can't jump to conclusions."

"There has to be a connection. The question is, why should someone want to murder two cousins? They must have been mixed up in something illegal, don't you think?" Nora waved her spoon to underline her point. "And I can't stop thinking about the fishing net. How does that fit in?"

"No idea. It might have been sheer coincidence. There isn't even a guarantee that the net belonged to someone on Sandhamn. It could belong to someone from one of the other islands."

Nora nodded. "What did it look like, by the way?"

"Torn—a mess. But it had been in the water for months, so that's hardly surprising."

"What if it was old? Nets can be used for years, if you look after them and mend them when they tear," Nora said. "It could be a really old net, one that belonged to a different generation." She was struck by a sudden thought and leaned eagerly toward Thomas. "There was actually someone on Sandhamn who had the initials *GA*. Someone I didn't put on the list. Do you remember Georg Almhult, Jonny's father? Jonny lives on the island—he's a carpenter, and he also paints pictures. He helped us out the other week when the fence needed mending. Jonny's father's initials were *GA*. What if it was his dad's net, even though he's dead?"

"You mean Jonny might have had something to do with Krister Berggren's death?"

Nora waved the question aside. "I've no idea, but if you could trace the net, it would at least be a start. It's worth looking into, isn't it?"

She gazed at him and leaned back in the white garden chair, pulling her jacket more tightly around her. There was definitely an evening chill in the air, and a cool breeze blew in off the sea.

Nora pictured Jonny Almhult.

When Nora was twelve years old, Jonny was one of the cool teenagers who hung out down by the harbor. He was a talented artist, and in seconds he could produce a pencil sketch that bore an almost creepy resemblance to his subject. He had been painting watercolors for years and had probably dreamed of going to art school in the city.

There was a long-standing artistic tradition on Sandhamn; both Bruno Liljefors and Anders Zorn had spent time on the island, and Axel Sjöberg had been a permanent resident.

But Jonny never did get away. He remained on Sandhamn with his parents. As the years went by, he got stuck in a rut. Like many other lonely bachelors, he drank too much and never managed to find a steady girlfriend. He made a living as a carpenter and general handyman, working for the summer visitors, and from time to time he sold the odd picture, featuring an archipelago motif. Nora remembered Georg, his father, clearly. He had been Sandhamn's stonemason. He had looked exactly like his son: wiry build, medium height, not particularly striking.

He had been fond of the bottle, too.

When he died, his widow, Ellen, had only Jonny left. There was an older sister, but she had left the island long ago. She was married to an American and lived overseas, if Nora remembered correctly.

Thomas interrupted her train of thought. He had also met Jonny over the years. "I find it difficult to imagine Jonny as the brains behind some sort of criminal enterprise," he said.

"But as somebody else's sidekick?" Nora asked. "Someone who needed a hand to deal with a person who was causing problems? A person who needed frightening into keeping their mouth shut, for instance?"

"I think you might have watched one too many crime shows."

"Seriously," Nora insisted. "Everyone knows he has a problem with booze. Maybe he's prepared to do whatever it takes to get money. What if there's some kind of link? Surely it's worth having a word with him, isn't it? And at least you know where he lives."

Thomas thought for a moment, then he looked at his watch. "Time I made a move. I'll go to Jonny's. If I leave now, I can be there before it's too late." He gave Nora a brief hug. "Thanks for dinner. I'll call you."

Chapter 26

Jonny Almhult's house was dark and deserted. Thomas decided to knock on Ellen's door; she lived in a larger house right next door. It wasn't uncommon in the archipelago to build more houses on the same plot as the family increased.

Jonny's mother opened the door wearing a fleecy pink robe. She looked surprised to see him.

"Good evening, Ellen, do you remember me? Thomas Andreasson. I'm with the Nacka police now," he said.

She stared at him.

"Sorry to disturb you at this late hour. I need to talk to Jonny, but he doesn't seem to be home."

Ellen still looked surprised but not quite so alarmed. "He might be at the bar," she said. "Or asleep. He's not that easy to wake. Would you like me to go and see?"

"That would be great, since I'm here."

Ellen picked up a key, and they went over to the smaller house.

Thomas looked around. The compact house was painted Falu red, like so many in the archipelago. White eaves and wooden cladding.

There was a pile of unused wood in the garden, along with several defunct boat engines.

Two tubs of glorious pelargoniums stood by the door, and a pot containing a big lilac petunia was hanging in a birch tree.

"Do you do the gardening?" Thomas asked.

"No, that's Jonny's job," Ellen said. "He's got green fingers, believe it or not. He even reads those gardening magazines. He's all grown up now."

She shook her head. Thomas couldn't work out whether she was proud of her son or worried about him.

Ellen opened the door and went inside. "Jonny," she shouted. "Jonny, are you home?"

Thomas followed her. It was a typical island bachelor pad. Sand on the floor on the porch, wet-weather gear hanging on the wall. 1950s kitchen. More beautiful pelargoniums on the windowsill. Jonny had a knack for flowers, that much was clear.

A huge television dominated the sitting room; presumably it helped to pass the long, dark winter evenings when the village was deserted and the summer cottages long since closed up. Several attractive watercolors hung on the walls; they were signed *JA*.

A row of empty beer cans were on the table, along with an ashtray full of cigarette butts. Thomas noticed that several bore the marks of lipstick.

The house smelled stale and stuffy. Nobody seemed to have aired the place out for several days. There were beer bottles on the dish rack, and even more cans next to the fridge.

Ellen disappeared into a room beyond the kitchen.

"He's not in the bedroom," she said when she came back. "He must be at the bar. That's where he usually is if he's not at home. Have you tried his phone?"

"I don't have the number, but if you could give it to me, that would be great." Thomas took out his notebook to write down the number. "Have you spoken to him today?"

"No. He hasn't been very well, so I didn't want to disturb him."

It was obvious that Ellen was uncomfortable; she spoke slowly and avoided looking him in the eye.

"What do you mean by 'not very well'?"

Ellen looked unhappy. She tightened the belt on her robe and pushed her hands into her pockets. She sounded embarrassed as she answered. "He'd been drinking the last time I came over."

"When was that?"

"Saturday."

"What time?"

"I can't remember exactly. In the middle of the day, I think. Around twelve."

"And he was drunk?"

"Yes, but not very drunk. He'd had a few beers." Ellen pursed her lips. "I know what men look like when they've had a few."

"Does Jonny have a girlfriend?"

"Not as far as I know. He's never been that popular with women. He's shy, just like his dad." She hesitated. "But he's kind, very kind. He wouldn't hurt a fly."

Thomas glanced at the coat hooks in the hall, where a white denim jacket adorned with sparkling studs hung alongside the wet-weather clothing.

"Is that yours?" he asked, against his better judgment.

"No," Ellen said. "It's not exactly suitable for someone my age, is it?"

"Do you know whose it is?"

"I've never seen it before."

Thomas took down the jacket and carefully checked the pockets. In his mind's eye he could see Kicki Berggren when he went down to reception in the police station to meet her. She had been wearing an identical jacket. It couldn't be a coincidence.

In one pocket he found a half-empty packet of Princes. The same brand Kicki had had in her handbag, the same brand she had fiddled with throughout their interview. In the breast pocket there was a comb with several long blond strands of hair; more than enough for DNA analysis.

He moved toward the front door, then changed his mind and went back into the sitting room. Something had caught his attention. He looked over the walls. He stared at the sofa, the TV, the stereo.

Then he realized what it was.

There was a radiator under the window, the same kind of ugly gray radiator found in thousands of Swedish homes. Rectangular, with a valve at the bottom to regulate the heat. On one corner he could see something brownish and dried. It looked as if a strand of blond hair was stuck to the brown patch. It wasn't a big mark, but it was definitely there.

He stopped himself from touching it. "Ellen, I need to bring in a forensics team to go over the house. You mustn't come back in until they've finished."

Ellen looked terrified. "What do you mean? Why would the police need to go over Jonny's house?"

Thomas sympathized with her. Her arms were tightly crossed over her chest, as if to defend herself from something she didn't want to hear. Her pale lips were barely visible as she clamped her mouth shut, trying to suppress her anxiety.

"I have another question," Thomas said. "Have you or Jonny kept any of Georg's nets?"

Ellen didn't understand the question. "Nets?"

"Fishing nets, I mean, with needles marked *GA*? Have you kept any of those?"

"I suppose so," Ellen said, "but I don't remember how many. I'll have to look in the boathouse." Her hand flew to her mouth as she was struck by a sudden realization. "You don't think Jonny had anything to do with the deaths of those two cousins, do you?"

"I'm not at liberty to say at the moment. We'll have to wait and see. If Jonny comes home or calls you, please ask him to contact me immediately. It's extremely important."

He put his arm around her shoulders and guided her gently toward the door.

"I need you to give me your keys to this house. And the boathouse."

Ellen's hand was shaking as she passed over the keys.

She looked lonely and frightened. Thomas felt sorry for her, but there wasn't much he could do. The most important thing was to get a team over as soon as possible, so they could find out if Kicki Berggren had been in Jonny's house.

He was fairly sure the answer would be yes.

"Do you have any masking tape or something along those lines, so I can seal the door while I'm waiting for backup?"

Ellen nodded. "In the kitchen. My kitchen," she said as she walked out.

Thomas accompanied her back to the big house. He waited in the hallway while she fetched the tape. Through the door of the sitting room, he could see a tall Mora clock in one corner. The furniture looked dark and old-fashioned.

Thomas yawned. He was exhausted after a long day's work. The thought of traveling back to town first thing tomorrow morning wasn't exactly appealing, but he would have to live with it.

"Go to bed, Ellen," he said when she returned. "It'll all work out, you'll see."

He went out and closed the door behind him, then took out his cell phone to call the station. With a bit of luck they might be able to send a team over right away by helicopter.

Perhaps it wouldn't be such a late night, after all.

Tuesday,

the third week

Chapter 27

Thomas stared at the preliminary autopsy report, which had been sent over to Nacka by the pathologist.

It described the body of a female, medium height, normal build, whose death had occurred sometime between five and ten on Saturday morning.

According to the report, the woman had received a blow to the right temple. This blow had resulted in internal bleeding around the temple and right eye, with some damage to the skin. The left-hand side of the back of the head had also sustained damage; it had been struck at an angle and from below the victim with considerable force. The attacker had used something hard and pointed. There was evidence of limited bleeding just behind the right ear. A major hemorrhage had occurred in the brain; this was likely the cause of death, but there had also been a number of hemorrhages in the chest cavity and stomach, as well as inside the mouth and pharynx. Traces of blood had been found in the intestines.

He continued reading the clinical text. It was hard to believe that it concerned a human being, a flesh-and-blood individual who had laughed and loved and appreciated life. If that had been the case, he thought, remembering her apartment in Bandhagen.

Samples of blood, urine, aqueous humor from the eye, and a liver biopsy had been taken and would be sent to the National Forensics Laboratory in Linköping as soon as possible, with a request for priority analysis.

He suddenly stopped reading.

The report stated that the cause of death could not be established beyond doubt. It had not been possible to ascertain what had caused the extensive internal bleeding.

Kicki Berggren had probably been killed by hemorrhage in her brain, caused by either the blow to her temple or the back of her head. But there was no explanation for her other internal bleeding. There had to be more to this.

Thomas knew from experience that forensics hated sending a report that contained so many question marks. When there was no logical explanation for the injuries found, this was meticulously spelled out. It was then up to the police to conduct a thorough investigation in order to find the cause.

Thomas frowned. Now they would have to wait for Linköping to see if there was an answer in the tissue samples. That would take at least four or five days—if they were lucky.

In his frustration, he managed to knock over his cup of tea, and the hot liquid quickly spread across his desk. As he tried to stem the flow with a napkin that was far too small, he felt more uncertain than ever about where the investigation was heading. He was also worn out. He had slept for a little while on the boat, but it had been hard getting up at five thirty to catch the first ferry back to Stockholm.

It had been almost midnight by the time he got the investigative team over to Jonny's house, so he hadn't had much sleep. Admittedly he wasn't someone who needed eight hours every night, but he could certainly feel how tired he was today.

He went to the washroom and splashed cold water on his face. It didn't help much, but it made him feel slightly better. He picked up the report and headed for the conference room.

Persson was already in his usual seat, with Carina next to him. She smiled at Thomas when he glanced at her. He was struck by how pretty she was in the sunlight filtering in through the window. She also looked cheerful, in sharp contrast to his other colleagues, whose gloomy expressions no doubt mirrored his own. Kalle was sitting next to Carina, with Erik opposite her.

A speakerphone was in the middle of the table. Thomas guessed that Margit had been called, despite the fact that she had just started her vacation. But at least this meant she didn't have to abandon her family and travel all the way back to Stockholm.

Persson took a sip of coffee and cleared his throat. "Thomas, can you start us off? What have we got?"

Thomas held up the autopsy report. "We have a woman who has been subjected to physical violence, although not of a particularly excessive nature, according to the report. She received a blow to the back of her head and another to her right temple. The blow to her temple was not fatal and was comparatively light, and since the blood vessels are close to the surface around the eye, the injury looks much more serious than it actually was. She also suffered internal bleeding, which does not appear to have been caused by the assault."

"So what was the cause of death?" Persson was looking impatiently at Thomas.

"According to the pathologist, she appears to have suffered a brain hemorrhage as a consequence of the back of her head coming into contact with something hard, either because she fell or because someone hit her. It could be a combination of both. The autopsy doesn't tell us whether death occurred as a result of violence or a fall, for example. And as I said, there is no explanation for the internal bleeding, so a number of samples have been sent to Linköping for analysis." Thomas fell silent. He had tried to relay the contents of the report as accurately as possible, but it wasn't easy. "It is highly likely that the injuries were sustained in Jonny Almhult's house; we found her jacket there, and there were traces of blood on a radiator in his living room. If the blood turns out to be Kicki Berggren's, that could explain the injury to the back of the head. Somehow she got back to the Mission House, where she was found the following morning."

Suddenly the telephone crackled to life. Margit was trying to make herself heard. "Have I got this right? Kicki Berggren was assaulted, but we don't know if it was fatal? She has major internal bleeding which can't be explained? Can I ask what we actually *do* know?" Margit snapped.

Thomas tried to provide a chronological account. "We believe Kicki arrived on Sandhamn shortly after one o'clock last Friday. We've spoken to one of the girls in the kiosk who remembers her, and according to the timetable, a ferry comes in at that time. Kicki asked about somewhere to stay, and it appeared she had just arrived on the island. The girl suggested the Mission House. Since Kicki's injuries must have been sustained at a later stage, the person who attacked her must also have been on the island."

"Are there any witnesses who saw her with anyone?" Margit asked.

For a moment her question was drowned out by the sound of children laughing. She was obviously outdoors, probably on the beach.

"We've spoken to the staff in all the cafés and restaurants, and no one recognized her," Thomas said. "But there are a couple of people who only work weekends, and they won't be back until Friday. I've got their phone numbers. I haven't managed to get ahold of them yet, but I'll try again when we finish here." He flexed his left foot, which boasted a huge blister—the result of tramping back and forth all over Sandhamn. "We've also knocked on the door of virtually every house on the island, but we haven't found anyone who saw her. Not so far, anyway."

Persson scratched his throat. He had a large, angry red mosquito bite just above his left collarbone. "Do we have any idea why this Almhult might have hit her?" He looked at Thomas.

"We don't even know if it was Jonny Almhult. He's disappeared, and we haven't managed to track him down." Thomas held up a photograph of Jonny Almhult; it showed a man with weak features and brown eyes. He had a broad nose, and his dark hair needed cutting. His face was tanned and freckled.

"He's never been violent toward women before, as far as we know. He doesn't have a criminal record. According to his mother, he's pretty lonely and a little shy. She's at her wits' end; she has no idea what's going on. The last contact she had with him was on Saturday, when he had either been drinking or had a bad hangover." Thomas paused. "Erik spoke to Almhult two days ago, on Sunday morning, but he claimed he didn't recognize Kicki's photograph—isn't that right, Erik?"

Erik nodded. "Exactly. I was only there for a couple minutes. He wasn't looking too good; he seemed pretty hungover. When I asked whether he'd had any contact with Berggren, he said he didn't know who she was. Then he apologized and said he wasn't feeling well, so I left." Erik looked unhappy, as if he were reproaching himself because he hadn't realized that he ought to have questioned Almhult more closely.

"I've known of Jonny Almhult since I was a teenager," Thomas said, "and there's never been anything suspect about him. There is no obvious reason why Jonny would suddenly pick up a total stranger and start knocking her around."

"You say she was a stranger, but we don't actually know whether they already knew each other," Persson said as he carried on scratching the mosquito bite, which was now bleeding slightly.

"No, you're right," Thomas said. "I've checked Kicki Berggren's apartment, and there's no trace of anything that might explain what's happened. We haven't found anything linking her to Sandhamn or

Jonny Almhult, apart from the fact that she visited the ferry company's website."

The speakerphone crackled again. "What about her colleagues? Was there anyone at work who had a grudge against her?"

"I've spoken to the company that runs the casino. She'd worked there for over fifteen years. They didn't have much to say—she did her job, didn't take any more sick leave than anyone else, and was generally regarded as honest and reliable." He looked down at his notebook where he had jotted down the salient points from his telephone conversation with Kicki Berggren's boss, a miserable man who had shown little interest, in spite of the fact that one of his employees had been murdered. "The only thing unusual, as I understand it, is that she'd worked there for such a long time. Most croupiers pack it in after five or six years. It's not the kind of profession people stick with, at least not if they have a family. The hours are terrible—evenings only, and late nights, of course. Nor is the working environment all that great."

"She'd spent some time in Kos recently, hadn't she?" Persson asked, leaning forward to grab a cookie.

"Yes. She asked for a four-month leave of absence on very short notice," Thomas said. "The casino where she worked was due to be renovated at the same time, so her employer was happy to agree. Otherwise they would have had to find her a temporary post elsewhere because she had a permanent contract with them."

"I'm just wondering whether there might be some connection between her place of work and her cousin's. Neither the gambling world nor the alcohol trade are exactly whiter than white," Margit said.

Thomas leaned forward so that she could hear him more clearly. "What are you thinking, Margit?"

"Krister Berggren worked for Systemet. I'm just wondering whether there might be a link there. Something to do with smuggling booze or drugs, perhaps? Possibly with a Greek angle?"

"Or the former Yugoslavia." Kalle straightened up, his face slightly pink with the excitement of having spoken up. "The Yugoslav mafia might be mixed up in this."

"I think that might be taking things a little far," Margit said, "but what if Krister Berggren was involved in something illegal at Systemet, and his cousin was helping him out? He could have been dragged into something. Or perhaps he was trying to put an end to it. Kicki Berggren might have known about whatever it was or been mixed up in it, too. I mean, a great deal has happened within Systemet in recent years that wouldn't stand up to close scrutiny."

"Some illegal scheme that meant he had to go over to Sandhamn, then she followed him," Kalle chimed in.

"Something along those lines," Margit said. "Thomas, you met her—what was your impression of her?"

Thomas closed his eyes and thought about Kicki. The image of a lonely, disappointed woman with good intentions came to mind. They had talked for about half an hour. She had seemed genuinely upset about her cousin's death. And surprised. "She said they were close, but she hadn't spoken to Krister once during all the time she'd been in Kos. They didn't seem to have had any contact for months. I found a postcard from her in his apartment, asking him to call her." Thomas flipped through his notebook to refresh his memory. "I didn't really get a satisfactory explanation as to why they hadn't been in touch. We started talking about his mother's death instead; evidently Krister had taken it very badly. It seemed to be a possible explanation for suicide." He fell silent for a moment. "I should have asked more questions."

Persson leaned back in his chair, which creaked in protest. His thighs spilled over the edges of the seat, and his round face was tanned by the summer sun. "If we assume for a moment that this involves smuggling, what would that have to do with Sandhamn?"

"Wasn't there some drugs case out there years ago?" Margit asked.

Thomas glanced around the table at his colleagues. "There was. I was only a little boy at the time, but there was a hell of a fuss. The Yacht Club restaurant was owned by a notorious guy named Fleming Broman. It turned out he had been spending his days serving food and his nights peddling drugs. It was a huge scandal, and the drugs squad was out in full force when they finally realized what was going on."

Thomas recalled the placards outside the newsagent's on his way home from school, the thick black headlines.

And now it was happening again.

"Do you think we could be looking at another drugs case?"

"It's more likely to be booze," Persson said. "If there was a way into Systemet via Krister Berggren, his cousin could have been involved as well. But that still doesn't answer my question about the link with Sandhamn."

Margit's voice came from the speakerphone again. "Let's assume Kicki Berggren knew her cousin was involved in smuggling alcohol to or from Systemet in some way. She comes home and finds out he's dead. If she knows who his contact is, perhaps she decides to go and see him, either to exact revenge or to demand money, which is far more likely. If this person has property on Sandhamn, it would be logical to go over there, wouldn't it? It's the middle of summer, after all, and that's also where her cousin's body was found. And if this contact person murdered Krister because he was afraid of being exposed, then he might have killed Kicki as well."

Thomas linked his hands behind his head and gave the suggestion some thought. "Kicki's stay in Greece might be totally irrelevant, but the trip to Sandhamn is key," he said. "In which case, Krister Berggren might have been found on the western shore because he too went over to Sandhamn to meet his accomplice over Easter, when he disappeared."

"A meeting that somehow went wrong," said Margit.

Thomas went through his notes from his conversation with Krister's boss at Systemet, a balding man of about fifty by the name of

Viking Strindberg. He hadn't had much to say, in spite of the fact that Krister had worked there for almost thirty years.

He hadn't regarded Krister as being particularly talented or bright. He had described him as a restless soul who thought life had treated him unfairly. He had confirmed that Krister had taken his mother's death very hard and had started drinking heavily. His mother had also worked at Systemet all her life, but Strindberg had never met her. She had worked at the branch in Farsta, if he remembered correctly.

"I spoke to Krister's boss last week," Thomas said. "Krister's main role was receiving deliveries at their big depot outside Stockholm. It wasn't a particularly demanding job, but his pass card gave him access to the entire depot."

"Is it possible he was selling alcohol as a little enterprise of his own and fiddling the books?" Margit wondered.

"But could you really steal enough alcohol to make it worth killing someone—or more than one person—to avoid being discovered?" Thomas said.

Persson stroked his chin. "People commit murder for the strangest reasons. And for much less money than you might think. Don't imagine someone won't kill for a couple hundred thousand kronor. Let's find out if there's a link between Sandhamn and Systemet, the alcohol trade, or other related areas."

"That sounds sensible," Margit said.

Persson cleared his throat and went on. "We'll continue with the investigation on Sandhamn so we have a complete picture of Kicki Berggren's movements from the moment she stepped ashore until her body was found."

Thomas didn't speak. What did Persson think they'd been doing on Sandhamn so far?

"Thomas." Persson turned to face him and underlined the importance of his words with a stabbing finger. "We also need to find this Jonny Almhult as soon as possible. Have you put out an alert?"

"I wanted to wait until after the meeting," Thomas said.

"Put out an alert across the region. Then get back to Sandhamn with Kalle and Erik. Turn Almhult's place inside out. There might be something hidden there that will shed some light on the case."

He scratched the mosquito bite again. "Why does this kind of thing always turn up in the middle of the summer?"

The speakerphone crackled. "Do you want me to come back?" Margit asked.

Persson shook his head. "I think we're fine for the time being. Thomas seems to be on top of things, and his local knowledge is improving with each day." He was almost chuckling. "You look after the children and that husband of yours. I'll let you know if I change my mind." He looked at Thomas again. "I think we're nearly done. By the way, have you been in touch with the prosecutor yet? It's Öhman, isn't it?"

Thomas nodded. Charlotte Öhman was the name of the prosecutor with the court in Nacka who would lead the preliminary investigation. He didn't know her, but she had a reputation for being practical and easy to work with. No doubt she, too, had been hoping for a quiet summer with nothing more challenging than paperwork.

Another person who had had to change her plans.

"I'm seeing her first thing tomorrow. We're keeping her informed."

As Thomas was leaving, it occurred to him that he ought to get in touch with Kicki Berggren's friend, the one who had persuaded her to go to Kos. He needed to find out who Kicki had met down there and whether she had said anything about her relationship with Krister. Perhaps Agneta would be able to explain why Kicki had sent that postcard to Krister.

He caught up with Carina in the corridor before she reached her office.

"Can you help me track down Kicki's friend, Agneta Ahlin? Try and get ahold of a phone number as soon as possible, then call me. I don't care how late it is."

WEDNESDAY, THE THIRD WEEK

Chapter 28

Charlotte Öhman, the prosecutor, peered at Thomas. Her light-brown hair was fastened at the back of her neck, and she had pushed her glasses up on top of her head. She was rolling a pen between her thumb and forefinger as she tried to grasp the situation.

"If I've understood this correctly, we have one deceased cousin where we know the cause of death, but we have no idea if he was killed by someone. Then we have another deceased cousin whom we suspect was murdered, but we are unable to establish that fact at the moment."

"Exactly."

The prosecutor made a note on her pad. She was left-handed. She had a furrow of concern on her forehead that resembled a figure eight. Thomas had never seen anything like it.

"And how are you intending to proceed?"

Charlotte raised her eyebrows a fraction. She didn't seem particularly impressed by the investigation so far. Hardly surprising, Thomas thought, given that they had made so little progress.

He went over the points the team had raised the previous day and outlined the way in which they intended to move the investigation forward. He summarized what they had done so far and the conclusions they had been able to draw.

The room fell silent, and Charlotte leaned back in her chair. She unclipped the barrette holding her ponytail in place, then refastened it—a ritual seemingly designed to give her time to think.

"I'm not sure if there's much substance to this smuggling idea, but I agree that you ought to look into it. The most important thing at the moment is to track Kicki Berggren's movements on Sandhamn and find the people she met."

"I've spoken to Inger Gunnarsson, the waitress who served her that Friday evening. According to her, Berggren was in the bar with Jonny Almhult for several hours. They ordered several rounds of beer, and it seemed as if they were getting along well. She certainly didn't have the impression that Kicki Berggren was in any way afraid of Almhult."

Charlotte made notes and nodded. "That sounds good," she said. "Sandhamn is a small island, so it seems reasonable that a number of people must have met her." She unfastened and refastened the barrette again. "When are you expecting the detailed analysis from Linköping?"

"I expect it will take a few more days; by the end of the week at the earliest, I think. We've asked them to give it priority, but they're short-staffed in the summer, just like everyone else."

The prosecutor smiled. "I appreciate that it could take a while before we have definite information, so just carry on as best you can."

"Of course."

"Keep me informed." She jotted down a few additional points. "By the way, have you checked on the financial situation?"

"There are no large sums of money floating around. Krister Berggren had a savings account containing a few thousand kronor; Kicki Berggren had a monthly savings plan, but we're not talking unusual amounts."

Charlotte nodded. "So if they were making money from smuggling booze, there's no sign of it in their bank accounts," she said. "Did either of them have a safety deposit box?"

"Not that we know of, but that doesn't mean it doesn't exist. We'll keep looking."

Thomas stood on the steps outside the prosecutor's office. It was a glorious day, perfect for sitting in the sunshine with ice cream. You could hardly imagine more unsuitable weather for a murder investigation.

He shaded his eyes with his hand and looked at his watch. There was a boat back to Sandhamn after lunch; with a bit of luck he might catch it.

CHAPTER 29

Strindberg's Café was almost full as Thomas, Erik, and Kalle sat down with cups of coffee.

Just a few yards away a young girl in a white apron was making waffles, using big black old-fashioned waffle irons. They were obviously popular, because they disappeared as soon as they were ready. She had a large bowl of whipped cream in front of her and another of dark-red strawberry jam, both of which she heaped on generously.

Thomas thought they looked delicious, in spite of the warm weather. The golden waffles reminded him of when he was a little boy and used to come over from Harö with his parents. If he were lucky they would come to Strindberg's.

They were sitting in one of the booths, which was made from a skiff standing on end. A fishing net was draped over the prow for decoration. It didn't provide much in the way of shade, but it did create an authentic atmosphere.

The name of the café came from the fact that August Strindberg had spent the night there when he'd visited Sandhamn in his youth. When he spent time on the island later in life, during his marriage to Siri von Essen, he had stayed elsewhere, but the café had borne his name ever since.

Thomas noticed that the dish of the day was fried herring with mashed potatoes. What could be better out here in the archipelago?

As Erik and Kalle discussed the forthcoming Stockholm derby between Hammarby and Djurgården, Thomas's thoughts returned to his conversation with Kicki Berggren's friend, Agneta Ahlin.

It had taken Carina just a few hours to track her down on Kos, where she was still working, and she had passed on a number where Agneta could be reached. The conversation hadn't made things any clearer. Thomas had explained what had happened and said that he would like to ask her a few questions. Agneta had become distraught and had wept most of the time. She had been unable to accept that Kicki was dead. She had no idea why anyone would have wanted to kill her friend or Krister, whom she had met only once. The police already knew more or less everything she could tell him about the relationship between the cousins, and she didn't have much else to add.

Agneta did, however, tell him that Kicki had called her the day she found out Krister was dead. Kicki had been devastated, and they had talked for a long time. Toward the end of the conversation Kicki had hinted that she had an idea why her cousin had been found dead on Sandhamn. She had made some cryptic remark, said that was where the money was, but then she had changed the subject and talked about other things. She hadn't told Agneta that she was intending to travel to Sandhamn.

Kicki had talked a lot about money, according to Agneta, and was always complaining that she was broke. She was fed up with her job but didn't know how she could afford to give it up or get another job, because she had no qualifications. While she was in Greece she had given some thought to how she could earn more money. The question had come up on several occasions.

After the call, which was memorable largely for the sound of Agneta sobbing, Thomas wasn't really any the wiser.

But the information that Kicki needed money was interesting. If she had known that her cousin was involved in something illegal, she might well have decided to exploit this knowledge in order to make some cash—the easy money she had been wanting for so long.

Sandhamn, that's where the money is, Kicki had told her friend.

Thomas thought about the comment. Was it a failed attempt to get ahold of that money that had led to her death?

THURSDAY,
THE THIRD WEEK

Chapter 30

Why do kids enjoy playing in the sand so much? Nora wondered as she spread the beach towels out on the shore at Trouville. The boys had been nagging her for several days to bring them here. She thought they might have had enough of swimming, since they were taking lessons every day, but a trip to the beach was still the best thing in the world.

The beaches at Trouville were among the finest stretches of sand in the archipelago. There was a reason the real name of the island was Sandön, or Sand Island, although most people these days called it Sandhamn. It was one of the few islands in the Stockholm archipelago that didn't consist mainly of rocks.

As soon as they woke up, both boys had started campaigning for a trip to the beach. Adam had asked if they could miss their swimming lessons for today, and Nora had allowed herself to be persuaded. Once in three weeks wasn't the end of the world, after all. In addition, the water was unusually warm: seventy-two degrees. It wasn't often possible to swim in water like that in the outer archipelago.

Once breakfast was eaten and cleared away, Nora packed their swimming gear and beach towels. Simon found their brightly colored plastic buckets and spades, then they cycled across the sand, past the tennis courts, and through the forest until they reached Trouville.

Adam complained that they were cycling too slowly, but Simon was pedaling as fast as his little legs could go. Nora hadn't the heart to tell him to hurry up.

After a mile, the Trouville road ended in a fork, and they headed off to the right. Just a few hundred yards along the track they reached the shore.

As it was still quite early, the tourists from Stockholm had not yet arrived. When they came on the ferry from the city at about eleven o'clock, the beach was usually packed, but it was still only ten, so Nora and the boys could choose where they wanted to set up.

Nora certainly didn't begrudge the tourists their enjoyment of the islands, but she couldn't help thinking how nice it had been when she was a child and the stream of visitors was a mere trickle. Now she could almost imagine the island was going to sink when she saw all the people pouring off the ferries in July.

Henrik had arrived home late and left early. He would be out sailing all day. She had tried raising the issue of the post in Malmö again, but he made it clear that he wasn't interested in talking about it. The recruitment company had contacted her, just as the HR director had said they would. They had agreed that she would come into Stockholm the following week for an interview. Nora really wanted to hear more about the new job, but a meeting presupposed that she and Henrik had decided it was a good idea to continue the discussions.

As she dug out sunscreen and sunglasses, she couldn't stop her thoughts from running away with her. Why not go and meet the consultant, Rutger Sandelin? It couldn't do any harm, could it? It was just like any other interview really, even if it was being held somewhere other than the office. If she didn't bother turning up for the interview, HR would think she was crazy. She'd been offered a really exciting job, and yet she couldn't even be bothered to go through the motions.

She squirted plenty of sunscreen on her shoulders and arms, then rubbed it in with a frenzy that suggested it was a matter of life and death, rather than the avoidance of a sunburn.

With a deep breath she decided she would at least find out what the job involved. The boys could spend the day with her parents. She and Henrik could discuss it later, when she had something concrete to tell him. At the moment it was all quite vague; it wasn't worth making a stand until she knew more.

The simplest thing would be to say that she had to go into the office for the morning. It wouldn't be the first time she'd had to make a quick dash into work during the summer. Since it took her only a few hours to get into the city, it was easy to call her in when something urgent came up. At least that's what her ghastly boss thought. He parked himself and his family on Gotland for the entire summer and refused to get himself back to Stockholm unless it was absolutely essential. Which meant a message either came down from the managing director of the bank or God.

In that order.

Somewhere deep inside she could hear a little voice asking what was really driving her. Why couldn't she be satisfied with what she had? Appreciate her life, which gave her the opportunity to combine an enjoyable job with a husband and children. A happy marriage, wonderful kids, and enough money to be able to afford the house on Sandhamn. Why turn everything upside down? Why challenge Henrik, instead of paying attention to the clear signals he had given her?

She took the bottle of cold juice out of the beach bag and set it in the shade. She could see her uncertainty and anxiety reflected in its chrome surface. She wasn't at all sure where she and Henrik were heading.

Suddenly she decided to forget the whole thing. It could only lead to trouble in their marriage. No new job was worth that. No boss was so useless that she couldn't put up with him. It was better to stay where she was than to start something when she didn't know where it would lead. The whole thing was ridiculous, just a whim. How could she even think of sneaking off to town behind Henrik's back?

She took out her cell phone and called Rutger Sandelin to tell him that she couldn't come and see him, after all, that she'd changed her mind. He could inform HR that she was no longer interested. The number was busy. She sat there with the phone in her hand, then pressed redial. Still busy. Then she started to have second thoughts.

What harm could it do to go and see Sandelin? She had never met anyone from a recruitment company, and she was curious. Plus, her only aim was to find out what he had to offer before she brought the matter up with Henrik again. She was bound to learn something from the experience.

Nora cursed herself. She was being ridiculous. The idea of calling and turning the job down before she had even met Sandelin was just stupid. Of course Henrik would agree that she ought to at least go and see him before making a decision.

She put the phone back in her bag. One meeting wouldn't do any harm.

Chapter 31

The sun was blazing down in spite of the fact that it was only eleven in the morning. Even the cry of the gulls sounded more tired than usual in the heat. The boys had spread out their buckets and spades and had started to build a sandcastle down by the water.

Nora had positioned herself so she could keep an eye on them while reading her book. It was by an English author and was about combining life as a professional woman working full-time with bringing up young children. She was completely absorbed by a hilarious chapter where the mother discovers late one evening that her daughter is supposed to take mince pies into school the following day for a bake sale. In desperation she buys a batch from the supermarket and bashes them with a rolling pin to make them look homemade.

Nora understood exactly how she felt. She stretched in the sun, enjoying the heat. Then she shaped the sand under her towel to provide better support for her neck. Little piles of fine sand had already accumulated in the towel's creases, in spite of the fact that she had only been lying there for a short while.

Simon came rushing over with his bucket. "Come and help us build a sandcastle!" He threw his sandy arms around her neck.

Nora smiled and kissed his forehead. "Why not?" she said. She put down her book and picked up a spare bucket and spade. She adjusted her bikini and walked down to the water, glancing out across the waves. In the distance she could see an odd shape, a long, dark lump, floating some distance offshore. It looked like an old, rotten log, bobbing awkwardly with the movement of the water.

Something wasn't right.

"Hang on, I'm just going to look at something," she shouted to the boys. "I'll be there in a minute."

She waded out a little way, but it was difficult to see because of the bright sunshine reflected on the water. She tried to shade her eyes with one hand as she moved farther out. The light was so intense that it dazzled her, however much she screwed up her eyes. Soon she was a good thirty yards from the shore and was able to make out more than a vague outline.

Then she realized what it was.

Her hand flew to her mouth in horror.

"This can't be happening," she whispered. "Not again."

She took a deep breath and cautiously moved closer. A man's body was floating facedown in front of her. He was wearing jeans and a T-shirt, and had longish brown hair. She couldn't tell whether he was dead or not, but she started to run through the water as fast as she could. It was hard work, and it felt as if it was taking an eternity to cover those last few strides.

When she reached the body she grabbed an arm. Touching it felt strange, but it was surprisingly easy to turn the body over. Once it was on its back, she recognized the man immediately.

Jonny Almhult, Ellen's son.

Jonny who had mended their fence and lived just a short distance away.

Nora felt the cold sweat break out on her forehead. It was the first time she had touched a dead body. It was almost like a film, but this was real.

She fought off the impulse to throw up and bit her lip hard. Jonny's body must be brought ashore. The police must be informed immediately.

She glanced over at Adam and Simon. They were still playing and didn't seem interested in what she was doing.

They mustn't see the body.

Nora tried to wave to some people on the beach to show she needed help, but none of them noticed. She didn't yell, because she didn't want to frighten the children. Instead, she took ahold of Jonny's T-shirt and started dragging him toward the shore. It took all her strength, and her arms began to ache after only a couple of minutes. She ended up nudging the body along, as far away from the boys as possible. When she finally got him to the water's edge, both sweat and tears were pouring down her face.

"Don't come over here," she shouted to the boys, waving them away. "Stay where you are."

She ran to her bag and grabbed her phone. She called Thomas as quickly as she could. "It's Nora. I'm on Trouville beach. I've just found Jonny Almhult. He was floating in the water. Like a lump of wood. He's dead." She started giggling hysterically and pinched her arm to stop herself. "Sorry. It was just so horrible. I'm here with the boys. I don't know what to do." The last sentence ended in a sob. She felt dizzy and could hardly stay on her feet.

Thomas's familiar voice was a relief. It was the first time she had encountered him in a professional capacity. Just talking to him calmed her down.

"Listen to me, Nora. Take deep, slow breaths. You're starting to hyperventilate; you need to calm down."

"OK." Nora could hear her own voice as if it were coming from a distance. It sounded weak and breathless.

"Sit down on the sand. Are you going to faint?"

"I don't know," Nora said.

"Put your head down, and try to slow your breathing."

Nora did as she was told, and after a few minutes she started to feel better.

"You need to stay there until I get to you," Thomas said. "Can you do that?"

"I'll try."

"I'm already in the village. I just need to borrow a bike. You can do this. I know you can. Just stay calm. I'll be there in no time."

Nora tucked her legs beneath her on the warm sand. It was unreal, seeing a dead body just a few feet away.

In the distance she could see Adam looking anxiously in her direction. He probably thought her blood sugar was low because of her diabetes. Which was better than him finding out what had really happened.

She waved at him.

"Play with Simon," she shouted. "I'll be there soon."

Chapter 32

In the afternoon, Jonny's body was taken to the forensic pathologist in Solna. After that, Thomas spent a few hours at the local station, which by this time was starting to feel like home. He settled down in the small interview room on the first floor, which had been transformed into a temporary office. He did all the necessary paperwork and called both Persson and Margit to inform them that Jonny Almhult was no longer missing.

Dead. Probably drowned.

With some difficulty he persuaded Persson to allow him to remain on the island, rather than travel back to the mainland to attend the press conference, which had been arranged for seven o'clock that evening—just in time to make the evening bulletins.

Thomas insisted that someone had to inform Ellen Almhult that her son was no longer alive. He wasn't looking forward to the task, but common decency dictated that it couldn't be entrusted to anyone else. Besides which, the idea of participating in a press conference wasn't remotely appealing, and there were plenty of others who enjoyed that kind of thing.

Persson raised objections but eventually gave in after complaining about all the idiots who kept asking him for information he didn't have. The chief constable wanted to be kept up to date daily, while at the same time making it clear that he wasn't happy about the fact that *his* vacation was being interrupted.

What was he complaining about? At least he was having a vacation!

Persson didn't have much time for bureaucrats within the police service who spent their time breathing down the necks of officers in the field. They must be allowed to carry out their investigations without interference; that was his mantra, which he repeated to anyone who tried to meddle.

Thomas stared at the calendar on the beige wall. Eighteen days had now passed since the bright summer morning when Krister Berggren's body had been found on Sandhamn's western shore. Eighteen days, which meant it was four hundred and thirty-two hours since the first body turned up. If his minicalculator was working, they'd had 25,920 minutes at their disposal to work out why first Krister Berggren and then his cousin had lost their lives.

If they had succeeded, perhaps Jonny Almhult would have been alive today, instead of having been found floating facedown off Trouville beach.

And Ellen Almhult, who was already a widow, would not have lost her only son.

Deep down Thomas firmly believed all three had been murdered by the same person. His instincts told him that the deaths were linked and that someone who had no hesitation about killing those who stood in his way was hiding in the shadows.

But how were they going to find him?

Thomas clenched both fists so tightly that his fingers ached. He hadn't a clue why someone had taken the lives of three people. The only thing he did know was that there was a murderer on the loose on Sandhamn.

And that the police had no idea who it was or how to prevent the next murder.

Chapter 33

The atmosphere in the station was subdued and oppressive. Routine matters were dealt with unenthusiastically. Most people sat around talking in small groups after their shift; even those who had finished for the day stayed on and chatted.

Everyone knew Ellen and her family.

Jonny's father, Georg Almhult, had been a part of the village community, an islander born and bred on Sandhamn. He might have had a few too many drinks now and again, but he had never been violent or unpleasant. Ellen Almhult had had a sharp tongue when she was younger, so there had been a certain amount of sympathy when her husband occasionally turned to the bottle. She had fallen out with various people over the years, but at a time like this, all the old grudges were forgotten.

The sorrow at losing a villager was mixed with fear over what had happened—and could happen again. Anxiety seeped through every façade and was reflected in the eyes of all those present. Some of the women were weeping as they talked. No one would be leaving the front door unlocked tonight.

"Thomas," said Åsa, one of the girls who worked at the station. She had moved to the island a few years ago when she had gotten together with a man who lived there. "Come and have some fresh coffee. Should I make you a sandwich? You look worn out."

Thomas smiled at her. "Thanks. That would be great. I don't think I've eaten much today."

Thomas went upstairs to the break room, and Åsa soon arrived with a substantial cheese sandwich and a cup of coffee. The room was sparsely furnished; there was a plain wooden table and two chairs by the window, and at one end of the room someone had managed to squeeze in a bed, which barely fit.

This was where Thomas used to spend the night when he was with the maritime police and couldn't get back to Harö or the mainland.

He attacked the sandwich while gazing out at the old sandpit where sailing ships had collected sand as ballast for hundreds of years at the price of two öre per ton. It had been abandoned and fenced off long ago, and only an angular, unnatural sandy slope bore witness to its past.

Åsa broke the silence. "Is your sandwich OK?"

Thomas took another bite. "It's delicious, thank you. I feel much better. That was just what I needed."

They both fell silent. Åsa looked upset; it was obvious that she had been crying. "I just can't understand why anyone would want to kill poor Jonny," she said. "You couldn't find a more harmless soul. I don't think he's done a bad thing in his life."

"I don't know, Åsa. Sometimes things happen, and we just can't understand them."

"And I can't work out what he had to do with those cousins. I've never even heard of them before. They weren't exactly familiar faces here." She let out a small sob.

"I think there has to be a link we're just not seeing," Thomas said. "Jonny and Kicki Berggren somehow bumped into one another, but right now we don't know how or why."

"I don't see how there can be a link. Jonny didn't have many friends, particularly outside Sandhamn. He hardly ever left the island unless he had to. He hated going over to the mainland. He used to say he couldn't breathe in the city." She shook her head.

Thomas stretched his weary muscles and gazed out at the sandpit once more. It must have been a hard life, loading sand onto the passing ships that moored at the huge anchors that had been buried in the harbor way back in the eighteenth century. Many of the workers died young, worn out by their labor.

He finished the sandwich and wiped his mouth with a napkin. "Thanks again. I'd better make a move; I've still got a few things to do." He paused in the doorway. "Listen, I might grab a few hours of sleep here if it gets too late to travel back to Harö. I probably won't make it to the city tonight."

Åsa nodded and managed a little smile. "That's no problem. You can have the room overnight if you need it. You've got a key, right?"

Thomas suddenly felt a rush of nostalgia as he thought of all those late nights when he was with the maritime police. "I do. It'll be just like the good old days, when we only had drunk teenagers and the odd stolen boat to worry about." Thomas tried to muster an encouraging smile, but it turned into more of a grimace. He didn't want to let Åsa see how worried he really was. It was difficult to maintain a positive approach in the face of the anxious expressions around him.

They had to find a pattern, or they would never be able to track down the murderer. Somewhere there was a clue they had missed. There had to be.

***

When Thomas left the center he took the narrow lane to the right leading down to the promenade, which passed between two yellow wooden houses built at the end of the nineteenth century.

He stopped at the kiosk and looked at the newspaper placards; they were designed to attract maximum attention.

"Extra," they said in thick black letters. "Another Murder on Sandhamn! Second Man Found Dead!"

It was incredible how quickly the press found out about what had happened. They'd only just got the body to Solna, and the stories were already in print.

One thing was certain: Persson wouldn't be pleased about the fresh speculation in the media.

Chapter 34

By the time Thomas knocked on Nora's door and walked in, she was feeling a little better. She had curled up in a wicker chair on the veranda with a blanket wrapped around her. On the table next to her were a big cup of tea and a pastry, which she had crumbled into tiny pieces.

Her parents had taken the boys down to the harbor to give her some space and the chance to recover from the shock of finding Jonny's body.

Nora really wished Henrik were home, but he was still out sailing. The regatta wouldn't end until about five o'clock, and the idea of calling him on his cell phone when he was in the middle of a competition was out of the question.

She was so sick of his sailing that she could have screamed. Where was he when she needed him?

Even though there was brilliant sunshine outside, Nora was so cold she couldn't stop shaking. Her brain registered the fact that it was warm inside the house, but the goose bumps on her arms and legs told another story.

She couldn't get the image of the dead body in the water out of her mind. Those unseeing eyes staring at her when she turned him over. A thin strand of hair bobbing up and down with the movement of the sea. A limp arm floating on the surface.

Who would dare to visit Sandhamn after this? Who would be next? What if a child were killed? She shuddered again.

When Thomas and his colleague had arrived in Trouville, they had quickly taken charge of the situation.

The other people on the beach had been asked to leave. An area covering half the shore had been cordoned off with police tape—a familiar sight to many residents of Sandhamn by this time.

Shortly after, a police launch appeared and moored by the rocks. The same rocks from which Nora had once dived for her bronze and silver medals.

The launch dropped off an investigative team that quickly went to work. When photographs had been taken from every possible angle and any piece of available evidence had been secured, they respectfully prepared the body for transportation to Stavsnäs, where a hearse was waiting.

Thomas called Nora's parents, who cycled over to pick up the children. Lars and Susanne looked around with horrified expressions but did their best to remain calm. The boys didn't want to go. There were far too many exciting things going on. There were police officers everywhere by this stage, and Adam could hardly wait to tell his friends at swimming lessons about the big police launch.

In the end, Thomas spoke to them in his most authoritative police officer's voice in order to get them to cooperate; the fact that they were also promised big ice cream cones probably helped, too.

Once the boys had gone off with their grandparents, Thomas gently asked Nora a few questions. Then he told her to go home and rest. Quietly think over everything that had happened.

They agreed that Thomas would stop by later so she could tell him in more detail about how she had found the body and what she had seen.

While she was waiting for Thomas, she fell asleep and dreamed that she was desperately swimming to reach the shore, while unattached legs and arms floated around her. The water was red with blood, staining her bikini.

"Can you tell me what happened?" Thomas began.

He had made a fresh pot of tea and settled down in a white wicker chair next to Nora on the veranda. The only sound was the gentle ticking of the kitchen clock. He waited patiently for her to find the right words.

After a while she began a hesitant account of the whole course of events, from seeing the odd, motionless shape in the water to the moment Thomas arrived.

"Did you notice whether the body was floating from a particular direction?" he asked.

Nora closed her eyes, her expression uncertain. "He was just lying in the water. There was hardly a breeze."

"Was there anyone else on the beach who could have thrown him in?"

"There was hardly anybody there when we arrived. I noticed two or three people over toward the little beach but nobody on the side where he was floating."

"And you didn't see any boats that could have dumped the body in the water?"

Nora looked doubtful. "It was really quiet. I remember thinking we were early, because there were so few people on the beach."

She fell silent, as if she were trawling through her memory. Then she told him about the bright sunshine that had almost dazzled her as she tried to make out the shape. "I didn't really see anything else."

"Do you remember anything unusual, anything that seemed out of place?" Thomas leaned forward. "Try to remember everything you can. Someone you didn't recognize, or someone behaving oddly."

Nora plucked at the Kleenex in her hand. Little bits of white fluff were starting to come off; it wilted immediately in the face of Nora's despair.

In his mind's eye Thomas could see Kicki Berggren sitting opposite him just a couple of weeks earlier, shredding a paper tissue in exactly the same way as she learned of her cousin's death.

"I'm sorry," Nora said, "but I can't remember anything special. Nothing that might explain how Jonny ended up in the water." She started to cry again, clutching the teacup with both hands. "It just feels so unreal. I can't believe Jonny's dead."

Thomas patted her hand. "I know. This sort of thing just shouldn't happen. If I knew who was behind it I'd put a stop to it, I can promise you that." He sank back in the chair and linked his hands behind his head. He was worried about Nora. She looked pale and frozen beneath her tan. The shock was clear in her slow movements. Her eyes were crimson from crying, and her nose was swollen.

"When will Henrik be back? I don't want you to be alone."

Nora shrugged. "I expect he'll be back in a few hours. But I'll be fine—don't worry. The boys are with Mom and Dad. I can easily go over there if I need some company." She grabbed a fresh tissue and blew her nose. "I think I might try to get some sleep, actually. You go—I know you've got things to do."

Thomas gave her an encouraging nod. "A few hours of sleep will do you good. Call me if you think of anything or if you just need to talk. I'll keep my phone on. If I don't hear from you, I'll call you in the morning."

***

Thomas stood on the steps for a moment, weighing his phone in his hand as he wondered whether to call Henrik or not. He was always pleased to see Henrik and Nora, but right from the start Thomas had been aware of a kind of resistance on Henrik's part, something that stopped Thomas from feeling relaxed in his company. It was as if Henrik couldn't quite come to terms with the solid, understated friendship between Nora and Thomas. Thomas didn't think Henrik was jealous; it was more as if their friendship somehow encroached on the private territory that Nora's husband believed should be reserved for a marriage.

There was an underlying distance between the two men that never quite disappeared in spite of the fact that they had known each other for a long time. Henrik's upper-middle-class background and deeply conservative values didn't exactly improve matters.

On top of that, Henrik was a doctor and was used to everyone listening to him whenever he had something to say. There was an element of authoritativeness in him that sometimes annoyed Thomas. And the way in which Henrik would interrupt Nora in the middle of a sentence or the irritation that was apparent when she didn't always agree with him made Thomas wonder occasionally about the balance within their relationship.

He decided that he would call Henrik and leave a message, so he would know what had happened before he got home. With a bit of luck he might realize that his wife needed him.

FRIDAY,
THE THIRD WEEK

Chapter 35

When Thomas arrived at the police station in Nacka on Friday morning, it was blissfully quiet. It seemed most of his colleagues who weren't on vacation had opted for a late start. Even those who were normally in first thing were conspicuous by their absence.

He had caught the early morning ferry once again, and his reward was time alone in the office. Thomas appreciated the silence. It had been an intense week, and it wasn't over yet. Being able to sit down at his desk without having to talk to anyone felt liberating. He went along to the kitchen with his mug, which was large and sturdy and bore the logo of the maritime police.

A selection of teas was arranged on a shelf. After some consideration he settled on Earl Grey. Not very original, perhaps, but a good choice first thing in the morning. Two teaspoons of sugar and a drop of milk—perfect.

He walked back down the corridor to his office. Apart from the obligatory desk, two birch wood chairs for visitors, and a neutral bookcase in the same pale wood, it was virtually empty. On the desk were piles of papers and documents. There were no photographs or potted plants to make the room homier.

He used to have a large photo of Pernilla next to the phone. He had loved that picture. It had been taken on Harö at sunset. Pernilla's hair had been bleached by the sun, and the picture captured that special evening light that exists only in summer in the archipelago.

She had been sitting at the end of the jetty gazing out to sea, just as the sun was going down. She hadn't noticed that he was taking the photograph, which was why it had turned out so well. A wonderful moment tenderly captured.

After the divorce he had put the picture at the bottom of a desk drawer.

He couldn't have a photograph of Emily on display either. It was just too hard. Whenever he thought of Emily he saw her tiny hand resting in his. He had sat by her for hours before they came to take her away, just stroking those little fingers as they lay lifeless on his palm.

It had been impossible to grasp that he would never again be able to touch her soft cheek, never hold her in his arms. In the end, when the paramedics had insisted on taking her away, he had gone crazy, clinging to her as if he could make her start breathing through sheer willpower.

He had howled like a wounded animal. When they took his daughter from him, he had sobbed helplessly. Nothing had been as painful as watching the ambulance drive away with his daughter's body—not the funeral, with the tiny white coffin in front of the altar, nor the unavoidable separation from Pernilla.

There was an envelope with his name on it sitting on his desk. He slit it open and immediately saw that it was the report from the national forensics lab in Linköping giving the results of the more extensive tests on the samples from Kicki Berggren's body.

They had worked fast, he thought. He began to read. The report wasn't what he had expected. And it didn't cast any further light on what had happened on the island.

Quite the reverse, in fact.

He scratched the back of his neck and stretched. Persson would be even more annoyed. New information that didn't help at all. It would probably be best to ask the prosecutor to attend their next meeting. She needed to hear this. She was leading the preliminary investigation, after all, which made her technically responsible for the case as a whole.

He picked up the phone to call Margit; she, too, must be informed. This was something the two of them needed to tackle.

Chapter 36

The meeting began at nine thirty on the dot. Persson believed in punctuality. If you couldn't turn up on time, then it didn't say much for your character, in his opinion.

When Thomas walked in to the conference room, both Persson and Charlotte Öhman were already there. Kalle and Erik were sitting opposite, and Carina was next to them with her pen at the ready. Thomas noticed that she was wearing a barrette, but a few strands of hair had escaped. Her pink blouse looked pretty against her tanned skin.

Carina pointed to a plate in the middle of the table. "Help yourself to a cinnamon Danish, Thomas. I passed a bakery on the way in, and I thought a treat might help."

Thomas nodded. "Thanks. Anything that raises the blood sugar and provides energy is welcome."

Persson cleared his throat. "Right, let's start. Is Margit with us?" He stared at the telephone.

The answer came loud and clear. "I'm here. How are things in Stockholm? It's seventy-seven degrees here, and the water is almost as warm."

"We can't complain. So, let's find out where we're at." Persson leaned back in his chair. "Thomas, you first."

Thomas quickly summarized the events of the past twenty-four hours, then picked up the report from the lab. "According to the forensic analysis, Kicki Berggren was poisoned."

Confusion spread around the room; they were all looking at one another without really knowing how to interpret this new information.

"Probably rat poison," Thomas went on.

"You mean the cause of death was rat poison?" Carina asked.

"The underlying cause of death," Thomas said. "The report states that she had ingested a fatal dose of warfarin, which is a component of rat poison. Indirectly, this is what killed her, by causing internal bleeding in the brain and other organs."

"What do you mean, indirectly?" Erik asked.

"Warfarin works as an anticoagulant, which means it prevents the blood from clotting. The blows or the fall that Kicki Berggren suffered were the direct cause of death, because her body was unable to stop the bleeding they caused."

"But otherwise she wouldn't have died?" Kalle looked at Thomas.

"Probably not. The violence to which she was subjected would normally have resulted in nothing more serious than some nasty bruises and a small amount of bleeding. It would have been obvious that somebody had slapped her but nothing worse than that."

"How do you think she consumed rat poison?" Margit asked.

"We need to check on that. It certainly seems odd," Thomas said. Who could possibly consume something like that by mistake, particularly in view of the fact that the container was usually marked with a clear warning?

Margit spoke again. "I recognize the name warfarin; isn't it used for people, too?"

Thomas nodded and skimmed through the report in his hand. "Warfarin is also a pharmaceutical drug used on humans under a number of different brand names," he said. "It's commonly prescribed after a stroke, because it reduces the formation of blood clots. However, it can also cause internal bleeding if it's administered in large doses. That's what happened to Ariel Sharon, the former prime minister of Israel. He suffered a blood clot to begin with, and when he was treated with blood-thinning drugs, it resulted in a major brain hemorrhage."

"I heard about that on TV," Carina said.

Thomas went through the report and tried to summarize the contents. "Forensics routinely checks for warfarin. Therefore it wasn't particularly difficult for them to find traces of an extremely high dose and to make the connection with rat poison. This dose would also explain the other bleeding discovered during the autopsy."

Persson drummed his fingers on the table, his impatience clear. "So, when did she take this rat poison?"

"According to the lab, it takes between twelve and twenty-four hours for the poison to achieve its maximum effect. The blow or blows she appears to have received at Jonny Almhult's place are likely to have exacerbated the situation. She was found at around twelve o'clock that Saturday. According to the pathologist, she had been dead for several hours by then, which means she must have been poisoned at some point Friday, if we work backward."

"In that case, it probably happened on Sandhamn," Kalle said. "She arrived on the island after lunch on Friday; at least that's what the girl in the kiosk said when we showed her Kicki's photo." Kalle seemed pleased that he had been the first to reach this conclusion. He looked around the table, radiating satisfaction.

Margit's voice came through the speakerphone. "Are you sure she couldn't have ingested the poison somewhere else?"

Thomas looked doubtful. "I suppose we can never be one hundred percent sure, but the analysis is clear. This kind of poison works within this time frame. It doesn't seem likely that she was poisoned anywhere other than on Sandhamn, but of course we can't completely exclude that possibility."

"Who has access to rat poison?" Erik asked.

"Most people, I presume," Thomas said. "You can buy it all over the place. But of course that's something we need to look into." He turned to Kalle. "Could you call the toxicology unit when we're done here? Find out where you can get ahold of rat poison. Can anyone buy it, or are purchases traceable? Someone should be able to help."

"Try Anticimex as well," Carina suggested. "They're the biggest pest-control company; they ought to know about rat poison and how people can get it."

Persson reached out for his third cinnamon Danish and bit into it angrily, glaring at the speakerphone as he chewed. "So to sum up: we have a situation where this woman somehow ingested a fatal dose of rat poison. Then she was subjected to violence from an external source, although this violence was not sufficient to cause death under normal circumstances. However, she had so much rat poison in her system that the blow or blows did in fact prove fatal. And all this happened on Sandhamn, presumably in the company of a person who has since been found drowned, also on Sandhamn. Have they gone completely mad over there? Is it something in the water?"

Carina scribbled as if her life depended on it. The atmosphere around the table was tense. They were all looking down at their papers, avoiding eye contact. The situation was serious, to say the least.

Thomas cleared his throat. "I have something else to report. The manager from the Mission House contacted me this morning."

Persson looked up from the report, which Thomas had passed over. "And?"

"It seems Kicki Berggren had asked her for directions to the house of someone who lived on the island. When we spoke to her before, she couldn't remember anything because of the shock. But now a few details have come back to her. She thinks Kicki Berggren was asking about someone called Fille or Figge or possibly Pigge."

The room was silent.

"Last name?" Persson asked.

"The first name was all she could remember. She also has a very strong accent, so that will probably affect the pronunciation. But it's definitely worth looking into."

"OK," said Persson, turning to Carina. "Go through every homeowner on the island and check if anyone has a name that sounds similar. Try and get ahold of someone in the housing department as soon as possible. I hope they're not closed on Fridays this time of year." He shoved the rest of the Danish into his mouth and looked around. "By the way, do we know any more about Jonny Almhult?"

Margit didn't speak, so Thomas took the lead. "No more than we established yesterday. The most likely scenario is that he drowned. There was extensive bruising, but we won't know for certain until we have the report from forensics. I've called them twice and asked for priority, so we'll see if that helps."

"Anything from where the body was found?" said Persson.

"It wasn't possible to secure any evidence from the beach. Nothing that could lead to a possible perpetrator. It's as if Almhult's body just popped up out of the water."

"For God's sake," Persson said. "Do you have any idea where Almhult had been before he floated along in Trouville?"

"I'm afraid not. The call went out on Tuesday morning, but so far nothing useful has come in. I'll contact the national CID again as soon as we finish here. At the moment we don't know where he'd been since his mother last saw him."

Persson shook his head. "And what about the link between Systemet and Sandhamn?"

"Nothing there either," Thomas said, looking worried. "I thought I might go and see Berggren's boss at Systemet again this afternoon to see if we can get any more out of him. I'll take Erik with me." He started to gather his papers. "We need to go through all the statements we've taken this week, look closely at every scrap of information we have. Kalle, you concentrate on Jonny Almhult, and the rest of us will stay focused on the cousins."

Charlotte Öhman cleared her throat and spoke for the first time since the meeting began. Her hair was up in a ponytail just like the last time, and she looked cool and composed in a white blouse and blue skirt. "Haven't we been rather cavalier when it comes to the question of motive? Shouldn't we have a more fully developed hypothesis with regard to the reason behind the murders by this stage?"

Persson turned to look at Charlotte as if he had only just noticed her presence. "Are you suggesting we haven't been doing our jobs properly?" he said. "We're still in the process of building up a picture of the victims. Obviously a motive will form part of that picture."

The prosecutor's cheeks flushed, but she stuck to her guns. "And that's exactly why we need to think very carefully about any possible motives, so we can find the perpetrator." She looked Persson in the eye. "Or perpetrators. We can't rule out the possibility that we're dealing with more than one murderer." She took off her glasses and swept the room with her gaze. "Unless anyone has any other ideas?"

Persson glared at Charlotte. "One thing I've learned over the years: sometimes murders are committed without there being a logical motive. People aren't always as rational as we might think."

Thomas tried to mediate. "Obviously we've considered various motives to try to establish a link between the three deaths. The problem is that the only clear connection between the first two is that they were cousins. We haven't been able to find any direct link between them and Jonny Almhult's death that explains why someone would want to take the lives of these three people. Neither their backgrounds nor lifestyles suggest any kind of common ground. But we're devoting a lot of time to this aspect."

He looked at Charlotte, who gave him a wry smile. Her expression was skeptical, but she seemed prepared to accept Thomas's explanation. For the time being, at least.

"Good. But every possible scenario in this situation must be examined. I'm sure I don't need to stress the seriousness of this case. We can't risk another murder," she said.

"Margit," said Persson, reaching for another Danish. He stopped when he saw the expression on Carina's face.

It's hardly surprising that he looks the way he does, Thomas thought.

"I want you back here on Monday so the prosecutor doesn't need to worry about our resources being overstretched. Thomas could probably do with some help, and I think Ms. Öhman would prefer you to be here for the rest of the investigation."

"I understand. I'll be there."

Margit was well aware of what the situation required and made no objections. Things were serious. Three dead bodies within the space of just a few weeks, and no resolution in sight.

CHAPTER 37

Erik and Thomas looked around the Systemet warehouse. There were bottles as far as the eye could see in all directions. The walls were lined with pallets stacked with boxes containing wines and spirits.

"I've never seen this much booze in my life," Kalle said. "If you don't turn into an alcoholic working here, you never will."

He walked over to one of the boxes and peered at the bottles. "Look, it's Dom Pérignon. A bottle like this costs over a thousand kronor, I think. Not bad for just five or six glasses, right?" He picked up a bottle and pretended to drink from it.

Thomas laughed; it was almost inconceivable that so much alcohol could be gathered in one place. He wondered what the total value of the contents of the warehouse might be. An enormous amount, no doubt. He hoped Systemet was well insured against fire; it would be no joke if the place burned down. It would probably provide the biggest fireworks display since the millennium party.

Krister's boss came over to them. He introduced himself to Erik, who had some difficulty in suppressing a smirk when he heard the man's name: Viking Strindberg. The name suggested a tall, well-built figure of a man, but in reality Viking Strindberg was small and skinny, with round glasses perched on the end of his nose. He looked as if he belonged behind a desk rather than in a place like this, surrounded by bottles and forklifts.

He asked if they would like coffee and pointed to a machine in the corner.

Thomas declined. The machine looked alarmingly like the one in Nacka's police station. Erik, however, who would happily drink engine oil if it were offered, accepted a cup without hesitation.

They followed Viking Strindberg to a conference room at one end of the depot. There was an oval desk in the center of the room, surrounded by blue chairs. Along one wall a range of Absolut spirits was displayed on a narrow table.

Erik and Thomas sat down across from Viking Strindberg.

"I thought you'd found out everything you wanted to know last time we spoke," Viking Strindberg began, glancing at Thomas.

"Not quite. We'd just like to check one or two more things," Thomas said as he worked out how to phrase his first question. No point beating about the bush. "Do you have any reason to believe Krister Berggren may have been involved in any kind of organized crime related to Systemet?"

"Absolutely not," came the swift response. "It's out of the question."

"How can you be so sure?"

"If you'd met Krister, you'd understand. He just wasn't the type. I don't think he would ever have had the nerve to do such a thing. He might have taken the odd bottle home from time to time, but that's not something I've looked into. Certain things just aren't worth making a fuss over," he said with a shrug.

"If I worked here I think I might be tempted to start selling booze on the side. So that wouldn't be picked up, then?" Thomas said with a meaningful look at Erik.

"We have excellent security procedures, I can assure you."

"But you just said Krister probably took home the odd bottle—your security procedures didn't pick that up, did they?"

Viking straightened up and took a sip of his coffee. To be on the safe side he took another sip before putting the cup down on the table. He didn't seem all that happy with the turn the conversation had taken.

"I've already spoken to you about Krister Berggren. I don't understand what else there is to say."

"I think there's plenty to say." Erik joined in. "You mean there's no wastage here?"

"Of course there is, but I don't see what that has to do with Berggren's death."

"That depends what kind of volume we're talking about." Thomas leaned forward. The little man's arrogance was annoying him. He could at least cooperate with the police in an investigation into the death of an employee. "According to my research, Systemet sold something in the area of two hundred million bottles of wine last year. Let me see," he said. "If my calculations are correct, that means that as little as one percent of that volume corresponds to two million bottles. Just half of one percent equals one million. Most companies within the retail sector allow for a considerably higher level of wastage than that."

Viking Strindberg was looking at Thomas like he wanted to kill him. "I can't tell you the exact level of wastage or the sums of money involved," he said. "That's confidential information. But I don't think it's anything serious. Definitely not." He tapped the desk with the palm of his hand to emphasize what he had just said.

Thomas wasn't impressed. References to confidential information were irrelevant in the middle of a murder investigation. "Please bear in mind that you're talking to the police. Now let me ask you again: Do you have any wastage here?"

Strindberg didn't look quite so cocky now. He took off his glasses and put them back on again. Then he ran his hand over the small amount of gray hair he had left. "We do have a certain amount of wastage, of course; it's unavoidable. Particularly in this trade. But we have very good procedures for dealing with that kind of thing."

"If someone could sell hundreds of thousands of bottles on the side, how much would they be able to make?" Erik asked the question as if it were routine.

It took Viking Strindberg a long time to answer. He ran his hand over his head once again before he spoke. "It's hard to say. Obviously it depends on how much you charge. We could be talking about big money."

"Big enough to murder someone over?" Erik asked.

Viking Strindberg looked quite ill now. "I can't possibly answer that." He glanced around. "You'll have to contact our security department if you want to discuss that kind of thing."

Erik wasn't prepared to give up. "Who would be interested in buying cheap booze?"

Beads of sweat appeared on Strindberg's forehead. "I've no idea what they get up to in the catering business. It has nothing to do with me."

SATURDAY,
THE THIRD WEEK

Chapter 38

"Turn that damn music down!" Henrik shouted from upstairs.

"What did you say?" Nora shouted back.

"I said turn the music down!"

Nora smiled. Bruce Springsteen was reverberating through the house. The neighbors' windows were probably rattling. She shouldn't really be playing such loud music in a densely populated area like Sandhamn village, but today she couldn't care less.

The regatta was over at long last, and there were celebrations that evening. Prizes would be awarded by King Harald of Norway, who had participated in the competition, and then there was a gala dinner at the Yacht Club.

Nora would be wearing a new dress in shades of turquoise, together with white high-heeled strappy sandals. After the terrible events of the past few days, she was desperate for some frivolity. She was looking forward to spending an evening with her husband, who hadn't exactly honored the family with his presence lately. Nora felt a powerful urge to enjoy herself, to get slightly tipsy and forget everything. She had wondered whether it was appropriate to attend the dinner in view of the recent deaths. The Yacht Club board had evidently been considering the matter, too; she had heard rumors that they were thinking of postponing the whole thing. However, they had eventually decided to go ahead as planned. After all, this was an international sailing championship, with participants from all over the world. With a bit of luck, many of the overseas participants might have missed all the commotion on the island, since they didn't read the local papers or watch Swedish television.

Nora just wanted something else to think about.

When she got over the initial shock of finding Jonny, she tried to fill her mind with anything but the sight of his dead body. She had slept for almost twelve hours straight and had felt much better afterward. A long walk in the forest had also helped clear her head. But the best medicine of all had been a game of Monopoly with the boys. Sitting there with Simon on her knee as they tried to decide whether to buy Norrmalmstorg, the most expensive lot in the game, was pure therapy.

Thomas had been careful not to release her name to the press, so hardly anyone knew that Nora had found the body and dragged it ashore. She blessed his thoughtfulness and his ability to keep tabs on something like that in the middle of everything that was going on.

She went into the kitchen to pour herself a glass of wine before she got changed. The boys were staying over with her parents, so she and Henrik would have the night to themselves.

Ever since she was a little girl and used to go there with her parents on Sundays, Nora had loved having dinner in the Royal Swedish Yacht Club's old clubhouse, where the traditions of competitive sailing were a part of the very fabric of the place. Wonderful old photographs showed elegant ladies in full-length dresses strolling along with their parasols as they admired the beautiful wooden boats, which in those days were regarded as the greyhounds of the sea.

The contrast with today's competitive sailing craft, which didn't even have as many bunks as crewmembers because the crew worked in shifts, was almost laughable. In the old days, sailing had been all about sleek boats that combined beauty with speed. Today the major competitions were a complex and commercial machine, where technology and sponsorship were of equal importance.

But the old clubhouse retained the atmosphere of those bygone days, and it wasn't difficult to picture its inauguration under the patronage of Oscar II, with bearded gentlemen and gleaming mahogany sailboats.

Nora and Henrik's party would be seated on the eastern veranda, with a perfect view of the sea. On a clear day you could see all the way to the lighthouse at Almagrundet, which lay some ten nautical miles southeast of Sandhamn.

She did a little dance of sheer joy. It had been ages since she and Henrik had gone dancing. These days they mostly went to dinner with other families, and the conversation centered on the children, how tired they all were, and how difficult it was to get everything done. Once they were all agreed on such matters, it was time to go home.

She picked up her glass of wine and went upstairs. Henrik was lying on the bed, gazing idly at some sports program on television.

"Shouldn't you be getting changed?" Nora asked.

Henrik grinned and winked at her. "I've got a better idea. Come here!"

Nora perched on the edge of the bed. "And what might that be?" she said with a teasing look.

"I was thinking of claiming my conjugal rights."

"Have we got time?" She couldn't help glancing at the clock. The drawback of being a mother. No wonder people said that having small children stopped you from having any more.

"Of course we've got time." He pulled her gently onto the bed. "When you've got kids you have to make the most of every opportunity!" His hand found its way under her top. Nora put down her glass and moved close to him. She kissed the hollow at the base of his throat and breathed in his familiar scent. He had virtually no hair on his chest;

it had always been that way. She used to tease him and say he was like David Beckham, minus the razor.

Everything was going to be all right, she thought. Whatever happened with the job.

CHAPTER 39

By the time they arrived at the Yacht Club, the pier was already full of happy people. The naval flags hoisted on the tall flagpoles fluttered in the wind. Waiters carried trays of champagne flutes. Everyone was dressed for the occasion, and there was an air of excitement.

Several of the sailors were in uniform, old-fashioned ceremonial dress that reminded Nora of the 1930s. Henrik had once said, half in jest, that he was thinking of buying one, but Nora's somewhat acid comment about looking like a circus performer had made him change his mind.

She had no problem with nostalgia, but there had to be a limit when it came to romanticizing the past. She also thought the Royal Swedish Yacht Club with all its traditions could be rather too much of a good thing sometimes, but she kept that to herself.

Henrik had grown up in a sailing family; his father was a prominent figure in the Yacht Club, so all the business of kissing each other on the cheek and preserving traditions was second nature to him. Nora, on the other hand, had never felt at home in this environment.

Admittedly, she had spent every summer on the island since she was born, but her view of Sandhamn was completely different. To

Nora, Sandhamn meant proximity to the sea, great expanses of silence broken only by the cry of the gulls. You caught your own fish and picked blueberries in the pine forest. On sunny days, you took a picnic down to the beach. In the evening, you fired up the barbecue down by the jetty. It was the simple life that Nora loved, the peace and quiet. The children could run free without anyone having to worry about traffic. Everyone knew everyone else. It was a feeling reminiscent of the novelist Astrid Lindgren's Bullerby books, and it wasn't so easy to find these days.

Deep down she regretted the development that had turned the island into a symbol of expensive sailboats and the beautiful people who followed in their wake. At the same time, it helped to keep the island alive. Far too many islands in the archipelago were already depopulated, and it wasn't easy to find work here. Regattas and other events made sure that Sandhamn was on the map, creating permanent jobs year-round.

You had to take the rough with the smooth.

Since Henrik loved sailing and felt completely at home at the Yacht Club, there wasn't really much to say. In any case, Nora couldn't imagine spending the summer anywhere other than Sandhamn, so what did she have to complain about?

The huge table was covered with silver cups of all sizes, and bottles of champagne were lined up at the ready. The odd paparazzo wandered around, searching for famous faces. Members of the royal family sometimes took part in various sailing competitions, so there was a good chance of success for the photographers.

Henrik spotted his crewmates and skillfully piloted Nora through the crowd to reach them. He scooped up two glasses of champagne in passing without so much as breaking his stride.

Nora cheerfully greeted Henrik's friends and their respective partners. She had met the other wives before, but they weren't close friends like the men. Most of the women either worked part-time, or not at all. Those who did work had some "appropriate" occupation, such as standing behind the counter at an interior design shop.

Nora, who struggled to combine her full-time job as a legal adviser with the bank and her role as the mother of two young boys, always felt slightly out of place in their company. She would think carefully before saying anything about how she spent her days. If someone had just been talking about the difficulty of getting an awkward customer to choose a particular fabric for her sofa, the contrast would be quite marked when she started describing negotiations involving loans worth tens of millions of kronor.

She always had the feeling that the others secretly shook their heads at her ambition, her determination to pursue a career.

As they took their places at the table, Nora realized how hungry she was. She polished off the ridiculously small starter of whitefish roe on toast in just a couple of bites while attempting to converse with Johan Wrede, one of the guests at their table.

Johan and Henrik had studied medicine together, and their families had known each other since forever. When she and Henrik got married, Johan had given a long and boring speech detailing every single sailing incident they had been involved in, none of them of any interest whatsoever to anyone else.

"So, how are the children?" Johan asked as he raised his glass to Nora.

"Fine, thanks," Nora said, nodding to acknowledge the gesture. "They love spending the summer here."

"Have they got many friends?" Johan asked. His children were younger; he had a three-year-old girl and a little boy of nine months.

"Tons. The island is crawling with kids. There's no shortage of playmates around here."

"It seems as if quite a lot of new summer residents are coming over these days. There have been a fair number of houses for sale lately, hasn't there?"

Nora could only agree. Despite the sharp price increases, low interest rates in recent years had led to dream deals on attractive properties with a sea view. Unfortunately, this also meant that many siblings could no longer afford to buy each other out when their parents passed away, so even more properties came onto the market for prospective buyers to fight over. The buyers were often rich Swedes who lived abroad, spending just a few weeks each summer on the island. For the rest of the year the houses stood silent and empty, making the little community even more desolate in winter.

"You're right. Several old houses that have been in one family for generations have been sold over the past few months. I think it's really sad," Nora said.

Johan looked at her, curiosity shining in his eyes. "Wasn't there some place that went for six or seven million last year?" He gave a long, low whistle. "Just for the summer!"

Nora grimaced and nodded. "Yes. And another in the middle of the village went for almost as much. It's crazy, when you think about it." She speared a piece of steak with her fork and went on. "It's a terrible state of affairs. Soon ordinary people won't be able to buy out here at all."

Johan held out his glass to a passing waitress for a top off. "So what are they like, these people who spend millions on a house?"

Nora thought for a moment. She pictured several of the families who had come to Sandhamn over the past few years. "They're like anyone else, I suppose. But with more money. Some of them try to fit in as best they can, while others have no sense of community at all. Some families spend a fortune restoring the property they've bought, while others ruin the place by getting rid of everything and doing it up to fit in with the latest trends. Or they build ghastly extensions that don't look right at all." She fell silent, thinking about a house that had been particularly dilapidated. "One or two have turned out really well, I must admit. So in a way you could say it's a kind of cultural bonus."

"If you spend that kind of money on a place just for the summer, I suppose you can do what you like," Johan said.

Nora shook her head. She didn't agree with that at all. "If you come to a place like Sandhamn, you have to adapt and follow the unwritten rules. For example, it's always been tradition that everyone can walk right around the island. You can't just buy a house and build a fence right down to the water's edge, even if the land forms part of your property. If you don't like the local customs, then you can take your millions and buy an island of your own. I mean, they obviously have the resources." The last comment came out more sharply than she had intended. But she couldn't hide her frustration over recent developments and the careless attitude many of the new owners displayed toward both permanent residents and visitors who had spent their summers on the island for many years. Suddenly the original benefits, like the opportunity to fish or hunt, had begun to be valued in a completely different way. Many things that in the past had been an integral part of life on Sandhamn were now being reassessed, and came with a price tag. It gave Nora the unpleasant feeling that everything was for sale. Everything could be bought or sold.

But there was no point in sitting here at a wonderful dinner and getting annoyed. She quickly raised her glass to Johan in order to take the sting out of her words. "Let's drink to the excellent results of the regatta," she said with a smile.

As usual, the restaurant got hot and stuffy as the guests dived into the main course; the ancient clubhouse had never had much in the way of air conditioning. The waiters scurried between the tables in spite of the temperature being around eighty-six degrees, and the gentlemen had removed their jackets long ago.

Everyone was laughing and chatting. The atmosphere was perfect. No one even mentioned the recent deaths.

Chapter 40

The dancing began after dinner. The same band had been playing at the Yacht Club for the past eighteen years. Nora had been a teenager when they'd first started, and the boys in the band just a few years older. At the time she had thought the guitarist was the best-looking boy she had ever seen.

Not anymore.

Henrik asked Nora to dance as the band struck up with "Lady in Red." She had always thought they danced well together; they both had rhythm and found it easy to keep the beat. Nora felt much better about everything now. And things were bound to work out with the job in Malmö. If she got it. She ran her fingers down Henrik's spine and breathed in the scent of him. She could never remember the name of his aftershave, but she would recognize it anywhere. She closed her eyes and gave herself up to the music, feeling the melody all through her body.

After one more dance they went out onto the veranda to get some fresh air and cool down. The packed dance floor created an almost sauna-like heat.

Outside, it was pleasantly warm, with hundreds of masts silhouetted against the dark-blue sky. One or two boats were still flying their ensigns, in spite of the ancient custom that dictated that all flags should be lowered at nine o'clock in the evening in the summer. Many sailors were still on board, enjoying the beautiful evening.

Over by the pool, they could see motorboats whose owners had gathered to celebrate this Saturday evening, untroubled by the dramatic events of recent weeks.

The biggest motorboats, the *Storebro* and the *Princess*, lay side by side at the Via Mare jetty. There was a fine line between what constituted a boat and what was actually a floating summer cottage. Some of the boats were so enormous they could only berth in Sandhamn or Högböte, the harbor that was home to the Royal Motorboat Club.

Nora had once asked one of Henrik's sailing friends how much a vessel like the *Storebro* would cost. He had given her a look and said, "Don't worry about what the boat costs—worry about what it costs to fill her up!" She hadn't asked any more questions after that.

Henrik interrupted Nora's thoughts. "Did you enjoy dinner?"

He put his arm around her shoulders as she shivered in the evening breeze.

"I did. Johan is easy to talk to, even if his account of the qualities of your new mainsail did take up most of the main course." Nora smiled at him. "But it's lovely to have a pleasant evening together for a change. I've missed this." She snuggled a little closer and gently stroked his cheek. "Have you given any more thought to the idea of moving to Malmö? It all sounds very exciting, doesn't it? It would be a terrific opportunity for me." The sense of pride at having been asked to apply for the post gave her a warm feeling. She gazed up at her husband, smiling.

Henrik looked back at her, surprise written all over his face. "I thought we'd finished talking about this. We can't move the entire family to Malmö just because somebody offers you a job there."

Nora was shocked. "What do you mean? Why can't we move to Malmö just because somebody offers me a job there?"

"I can't move, and I have no desire to do so. I'm very happy at the hospital in Danderyd. I have absolutely no wish to start again somewhere else." He half turned and waved to a passing acquaintance. "Shall we go back inside? The others will be wondering where we've gone."

Nora was at a loss for words. Then she furiously shook off his arm. The happy atmosphere was gone in a second; suddenly the gala and all those people laughing and dancing seemed a long way off.

"How can you possibly say we've finished talking about this? We haven't even discussed it properly!" She pushed a strand of hair back from her face and continued. "Have you even heard what I've been trying to tell you?" To her surprise, her voice was shaking. "I thought we had a modern relationship, an equal marriage, where both our jobs were important, not just yours."

"Calm down," Henrik said. "Let's not get carried away. I just meant that you need to be a little more realistic about the future. After all, I'm the main breadwinner. Our family and friends are in Stockholm. And I've got the boat here, of course." He took a step back and looked at her. "There's no need to be so melodramatic when I don't agree with you."

Henrik sounded exactly like the clinical practitioner he was. His voice was cool and distant, and he was looking at her as if she were a small child.

"I'm not being melodramatic."

Nora blinked away a tear, even more angry because she was starting to cry. The injustice of it all took her breath away. She swallowed, partly to get rid of the lump in her throat and partly to prevent the tears from falling.

Henrik was expressionless. He took a few steps toward the door. "Yes, you are. Now pull yourself together so we can go back inside." He took another step.

Nora clenched her fists in rage. Every time Henrik wanted to go away for a competition, the family simply had to make it work. His training sessions and sailing competitions already took up most weekends during the spring and autumn, and their entire summer vacation was arranged according to the various regattas. But when her job happened to be in the spotlight for once, she was being melodramatic.

Henrik was leaning impatiently against the doorframe. "Come on, Nora. Surely you don't have to make a scene tonight of all nights. Can't we just go back inside and enjoy ourselves? Is that too much to ask?"

Nora glared at him. "Yes," she said. "It is." She dashed away another tear. "I'm going home. This evening is over as far as I'm concerned." She ran down the steps. The night was ruined. Henrik could come up with some explanation for his friends—she really didn't care.

It had been a terrible week. Perhaps it was only fitting that it had ended with a terrible evening.

SUNDAY,

THE FOURTH WEEK

CHAPTER 41

The attempt to clear his mind by going over to Harö hadn't exactly been a success. By the time Thomas got there on Saturday afternoon he was far too pumped up on adrenaline to unwind completely. Instead he had gone out for a long run, followed by a refreshing dip from the jetty.

He had gone to bed early to try to catch up on the sleep he had lost during the week, but it had been a waste of time. He found it impossible to stop his mind from dwelling on the case. Fragments of conversations with potential witnesses and disjointed images of the victims whirled around in his head.

At about two o'clock in the morning he gave up, grabbed a beer, and went to sit on the jetty. The sun had already begun to rise; it didn't stay below the horizon for very long at this time of year.

Thomas sat there thinking about the murders, and eventually he nodded off in his chair. His mother woke him when she came down for her morning swim.

"Have you been out here all night?" she asked, looking puzzled.

Thomas blinked at her, still only half-awake. "I couldn't get to sleep, so I came down here."

He sat up and ran his hands through his hair, then stretched to ease the muscles in his back, stiff from sitting in an awkward position in the chair.

It was a beautiful, still morning, with gentle ripples on the surface of the water. A little family of eider ducks with three ducklings came swimming along; one little ball of fluff almost got tangled up in a piece of floating yellow seaweed.

His mother shook her head, looking concerned. "You need to take things easy. You sleep badly and you eat badly. I'm going to make you a proper breakfast after my swim."

Thomas smiled at her. He knew that his parents worried about him. Emily's death had hit them hard. They had so looked forward to their first grandchild and had been utterly devastated by what had happened.

It suddenly struck him that they were both over seventy. Two living, healthy parents was no longer something he could take for granted.

He got up and gave his mother a great big bear hug. She almost disappeared in his embrace.

"Breakfast would be fantastic. I'm starving."

After lunch, he abandoned the attempt to think of anything other than the investigation. He took out his laptop and logged on. He spread out all the relevant documents on the kitchen table, including information from the general public and the various reports that had been handed in during the week. Methodically he went through it all.

It was clear that few people had noticed Kicki Berggren's visit to Sandhamn. Among the crowds of summer visitors, sailors, and tourists, hardly anyone had noticed a lonely woman of about fifty.

In spite of the fact that they had knocked on every single door in Sandhamn—more than once in some cases—their inquiries had produced little. Thomas rubbed his eyes and yawned. The only point of interest was a statement Erik had handed in. He had spoken to a woman who lived in the older part of the village who thought she remembered Kicki Berggren walking past the bakery heading toward Fläskberget—going west, in other words. The woman had noticed her because she had been wearing such high heels and had had some difficulty walking on the sand.

"These are much better," the old lady had said, pointing to her white sneakers, the laces tied in a neat bow.

According to the report, Kicki Berggren had been looking around as if she didn't really know where she was going.

The woman had also noticed that Kicki had spoken to someone, but she couldn't remember who it was. She couldn't for the life of her come up with any distinguishing features about the person Kicki had been talking to. She couldn't even recall whether it was a man or a woman, let alone the person's age or appearance. Just that Kicki seemed to be asking questions.

"I'm sorry, but it was all so quick. It was just something I saw out of the corner of my eye. I was too busy wondering how she could walk in those shoes," she had explained when Erik pushed her for more details.

Thomas got up and went to make a cup of coffee. Two spoonfuls of instant coffee, hot water, two sugar lumps, and a little milk. He stirred thoughtfully as the sugar dissolved. Then he opened the cupboard to see if there was anything to eat. There wasn't much, but he managed to locate an open packet of slightly stale cookies.

He took his coffee and the cookies back to the computer and sat down. He read through Erik's report one more time as he pondered. If Kicki Berggren was going to visit someone, but didn't know where that person lived, it was only logical that she would ask the way. The bakery was a natural meeting point on Sandhamn. Everyone who lived on the island went there on a regular basis to buy bread.

The woman had seen Kicki at some point on Friday afternoon. If one assumed that she was intending to visit someone who lived on the island, then she must have asked a resident. A sailor or a tourist probably wouldn't have been able to help. Therefore, there had to be someone who had spoken to Kicki and who knew what questions she had asked.

The problem was that they had yet to find this unknown person. Nor had anyone come forward.

On the other hand, Thomas was well aware that he or she wasn't necessarily still on the island. Many families shared the houses they had inherited, which meant that they spent only part of their vacation on Sandhamn. If this mysterious individual had left the island and gone somewhere else, perhaps to a different part of the country or even abroad, that would explain why the police hadn't managed to track him or her down. There could also be an even simpler explanation: the person might not realize that he or she had spoken to the woman who had later been murdered and that the police would be interested. If this was the case, the chances of finding him or her were probably infinitesimal.

Thomas drank the last of his coffee. If they could find out whom Kicki Berggren had spoken to, it would provide an important piece of the puzzle.

He decided to post Erik at the bakery for the entire next day with a photograph of Kicki. He would ask him to speak to every person who turned up to find out if anyone had seen or spoken to her a week ago.

They also needed to question the bakery staff again. There was no guarantee that the girls who had been working there when the police turned up were the same as when Kicki stopped by. He remembered working in a bakery when he was a teenager; the employees had different shifts, coming and going all the time.

Thomas closed his eyes and tried to visualize the bakery. If you headed west from there, where would you end up?

In his mind's eye he saw the lane where the red building housing the bakery was located. It led past one of the oldest houses on Sandhamn, a little cottage dating back to the eighteenth century where someone by the name of C. J. Sjöblom had once lived. The name was etched into the rock at the bottom of the steps leading up to the cottage. Apparently another past resident, an old woman, had made a living taking in laundry for the islanders.

The very thought of washing clothes by hand in winter in the ice-cold water made Thomas shudder.

He continued walking through the village in his mind.

If you carried on along the lane, you passed the little hill where children of every age wore out the seat of their pants by sliding down and landing on the sand.

Then came a row of old houses, followed by the marina for small boats to the north, then Kvarnberget.

Eventually you reached Fläskberget, an attractive sandy shore, which many families in the village preferred to the more famous Trouville beach, which was often packed with tourists.

Finally you came to Västerudd, the western point of the island, which consisted mainly of pine forests and low-growing blueberry bushes, with the odd large house and garden dotted around. It was on the beach between Koberget and Västerudd that Krister Berggren's body had been found, next to a house owned by the Åkermark family. A stretch of sand with virtually no sign of habitation.

Thomas realized that if Kicki Berggren had been on her way to the western side of the island, it meant that the Trouville area could be discounted completely. This in turn meant that the search area was significantly reduced.

A welcome thought under the circumstances.

He decided to spend the following morning concentrating on the area between the bakery and Västerudd. With a bit of luck they would be able to find someone who had seen a blond woman in high heels wandering around last Friday.

Thomas stretched. He had earned a cold beer down by the jetty. At least he felt like he was getting somewhere.

Chapter 42

"What time are we leaving, Mom?" Simon patted Nora's arm and planted a soft kiss on her cheek.

Nora looked around, only half-awake. The digital clock showed that it was only 7:20. Far too early to get up, at least if she had anything to say about it.

"What do you mean, sweetheart?"

"What time are we leaving for Alskär? We're going there with Fabian's family, remember? That's what you said yesterday."

Nora suppressed a groan. She had completely forgotten that they had promised to take the children to the little island immediately northeast of Sandhamn, just a ten-minute boat trip away. There was a natural sandy beach on Alskär, plus a tiny island opposite that you could wade to. The children loved going there and making their way across the little sound.

Yesterday afternoon, when she was in a really good mood, she had happily agreed with Eva Lenander that they would spend Sunday on Alskär together. Eva's son, Fabian, was Simon's best friend on Sandhamn, and the Lenanders lived just a few minutes away.

A lovely day out with a picnic on the beach. Today it didn't have quite the same appeal.

She turned her head and gazed at Henrik, who was still fast asleep.

She had been furious and disappointed when she'd gotten home last night. In spite of the fact that she was still awake when Henrik arrived soon after her, she'd pretended to be asleep. She hadn't had the slightest desire to speak to him.

A trip with the Lenanders would mean they wouldn't have the opportunity to sort out last night's argument. Instead they would have to keep up the pretense all day, acting as if everything were fine. That didn't feel right.

"Come on, Mom, when are we leaving?"

"Sweetheart, do you know what time it is? Come and cuddle and try to sleep for a bit longer. It's much too early to go anywhere."

Nora drew Simon close and pulled the covers over him. She could already feel the beginnings of a headache, but she couldn't work out whether it was due to the lack of sleep or her anger at Henrik.

"Just for a little while," she said.

Nora closed her eyes and tried to get back to sleep. It was easier said than done. Simon was wide awake and incapable of keeping still. If he wasn't kicking her in the kidneys, he was pushing his little face up against her ribs. At around eight o'clock she gave up.

"OK, come on. We'll get dressed and cycle down to the bakery for some fresh bread."

At the bakery, they were met by the aroma of freshly baked bread and warm cakes. Other summer visitors who were up bright and early stood around in small groups, waiting for the shop to open. Nora chatted with several people she knew while waiting in line.

She bought fresh rolls and a loaf of bread. Simon was allowed to choose which cakes they should take with them to Alskär. He settled for two Sandhamn knots flavored with cardamom and two flaky Danish pastries with a generous dollop of vanilla in the center.

With Simon on the luggage rack, she carried on to the kiosk to buy a morning paper. There was no line when she got there, just a dog racing around with his tail in the air in spite of the fact that his owner was calling to him. A few hungry gulls circled overhead, searching for some discarded delicacy on which they could feast.

"Morning," Nora greeted the woman in the kiosk, whose family she had known ever since she was a little girl. "Could I have a nice fresh morning paper, please?"

She held out her money and was met with a wry smile.

"I should think so. If you want to read the paper, that is. There seems to be no end to the nonsense they can come up with about the Sandhamn murders. And then there are the evening papers. We'll see what nonsense they've made up after lunch."

Nora took the paper and tucked it under her arm. "Have the deaths made a difference in your sales?"

"I'm afraid so. We usually have a line here in the afternoons at this time of year, but it's been much quieter, and I should think it'll get worse now that the regatta is over. I hope the police catch the killer soon. Otherwise businesses out here are going to be in trouble. We make our living in the summer."

Nora stayed and chatted for a little while, then she lifted Simon back onto the luggage rack and cycled home. She hoped Henrik was still asleep. She almost wished he were still out sailing. She needed to think things through before she spoke to him.

***

As soon as breakfast was over, Nora started packing for their day out.

It was quite a task. Four beach towels, a picnic blanket, a mountain of beach toys in various colors, a big basket of sandwiches, pastries, juice, and a thermos of coffee. At the last minute she remembered to put in a roll of toilet paper; it always came in handy. Sunscreen and four life jackets, and she was ready.

The cordless phone rang, and she answered it.

"Nora, my dear." Her mother-in-law's domineering voice filled the receiver. Nora stiffened; the harsh sound of Monica Linde filled her entire body with distaste. "I want to speak to Henrik. Bring the children, and come over to Ingarö right now. I've already prepared the guesthouse. You can't stay on that island while there's a murderer on the loose."

Nora sighed and forced herself not to lose her temper. She would rather stay on Sandhamn with ten murderers than spend one night with Monica at their country house on Ingarö. The long tradition of spending Christmas there with the entire Linde clan was more than enough. Monica ruled the roost, and Nora made such an effort to keep her mouth shut that her jaws ached. Henrik didn't notice a thing, as usual. Once he was back in the home where he grew up he reverted to a spoiled teenager, letting his mom do everything. Meanwhile, Nora ran around trying to keep the boys in order and helping out as best she could. Her father-in-law usually fled to the sauna with an enormous drink, but she didn't have that luxury.

"I'm sorry, Monica. Henrik is already down at the jetty. We're going out for the day. I'll ask him to call you when we get back."

She quickly ended the call in spite of Monica's protests. Henrik had in fact gone down to the boat to get everything ready and check that there was enough fuel in the tank.

Nora slipped on her life jacket and turned the key in the door. She didn't usually bother to lock up; on the contrary, she often left the veranda door open, both to let in some fresh air and to show that they were home. But at the moment it just didn't feel safe, particularly as they were going to be out all day.

As she was passing Signe's house, the kitchen window opened, and a familiar face appeared.

"Are you going sailing?"

"It looks that way," Nora said. She really was fond of her neighbor. "We're going to Alskär; the kids love it. We're going with the Lenanders—you know, Fabian's parents."

"What a good idea—Alskär is a wonderful place."

Nora smiled at Signe. Just the thought of a boat trip made her feel more cheerful.

"Take these for the boys." Signe passed a bag of jam tarts out of the window. "I know they love them, and I expect even you and Henrik might manage one or two."

"That's so kind of you—thank you!" Nora took the sweets, placed them carefully in her beach bag, and waved her grateful thanks to Signe before heading down to the jetty.

Henrik had already cast off, and the boys were sitting in the prow. As usual Adam had been pestering Henrik, demanding to steer; Henrik had promised that he could have a try as soon as they were out in open water.

Nora sat down in the middle of the boat, at a safe distance from Henrik.

They had maintained a polite and neutral tone all morning and had discussed only practical matters. Neither of them had mentioned the previous night's argument. Fortunately the boys had been jumping around, full of excitement about the day's outing, and it had been easy to hide behind their eager chatter.

***

The Lenanders were already there when they arrived. Henrik maneuvered in among the rocks and dropped anchor. Alskär had a natural harbor, so it was just a matter of finding a suitable place to moor the boat. Everyone tried to avoid dragging the boats up onto the shore so that the little beach was left free for the children to build their sandcastles.

After their picnic Nora went for a walk with Eva. On the other side of the island there was an area of completely flat stones, worn so smooth by wind and water that it felt like a baby's bottom when you ran a hand over the warm rock. Nora and Eva sat down for a while.

It was a beautiful spot. Far away they could just see the tower of the lighthouse on Korsö, with lots of yachts in the distance. The sky was a perfect shade of blue, with the odd wispy cloud here and there. They looked like little scraps of the finest cotton wool, dotted across the sky. A herring gull swooped after food on the surface of the water.

"So, how are things?" Eva asked. She had become a good friend in recent years. Nora saw her almost every day, since Fabian and Simon attended swimming lessons together. Eva was one of those rare individuals who really seemed to care about other people and was always in a good mood.

Nora met Eva's concerned gaze. She knew she had been unusually subdued all day.

"Could be better. It hasn't been a great week, has it?" Nora said.

"Did you have a good time last night?"

"Not exactly. We had a massive fight about that job I mentioned the other day."

"Do you want to talk about it?" Eva placed a consoling hand on Nora's shoulder.

Nora tucked her knees up under her chin and wrapped her arms around her legs. She thought for a moment before she answered. "Henrik can't understand why I'm interested in working in Malmö. He won't even try to listen. He doesn't want to move away from Stockholm;

he thinks we have a good life at the moment, and there's nothing to discuss." She picked up a small pebble and skimmed it across the water. It bounced three times before sinking. She found another that was nice and flat and tried again. This time she counted four. Her personal best was seven, but that must have been at least fifteen years ago—maybe even twenty. "It's as if his job is the only one that counts."

"But you do have a good life, don't you?" Eva said.

"That's not the point. We have a great life, of course we do, but at least we ought to be able to talk about this before he dismisses the whole idea. What do you think would have happened if it had been the other way round? If he'd been made a terrific offer from Sahlgrenska University Hospital in Gothenburg?" She picked up another pebble and hurled it furiously into the sea. It sank immediately. "I just can't stand the thought of going back after our vacation and working with Ragnar again. The man is a complete idiot." She ran her hands through her hair in frustration. "And I'm an idiot if I don't move. Particularly when the bank is offering me an opportunity like this."

Eva patted her on the shoulder again to show her sympathy. Then she adjusted the strap of her red swimsuit and lay down on her stomach on the warm rock. "This hasn't been an easy week for you. How's the investigation going, by the way? Have you heard anything from Thomas?"

Nora shook her head. "I haven't spoken to him—we've just exchanged some texts. He's been so busy. He sent a message to tell me he'd be on Harö this weekend, mainly to get some sleep, I think. He's been working all hours. The last time I saw him he looked absolutely shattered."

"There was something I wanted to talk to him about . . . I think."

Nora looked at Eva, who frowned and started chewing her thumbnail. "What do you mean?"

"We had visitors from Stockholm last Sunday. Malin called me last night to say thanks." Eva hesitated. "She said she was almost certain she'd been sitting a couple seats away from Jonny Almhult on the ferry back to Stockholm."

Nora sat up and turned her head so she could see Eva more clearly in the bright sunlight. "Is she sure?"

"She said she remembered him because he stank of stale booze. They were only a few feet apart. Her oldest daughter wanted to know why he smelled so horrible. You know, the way kids do."

"Go on."

"That's it. They disembarked, and she didn't give it another thought until Jonny's body was found, and she saw his picture in the paper. That was when she realized he'd been sitting near them on the ferry." She fell silent and looked anxiously at Nora.

"Has she called the police?"

"I don't think so. It didn't sound as if she had. Should I mention it to Thomas?"

"Definitely," Nora said. "Thomas told me every piece of information is valuable. They're trying to find out where Jonny was before he died. Did your friend see where he went when they got to Stockholm?"

"I don't know. I didn't think to ask," Eva said.

Nora got to her feet. "Come on. Let's go back. We need to call Thomas."

Monday,
the Fourth Week

CHAPTER 43

Margit had left her family and traveled up from the west coast. She was sitting at her desk reading through all the case notes, and she was in a foul mood. Any hope of a restful, uninterrupted vacation had been shattered. The situation was not improved by the fact that her teenage daughter had immediately found soul mates of her own age and was more than happy to escape her mother's watchful eye.

Thomas and Margit had gone through the entire investigation from start to finish, and he had summarized the events of the past week.

They were still unable to find a link between Krister and Kicki Berggren and Sandhamn. Neither their background nor a search of their respective apartments had come up with anything that could lead to someone on the island. They had received a number of calls from the public but nothing of any real value.

The money was on Sandhamn, Agneta Ahlin had said. Thomas kept thinking about that. What money? And where was it?

As expected, the forensic report had confirmed that the dried blood on the radiator in Jonny Almhult's house was Kicki's. The jacket hanging in his hallway also belonged to her. Therefore, there was clear evidence that she had been there, but it had been impossible to establish where she had ingested the fatal poison.

Thomas wondered when he had last felt properly rested. His sleep deficit was beginning to reach unimaginable levels. He remembered how tired he had been during those first few months after Emily was born, but it had been easier then because he had been so amazed at the miracle of becoming a father.

At the moment, he was utterly exhausted. Either he was trying to talk to people on Sandhamn or he was trying to piece together information as it emerged. They had brought in extra staff to go through everything one more time with a fine-tooth comb.

Thomas went off to the coffee machine. It felt like an admission of defeat, but the only thing that enabled him to think clearly at the moment was unlimited quantities of caffeine. With a certain amount of distaste he got a cup for himself and one for Margit, then went back to her office.

"Here," he said. "This might help. Who wants a family vacation when you can sit in a stifling hot police station and solve a murder?"

Margit looked at him, her expression grim. "Very funny. I promised the girls we'd have four weeks together this year. And it was a nightmare trying to find a decent place to rent in July that didn't cost a fortune."

Thomas leaned back in his chair. "But the family's having a good time, right? They're still down there?"

"Oh yes, the girls are absolutely fine. But Bertil wasn't at all pleased when I said I'd have to come back here." Margit glanced apologetically at the photograph of her husband that stood on her desk. She put her head in her hands and groaned. "I just don't understand how Jonny Almhult comes into the picture. Everyone you've spoken to describes him as a fairly innocuous person, not a violent character. Definitely not a ladies' man. It's hard to imagine him beating Kicki Berggren after drowning her cousin."

"And even if he did," Thomas said, "we still have no explanation as to why Jonny is also dead." He linked his hands behind his neck as he gave the matter further consideration. "What if there's a fourth person involved?" he said. "Perhaps someone Jonny used to work for, before something went wrong. If he was acting on behalf of someone else, that could explain why he was killed. In which case we have a murderer who has killed three people and possibly got rid of Jonny in order to cover his tracks. Which takes us back to the question of why the two cousins were killed."

Thomas gazed at the sparkling blue waters of Nackafjärden through the window. It was a perfect day for sitting on the jetty with a cold beer, instead of drinking tepid coffee in a stuffy office.

With a huge effort he forced himself to gather his thoughts. "We're getting nowhere fast," he said. "We haven't even managed to find the person Kicki Berggren allegedly spoke to outside the bakery. And if it was someone who was visiting for a few days, the chances of doing so are almost nonexistent."

Margit took a sip of coffee. She ran a hand through her hair, which didn't make her look the least bit better, then started rummaging through the pile of reports. "If your theory that Kicki was heading west on Sandhamn holds, then at least we have a limited area on which to focus. Plus Krister's body was washed up on that side of the island," she said as she skimmed the document in her hand.

Thomas picked up a large map showing every property on Sandhamn. He spread it out on the desk and drew a large circle around the northwestern section, from the bakery to the outermost point of Västerudd.

"There are approximately fifty houses inside this circle," he said, carefully examining the map.

He got up and went out into the corridor to call Carina, who appeared in the doorway a minute later.

"I'm just wondering about that check on property owners on Sandhamn that we talked about on Friday," he said. "Did you manage to find anything that matched the name the Mission House manager thought she remembered?"

Carina shook her head. "Sorry, no. The land registry office is closed on Fridays; they open at nine this morning, so I'm going to call them as soon as possible."

She looked like an abandoned kitten, with her heart-shaped face and a little dimple in one cheek.

Thomas gave her an encouraging smile, and she seemed to relax.

"Don't worry," he said. "But let us know as soon as you find out anything. We'll be here for quite some time."

He was rewarded with a beaming smile. "I'll come and tell you right away, I promise."

"Try to find out which of them are permanent residents and which are summer visitors, if you can," Margit said. "I have a feeling Kicki was looking for a summer visitor. I find it difficult to believe a resident would be involved in something like this. Small communities usually exercise a high level of social control. If someone is smuggling alcohol, I don't see how you could run it from the archipelago. It would be very complicated, anyway."

"Jonny Almhult was a resident; that contradicts your theory," Thomas said.

"But we think he was working for somebody else, don't we? And didn't he do a lot of little jobs for summer visitors?"

Thomas figured as a carpenter, Jonny must have had plenty of opportunities to join forces with someone who might want slightly more demanding tasks carried out. Striking fear in a third party, for example. Jonny must have met most of the homeowners over the years. But would Jonny have poisoned Kicki and then slapped her around? That couldn't be right.

"How likely is it that Jonny could lead us to the real killer?" Margit asked. "The indications are that Kicki ingested the poison before she met him. She might just have picked up Jonny in the bar; perhaps they bumped into one another, and there was no connection with the person who gave her the poison." Margit looked at him, waiting for a response.

Thomas had to admit that she could be right. "It's possible." He picked up a pen and doodled in his notebook as he tried to come up with something sensible. "We have no evidence Jonny was in collusion with the person who murdered Kicki and presumably killed her cousin. But isn't it a bit far-fetched to assume it was pure coincidence?"

Margit looked skeptical. "Most things seem to be a bit far-fetched in this case. Nothing has been straightforward so far."

"I still think we should stick to the hypothesis that Jonny has some kind of relationship with the poisoner, who is also involved in Krister's death," Thomas said. "Think about the needle threaded through the net around Krister's body. It was marked with Jonny's father's initials. I can't believe Krister's death has nothing to do with everything else that's happened."

Margit had nothing to say. She took the top off a marker and went over to a flip chart in the corner. She drew two stick men and a stick woman side by side. Above them she wrote *Known Facts*. "The deceased were two cousins, plus one person previously unknown to them. None of them was married or had children. All three made little money. Two seem to lack any connection with Sandhamn; one was a resident. There is no obvious motive for any of the murders; all we have is speculation."

Thomas gazed at the flip chart. "Aren't you going to write down that we don't have a perpetrator either?" he said sarcastically.

Margit smiled. "I haven't finished yet." She picked up another marker.

> *Cause of death: two drowned, one poisoned, violence a contributory factor.*

Residence: two lived in Stockholm, one on Sandhamn.
Relationships: two knew each other very well, the third probably a passing acquaintance of one of them.
Work: warehouse worker, croupier, carpenter.

When she had finished she took a step back and read through her summary. Then she went back to her seat and put down the marker. She rubbed her eyes and blinked a few times. She had reorganized the information they had, but it provided no fresh insights.

Thomas gazed at Margit's notes. He chewed on a marker for a little while, then went over to the chart and carefully wrote *Sex*. He stood there for a moment, then added a question mark. "Try this. The murderer gives Kicki a bunch of rat poison, but he's not sure it's enough. On top of that, he doesn't want to take the risk of her babbling about what she knows. So he tells Jonny to go and find her, just to be on the safe side, and to keep an eye on her. It wouldn't have been particularly difficult to track her down on the island. He bumps into her in the bar according to plan. They have a few beers together, and she goes home with him. Then something goes wrong."

Margit was looking intently at Thomas. "Perhaps Jonny thought he might get something out of it for himself. He would do what he had been told to do, but he would go to bed with her as well."

"And when she wasn't interested . . ."

"He lost his temper and hit her."

"Not because he'd been told to, but because she turned him down."

"And the desired result was achieved after all: Kicki died."

"And everyone was happy."

"Except perhaps Jonny," Margit said. "Violence instead of sex doesn't really sound like a great result."

Thomas couldn't argue with that. "If we can track down Jonny's contact, we'll probably have our killer," he said.

"Very possibly. We need to carry on tracing Jonny's movements and finding out who he met up with."

Thomas yawned and put down the marker. "But what we really need to know is who Kicki was asking about. Let's hope Carina's inquiries get us somewhere. And soon."

CHAPTER 44

The pressure was intense and increasing all the time. Persson had held several press conferences over the past few days and was doing his best to keep the top brass informed. The press officer was working furiously to deal with all the phone calls so that the investigation could be conducted without interruption, but his constant requests to Persson for updates had fallen on stony ground.

Now Persson was growling as soon as the phone rang.

The cases of the multiple deaths in the middle of summer had shaken all those involved. The number of tourists heading over to Sandhamn had dropped significantly, and the chamber of trade had contacted the local authority and the chief constable. The problem must be solved, and soon.

The Waxholmsbolaget ferries were carrying far fewer passengers than they should be at this time of year.

The leader of the local council in Värmdö had called a press conference of his own to put forward his view of events, which consisted of a hastily cobbled together conspiracy theory touching on Mafia involvement from the Eastern Bloc. Which hadn't been of any help to the investigation whatsoever. On the contrary, it had served to increase confusion and had given the media even greater opportunity to speculate on a range of theories.

"Remind me not to vote for that idiot next time we have a local election," Persson had said with ill-concealed disgust. Then he had wadded up the newspaper in which the council leader had been permitted to outline his homespun analysis and hurled it into the trash.

Persson had also been contacted by the chairman of the Royal Swedish Yacht Club, a well-known figure from the world of industry, who had spoken with great authority, demanding to be informed about what was happening and how the investigation was progressing. The chairman had pointed out how important it was for Sandhamn's reputation as an international center for competitive sailing that the case should be brought to a conclusion without delay. He had spoken about the long tradition of holding competitions based on Sandhamn and of the youth project on Lökholmen, where children from the Stockholm area gathered to attend sailing and confirmation camps. Anxious parents were calling him up, reluctant to let their offspring travel to the island.

"The situation is extremely worrying," the chairman said. It was vital that the police understood how serious it was and did their utmost to sort things out. The Yacht Club had even discussed the matter at their board meeting that week. They had noted in the minutes that the police must find the guilty party as soon as possible.

Persson did his best not to explode during the conversation. He was dangerously close to losing his temper several times, and his face, which was normally red, could now be described as scarlet. He gritted his teeth and informed the chairman that the police were well aware of the seriousness of the situation. All available resources had been deployed on the case, including an officer with excellent local knowledge. The investigation was being given top priority.

But when the chairman insisted that he be kept informed on a daily basis, Persson almost lost it.

"I am conducting a murder investigation. I am not an information service. You're not the only person calling and demanding information I don't have," he said.

"Now, now, my good man," the chairman said. "Let's not get worked up. It's essential to maintain a good working relationship between the police and the Royal Swedish Yacht Club. We have nothing to gain by losing our temper."

Persson almost burst.

"As I was saying to my good friend the commissioner the other day," the chairman carried on, "I have every confidence in the way the police are conducting their investigation, but naturally I wish to be kept informed. In my position, I must be able to follow your work. Surely you understand that?"

Persson's complexion changed from scarlet to dark purple.

"Don't hesitate to contact me if you have a breakthrough. I can always be reached through the Yacht Club's main office. Don't worry about disturbing me if it's something important."

The receiver was nearly crushed in Persson's viselike grip. With some difficulty he refrained from shouting again and managed something that could have been interpreted as a polite good-bye.

He ended the call and went into the conference room. It was two o'clock in the afternoon, and the team had gathered for a briefing. His irate expression and aura of rage rang alarm bells as soon as he walked in. Not even Carina—his own daughter—dared to ask what had happened, and most of those who had heard fragments of the telephone conversation reverberating down the corridor realized that if they wanted to save their own skins they would be well advised to keep a low profile.

"If one more fucking idiot asks me how this investigation is going, I swear I'll punch him," Persson said.

No one doubted his ability to keep that promise. He sat down on a chair that was already too small; it creaked in protest.

"So, how's it going? Thomas, status report, please." It wasn't a question, merely an order barked from the corner of his mouth.

Thomas looked down at his papers and took a moment to gather his thoughts. "Carina has gone through all the property owners in the part of the island where we think Kicki Berggren was headed. We have two names that could be of interest: Pieter Graaf and Philip Fahlén. Both are summer residents and have names that could to some extent match the name given by the manager of the Mission House. Philip Fahlén's house is very close to the spot where Krister Berggren's body was found; Pieter Graaf's isn't far from the Mission House, on the way to the beach at Fläskberget. Margit and I will be going over to Sandhamn to interview the two men as soon as possible."

Persson looked a little less angry; he leaned back in his chair, which wobbled. "Well, at least that's something to go on," he said. "What do we know about Kicki Berggren's other contacts on Sandhamn?"

"Erik will be standing outside the bakery all day today in order to try to find the person she spoke to," Thomas said.

Persson looked at him impatiently. "How's it gone so far?"

Thomas looked down at the table. "Nothing useful yet. However, I have spoken again to the girl who was working in the bar the night Kicki Berggren was there." He flipped through his notebook. "Inger Gunnarsson. She had remembered something after our conversation last week. It seems Kicki had complained of an upset stomach; evidently she asked if they had any kind of antacid behind the bar."

Margit folded her arms and gazed around the impersonal conference room, where a single wilting Busy Lizzie was the only attempt to make the place look better. Without the view of the blue waters of Nackafjärden through the window, it would have been depressingly bare. "Presumably she was beginning to feel the effects of the poison," Margit said. "That would fit in with the pathologist's report. If it was after eight o'clock, she would have started to feel ill. But she had drunk a fair amount of beer, so she might well have attributed the symptoms to something else."

Persson changed tack. "Have we heard anything about Almhult from the pathologist? Do we know what the cause of death was?"

Thomas picked up a document that had been faxed through that morning. "Cause of death was drowning. There was evidence of a high level of alcohol in the blood. He must have been very drunk when he drowned—paralytic, in fact."

"Any trace of poison?" Persson looked at Thomas. It was obvious that he was hoping for a negative response.

"No chemical substances whatsoever, at least in the preliminary report. However, they have sent samples to Linköping for analysis, and it's difficult to be certain until we've heard from them."

"Anything else?"

"Crush injuries."

"What?"

"Crush injuries to the head and the rest of the body, as if he'd hit something with tremendous force, or as if someone had hit him with a blunt object. He had a number of broken bones, along with severe bruising."

"Any idea what might have caused all that?" Margit asked, looking at Thomas.

He looked down at his papers again. "The report only describes the injuries; it doesn't suggest how they might have happened or what caused them."

Margit raised her eyebrows. "It seems as if our friends in pathology have taken the easy way out this time. I think we should call and ask if they have some kind of theory we could work with." She leaned back with an expression that made it clear she expected more substance from the medical profession. She was making no attempt to hide her bad mood.

Persson was also unhappy. He sighed and turned to Margit and Thomas. "So what's the next step?"

"We've had a call about Almhult," Thomas said. "It seems someone saw him on the ferry to Stockholm just over a week ago. We'll check that out right away. We've also put up posters all over Sandhamn, asking anyone who spoke to Kicki Berggren to contact us. That might help."

He looked at Margit, who nodded.

"We're also going to look into any possible connections between the house owners and Systemet, anything that might link one of them to Krister Berggren," Thomas said.

"Right," said Persson. "As you know, I was intending to take my vacation next week, so if you could solve the case by Saturday, that would be great." His feeble attempt at humor didn't go down very well. He stood up and wiped the sweat from his brow with a handkerchief that looked well used.

The meeting was over.

CHAPTER 45

The woman who opened the door the third time the bell rang had blobs of something that looked like vegetable puree all over her T-shirt. She looked stressed and was clutching a dish towel in one hand. The sound of children screaming emanated from the house.

"Are you the person who called from the police?" she asked, glancing over her shoulder where the piercing screams had turned into something more like a furious roar.

Thomas nodded. "My name is Thomas Andreasson, and this is my colleague, Margit Grankvist. May we come in for a few minutes? We'd like to ask you a few questions, if that's OK."

The roaring continued, and the woman looked even more stressed.

"Come in. I've left my daughter on her own in the kitchen, and I need to get back to her."

She disappeared down a narrow hallway to the right of the entry, and Margit and Thomas followed.

It was a pleasant house, cozy and well cared for, in the middle of Enskede, one of Stockholm's older suburbs. A typical old-style house with a yellow wooden façade, white eaves, and a small south-facing garden. Thomas counted four apple trees and one plum tree.

A gray cat slid past, uninterested in the visitors.

In the kitchen a very cross little girl was sitting in a high chair, banging her spoon on the table. The remains of something orange were strewn across the floor; it was the same color as the blobs on her mother's T-shirt.

The hard-pressed mother pushed a strand of hair from her face with the back of her hand. She wiped her hands on the dish towel and extended her right hand. "Malin. Sorry about the mess. My daughter seems to have woken up in something of a temper today. Please, sit down."

Margit tried to discreetly check whether there was anything orange on the kitchen chair before she sat down.

"You wanted to talk to me about my journey home from Sandhamn?"

Margit nodded. "We heard that you and your family were on the same ferry as the man who was found dead on the island just a few days later," she said.

"I think so." A fleeting expression of uncertainty passed over the woman's face. "There was a man sitting just a few seats away from us who looked exactly like the picture in the paper."

"Could you describe him?"

Malin thought for a moment; she wiped a blob of carrot puree off the table before she answered. "He was a real mess. Kind of shabby and run-down, you know? He was wearing a hoodie with the hood pulled tight, so I didn't see him very clearly. But he certainly stank. Sorry. I don't want to speak ill of the dead. But he smelled gross—like stale booze or something. That's why my eldest daughter, Astrid, asked about him. She's four."

"Did he do anything in particular during the crossing?"

"Not that I can remember, but I wasn't really paying attention." She smiled and pointed to the little girl, who had calmed down and was now clutching her sippy cup. "They keep you busy when they're that age."

"Could you tell us if you noticed anything else?"

"I'm sorry. There isn't really much I can say. He sat there during the whole trip, as far as I can remember. It takes about two hours."

"So he went all the way into Stockholm? He didn't get off beforehand?"

"No, we were quite late getting off. It took forever to pack up all our stuff. He got off about the same time; I remember that quite clearly."

She glanced at her daughter, who was now fully occupied in trying to remove the lid of her sippy cup so she could pour water all over the table.

Thomas thought for a moment. If Jonny Almhult had been sitting there with his hood pulled down, it was hardly surprising that no one from the ferry company remembered him, in spite of the fact that they had shown his photograph and questioned the crews of all the ferries serving Sandhamn.

He bent down and picked up the sippy cup, which the little girl had dropped. She took it and immediately threw it on the floor again, beaming at him.

An entertaining new game.

"And you didn't see him after that?"

"No, I don't think so." She seemed hesitant. "Or did I? I'm not absolutely certain; I might have seen him on Skeppsbron. My husband picked us up in the car, and as we were waiting under the lights outside the Grand Hotel, I thought I saw him walking toward Skeppsbron." She picked up the cup her daughter had just dropped for the fifth time. "But I can't swear it was him. I mean, it could have been anybody wearing a gray hoodie."

***

Thomas reversed the Volvo out of the little cul-de-sac and drove back the way they had come. Enskede was really charming, with old wooden houses surrounded by a variety of fruit trees. Just the kind of place you would want to live if you had a family.

Children.

Margit broke the silence. "It was well worth coming out here to speak to her, don't you agree?"

"Absolutely. Now we know Almhult came into town four days before his body was found. But where did he go after he got off the ferry?"

Margit thought for a moment, then opened the glove compartment and started rummaging around.

"What are you looking for?"

"A street map of Stockholm. Every police officer has one in the car, right?"

Thomas laughed.

"Really? Have you got one in your car?"

Margit pretended not to hear and kept on looking.

Thomas glanced at her. "Try the door pocket instead."

Margit fished out a well-thumbed wad of pages edged in red and held together with a paper clip. "You've torn out the map section from the Yellow Pages!" she said, shaking her head.

"Pernilla took the A–Z when we split up. I'm going to buy a new one as soon as I get around to it. Stop complaining. That works perfectly well. What do you want it for?"

Margit didn't answer. She ran a hand through her short, spiky hair as she studied the index of street names. When she found what she was looking for, she turned to the relevant page and placed her finger on the map. "Stop the car and I'll show you."

"What?"

"Stop the car. You can't drive and look at the same time. You're a police officer. You have to obey the law."

Thomas looked at her dubiously, then gave in and pulled over at the nearest bus stop. There was no point in arguing with her.

"What have you come up with?"

"Look at the map." Margit held out the page that showed the area of Stockholm around Skeppsbron. "If you go straight on from Skeppsbron, where do you end up?"

Thomas thought about it. He pictured the Grand Hotel, the ferries to the archipelago, and Skeppsbron. If you walked across Skeppsbron, where would you end up? "Gamla Stan—the old town? Slussen?"

He shrugged and looked at Margit.

"Keep going. You live in Stockholm, don't you? Where's your local knowledge? If you carry on past Slussen and walk along the water, where will you end up?"

"Stadsgården, down at the bottom of Fjällgatan."

"Exactly. And what will you find there?"

Suddenly it hit him. "The terminal for the ferries to and from Finland!"

"Bingo, Einstein!"

Thomas smiled sheepishly. He ought to have worked that out for himself. Margit was sharp.

"If you're on the run from the law—or from someone you work for who isn't too happy with you—and you want to disappear for a while, and aren't the type to hop on a plane to Brazil, where do you go?"

"To Finland, on the ferry." Thomas could have kicked himself. It was such a simple explanation.

"And if someone follows you and pushes you overboard as you're taking a last look at your home on Sandhamn," Margit went on, "what are you going to look like?"

"Bruised and battered, with broken bones that will be discovered postmortem."

"Exactly. If you fall from the top deck of a ship that size, it's like jumping off a tall building. The surface of the water is rock hard when you fall from a real height."

Thomas nodded.

"And where are you likely to be found?"

"On the beach at Trouville, a few days later."

"Exactly."

"We need to speak to the staff at the departure terminal. And we need to see their passenger lists for the crossings between the Sunday when Almhult arrived in Stockholm and the Thursday when he was found."

"Correct."

"Presumably we now know how Jonny Almhult lost his life."

"Correct."

With a triumphant smile Margit sank back into the warm car seat. Thomas felt like a schoolboy having his homework corrected.

Tuesday, the Fourth Week

Chapter 46

There was a thick mist lying in the Sandhamn Gap. Between Telegrafholmen in the north and Sandön in the south lay a sound that formed the natural passage into Sandhamn from the mainland. The sound was extremely deep, but barely sixty yards across at its narrowest point. It was only just wide enough for the ships that passed during the day.

The fog had rolled in overnight, transforming the beautiful evening sky of the previous day to a billowing mass of cloud. When Nora woke she could hear the faint sound of the foghorn at Revengegrundet lighthouse in the distance, a sure sign of poor visibility. Its mournful echo gave sailors a fixed point by which to navigate. Each lighthouse used the first letter of its name in Morse code as its signal. *A* for Almagrundet, *R* for Revengegrundet, and so on, helping those at sea to find their way if they had gone astray in the fog.

Ever since Nora had gotten lost many years ago in an evening mist just off Sandhamn, she had held a deep respect for the weather. She had been heading over to Skanskobb, a little island opposite the Trouville jetty that was the finish line for some of the sailing races. It was only about one nautical mile from the Yacht Club marina, if that. She was supposed to be helping out for a few hours in the Round Gotland Race, a major annual event.

In spite of the fact that she knew the waters around Sandhamn like the back of her hand and had sailed out to Skanskobb countless times in the past, she missed the island completely and suddenly saw a lighthouse looming ahead of her. She had passed Skanskobb and was about to crash into Svängen, the caisson lighthouse to the south of Korsö. If she hadn't ended up there, she could well have carried on out into the Baltic. After that she had never underestimated the difficulty of navigating in fog.

Nora looked at the digital clock. The red numbers told her it was six fifteen. Too early to get up, too late to go back to sleep. She had slept poorly over the past few nights. The atmosphere at home was still tense, though not quite as bad as it had been.

After a great deal of thought, she had decided to go to the meeting at the recruitment agency the following day. She had concluded that there was no point in discussing the matter with Henrik again; it would be better to have the meeting before she brought it up once more.

She slid out of bed and pulled on a pair of jeans and a top, along with a pair of old sailing boots she'd had since she was a teenager. The rubber had begun to crack up the sides, but they were easy to slip into. Then she put on an old sailing jacket that someone had once left behind and grabbed an apple from the fruit bowl.

The air was fresh, and a fine damp mist immediately covered her face. The silence was absolute, every sound deadened by the thick fog. She couldn't even hear the cry of a single gull. When she looked out over the sea, she couldn't see a thing.

The familiar contours of the islands off Sandhamn had been swallowed up by the gray dampness. Beyond the edge of the jetty the world became nothing but mist, a ghostly horizon with neither a beginning nor an end. Nora pulled up her hood and pushed her hands deep into her pockets, then strode off across the sand and into the forest.

The soft moss and heather combined to form a springy mat that gave as she walked. Only her footprints in the drifts of pine needles covering the path bore witness to her progress. She closed her eyes and took a deep breath.

There wasn't a soul in sight.

Total peace and quiet.

After a long walk through the forest she emerged on the northwestern side of the island. There were only a few isolated houses, set in large tracts of land covered in pine trees and blueberry bushes. This was in sharp contrast to the tiny plots in the village, where most of the space was given over to flower beds.

The wind soughed gently in the tops of the tall pines. The fog seemed to have lifted slightly; visibility was better, and she could just see the water's edge.

Nora turned to the right and followed the narrow forest track leading back to the village. As she passed the little churchyard surrounded by a simple white fence, she impulsively opened the gate and stepped inside. She stood there contemplating this tranquil place.

Sandhamn's churchyard had been established during the great cholera epidemic in the 1830s. Many of the graves were beautiful and elaborate, made of marble and granite. Some were overgrown with lichen, the inscriptions eroded to the point where it was almost impossible to read them. The gravestones could provide a great deal of information about the population in years gone by and about how people had made a living in those days. Every stone carried the name and occupation of the person who was buried there. Many master pilots and customs officers had been laid to rest here, often beside a faithful wife, whose name was always below that of her husband.

Nora recognized many of the surnames; they were families who still owned property on the island, houses that had been passed down from one generation to the next. They were often made up of sections of older houses that had been transported to Sandhamn from other islands.

There was an air of peace about this place, which lay just behind the beach at Fläskberget. The graves were surrounded by sand, its surface covered in needles and cones. Here and there the ground was crisscrossed by the gnarled roots of the pine trees, which gave the impression of an irregular pattern laid out at random, like a skewed chessboard.

A beautiful laburnum tree had been planted next to the modest grave belonging to Avén, the former lighthouse keeper who had been responsible for the lighthouse on Korsö for the latter part of the nineteenth century. People said he was a real gardener, who created an unparalleled display of flowers during his time on the island, with rose bushes and flower beds wherever you looked.

Nora wandered slowly among the graves. She had always loved the atmosphere in this churchyard and the feeling of stillness that came over her whenever she visited.

Up in the left-hand corner there was a memorial grove to commemorate those who had not been laid to rest in a grave of their own. A heavy black chain fenced off the area, and beside the great anchor in the sand there were fresh flowers and candles. For a moment she wondered who had put them there; perhaps it was some kind soul thinking of poor Kicki Berggren, who had recently lost her life on Sandhamn, or a resident wishing to honor the memory of a relative lost long ago.

Nora stopped at the Brand family grave, the resting place of every member of Signe's family who had passed away since the churchyard was established. The last name on the large gravestone was Helge Brand, Signe's brother, who had died of cancer at the beginning of the nineties.

Nora didn't have very clear memories of Helge. He had left the family and spent many years abroad and at sea. By the time he returned home to Sandhamn, he was already marked by the illness that would take his life. Signe cared for him in their childhood home until the end. She had refused to let him go to the hospital, insisting that she could care for him better than strangers.

Nora bowed her head as a mark of respect and slowly walked away, lost in thought.

People's lives could turn out so differently. One minute out on the seven seas, the next marked by death. Helge Brand had returned to Sandhamn as his life neared its end, while Kicki Berggren had been on the island for such a short time when she died. And Krister Berggren was already dead when he reached the island. None of them could have foreseen what a short time they had left to live.

Would they have done anything different if they had known what was coming? Nora wondered. *Would they have appreciated life more if they had sensed how quickly their time was running out?*

In a moment of ice-cold clarity Nora realized she wasn't prepared to compromise simply to appease Henrik. The injustice of the way in which her own wishes had been casually waved aside caused her physical pain. The anger at not being taken seriously felt like a solid lump in her chest. Never before had Henrik spelled out so clearly what really mattered.

She was so preoccupied that she stumbled over a tree root sticking out of the sand and almost lost her balance. The fog had come down once more, and she could taste the fine drops of rain on her tongue. She decided the boys could miss their swimming lessons today. In this weather they might as well sleep in.

Chapter 47

Margit and Thomas walked out into the police station parking lot to drive to Stavsnäs, where they would catch the morning boat to Sandhamn. Even though it was only nine thirty, the blazing sun had transformed the interior of the Volvo into something resembling a Finnish sauna. A wave of heat struck them as they opened the doors.

Thomas started the engine, and as he put the car into reverse, he turned to Margit. "Do you remember what work those two property owners on Sandhamn did? I meant to look, but something came up."

"I can't remember. I should have checked."

Thomas pulled out onto the highway heading for Stavsnäs. As they were approaching Strömma, his cell phone rang, and Thomas switched to speakerphone. The sound of Kalle's voice filled the car. He had new information about the rat poison that had killed Kicki.

"I finally reached somebody at Anticimex, the pest-control firm. Nobody at the hospital in Huddinge was willing to say anything definite, even though I've spoken to several different people. They all referred me to some guy who's a clinical pharmacologist, but of course he's on vacation abroad and isn't answering his phone."

"So what did Anticimex say?" Margit broke in.

"He was very dubious about the idea that someone could die from warfarin. He said anyone who consumes rat poison must either be blind or unusually ready to die. Rat poison consists of quite large granules, usually colored green or blue to show they're dangerous."

Margit leaned forward to speak into the phone, which was in a dock below the windshield. "What else did he say?"

"The amount you would need to consume to produce a fatal effect is more or less the equivalent of an entire meal. You have to ingest a significant amount for it to be dangerous."

"It doesn't seem credible that a person could consume that much without noticing anything," Thomas said.

"Exactly," Kalle said. "And another thing: it usually takes a couple of days to work, according to Anticimex. The idea is that the rats leave the house, so they don't die down in the basement. Nobody wants to find rotting rat corpses in their house."

Margit gave Thomas a look as she digested the information. "I presume we can rule out the possibility that Kicki tried to take her own life by eating rat poison," she said. "If someone wants to commit suicide, there are plenty of ways that are quicker and simpler; a handful of sleeping tablets and a bottle of whisky usually does the job in no time." She let out a cynical little laugh; it was a typical coping mechanism among police officers, to deal with unpleasant matters by using dark humor.

Thomas quickly changed the subject. "Kalle, can you check the professions of those two homeowners on Sandhamn? I was in a rush and forgot."

"Hang on." There was the sound of rustling paper as Kalle went through his notes. "Pieter Graaf is an IT consultant, and Philip Fahlén has his own company supplying equipment for catering facilities."

Margit whistled. "Catering facilities—that means restaurants. I'm just wondering if Philip Fahlén supplies more than kitchen equipment to his clients." She glanced at her watch. "It's high time we had a chat with those two gentlemen."

They arrived on Sandhamn after nearly an hour. Sometimes the ferries sailed directly from Stavsnäs to Sandhamn, which took no more than thirty-five minutes, but sometimes it seemed as if they were intent on calling at every single jetty in the southern archipelago. This time they had dropped off passengers on Styrsvik, Mjölkkilen, and Gatan before they reached their destination, but now the harbor opened out in front of them.

Thomas and Margit waited patiently in the line of families and day-trippers. They handed over their tickets and finally disembarked.

People were waiting on the pier to meet the new arrivals. Children and teenagers leaned on their bicycles as they ate Popsicles. Over by the kiosk, several people were going through the newspaper. In his peripheral vision Thomas could see that some of the headlines still featured the murders. And yet the harbor looked more or less the same as usual.

Except that it was quieter. With fewer boats.

Once ashore, they quickly set off for the western side of the island, where both Graaf and Fahlén lived. As soon as Thomas had looked at the map showing all the properties on Sandhamn, he knew exactly which houses they were.

They took the lane to the south of Strindbergsgården; it led into the heart of the village and through the old quarter. On the way they passed a little house painted Falu red, which reminded Thomas of a gingerbread house. Everything was extremely well maintained but in miniature. The garden extended no more than two yards around the property. The flag was flying, and the whole of the south-facing wall was covered in trellises weighed down with heavy bunches of luscious blackberries, in spite of the fact that it was only July. Pretty pots packed with plants were arranged by the fence; a tiny wooden deck area had been squeezed into one corner, and there was just room for a table and two chairs next to a compact woodshed with gray lichen on the roof.

It looked like an advertisement for summer in Sweden.

They cut across Adolf Square, the place where the traditional midsummer celebrations were held. The maypole was still standing, although it was somewhat yellow in comparison to what it must have looked like a few weeks earlier. One of the houses in the square had a climbing rose covering the entire wall; it looked like a pink firework spreading in all directions. There didn't seem to be a single house where the beds weren't full to bursting with glorious blooms.

Thomas wondered whether Sandhamn enjoyed some kind of microclimate that was particularly good for perennials. Either that, or all the people on the island must spend all their time tending their gardens. Watering alone must take forever.

He turned to Margit. "Have you been to Sandhamn before?"

"Yes, but it was a long time ago. My daughters have been over here a few times with their friends; it seems to be a popular place with teenagers. Bertil and I haven't been here for ages. Not since one summer twenty years ago, when the whole place was packed with wasted teenagers. It was indescribable. Drunken adolescents staggering around and not an adult in sight."

"I know what you mean," Thomas said. "When I was with the maritime police I picked up one or two who needed a lift home. But I think the situation has improved in recent years. These days most places are closed on Midsummer's Eve, and there aren't as many places to camp either."

"That must have had an effect."

"You can't imagine. One year when the weather was really bad, a group of kids actually broke into the police station so they'd be taken into custody. A kind of reverse outreach activity, if you like." Thomas laughed at the memory.

They continued quickly toward Västerudd. On the way, Thomas took a small diversion to point out Nora's house and to explain that his godson's family lived there.

"What a beautiful gate," Margit said. "I haven't seen that sun pattern before."

"I think Nora's grandfather made it. She inherited the house from her grandparents about ten years ago, and that gate has been there for as long as I can remember."

"It's exactly right." Margit nodded. "It's good when people preserve a craftsman's work like that."

"Perhaps we could stop by and say hello when we're finished," Thomas said. "It would be nice to see Simon if we have time."

Margit nodded.

Chapter 48

Pieter Graaf lived in a typical 1950s house surrounded by a large sandy garden containing a swing and a few stunted pine trees. It could have been in any suburb on the mainland and looked like a classic that was popular after the Second World War, when everyone decided to move out of the city. A couple of bedrooms, small windows, a kitchen, and a living room. Yellow wooden façade on a gray concrete base, surrounded by a white fence.

Margit looked at Thomas, who explained that the area had been established just after the war. Land had been divided up and houses built to provide accommodation for the families of pilots who had moved to Sandhamn.

Graaf was about thirty-five years old. He wore jeans and a tennis shirt spattered with something suspiciously like the green paint adorning the hut in one corner of the garden. He also wore a baseball cap with the logo of a well-known sports shop.

As they approached the house, Graaf was kicking a ball with a little boy who looked about three years old. The child was dressed in only a T-shirt and was as brown as a berry. He doubled over with laughter as his father deliberately missed the ball.

Margit and Thomas introduced themselves and explained that they had some questions relating to the recent deaths on the island. Did he have time for a chat?

Graaf looked surprised. He said he had already spoken to a police officer who had come by the previous week, but he broke off the ball game and invited them to sit down. He politely offered them a cold drink and said he would do his best to answer their questions.

The conversation was brief and not particularly useful.

Graaf had never set eyes on Kicki Berggren. He hadn't even been on the island during the weekend when she was murdered. He had been in Småland visiting his in-laws. Nor had he met Kicki Berggren's cousin. All he knew about the two of them was what had been in the papers.

Thomas considered him. The afternoon sun cast long shadows across the garden. There was virtually no sun where Graaf was sitting. He swung gently on the garden seat, which moved in time with the almost imperceptible movements of his body. From time to time a few pine needles drifted down onto the sand. He appeared to be an honest and pleasant person; he seemed genuinely surprised to receive a second visit from the police.

Many years' experience had taught Thomas that his first impression wasn't always accurate. But his gut feeling told him that he was talking to a perfectly ordinary father, not a cold-blooded killer.

"The day before Kicki Berggren died, she was asking about a man with a name similar to yours. Can you think of any reason why she might have wanted to speak to you?"

Graaf looked concerned. He bent down and kissed his son's forehead; the child had clambered up onto his knee and settled down. The little brown body with the white-blond hair looked exactly like the picture on matchboxes available everywhere.

"No reason at all. I have absolutely no idea who she was or why she was on Sandhamn. I hope you believe me, because I don't know how to prove it. The first I heard of Kicki Berggren was when I read about the murder in the paper, as I said." He looked at his watch, which also showed the date. "That must have been about ten days ago."

"You're quite sure you've never met her?" Thomas asked.

"As far as I know, never."

"You live near the Mission House."

"True, but so do lots of people. And I wasn't even here the weekend she died."

"Where were you on Easter? That was when her cousin, Krister Berggren, disappeared," Thomas clarified.

"I was in Åre; we went skiing and stayed at Fjällgården." He looked slightly worried. "I've never had any contact with these people. I'm sure of it."

"Do you spend much time here in the winter?" Thomas asked.

"No, none at all. We close up the house in October and come back at the end of April. We're only here in late spring and summer."

Margit cleared her throat. "Do you know anyone who works at Systemet?"

"Not really. Why?"

She explained that Krister Berggren had worked at Systemet until his death, and that they were interested in any possible connection between Berggren and Sandhamn.

"I usually go there on Fridays," Graaf said. "I stand in the line along with everybody else, wishing I'd gone earlier in the week." The comment was accompanied by a wink.

"Do you have anything to do with Systemet through your work?" Margit asked.

"Not at all; none of our clients are public companies. We work mainly with small or medium-size enterprises. In the private sector."

Thomas didn't say anything.

Graaf smiled and spread his hands wide. "I'd really like to help if I could, but I don't think I have anything useful to contribute."

Thomas decided to change the subject. "What about Jonny Almhult? Did you know him?"

Graaf looked puzzled. "Who's he?"

"He's the person who was found dead in the water just off Trouville beach last week. He was a permanent resident on the island who made his living as a carpenter. He was an artist, too, a painter."

"Sorry, I never met him. We haven't been coming here all that long, and we haven't really had much to do with the locals. The house was pretty well-maintained when we bought it, so we haven't needed any work done so far." He tapped the table with his index finger. "Knock on wood."

The little boy on his knee was obviously starting to get bored with the conversation; he was wriggling like a worm. "Play ball, Daddy. I want the people to go." He tugged at his father's shirt. "Go now," he said again.

Thomas smiled at the child. "We won't be long," he promised. "Just one more thing." He contemplated the man for a few seconds. "Do you have any rat poison here?"

"Rat poison?" Graaf looked perplexed.

"Rat poison," Margit said. "We're wondering if you have any rat poison on the premises."

Graaf thought for a moment, then gently lifted his son down and stood up. "I'll have to ask my wife," he said. "We might."

He went over to the open door and shouted. A slim woman with her hair in a thick plait appeared in the doorway. She looked at her husband and the two strangers sitting in her garden.

Graaf quickly explained the situation. "They want to know if we have any rat poison."

"There might still be some down in the cellar," she said. "In that little cupboard?" She turned to Thomas and Margit. "The previous owner left a bunch of stuff down in the cellar and told us to take what we wanted. There might be some down there; I'll go check."

She disappeared indoors and returned after a few minutes with a plastic container marked with a warning triangle. "Mouse and Rat Killer," it said in big black letters. She handed it to Thomas, who carefully opened the childproof cap. The container was full of blue granules.

After a few more questions about Graaf's contacts on the island over the summer, they brought the interview to a close and left. The little boy had grown tired of the adults and was playing with his ball again. At the moment he was fully occupied with trying to sit on it.

"That didn't get us very far," Margit said as soon as they were out of earshot. "There's no obvious connection, he has no motive, and he has an excellent alibi. What more can you ask? The only thing that counts against him is the rat poison."

"I agree," Thomas said. "And having rat poison in the house doesn't make you a murderer."

He wiped his forehead with his shirtsleeve. The air was ferociously hot. The wind had died away, and it would be a long time before there was any prospect of a cooling evening breeze.

Thomas looked at Margit. "Are you ready to tackle Philip Fahlén?"

"Absolutely. Lead the way."

Chapter 49

They headed off in the direction of Fläskberget and the churchyard, passing a number of more modern houses built from the sixties onward. They looked like typical summer cottages, far removed from the traditional style that characterized the village.

Thomas already had sand in his shoes; it was unavoidable.

There was no mistaking the fact that it was almost the end of July. The lilacs had long since finished flowering and had been replaced by dark-yellow sunflowers and currant bushes laden with fruit. Here and there the odd wilting tuft of grass was sticking up through the sand, evidence of brave efforts to put down roots in an impossible environment. The occasional feeble attempt at a lawn could be seen in a few gardens, but most people made do with flower beds surrounded by the ever-present sand.

Philip Fahlén lived on the northwest side of Sandhamn, where the spit of land was so narrow that you could see right across the island.

All the way to the beach where the unfortunate Krister Berggren had been washed ashore just a few weeks earlier.

They were only ten minutes' walk from the harbor, busy with boats and visitors, but this side of the island was quiet and peaceful. They could hear birds singing, and the sunlight filtered down through the tops of the pine trees. The blueberries were beginning to ripen; the bushes were full of fruit.

Fahlén's house was in a beautiful spot on the rocks, just a few yards from a wide jetty that extended a long way out. A splendid Bayliner day cruiser was moored there, and a huge hot tub made of dark wood stood by the water's edge, with a perfect view over the sea. On the other side was a boathouse with two small square windows; Thomas could just glimpse several fishing nets hanging on hooks inside.

The flag was flying, a sure sign that the owner of the house was on the island.

Margit was staring at the house as if she couldn't believe her eyes. Thomas, who had known what to expect, grinned at her.

The house was bright green.

In the middle of the idyllic archipelago, where virtually every single house was painted Falu red, someone had decided to paint the whole place bright green. Apart from the white eaves and steps, every last piece of timber was nauseatingly green. Without the eaves and steps you could easily have imagined you were standing in front of a giant marzipan cake. Only the rose was missing.

Margit looked at Thomas, who merely gave a resigned shake of his head.

"To each his own. It's looked like this for a long time."

"But why on earth would anyone even think of doing that? In a place like this," Margit said in disbelief.

"Perhaps they thought it looked nice. Or else they're color blind."

"Don't you have to get permission to do something like this? Surely it must be against building regulations?"

Thomas shrugged. "I expect the council tried, but they can't be bothered to follow up. People get away with quite a lot out here. You can't imagine how many houses have gone up without anybody paying much attention to building regulations."

Margit reached out and touched the wall, as if she weren't sure if the color were real or if it might come off on her hand. "Good grief. I've never seen anything like it."

A "Welcome" sign was hanging on the front door; fortunately it was painted in more traditional colors—blue and white. One of the windows was ajar, but no one answered when they knocked. They walked around the back of the house and saw that the doors leading to the patio were closed. There were no signs of life.

An enormous wooden deck ran along the back wall. It was dominated by a huge teak table and an unusually large gas barbecue on wheels. A short distance away several striped sun loungers were arranged, while through the wide panorama window they could see a dining table and chairs and a plasma TV on the wall. Bang & Olufsen speakers stood in each corner.

"You could certainly relax and recuperate here on a summer evening," Margit said.

She looked at the hot tub, from which a white plastic pipe ran into the sea. Presumably seawater was used to fill it. A wooden tray with three glasses and a bottle of whisky was floating on the surface. Evidently the owner wasn't worried about strangers wandering in and drinking his booze.

The expression on Margit's face was a mixture of fascination and horror as she contemplated the comfortable lifestyle. "I wonder how you come to afford something like this. It doesn't look particularly cheap. Either the owner must have won the lottery, or he must have his own business at the very least. What do you think?"

"I think he runs his own business. I imagine quite a lot of this stuff has been billed to the company," Thomas said. "Of course they'll go down as essential materials rather than a hot tub for his place in the country."

Margit gave a wry smile.

"Of course it depends on your conscience," Thomas said with a wink. "But I can't imagine someone's normal income paid for all this."

Margit looked around. There wasn't a soul in sight. "What now?" she asked. "There's no one home, and it could be a while before the Fahléns turn up."

"If they're out at sea they'll probably be back before too long; if they were going to stay away overnight, they'd have taken the Bayliner. They probably left in a smaller boat." He pointed to some ropes lying on the jetty that appeared to belong to another boat. "One you can use to lay nets," he said, mostly to himself.

"Do you want to wait?"

"We can come back later. I don't really want to call and warn them in advance. It's better to turn up unannounced with questions like this." He looked at his watch. "Let's get something to eat, then we can see Nora. I don't see the point of giving up now that we're here."

He set off toward the gate, then turned and smiled at Margit.

"And you'll get to meet my godson, too."

Chapter 50

"Thomas!" Simon came barreling through the gate and hurled himself into Thomas's arms. "Did you bring me a present?" He looked expectantly at Thomas, his eyes bright.

"Simon, you don't ask people for presents!" Nora gave him a reproachful look. "It's good to see Thomas with or without a present."

Thomas introduced Margit, and they gratefully accepted the offer of a cold beer—preferably low alcohol, as they were still on duty.

They sat in the garden, enjoying the scent of the roses drifting across from Signe's garden next door. The swallows were flying high, a sure sign of good weather.

"How's the investigation going?" Henrik asked as he poured their drinks.

Nora placed a bowl of potato chips on the table; Simon immediately grabbed a handful before she could stop him. Then he beamed, showing the gap in his bottom teeth. It was impossible not to smile back.

Thomas turned to Margit, who grimaced.

"It depends on how you look at things," Thomas said. "We know what killed Kicki Berggren, but we don't know how or why."

"So what killed her?" Henrik asked.

"Rat poison." It sounded more dramatic than Thomas had intended, and the effect was immediate. Both Nora and Henrik stared at him in surprise.

"I didn't think you could kill a person with rat poison," Henrik said.

"You can kill most people with virtually every kind of poison, if they ingest enough of it," Thomas said.

Henrik frowned. "If I remember correctly from med school, there are a number of notorious cases where people have tried to commit suicide by taking rat poison, or warfarin, but they haven't been very successful. They've just caused themselves a great deal of pain. You have to take enormous quantities in order for it to be fatal."

"You're right," said Thomas. "According to forensics the rat poison alone wouldn't have been enough, but she suffered a blow to the head, which caused a fatal hemorrhage."

"That explains it," Henrik said. "If there was a bleed and the clotting mechanism was impaired by the warfarin, then it would have been nearly impossible to save her. It wouldn't have taken many hours for her to die in that case." He took a few chips and went on. "Did she have any other symptoms to indicate that her blood wasn't clotting?"

"She'd also suffered a blow to the temple that apparently looked much worse than it should have."

Henrik nodded. "That fits with the effects one would expect. When the blood isn't clotting, any bleeding becomes much worse than usual, and it can look pretty serious."

Nora tried to save the bowl of chips from Simon's repeated onslaughts. "Rat poison," she said. "That's an unusual method."

Henrik nodded. "On the other hand, it's very easy to get. If you don't have access to medical resources where you can get the more common poisons, then perhaps you might think it would work, if you don't really know what you're doing. If you ask most people I think they'd expect it to do the job."

Thomas was all ears. "What do you mean by common poisons?" he asked, leaning forward.

"Arsenic, for example, or digitalis, which comes from ordinary foxgloves. A lot of people with heart problems take digitalis, but if you take too much, it's fatal. The monks used it in the old days when they wanted to do away with someone secretly because the substance was so difficult to trace." Henrik paused. He took another handful of chips, then continued, "Morphine works in the same way. A small amount eases pain; an overdose will kill. There are many pharmaceutical drugs that become a deadly poison if the wrong dosage is used."

"So the use of rat poison would suggest that the murderer wasn't familiar with its effects," Margit said. "An amateur, in other words."

"Absolutely. Rat poison is easy to find, and it looks dangerous. But it's far from effective if you want to be sure of success, so to speak."

Thomas considered Henrik's theory. "So if you're right, we're dealing with a perpetrator who acted deliberately but didn't really know how to go about it," he said.

Henrik shook his head. "Not necessarily. It could also be a murderer who wasn't prepared and simply used what was at hand."

"You mean he used the first poison that came to mind?" Thomas said, with a trace of doubt in his voice.

"That's right. If you haven't planned in advance to murder someone, but suddenly find yourself in a situation where you feel you have no alternative, then wouldn't you use whatever you had in the house?"

"Can you buy rat poison on the island?" Margit asked, directing her question to Nora.

Nora looked dubious. "I don't know, but you can certainly bring it over from town."

"Hang on. It's not that easy to fool someone into taking rat poison," Thomas said. "How do you get someone to polish off a plate of blue granules without making them suspicious? That's just not possible."

Nora picked a long blade of grass and wound it around her finger. She frowned as if she were trying to remember something. "I remember some kind of liquid rat poison from when I was a kid," she said. "My mother used it while we were here, because she used to keep the bottle on the top shelf, and she threatened us with no Saturday sweets if we so much as touched it. It was a dark-brown bottle, as I recall, and there was a skull and crossbones on the label."

Margit straightened up and looked at Nora. "Liquid rat poison. We should have thought of that. That has to be the explanation. You could just add it to a drink, and it would be easy to fool somebody who wasn't on guard." She turned to Thomas. "We'll give Carina a call; she can look into what's available. We need a fresh approach." She patted Nora on the shoulder. "Good thinking."

Nora looked embarrassed but graciously accepted the praise. Then she frowned again. "Why would the murder of Kicki Berggren be spontaneous, if the murderer had already killed Krister Berggren?"

The question hung in the air.

"We still don't actually know whether Krister Berggren was murdered," Thomas said.

"No," Margit said, "but if he was, no one was supposed to know that. The murderer probably thought he would never be found. That loop of rope around his body was almost certainly attached to a weight, so it would sink to the bottom of the sea. If the rope hadn't broken, and the temperature of the water hadn't brought the body to the surface so it was washed ashore on Sandhamn, nobody would ever have found out a murder had been committed."

Thomas nodded. "If Kicki Berggren hadn't been killed, her cousin's death would probably have been dismissed as an accident."

Margit said, "The discovery of Krister Berggren's body was unfortunate for the murderer. Then Kicki turns up. Somehow she knows, or thinks she knows, who killed her cousin. So she comes over to Sandhamn and confronts him."

"He panics," Thomas said, "and decides to get rid of her, too."

"Exactly," Margit said.

"And since the murderer wasn't expecting Kicki to turn up, he uses whatever he happens to have in the house, namely rat poison," Thomas said.

Margit leaned back in her chair, looking pleased with herself. The more they understood about the murderer, the better their chances of solving the case. Thomas knew from experience that an unplanned crime usually left a fair amount of evidence behind, and they needed all the help they could get in this investigation.

They didn't have to wait long for Carina to call back. Thomas could hear from the unmistakable excitement in her voice that she had something to tell them.

"I couldn't reach any of the pest-control people at this time of day, but I checked online. I found seven types of rat poison containing warfarin, all in the form of blue granules; the usual stuff, in other words."

"Was that all?" Thomas couldn't hide his disappointment.

"Don't be so impatient," said Carina. "I found something else. Something very interesting. There used to be a product called Warfarin Liquid Rat Poison. It was banned on December 31, 1990, but it was on sale until that date."

"Now we're getting somewhere." A big smile spread across Thomas's face.

"And another thing: it was far more concentrated than the rat poison you can buy today. It was almost fourteen times as strong as anything on the market now. Significantly more effective, in other words."

Thomas whistled. Carina was good. He pictured her face, and to his surprise an unexpected feeling of happiness suffused his entire body. "Terrific work, Carina," he said, feeling slightly confused as he ended the call. He sat there holding the receiver, startled by his reaction.

A comment from Margit brought him back to reality. "That explains everything. If the murderer had access to liquid rat poison, then obviously it would be much easier to dupe Kicki Berggren into taking a dose that was high enough to kill her."

"It would have been pretty straightforward," Thomas said. "All he had to do was mix it with something else she was going to drink." He finished off his beer and got to his feet.

"Time for a chat with Philip Fahlén, I think. We can always ask if he has any rat poison in the house. Liquid rat poison." He winked at Nora.

Carina sat for a while lost in thought after her conversation with Thomas. She had blushed with pleasure when he'd praised her over the phone. Over the past few weeks he seemed to have noticed her more than he had in the past. They had also spoken quite a lot. He often asked her to sort something out or to contact people involved in the investigation. And there had been a fair amount of small talk, too.

She felt as if she had gotten closer to him.

He had sounded delighted when she told him what she had discovered on the Internet. As soon as she found the information about the liquid rat poison, she knew he would be pleased. Really pleased. She could hardly wait to call and tell him.

When she heard his voice on the other end of the line, it made her tingle all over. She was sure he had felt it, too. It couldn't just be her imagination, could it?

She decided to suggest going out for lunch one day soon when he was back at the station. After all, everybody had to have lunch, and it wasn't quite as big a step as dinner.

She didn't dare ask him on a date, not yet.

She was humming to herself as she picked up her bag, ready to set off for the gym. You needed a high level of fitness to get into the police training academy, and by now even six miles on the exercise bike felt like a pleasant way to spend the evening. She smiled at her reflection as she passed the mirror in the foyer on her way out of the building.

Chapter 51

The shore at Fläskberget was almost deserted. Calm had descended after the invasion earlier in the day. A forgotten red plastic spade down by the water's edge was almost the only evidence of the hordes of families who had been there; a child's blue shoe was sticking up out of the sand.

Margit and Thomas crossed the small beach and turned onto the road leading toward Västerudd and the Fahlén house. As they approached, they saw a blue boat with an outboard motor moored alongside the day cruiser. A woman in shorts and a top that left most of her stomach bare was looking out a window. The large sunglasses pushed up onto her forehead made her look like a giant fly. She emerged from the house and came up to the gate when they were still a few yards away.

"Are you looking for someone?"

"We're with the police. We'd like to speak to Philip Fahlén, if he's home." Thomas took out his ID and held it out so she could see he was telling the truth.

"Phil, there's two police officers here—they want to talk to you." She looked anxious. "Has something happened? Are we in any danger?"

"We just want to ask a few questions. It won't take long." Thomas gave her a reassuring smile; Margit said nothing.

Philip Fahlén appeared in the doorway with a glass in his hand. He was a plump man, aged about sixty-five. He was very tan, and what little hair he had was cut extremely short, which drew attention to his slightly protruding ears. He was wearing blue pants and an open white shirt, with a blue-and-red scarf knotted around his neck.

Thomas thought with a certain amount of amusement that all Fahlén needed was a captain's hat to complete the impression that he was the captain of a luxury liner cruising the Mediterranean.

Fahlén showed them into the huge living room that overlooked the sea. He offered them a seat on the plush sofa, where there was hardly room to sit down with all the cushions. It was like sitting outdoors, and yet it wasn't. The view through the panorama window was astonishing: an endless series of islets against the backdrop of a glittering sea.

Glossy foreign magazines and several books featuring topics relating to the archipelago were arranged on the glass coffee table. Thomas recognized a book on lighthouses by the photographer Magnus Rietz, well known for his work on the islands. The entire room had a nautical theme. Pictures of various ships adorned the walls, and the cushions on the royal-blue sofa were patterned with international signal flags. Fabric made to look like maritime charts had been used for the shades of the floor lamps in each corner, and a blue-and-white-striped square rug completed the decor, along with a huge electrified kerosene lamp hanging from the ceiling.

It looked as if someone had gone crazy in a marine interior design store.

As Margit sat down on one sofa and contemplated the decor with a stunned expression, Thomas introduced himself and explained why they were there. He summarized the course of events that had led them to Fahlén and started by asking whether he'd had any kind of relationship with either Krister or Kicki Berggren.

"I didn't know those people at all," Fahlén said. "I only know what was in the papers. I've never met them." He stared at Thomas and Margit, frowning as if to express his astonishment that they could possibly think there was a connection.

"You're sure about that?" said Margit.

"Obviously. Otherwise I wouldn't have said it, would I?"

Thomas decided to change the subject. "Could you tell us a little bit about your company? Is it successful?"

Fahlén looked even more surprised; he clearly hadn't expected the police to be interested in his business. "Very successful. We supply white goods and dishwashers to restaurants and catering facilities all over the country."

"How many people do you employ?" Margit asked.

"Approximately fifty. I took over from my father, but of course I've expanded. You have to move with the times, after all."

"Where are you based?" Thomas asked.

"Our head office is in Sickla, but we serve all of Sweden. We have several well-known restaurants among our clients." It was obvious that Fahlén was proud of his company. He wasn't in the least embarrassed as he continued to boast about his successes and top-tier clients.

After a while Thomas attempted to steer the conversation toward Sandhamn. "Why did you decide to spend the summers out here? Do you have any particular link to the island?"

"Not really—I fell in love with the archipelago in the seventies and started coming here."

"Have you been living here since then?"

"No. For the first fifteen years, while my daughters were young, I rented a place in Trouville."

"And then you bought this house?"

"That's right. I bought it from old Mrs. Ekman when she was widowed and couldn't manage it anymore. Picked it up for next to nothing at the beginning of the nineties, long before prices shot up and everyone decided they wanted to buy property here." He leaned back among the cushions. "I'm sure I could sell it for many times the purchase price today. It's been an excellent investment, no doubt about it. But I've got a good nose for business," he said with a smug smile.

"Does your company have any contact with Systemet?" Margit asked.

Fahlén looked blank. "Not on a professional basis."

"Are your clients interested in buying more than just kitchen equipment?" Margit asked.

"What do you mean? Like what?"

"Cheap booze, for example. Contraband."

"How should I know? Where's this coming from?" Fahlén demanded.

Margit stared hard at him, keeping her eyes fixed on him for such a long time that he began to fiddle with the glass in his hand. A tiny bead of sweat appeared by his right temple.

Thomas decided to change direction. "Do you spend much time in this house?"

"Quite a lot. We enjoy life here."

"Do you come here in the winter? Were you here over Easter this year?" Thomas asked.

"As I said, we're here quite a lot."

"You didn't answer my question: Were you here over Easter?"

Fahlén looked confused, as if he were trying to work out why the question had been asked. "Probably—we often spend Easter on Sandhamn."

"Krister Berggren disappeared around that time," Thomas explained in a cool voice. "And then his body was washed ashore not far from this house. You can probably see the spot from your kitchen window." He got up and walked over to the window in question; beyond the pine trees he could just see the strip of shoreline where Krister Berggren's body had been found lying at the water's edge.

Fahlén was appalled; he shook his head. "I didn't meet that Berggren, or whatever his name was, over Easter. And I've never met the woman either. I've already told you, I know nothing about these people."

"What about Jonny Almhult? He lived on the island," Thomas said, his tone growing sterner.

Fahlén shook his head again.

"Are you absolutely certain?" It seemed to Thomas that Fahlén deflated slightly.

Seconds passed as Fahlén gave the matter some thought. "I might have met him once or twice. I definitely wouldn't say I knew him."

"So you have met Jonny Almhult before."

"Possibly. I don't understand why you're asking." Fahlén took a swig from his glass, which was adorned with golden knots all the way round.

"Obviously we're interested in any information relating to the three people who were found dead on the island." Thomas spoke slowly, hoping that the words would sink in. "Did Jonny Almhult do any work for you?"

"What kind of work?"

"You know that better than I do. Did he?"

"He might have helped us out with the odd practical job now and again. I don't really remember."

Margit looked at him skeptically. "Is that all?"

"I can't think of anything else."

"He didn't help you deliver messages to other people? Messages you didn't want to deliver yourself?"

"I have no idea what you're talking about." Fahlén had abandoned his relaxed posture and was now sitting upright on the sofa.

"You didn't ask him to contact Kicki Berggren on your behalf, for example?"

"Absolutely not." The response was swift and irate.

Thomas wondered whether to ask a few more questions about Almhult but decided he was unlikely to get any more information out of Fahlén unless he brought him in for a formal interview. He needed to give the matter some thought.

Instead he fixed Fahlén with his gaze once more. "Do you have any rat poison?"

"I haven't a clue. You'll have to ask my wife. Sylvia does all the shopping."

"Have you had rats in the house? Surely you must know that?"

"We might get them occasionally in the autumn. I can't really say."

"But you haven't gone out and bought rat poison?"

"I've already told you, I don't know!"

"What were you doing the Friday before last—ten days ago?" Margit interjected.

A look of uncertainty spread across Fahlén's face. He frowned, as if he were trying to remember where he had been. "I think I was here, working on the boat. The engine wasn't ticking over properly, so I was trying to fix it. At least I think it was that weekend."

"Is there anyone who can confirm that?"

"Sylvia was here."

"All day?" Thomas asked.

Fahlén looked slightly shifty. "Probably. Well, nearly all day. If I remember rightly she might have gone out on her bike for a while in the afternoon to meet some friends for a glass of wine. But you can ask her yourself. It's not easy to recall the exact details a week and a half later."

Thomas leaned forward so he was close to Fahlén, only a few inches from his face. Fahlén reeked of cigarette smoke. "Is it definitely true that you didn't know Krister Berggren or his cousin Kicki? Neither of them ever came here?"

"I've told you, no. Don't you think I know who's been in my house?" Fahlén said, his voice rising.

"You just said you didn't know Jonny Almhult, then you changed your mind."

"I'm getting very tired of this. Exactly what are you insinuating? If you are intending to continue with this line of questioning, I want my lawyer present." Fahlén stared defiantly at Thomas.

"That's one option, of course," Thomas said. "But it would be much simpler if you could just answer our questions, since we're here now."

Fahlén didn't share Thomas's point of view. He got to his feet, indicating that the conversation was over, and mopped his brow with a red handkerchief. Then he walked into the hallway, where he opened the front door wide. "Thank you for stopping by. Have a nice day."

Thomas couldn't help being fascinated by the fat man in the doorway. He hadn't expected Fahlén to pluck up so much courage; he had pegged the man as a philistine and pretty sly but certainly not brave. Thomas was almost impressed in spite of himself.

Thomas and Margit got up and headed toward the door.

Fahlén mopped his brow with the red handkerchief once again.

Thomas gave him one last look before leaving the house. "See you again," he said.

Fahlén didn't say good-bye.

Margit and Thomas set off along the path. The wind had started to pick up and could be heard blowing through the trees; their gray trunks provided a gentle contrast to the green of the blueberry bushes. Clumps of blue-green moss were scattered among the pines like soft cushions.

Margit glanced at her watch. "It's getting late. We'd better make sure to catch a ferry back to town." She turned around and looked back at the house. "What do you make of Fahlén? I've never seen such a fine example of nouveau riche. But I wonder if he's capable of three murders?"

Thomas scratched the back of his neck as he considered her question. "Hard to say. He didn't seem all that trustworthy—I got the feeling he was extremely nervous. I definitely think we need to take a much closer look at him. I think we can forget about Graaf for the time being, but there's something about Fahlén that just doesn't feel right."

He took one last look at the marzipan-green house behind them, then checked his watch.

"I think there's a ferry in half an hour. If we head back now, we'll be there in plenty of time."

Wednesday, the Fourth Week

Chapter 52

Nora looked around. The address of the recruitment company had led her to an old building in one of the better areas of Stockholm, known as Öfre Östermalm. It had an impressive entrance, with a red carpet in the foyer. The offices were three floors up in an old-fashioned patrician apartment, which must have been built as an elegant residence for some well-to-do family back in the day.

It was hardly surprising that the bank was working with such a conservative company; the financial world wasn't exactly famous for its progressive thinking.

She had caught the early morning ferry, and even though she was tired, it had been nice to get up so early. There was a special freshness in the air that was only discernible before eight o'clock in the morning on Sandhamn. It was wonderful to breathe in the pure air and enjoy the stillness before the archipelago came to life.

The boys would be spending the day with her parents while she was in the city; Henrik would be busy with his boat. As usual. Nora was intending to have a look at the summer sales while she had the chance. She didn't often have time to wander around town without keeping one eye on the clock.

She had told Henrik she had to go into work to sort out something that had come up unexpectedly. It didn't feel like a lie—it was more like waiting until a more suitable moment to tell the truth. It could well turn out that the new job wasn't worth considering, in which case she and Henrik would have fallen out quite unnecessarily.

The receptionist showed her into a conference room where coffee and mineral water were set out on a tray. Nora almost laughed; the room was exactly as she had imagined. On the mahogany table stood a vase of beautifully arranged flowers. Several attractive paintings adorned the walls. The impression was so warm and welcoming it could almost be someone's home.

Nora wondered what would happen if she met someone she knew. They might well be interviewing one of her colleagues from the bank's legal department. She assumed people must bump into one another occasionally if the interviews overran, but she hoped that wouldn't happen.

When Rutger Sandelin walked in and introduced himself, she immediately recognized his voice from their phone conversations. It was an unusual name, Rutger. It sounded English, like a medieval knight. She had pictured a muscular individual in leather boots and riding breeches. Instead he was an impeccably dressed man in his sixties, with a sprinkling of gray in his hair and a hint of plumpness.

"Thank you for coming," he said. "The bank asked us to see you in order to gain an objective view of your qualifications. The idea is that the appointment shouldn't be affected by internal considerations and relationships."

"I understand," Nora said. It all sounded very sensible.

They started to discuss the post in Malmö and the qualifications necessary for the legal adviser in the southern region.

As Nora answered his questions, she noticed that he had a greasy mark on the lilac silk tie that matched his shirt to perfection.

Presumably it was the result of an accident over lunch, but it helped to make him more human.

Nora told him about herself and her work experience. She had studied law in Uppsala and had been an active member of the students' union. After graduating, she had worked in the district court before beginning as a trainee with the bank. Eventually she had applied for her current post.

Her background was detailed in her file, but he seemed to want to go through everything, as if he were dealing with a completely new post outside the bank.

Nora also had to talk about her strengths and weaknesses, and how her colleagues would describe her. She had to tell him what she found difficult and challenging and how she handled stress and conflict.

She thought to herself that it was singularly pointless to ask the mother of small children whether she could deal with stress and conflict. If you couldn't sort out that kind of situation, you wouldn't last five minutes in her family. All children clashed at regular intervals, right? In addition, the combination of two parents working full-time, two boys aged six and ten, and an endless stream of notes from day care and school about excursions, packed lunches, and collections for this and that made the perfect stress generator.

Suddenly Sandelin asked how she would describe her relationship with her current boss. Nora was slightly taken aback.

What should she say? That Ragnar Wallsten was a spoiled brat who had been promoted far above his competence level? That his sharp tongue meant that most people were reluctant to stand up to him, but few sought out his company? That when she first started in the department she had watched him bully an older colleague into a bitter departure?

During the course of a few seconds she desperately tried to decide which way to go.

"We have a decent relationship, the way most colleagues do," she said. Her voice died away as she searched for something neutral to say. "He's not the kind of boss who interferes a great deal. He leaves people to get things taken care of." The last comment sounded so idiotic that she regretted it as soon as the words came out. "Of course he's very busy with major issues within the bank," she added.

Sandelin seemed to be aware of her embarrassment and smiled at her. He leaned forward and looked Nora in the eye. "I'll be honest with you. Opinion is divided on Ragnar Wallsten and his ability to lead the legal team."

Nora bit her lip. This sounded too good to be true. She was sick and tired of working with him.

When they had been talking for about an hour, Sandelin changed focus. Could she tell him about her husband's work?

"He's a consultant radiologist at the hospital in Danderyd. He's really happy there."

"And how would he feel about moving to Malmö?"

"We haven't really discussed it yet, but I'm sure he'd have no difficulty getting a job at one of the hospitals in the area."

Sandelin leaned back in his chair and brought his palms together, which made him look like an old-fashioned schoolmaster. "It's very important that couples are in agreement on an issue like this. When the whole family moves, it's a major readjustment. Everyone has to make an effort to do their best to adapt to a new environment." He gave her a searching look. "Do you think your husband is ready to make that readjustment?"

Nora swallowed. Everything Sandelin had told her about the new job sounded fantastic. Exciting responsibilities, excellent conditions, and a significant promotion. The bank would pay for the move and provide assistance in finding somewhere to live. In addition, the Öresund area was buzzing. The new bridge to Denmark had brought with it a huge upturn for the whole of southern Sweden; the continent had suddenly opened up. Just a few hours in the car, and you were on mainland Europe. The boys would love living so close to Legoland. Imagine being able to drive across to Copenhagen and wander hand in hand down Strøget, the lovely pedestrian shopping area.

"We need to talk about it in more detail, of course, but I'm sure Henrik will think it would be exciting for the family to move and have the chance to experience something new." Nora secretly crossed her fingers, even though she knew it was a childish thing to do.

Sandelin beamed at her. "You have an excellent reputation within the bank. Magnus Westling, who is the new boss for the southern region, has heard very positive things about you, and he thinks you would be an excellent choice for this position. Think it over for a few days and let me know how you feel; if you wish to proceed, we'll arrange for you to meet him. In the meantime I'll send a report to your HR department."

Back out in the street after saying her good-byes to Sandelin, Nora was both excited and depressed. How was she going to get Henrik to move to Malmö? She really wanted to accept the job.

She went into the nearest café and bought herself a latte. If Henrik had received an offer like this, there would have been nothing to discuss. Henrik and everyone else would have simply assumed she would pack up all their belongings and move. But when it was the other way round, the solution wasn't quite so self-evident.

On an impulse she called Henrik's phone, just to hear his voice. Over the past few days they had barely exchanged a word unless it had to do with the children. But his phone was switched off and went straight to voice mail.

Which presumably meant he was at sea. As usual.

Chapter 53

Thomas finally managed to get ahold of the forensic pathologist in the afternoon; the most likely hypothesis was that Jonny Almhult had fallen overboard from the ferry to Finland on that Sunday evening.

It normally took almost a week for a body that fell into the water to rise to the surface, but in summer, if the water was unusually warm, as it was this year, it could happen after only a few days.

As the body had been found on a Thursday, it was therefore unlikely that Jonny had fallen overboard any later than Sunday, when he was last seen alive. That meant he must have been on the ferry that left from Stadsgården at seven o'clock in the evening.

The *Cinderella* had arrived at Strandvägen from Sandhamn at five; there had been plenty of time for Almhult to cross Skeppsbron and catch the ferry to Finland.

Back at the station that morning Thomas and Margit had gone over the previous day's interview with Philip Fahlén. They had agreed that it was definitely worth taking a closer look at him; Kalle had contacted the economic crime unit to ask for their help in investigating Fahlén's affairs. They too were working with a reduced staff but had promised their assistance later in the week. Meanwhile the priority was to track Fahlén's movements.

Thomas made himself a fresh cup of tea and went back to his office. It was just after four o'clock. He had decided to call Fahlén and ask where he had been between Sunday and Thursday the previous week, the period during which Jonny Almhult had been missing before his body was found.

Fahlén answered immediately, almost as if he had been waiting for the phone to ring. When he heard who it was, his tone became significantly cooler.

"Could you tell me where you were between Sunday and Thursday morning last week?" Thomas said.

"What's that got to do with the police?" Fahlén snapped.

"You don't need to know that," Thomas said. "Answer the question, please."

"I was here on Sandhamn from Tuesday to Thursday."

"What about Sunday and Monday?"

"I needed to be in town, so I went over on the morning boat on Sunday."

"And what did you do when you got here?"

"I was in the office for a while. I had a few things to sort out."

"How long were you there?"

Fahlén sighed. "I don't know. A few hours maybe. My secretary can confirm that I was there; she came in to help me even though it was the weekend."

"What time did you leave the office?"

"About five thirty, if I remember correctly."

"And what did you do then?"

"Went back to the apartment. Had something to eat. Watched TV."

"Where's your apartment?"

"Vasastan."

"Were you at home all evening?"

"Yes. I didn't go out."

"And when did you travel back to Sandhamn?"

"On Monday."

"Can you remember exactly when you got back?"

"Sometime after lunch, I think." Fahlén had had enough. "What is this? An interrogation? I told you last time that if you're going to question me, I want my lawyer present."

Thomas tried to calm the irate man. "I only have a couple more questions. Isn't it easier if we deal with this over the phone, rather than bringing you all the way into town?"

Silence. Thomas wondered for a moment whether Fahlén had hung up but decided he probably wouldn't dare slam the phone down on a police officer.

"One last question," came the reluctant response.

"Is there anyone who can confirm that you were in your apartment for the whole of Sunday night?"

"No, there isn't."

There was a click in Thomas's ear. Philip Fahlén had hung up.

CHAPTER 54

Nora was sitting at her desk in the bank.

It was obvious that it was the middle of summer; the open-plan office was deserted. There was no sign of anyone from the legal department, and most computers were switched off.

It was refreshingly quiet on the eighth floor. Nora had placed her now lukewarm latte next to her computer. It had taken less than fifteen minutes to walk to the bank through the sultry heat of the city; the pavement was crowded with eager tourists, snapping away with their cameras.

She couldn't stop thinking about Philip Fahlén; Thomas had mentioned that they were on their way to see him the previous day. Since she was in town, she might as well take a closer look at his business. The sales could wait.

She logged on and quickly found the number of the local housing office for Värmdö council. A young man answered, wondering how he could help.

"Would you be able to tell me who owns a particular property, if I give you the reference number?" Nora asked.

"Of course, that's no problem. Where's the property?"

"On Sandhamn."

"One moment please."

There was a brief silence; Nora took a sip of her coffee, which had gone cold.

"The property is owned by a limited company."

Nora raised her eyebrows. Was it indeed! Philip Fahlén had let his company pick up the tab for his impressive house. She wondered whether he was paying the market rent to the company for the privilege of using the house in high season, as current tax regulations dictated he must.

"What's the name of the company?"

"Fahlén & Co. Ltd."

The company Philip Fahlén owned.

"Do you have a registration number for the company?"

"Certainly."

Nora was given a ten-digit number, which she carefully wrote down. Now she could find out lots of interesting information. First, she went into the Companies Registration Office website, where every Swedish company was listed. The bank was a subscriber and had access to their database, so she could get to all public information, including proof of registration and annual accounts.

Quickly she typed in the number she had been given, and within a second the latest available annual accounts appeared on the screen. She pressed "Print," then repeated this for the previous nine years. To be on the safe side she also printed out the company's annual registration certificate so she could see who had been on the board and access their personal details. This certificate also enabled her to see data on the company's activities.

She then logged into UC, the credit information service, to which the bank also subscribed. The site also provided details of any financial matters investigated by the police. UC registered everything about everyone, both companies and private individuals. It was an invaluable source for anyone who wanted to determine whether a business was creditworthy. Little could be hidden from someone who had access to UC's database.

Fahlén & Co. appeared to have behaved itself when it came to finances. There were no negative comments, no financial irregularities. The company's credit rating was good, because its liquidity was high and its debts low. Things were obviously going well.

As soon as Nora had gathered the information she wanted, which amounted to a substantial pile of documents, she put it in a blue folder and slipped it into her bag. Then she shut down the computer. It was time she made her way over to Strandvägen if she were going to catch the next ferry back to Sandhamn.

Chapter 55

As usual, the *Cinderella* was packed with people on their way to the archipelago, but as this was an evening boat mainly intended for commuters and late visitors, Nora had no difficulty finding a table on her own in a quiet corner where she could spread out all her papers.

She took out the blue folder and began to scrutinize the accounts Fahlén & Co. had submitted over the past ten years. As a legal adviser with the bank, she was used to reading accounts and balance sheets in a variety of contexts, and she had always found dealing with figures easy. She had also brought her trusty calculator.

Nora decided to start with the turnover for the past five years. Then she would look at the costs so she could get an idea of the company's profit margins. She was well aware that the catering industry was not known for its high profit margins; perhaps it was reasonable to assume that this also applied to their suppliers.

Quickly and methodically, she worked through the results for each year. Her fingers flew over the buttons, and her notepad was soon covered in calculations.

After about an hour she decided it was time for a reward, so she went to the cafeteria and bought a cold beer. She nodded to one or two acquaintances from Sandhamn and chatted for a couple of minutes to the man in the ticket office. He couldn't help commenting on the murders. They were still on everyone's mind.

She went back to her table and carried on with her analysis. A pattern was beginning to emerge, and with every calculation it was becoming clearer. She had to tell Thomas about this.

She took out her cell phone and called him.

"Hi, Nora."

"Thomas, I think I've found out something extremely interesting about Philip Fahlén's company. You need to see this as soon as possible."

"Where are you?"

"On board the *Cinderella*. I'll be there in about half an hour. What are your plans for this evening?"

"I was going to stay in town," Thomas said. "On the other hand, it would be nice to get away from this suffocating heat."

"Dinner on me at the bistro in the Yacht Club restaurant?" Nora offered, trying to tempt him. She had more to talk about than Fahlén's company; she wanted to take the opportunity to discuss her meeting with Rutger Sandelin. She needed a male perspective on the whole thing before she tackled Henrik. "You really do need to see this. I can't explain over the phone—it's far too complicated."

Thomas laughed. "OK, you win. But I'll have to catch the last boat. It leaves from Stavsnäs at seven thirty, so it'll have to be a late dinner."

"No problem," Nora said. "I'll be waiting by the steps at eight thirty."

Chapter 56

The bistro was the result of an extension to the original clubhouse, which had dominated the harbor for more than a century. The Falu-red creation with its turret housed both the offices of the Royal Swedish Yacht Club and its harbor administration, along with a number of restaurants. Countless sailors had passed through this building over the past hundred years or so. If the walls could talk, they would have had plenty of spicy stories involving kings and gentlemen. The Sailors Restaurant had seen many innkeepers come and go, from the legendary Åke Kristersson in the seventies and eighties to the notorious drug dealer Fleming Broman.

Nora was waiting by the steps leading up to the bistro when Thomas approached from the pier. She recognized his determined stride from some distance away, and as always she was struck by how good he looked. In spite of the fact that he had no interest in clothes, he always pulled off whatever he wore. Tonight it was a pale-blue polo shirt and faded jeans with a pair of aviators.

Nora saw a couple of giggling girls in their twenties turn around to watch him as he passed; Thomas, of course, was totally oblivious.

He broke into a broad smile as he reached Nora and got a big hug in return.

"How are you? Are you tired? What do you want to eat?" Nora said, ignoring the fact that she had just fired off three questions without waiting for an answer. She patted her stomach. "I'm absolutely starving. Let's go up." Without waiting, she turned and led the way.

A hostess dressed in black showed them to a table with a view of the harbor; she handed each of them a menu and left.

Nora looked at the list of dishes. There was plenty of fish, of course, but there were also some tempting meat courses. "What are you going to have?" she asked. "And remember this is on me; a promise is a promise."

"I know exactly what I want. There's really only one thing to choose here."

"And what might that be?" Nora smiled at him, well aware of what he had in mind.

"Sailor's toast, of course."

The classic dish known as *Seglartoast* had been served in the restaurant for as long as anyone could remember. It consisted of a large fillet steak on a piece of toast with a decent scoop of Béarnaise sauce, accompanied by a generous portion of fries.

"It doesn't exactly come under the heading of healthy eating," Nora pointed out.

"But it's damn delicious," Thomas said. "If you'll excuse my language."

When the waitress had taken their order and poured them each a glass of a dark-red Australian Merlot chosen by Nora, Thomas could no longer suppress his impatience.

"Right, so what have you found out about Philip Fahlén's business?"

Nora took out the blue folder and the pad with all her calculations. She quickly explained how she had gone about it and what she had examined more closely. "Look at this," she said, showing him a sheet of paper with lists of figures. "For a long time, the company had roughly the same turnover and the same profit margin; no real variation from one year to the next. But five years ago, the turnover rose sharply, and at the same time the profit margin increased by over three hundred percent."

She pointed to the number 300 to underline what she had just said.

"And what does that mean?" Thomas asked.

"It means the company is suddenly achieving a far greater income with no increase in expenditure." Nora took a sip of water and went on. "When companies boost their income, most experience an equivalent rise in costs. It usually goes hand in hand. Even if they can take on a certain amount of extra business within the margin, it's highly unusual to see a dramatic rise in income with no effect on costs. After all, the company has to supply something, which would normally involve more expenditure. But Philip Fahlén has done the exact opposite."

She produced another sheet of paper with different figures.

"You can see for yourself: suddenly the income is much higher than the expenditure. And I can't find a reasonable explanation. As far as I can tell from the annual accounts, he hasn't bought another company or signed some major contract. There are no sales profits to explain the upturn, nor any other income outside the norm. It's as if a fairy has suddenly waved her magic wand so he's making a lot more money than he was before."

Nora stopped and took a mouthful of her paella; she had been so eager to talk about her discoveries that she'd hardly touched it since it had arrived.

Thomas was looking at her with an expression of intense concentration.

"On top of that, the dividends paid out to the owner have also increased—and the owner is Philip Fahlén, of course. In the past, he took out quite modest amounts, but now he's starting to take significant sums of money every year. Which in itself is fine, because the profits have gone up so much."

"And what's the explanation for all this?"

"This is my theory. What if he's supplying his clients in the restaurant trade with something else, alongside his normal deliveries?"

"Like illicit booze," Thomas said.

Nora nodded. "Possibly. If that's the case, he can hardly put down the costs involved in generating the income, i.e., the amount he pays for the booze."

Thomas nodded as he shoveled down the last of his fries. His plate was almost clinically clean; there wasn't a drop of sauce left. "I can understand that. It would be pretty difficult to explain that particular deduction to the tax office." He smiled.

"Exactly. But at the same time, he needs the money to show up within the company so it becomes legitimate. It's not practical to have a bunch of random cash floating around. Where are you going to hide it so the tax officials don't catch you? All banks have an obligation to report company balances. He has to find a way of dealing with the part of his operation that handles this additional income."

Thomas put down his knife and fork and took a sip of wine. "That sounds logical."

"I think Philip Fahlén has doctored the invoices he sends out to the restaurants he's supplying illegally. If we're talking about alcohol, that is. He raises the price of his legitimate deliveries, which is perfectly legal. This means the restaurant can deduct its costs for the alcohol against a genuine invoice. Fahlén's company then has a significantly increased income, and therefore higher profits. This profit is then paid out by the company to its owner, and he uses that money to pay the person who is supplying him with illicit booze." Nora smiled at Thomas and held out another sheet of paper. "And abracadabra, the random cash no longer exists."

Thomas leaned back on his chair and linked his hands behind his head. It was an interesting theory that sounded plausible. Once again he recalled what Agneta Ahlin had told him: Kicki Berggren had said the money was on Sandhamn. Was she thinking about Fahlén's money?

Nora was waving yet another piece of paper. "There's more. The fees paid to board members have also increased significantly."

"During the same period when all this other stuff was going on?"

Nora nodded. "For a long time the board members received an annual payment of fifty thousand kronor. Four years ago that payment was increased to six hundred thousand kronor a year for each member. The amount has remained the same until now."

Thomas whistled. Six hundred thousand. That wasn't bad. Far more than most people could expect to earn in a year. "And who's on the board?" he asked as he gazed at the piles of documents on the table.

Nora found the registration certificate and passed it over to him. "There are only three members: Philip Fahlén; his father, who must be almost ninety judging by his ID number; and a woman called Marianne Strindberg."

Thomas took the certificate and studied it closely. He was so absorbed that he barely noticed when the waitress asked him for the second time whether he would like coffee or a dessert. He ordered a double espresso. No dessert. Nora did the same, after sadly concluding that the tempting chocolate mousse wasn't really suitable for a diabetic.

"Strindberg," Thomas said. "I recognize the name, but I can't place it. Apart from the famous playwright, of course," he said and smiled.

"She joined the board in 2000," Nora pointed out. "An interesting coincidence, wouldn't you say? The same year the company increased its profits so dramatically. Before that the board consisted of Philip Fahlén and his father, with his mother as a deputy member."

Thomas sipped his espresso, which had just arrived, relishing the deep coffee flavor. His face clearly revealed that he had just thought of something. "Viking Strindberg," he said as he put down his cup. "Krister Berggren's boss is called Strindberg."

"What if he's married to a woman called Marianne?" Nora said, excited.

"He seemed inexplicably nervous when I spoke to him," Thomas said. "I wonder if this could be a coincidence?" He raised his glass in a toast. "Here's to you, Nora. This is fantastic. I'm glad you persuaded me to come over. You're a master detective, no doubt!"

Thursday, the Fourth Week

Chapter 57

"How's it going?"

Carina looked up to see Margit standing in the doorway of her office. The day had hardly begun. The corridors were still silent, but Carina had been working since seven thirty. There was nothing wrong with her ambition. Her desk was cluttered with piles of paper.

"The ferry company sent this over yesterday, but I haven't had time to go through it all yet." She rubbed her eyes and stretched.

"Have you found anything?" Margit asked.

Carina shook her head. "I've hardly started. Do you know how many passengers a ferry to Finland carries? Thousands at a time. And they're listed according to the order in which they bought their tickets. The guy I spoke to said there was some kind of computer error that meant they couldn't sort the names into alphabetical order, and I've only got hard copies of everything, nothing digital." She held out a bundle of lists. "I'm looking for anyone with a name that's similar to Almhult or Fahlén; it could be misspelled." She looked down at the lists. Row upon row of names. "And then of course we don't know whether Fahlén used his own name. It might almost be easier to wait for the electronic file so I can sort it on the computer instead."

"But we can't afford to wait, so I'm afraid you'll just have to keep looking," Margit said. She turned away, then stuck her head in the door again. "You are starting with Sunday's departures, I presume?"

Carina raised her eyebrows. "Of course."

Margit smiled. "I should have realized. I know you're doing your best."

Carina shook her head. "No problem. I'll let you know as soon as I find something."

Margit went to get herself another cup of coffee. She looked at her watch: twenty to nine. Thomas was seeing Philip Fahlén this morning to push him harder. He had called her late last night to tell her about Nora's scrutiny of Fahlén's accounts and the conclusions they had drawn.

Margit and Thomas had agreed that he would stay over and visit Fahlén the following morning in order to confront him with the information. Better to try to take him by surprise one last time, rather than bring him in for a formal interview where he could have his lawyer present.

Things were certainly starting to look awkward for Mr. Fahlén, Margit thought. As soon as she saw that horrible green house she had felt that something wasn't right. Something didn't ring true.

Her task this morning was to chase details of his recent phone calls, and perhaps even get a warrant to tap his phone.

She called the prosecutor's number.

CHAPTER 58

Thomas had gratefully accepted the loan of the Linde family's launch so he could get over to his own house on Harö for the night and come back to Sandhamn the following morning in plenty of time to see Philip Fahlén. He moored the little boat at the Lindes' jetty and set off for Västerudd at a rapid pace. It was slightly cooler than it had been earlier in the week; the morning air was fresh and clear. A much more pleasant temperature than the stifling heat of the last few days.

As he walked he took the opportunity to call Carina. He asked her to find out if Marianne Strindberg was married to a man called Viking and if they both lived at the same address in Tyresö that appeared on the registration certificate for Fahlén & Co. When she confirmed that this was the case, Thomas couldn't help smiling.

Philip Fahlén opened the door as soon as Thomas knocked. Reluctantly he showed Thomas into the kitchen and pointed to a chair. He didn't look well; his face was red, and he had noticeable bags under his eyes.

"So," he said, "what is it this time?"

"I'd like to ask you a few more questions."

Thomas ignored the obvious antipathy coming from Fahlén. This time he was determined to back the man into a corner. He sat down; Fahlén moved to the other side of the table, as far away from Thomas as possible.

"I'm interested in your company. I believe it's been doing much better over the past few years? You've made an impressive profit since the millennium, as I understand it."

"What's it to you?"

"Could you answer the question, please?"

Fahlén glanced around. "Things have gone pretty well. There's nothing odd about that. We've been successful for years."

"How do you explain the fact that your profits have tripled?"

"We've put the effort in. If you work hard, you make money. It's no mystery."

"You must have worked extremely hard. As far as I can see, your profit margin is much higher than the industry norm."

"Is that against the law?"

"That's not what I said. But it's rather unusual. I'd be interested to hear how you've achieved such excellent results." He leaned back in his chair.

Fahlén stood up abruptly and went over to the sink. He took a glass out of the cupboard and filled it with water. He kept his back to Thomas as he drank.

"Did you understand the question?" Thomas asked.

No response.

Thomas spoke more sharply. "Answer the question."

Fahlén turned around, an aggressive look in his eye. "Are you deaf? I just told you, we've worked hard. Picked up new clients, secured large orders. That's what happens when you do business." He turned back to the sink. "Isn't a man allowed to work in this fucking police state these days without some asshole turning up and quizzing him?"

A thick silence spread through the room. Thomas waited, not moving a muscle.

The only sound came from Philip Fahlén's throat as he gulped down more water.

"Who's Marianne Strindberg?" Thomas asked.

Fahlén gave a start. "What?"

"Could you tell me who Marianne Strindberg is?"

"She's a member of my board."

"Why?"

"What's that got to do with anything?"

"I'd like to know why she's on the board. She hasn't been there very long, has she?"

"She's an economist. I thought it would be useful to have someone like her."

"And you suddenly realized this four years ago, having managed perfectly well for many years with only your father on the board?"

"What's my father got to do with this?" Fahlén was extremely agitated.

Thomas decided it was time for a change of tack. "How come the payment to your board members has gone up from fifty thousand to six hundred thousand kronor since Marianne Strindberg joined?"

"That's none of your business," said Fahlén, tearing off a paper towel and mopping his brow. "But if you must know, I thought it was time I paid the board members a little more. Is that not allowed?" He spread his arms wide and looked at Thomas.

"Of course, but it's rather unusual," Thomas said as he studied the fat man's expression. "Would you like to know what I think?"

"Not really."

Thomas decided there was no point in beating around the bush. "I think you raised the fees payable to board members because you had to pay Marianne Strindberg for the services supplied by her husband."

Fahlén tried to appear unmoved, but then he turned pale and reached out a hand to lean against the sink.

Thomas fixed his gaze on Fahlén. "I happen to know that Marianne Strindberg, who is a member of your board, is married to Viking Strindberg, who works for Systemet. And I have a feeling this same Viking Strindberg helps you out with special deliveries; he smuggles out wine and spirits, which you sneak into various restaurants along with the equipment you supply, and your clients reward you handsomely. This additional source of income is the reason your turnover suddenly increased so significantly, and it explains why you earn so much more than anyone else in the industry." Thomas leaned back and folded his arms. He stared at Fahlén with a challenging gaze. "That's what I think," he said after a moment. His words hung in the air, vibrating with energy long after they had been uttered.

Fahlén had had enough. He wiped his brow again; it was covered in beads of sweat. He pointed at the door with a shaking hand. "Out," he said. "Get out of my house. You have no right to come here making accusations. I'm calling my lawyer."

Thomas gazed at him calmly, wondering if he should stay and try to get Fahlén to answer a few more questions.

Fahlén was so agitated that there was spittle at the corners of his mouth. His chin was trembling, and a muscle just below his left eye was twitching.

Thomas decided to leave. There wasn't much point in trying to wind him up even more. It would be better to bring him into the station as soon as they were absolutely certain of his relationship with Viking Strindberg and had access to his phone records.

Thomas got up and moved to the door. As he opened it he turned back. "I'll be in touch," he said. "Soon."

"Get out," Fahlén panted. "Get out."

CHAPTER 59

Henrik walked into the kitchen, seething.

Nora, who was busy making pancakes for the following day's trip to Grönskär, raised her eyebrows. "What's happened?"

"What's happened is that our new perch net has a great big hole in it," Henrik said. "The boys have been playing in the boathouse, and now we have a ripped net and several tears in the flounder rig. It's going to take forever to repair them, and I was supposed to be out laying nets with Hasse Christiansson today."

Nora tried to look sympathetic. "It's not the end of the world."

Henrik looked angry, and Nora backtracked.

"I realize you're annoyed, but we can always buy a new one. I suppose that's why we get child benefits, to pay for all the trouble they cause," she joked.

Henrik was still mad. "They have to learn to be careful with things. I'm sick and tired of them leaving their stuff all over the place and breaking everything." He stood at the bottom of the stairs and shouted. "Simon, Adam, get down here right now. I want to talk to you."

"We haven't done anything," came the chorus from their bedroom.

"Get down here, I said."

"Couldn't you ask Signe if you can borrow a net? She's got lots," Nora suggested. She was trying to avoid a fight and to rescue the fishing trip at the same time.

Henrik allowed himself to be appeased and lowered his voice. "Can't you ask her? You know her better than I do."

"Of course," Nora said, relieved that the crisis seemed to have been averted. "I'll go over in a minute when I've finished these pancakes."

Nora opened the beautiful handmade double gate leading to the Brand house. She walked up to the front door and knocked. There were no doorbells on Sandhamn. The door would be left open, and you would just shout out a cautious "hello" before walking in, or knock loudly. Either approach was fine, as long as you announced your presence in some way.

Signe opened the door wearing her usual apron, the one Nora had seen her in for so many years. Sometimes Nora wondered whether Signe, like the Phantom with all his outfits in the Skull Cave, had an endless supply of identical aprons hidden away somewhere, so she could just bring out a new one when the old one wore out.

Nora greeted her cheerfully. "I wonder if we could possibly borrow one of your perch nets? Adam and Simon have managed to rip ours. They were supposed to be out laying nets today, so otherwise we'll end up with no dinner!" She winked at Signe. "As you can imagine, Henrik isn't pleased. He's just banned the boys from using the computer for two hours as a punishment. They'll never play in the boathouse without permission again!"

"Of course you can borrow a net. Just go down and take whatever you want."

Kajsa came to the door and pushed her wet nose into Nora's leg. Nora bent down to pet her. Kajsa was the sweetest dog in the world.

The gray hairs around her nose gave away the fact that she was getting old, just like her mistress.

Signe handed over the key to the boathouse. "Just make sure the net is clean before you put it back!"

Nora smiled. A net full of seaweed was no joke. Signe knew what she was talking about. You could beat the net with juniper branches forever without getting it really clean. It was Signe who had taught Nora that the best way of cleaning a really dirty net was to bury it in the ground for a few weeks. Somehow the enzymes in the ground broke down the seaweed; it simply disappeared, and the net was miraculously clean. An old archipelago trick that came in handy from time to time.

Nora went down to the boathouse, which was right next to the jetty belonging to the Brand property. It was absolutely typical, painted Falu red with a green door.

Many people on the island envied Signe the large jetty that had space for so many boats. The demand for moorings was always greater than the supply. The bulletin board in the harbor was always full of notes from boat owners who had no mooring. The going rate for a summer berth had shot up recently and had now reached several thousand kronor. Quite a number of residents made some extra cash by renting out vacant moorings at their own jetties. Signe allowed two families who had owned summer cottages on Sandhamn for a long time to rent berths at the Brand jetty for a reasonable sum.

Nora unlocked the boathouse door with the old, heavy key. It was quite gloomy inside, and the small light on the ceiling didn't really help much. Now where were the perch nets? She looked along the wall. Most of the nets were in a good state of repair, but the odd one was old and torn. Nora turned over the net needle in one of the worst and noticed that it bore the initials *KL* instead of *SB*. Obviously someone else was keeping nets in Signe's boathouse; perhaps it was one of the summer visitors?

She found the nets she was looking for at the back on the right-hand side. She unhooked two of them and carefully carried them out into the sunshine. She locked the boathouse, then carried the nets down to their own jetty, where Henrik was busy getting the boat ready.

"There you go." She handed the nets over carefully so they wouldn't get tangled. "I hope you catch lots of fish. I suppose we'll need to eat early if you're in the twenty-four-hour race. It starts at midnight, doesn't it?"

"If we eat around five that should give me plenty of time; I don't need to leave until nine," said Henrik, who had calmed down considerably. He smiled warmly at her, and it felt as if he were trying to smooth over the disagreements of the past few days.

"Actually, I've got something exciting to tell you," Nora said, crossing her fingers behind her back. "Something I'd like to have a chat about this evening. But you'd better set off now before it gets too late."

Henrik helped Adam into the boat. He had nagged and nagged to be allowed to go along and help with the nets.

Nora blew him a kiss. "Promise you'll be good?"

Adam looked at her and saluted. "Aye, aye, Captain. I'll be really, really good. Especially if I'm allowed to steer the boat," he said with a shy glance at Henrik, worried that his escapade with the nets might have scuppered his chances of taking the wheel.

Henrik laughed and ruffled Adam's hair. Harmony had been restored.

"Come on, Tiger. Let's go. Of course you can steer for a little while."

Nora wandered pensively back to the house, wondering how to tell Henrik that she really wanted to take the job in Malmö.

They hadn't mentioned it again after the argument on Saturday night. She hadn't found the right moment to tell him that she'd had a meeting in town with the recruitment agency.

Nora felt that she wanted to talk to him before he left for the race, so he would have time to digest it while he was away.

Tonight. After dinner.

That ought to be a good time.

Chapter 60

Call Marcus Björk at the ferry company, said the note on Thomas's desk when he got back to the station after catching the eleven o'clock boat back to the mainland.

I ought to get a season ticket for the Waxholmsbolaget ferries, he thought. It was such a nuisance keeping track of all the receipts that had to be handed in when he was claiming his expenses. Occasionally he managed to hitch a ride with the maritime police, but their schedule didn't usually fit in with his, and they had fewer and fewer boats these days.

A phone number was written on the note; he called Margit, and they sat down at his desk. Margit dialed the number and switched to speakerphone so they could both follow the conversation.

"Marcus Björk, how may I help you?" The voice sounded youthful and enthusiastic. Thomas pictured an ambitious, apple-cheeked young man.

"This is Margit Grankvist from Nacka police. My colleague Thomas Andreasson is also listening to this conversation. I believe you called us earlier?"

"Absolutely. Thanks for calling back. I work in the admin department of the ferry company; we supplied you with passenger lists for our ferries from Stockholm to Helsinki yesterday. I'm sorry it took such a long time, but we got them to you as soon as we could. We had a computer glitch that caused us all kinds of hassle."

"I understand."

"I've now spoken to the captain who was on duty on the Sunday you asked about, almost two weeks ago. He told me a couple of teenagers did actually report seeing someone fall overboard on that particular evening. However, they didn't report it until they were just about to disembark the following day, and there was nothing else to suggest anything had happened. It also appeared that the teenagers had been quite drunk the previous evening, so the captain made a judgment call and decided nothing had happened." Marcus Björk laughed nervously.

"So what happened next?" Margit asked.

"Not much, unfortunately. It was difficult to take these teenagers seriously. I can't tell you how many people claim all kinds of things that never happened." The last comment sounded rather anxious, as if Marcus Björk was afraid that someone might have made a huge mistake. "But as you'd asked for the passenger lists, I thought you'd want to know that something had actually been reported relating to that particular evening."

Thomas and Margit looked at one another; Margit gave Thomas a thumbs-up.

"Names?" she mouthed to Thomas.

Thomas leaned closer to the telephone. "Do you have the names of the two teenagers?"

"Yes, we have their names and addresses. The captain made a note of where they lived, just to be on the safe side. Thank goodness." Marcus Björk no longer sounded quite so enthusiastic; anxiety was taking over.

"Excellent," said Thomas, nodding at Margit. "Could you e-mail me the information as soon as possible?"

"Of course." There was a brief silence. "Please let us know if we can be of assistance with anything else," Marcus Björk said.

"Do you have CCTV cameras on board?" Margit asked.

"We do indeed, all over the ship."

"In that case we would very much like the tapes from the Sunday before last. Monday to Wednesday as well, if you don't mind. As soon as possible."

"Absolutely; I'll sort it out as soon as the ship gets back."

Margit looked at the clock and sighed. "And when will that be?"

"Let's see . . ." Judging from the sounds in the background, Marcus Björk was leafing through piles of paper.

"Surely he ought to know this off the top of his head," Thomas muttered to Margit.

"Late this afternoon. She's due out again at seven this evening."

Margit twirled a pen between her fingers as Thomas ended the conversation.

"Could we possibly be lucky enough to find that the CCTV cameras caught Jonny Almhult and his killer?" Margit said. She tore off the sheet of paper on which she had been doodling, crumpled it up, and threw it with deadly accuracy into the trash can in the far corner. Then she gave Thomas a skeptical look. "Or would that be too much to hope for?"

He leafed through his notebook, where he had jotted down a reminder about tapping Viking Strindberg's phone. "What did the prosecutor say about that phone tap we discussed?"

Margit rolled her eyes. "She didn't like it, of course. They never do. But I just had to quote the relevant section from the Code of Judicial Procedure, chapter twenty-seven." Margit knew it by heart. "Covert telephone surveillance may be used during a preliminary investigation into crimes that would incur a custodial sentence of no less than six months." She looked very pleased with herself. "If someone's smuggling booze worth millions from Systemet, then selling it tax-free to various restaurants, I think he'd go down for more than six months, don't you?"

Thomas smiled to himself as he thought about Charlotte Öhman's reluctance to give permission for the phone tap. The procedure didn't sit well with many people's perception of where the boundaries lay in a democratic society, but it was a powerful tool in a police investigation and often provided key pieces of evidence.

On this occasion the prosecutor appeared to have given in surprisingly quickly.

"It's being set up today if our colleagues do as they've been told," Margit said. "I've put Kalle on it. He's also going through all the calls over the past few weeks."

She raised her eyebrows. "Do you think he might possibly find the odd call from Viking Strindberg to Philip Fahlén?" She weighed her cell phone in one hand, gazing at it. "I'm always surprised at how lax criminals are when they use their phones. I mean, everyone knows it's possible to trace calls these days. We can even pinpoint the area where a call was made, more or less. It was easier to commit crimes back in the old days."

CHAPTER 61

Thomas looked suspiciously at his beeping cell phone. He was speaking to Margit on the landline; she had given up for the evening and had gone home for something to eat. She had only just sat down at the table when Thomas called. He had interviewed the captain of the ferry on which Jonny Almhult was thought to have traveled.

"Margit, hang on. I've got a text. I'll just check and see what it is."

Thomas opened the message:

`Philip Fahlén taken to the hospital by helicopter. Critical.`

The message had been sent at 6:57, from Carina's phone.

"What does it say?" Margit asked.

Thomas jumped; he had almost forgotten she was on the other end of the phone. He quickly read her the message.

"Does it say why?" she asked.

"No." Thomas hesitated. Should he briefly summarize his discussion with the captain of the huge ferry? The man had more or less repeated what Marcus Björk had said. Or should he find out what had happened to Philip Fahlén? He decided on the latter. "Listen, I'll speak to Carina and call you back."

He hung up and called Carina.

She answered immediately. "I tried to call you," she said, "but the line was busy, and I thought you'd want to know this right away."

"What's happened?" Thomas asked.

"Fahlén was picked up by the air ambulance on Sandhamn at around four o'clock this afternoon. They flew him to Danderyd hospital, and he's in intensive care."

"What's wrong with him?"

"I couldn't get much out of them; you know how sensitive patient confidentiality is."

Thomas tried to suppress his impatience. "So what did they say?"

"It seems to be a brain hemorrhage. Apparently he was unconscious when the air ambulance picked him up."

"A brain hemorrhage?" The surprise in Thomas's voice was unmistakable.

Carina went on. "I'll call again in an hour and see what I can find out. They should be able to tell me something about his condition, at least."

Thomas's thoughts began to wander. Had Fahlén suffered an ordinary stroke? Or had someone managed to get him to ingest enough rat poison to trigger a potentially fatal hemorrhage?

Which was what had happened to Kicki Berggren.

Was a pattern being repeated right before their eyes? And if so, who was responsible? If someone had poisoned Fahlén, then that person must also be behind the three deaths. They had no idea who that person was or where he might be, but it was absolutely essential to track him down.

"Call me as soon as you've spoken to them again, whatever time it is," Thomas said. "And find out when we can go and speak to him."

Carina sighed. "I've already asked, and it didn't go well. The nurse I spoke to emphasized the fact that he could die; his condition is extremely serious. He might never regain consciousness. She almost told me off for even mentioning it."

"Ask anyway. If he does come around, it's absolutely essential that we have the chance to speak to him."

"OK," came the subdued response.

There was a brief silence before the connection was broken.

"Before we have another murder on our hands," Thomas said.

CHAPTER 62

The fishing trip had been a great success. They had caught big, fat perch in the net, which had been lying in the water for several hours.

Adam was so proud when they got back. He was sitting in the middle of the boat, his whole face beaming, surrounded by the perch net, which was filled with seaweed.

"Look, Mom! Have you ever seen this many fish?"

When they had cleaned as many as they could, there was still a whole bucket of fish left over; they put those in the tank, a holding area that had been built inside one of the stone chests on the jetty. It served as an aquarium where the fish could live for a few days after they'd been caught. It was a very practical feature that had been part of the jetty for as long as Nora could remember.

The grilled perch with new potatoes and chanterelle mushrooms fried in butter made a perfect summer meal. Nora set the table in the garden so they could make the most of the fine evening.

Henrik didn't want to drink wine as he was going out sailing, but Nora had a glass of golden Chardonnay. They had strawberries and ice cream for dessert.

Now they were sitting over a cup of coffee; it would soon be time for Henrik to make a move. There were still several hours to go before sunset. The pennants that had been fluttering proudly in the breeze earlier in the day were now drooping. The bumblebees were buzzing. The boys had gone over to see their grandparents for a while, so Nora and Henrik were alone.

It was time to talk.

Nora turned to him. "I've got something to tell you. I hope you'll be pleased, because I think it's really good."

She reached out and squeezed his right hand.

Henrik took a sip of his coffee and looked at her with curiosity. "Sounds good. I'm all ears."

Nora decided to ignore the anxiety in her chest and made an effort to sound as positive as possible. "When I was in town yesterday I took the opportunity to meet up with that recruitment consultant I told you about. We had a really good talk. The job sounds fascinating. Just the kind of challenge I want. And the idea of getting rid of my useless boss . . . no more Ragnar!" A smile crossed her face as she described the meeting and the questions that had come up. As she was talking she waved her hands. She couldn't help getting excited, and the words came more and more quickly.

Until she noticed that she wasn't getting any response.

Henrik hadn't said a word.

When Nora stopped talking, the silence hung heavily between them.

At last Henrik said, "You mean you went and met him behind my back?"

Nora stiffened. Henrik's voice was ice cold, and he was sitting with his back straight, looking at her as if they hardly knew each other.

"I wanted to meet him first to see if there was any point in bringing it up with you again."

"Like I said, behind my back." The words sounded like the crack of a whip.

"There's no need to take it that way. I decided to meet Rutger Sandelin before I told you. Is that so terrible?" A huge lump was forming in her throat.

This wasn't Henrik, her husband, sitting opposite her. This was a stranger. A stranger with black eyes and a condemnatory expression.

"I won't have this," he said. "If you think you can play fast and loose with this family just to fit in with your career, then you're mistaken."

Nora swallowed. Her stomach was contracting, and a quiver of fear slithered through her abdomen and into her throat. She had assumed he would be surprised that she'd met the consultant, but she had been sure they could talk it through. How could he react like this? "You can't forbid me from seeing anybody I want to see." The words came out more sharply than she'd intended, like an insolent child.

"I can do whatever I like, since you seem to think you can do whatever you please without a thought for anything other than your fucking job." Henrik was furious, his lips white. "I want nothing to do with this. I'm incredibly disappointed in you. How selfish can you be? You've got two children; have you forgotten that?"

"So have you," Nora said. "But you can go sailing for hours on end—that's perfectly all right—while I try to cope with everything else." She got up so fast that the chair fell over. "How can you say that? You should be proud of me. Pleased that someone's offered your wife an exciting job." She took a deep breath and tried to control her voice, which was threatening to crack. "Instead you're just being nasty."

"I'm trying to take care of what we have. And look after the best interests of our children. But you're behaving like a spoiled brat who doesn't get her way. We're not your puppets. You can't pull our strings just because it suits you." He folded his arms across his chest and looked at her. The muscles in his arms were tense, his fists clenched.

Nora looked at him in distress. In vain she looked for a shred of understanding on his face. Some sign of the Henrik she loved.

The Henrik who was her husband.

He looked at his watch and got up from the table. "I have to go or I'll be late."

Nora couldn't speak. There were no words. She hated the thought that he was going to leave without them making peace, but she just couldn't continue the conversation with him. She was torn between her desire to let the anger take over, to scream at him to go to hell, and the realization of how terrible she would feel if he simply left without some kind of reconciliation.

Reason won over rage, with some difficulty. She bit her lip, then took a deep breath. Little more than a whisper came out. "You can't just leave like this."

"I don't think we're going to get much further. I have to be there on time," he said with suppressed fury.

"Henrik." The name came out like a sob. "You have to stay—we have to talk this through." Her voice was shaking with the effort of keeping it under control. She took another deep breath and smothered the sob that was on its way. All of a sudden it was very important that she didn't start crying.

The distance between them was terrifying. Impossible to cross.

An empty glance was his only response.

The man who had promised to love her for better and for worse walked into the house. She watched him pick up his things and his life jacket from a hook inside the door. When he came out again he made a point of changing the subject, without looking her in the eye.

"Say good-bye to the boys for me. I'll be back around midnight tomorrow, if the wind is with us."

He barely paused; she only registered the words when he had already passed her.

"I have no desire to talk about this matter any further. The discussion is over. You need to pull yourself together, Nora."

He opened the gate and left the house with rapid, determined steps. As he was walking, he shrugged on his life jacket. His kit bag swung in time with his steps. He didn't look back.

Nora stood in the garden and watched him go. The tears were building up in her eyes. She dashed them away with the back of her hand.

If the boys hadn't come running at that very moment, she would have broken down completely.

Chapter 63

Nora was sitting on the veranda. She had put the boys to bed and was trying to work out what had actually happened between her and Henrik. She couldn't remember the last time they'd had such a serious falling-out. She had never felt so unhappy in her marriage, not even when things had been at their most difficult, when the children were small and Henrik was working night shifts.

How could something that had started with such a positive piece of news turn into such a crisis?

She thought about calling Thomas but didn't want to bother him with her marital problems, even if she had known him for many years. Besides, he had his hands full with the murder investigation and had been completely worn out the last time she'd seen him.

Her anger and shock at Henrik's reaction was like a weight lying on her chest; she could almost feel it. Her arms and legs felt numb, and her throat ached, as if she were coming down with something. The tears were burning beneath her eyelids.

She had no idea how to react to Henrik's harsh words. If he was serious, she would have to give up all thoughts of the job in Malmö.

Or think about whether she was prepared to move to Malmö without her husband.

It was more painful than she could possibly have imagined.

Was the job as legal adviser to the southern region worth a wrecked marriage?

Of course not. But the answer wasn't that clear cut.

As she went into the kitchen and got out Henrik's favorite whisky to pour herself a generous glass, she wished yet again that she'd never received the call from human resources.

With glass in hand, she picked up her sailing jacket and walked down to the jetty. The boys were fast asleep. It was perfectly safe to leave them for a few minutes. She sat down on one of the chairs and gazed out over the sea. Being by the water normally made her feel better. Just the sight of the shining surface of the sea would bring her peace. But tonight it wasn't helping at all.

The weight on her chest was just as palpable as before.

The sound of footsteps on the gravel made her jump.

"Are you sitting here all on your own?" Signe was standing there, looking at her.

"It was such a lovely evening. I just wanted to watch the sunset." Nora's brave attempt to smile ended up as more of a grimace. She just couldn't help it; the tears poured down her face.

"But, my dear child, whatever's happened?" Signe looked anxiously at Nora.

"Nothing, really, it's nothing." She knew she didn't sound particularly convincing.

"But I can see something's wrong. Come on, now. Tell me what's happened." Signe sat down on the chair next to Nora and gently touched her arm. "It can't be that bad. Is it something to do with Henrik? Where is he, by the way?"

"Out sailing," Nora sobbed. "The twenty-four-hour race."

With the tears still flowing, she told Signe what had happened earlier that evening. She told her about the new job, the visit to the recruitment consultant, and Henrik's reaction.

Signe looked at Nora. The sun had gone down, and shadows were taking over. Nora could see the sorrows of a lifetime reflected in Signe's eyes.

"What do you want?" Signe asked.

"I don't know. Well, yes, I do. I want Henrik to want me to take that job."

"And if that doesn't happen?"

"Then I don't know what I want. But how can I turn down an opportunity like this? What are they going to say at the bank if I do? And I hate working for my current boss. He's an idiot." The tears started again. "I'll regret it for the rest of my life." By now Nora was crying so hard she was shaking.

Signe took a handkerchief out of her pocket and passed it to Nora. "There, there," she said. "My dear, there are many things you might bitterly regret in your life. I can promise you that turning down a job isn't one of them." Signe stroked Nora's cheek. "You're so young. You've got your whole life ahead of you and your wonderful boys to enjoy."

"Do you regret never having any children of your own?" The question slipped out before she could stop herself. She looked at Signe in horror. She had never asked anything like that before.

"Sweetheart, of course I would have loved children of my own. But sometimes things don't turn out the way you wish." She gazed out over the sea and slumped slightly. "There are a whole lot of things that don't turn out the way you wish. Things you regret when it's too late."

***

Nora walked back to the house deep in thought.

She brought in the cushions from the garden furniture and locked the outside door. The pelargoniums got a drop of water once the sun had gone down. Then she switched off the lights on the ground floor and went upstairs to the boys' room.

The only sound in the house was their gentle breathing as they slept.

As usual Simon was lying on his knees as if in prayer, sleeping with his head buried deep in the pillow. She bent down and stroked his soft cheek. He was sweating slightly in his sleep, making the hair curl above his ears.

She lifted him up and carried him to her own bed. He settled in without waking up. Slowly she got undressed and lay down beside him, as close to his warm little body as she could get. As the tears began to flow again she stroked his soft stomach, rising and falling as he breathed. She stared out into the darkness.

FRIDAY,
THE FOURTH WEEK

Chapter 64

When the digital clock showed 6:23, Nora abandoned the attempt to sleep.

Simon was rolled up beside her in a little ball. He had thrown off the covers, but his forehead was still sweaty. Through the open window she could see clear blue sky.

It was going to be another beautiful summer's day.

But it had been a terrible night.

She had slept only intermittently, her muscles tensed to the breaking point. It was as if she had been lying as stiff as a board with her hands by her sides, constantly on alert. Time after time she had woken up, and before she remembered why, she had been overwhelmed by the pain in her chest. Then she had relived that dreadful conversation with Henrik, and the tears had begun to flow again.

She had been tormented by terrifying dreams in which they split up. The house had to be sold, and the children were forced to leave their home.

Logically, she was able to tell herself that it was just an ordinary argument, but her body knew better. The entire basis of their life together was at stake. That was how bad it was.

She buried her nose in Simon's warm back and felt the tears welling up again, but his warm little-boy smell made her smile in spite of herself. Whatever happened, she had the children.

She forced herself to think about something else.

Today they were going to Grönskär. She had been looking forward to visiting the lighthouse for ages; it was a well-known landmark throughout the archipelago. Excursions with the Friends of Sandhamn were always enjoyable, and Nora's parents and Signe were coming, too.

But how was she going to be able to control herself during the day? If her mother found out what had happened, she would have to tell her the whole sorry tale.

That was unthinkable, especially with the children there.

Better to say nothing at all, even if it meant pretending everything was fine. Strangely enough, she didn't mind Signe knowing what had happened. She had no regrets about confiding in her; last night she had really needed someone to talk to. Besides, Signe wasn't the kind of person who would offer advice unless she was asked.

Unlike Nora's mother.

Nora took a deep breath and once again resolved to think about something else. Henrik would be back from the race soon enough, and then they would have to try to sort this out.

Until then, she would just have to switch to autopilot.

The boat to Grönskär was due to leave at nine thirty. The Friends had chartered a taxi boat to transport the forty participants. Everyone was to bring a picnic, plus a blanket to sit on. There would be a tour of the lighthouse, followed by a group picnic on the rocks nearby.

She looked at the clock again; they didn't need to leave for at least a couple of hours, but she might as well start packing the picnic basket. After all, it wasn't as if she had anything better to do. She managed a bitter little smile and headed down to the kitchen.

Yesterday's pancakes would be filled with jam and rolled up for the boys. Nora would be happy with sandwiches. She prepared some cucumber slices and carrot sticks, then added a thermos of coffee, a big bottle of soda, and a selection of buns.

She looked at the clock again. Quarter past seven. Still more than two hours to go.

She sighed and started setting the table for breakfast, just to give herself something to do. She wondered if she would be able to disguise her red puffy eyes if she used enough mascara and foundation. Probably not.

It would have to be dark glasses all day. Fortunately the sun was shining, so no one would wonder why.

Chapter 65

The boat was full of excited passengers. At least half of them were children, so the decibel level was high. Nora knew virtually everyone on board. Signe and Kajsa were sitting next to Nora's parents. Eventually the crew cast off, and they set sail for Grönskär.

They moored at Kolbranten just below the lighthouse. The old small-boat harbor on the northern side was shallow these days, but the sturdy concrete quay was easily able to accommodate larger boats.

The sight of Grönskär was striking. The lighthouse was known as the Queen of the Baltic because of its beautiful silhouette. It was owned by the Archipelago Foundation, which was responsible for its upkeep and took excellent care of it. The current lighthouse keeper—or curator, to be more accurate—was really passionate when it came to the lighthouse and its future.

The tower was almost eighty-five feet high; it dominated the little island, which was no more than four hundred yards in length. The lighthouse rose up as a memorial to seafarers' need for guidance during the hundreds of years when sailing ships sought safety in the sheltered harbor of Sandhamn.

The curator was standing on the quayside, legs apart, ready to welcome the visitors. The guide, a cheerful resident of Sandhamn, held forth enthusiastically about the history of the lighthouse as she led the group to the entrance.

"Grönskär lighthouse was designed by the famous architect Carl Fredrik Adelcrantz in 1770, and it was built of granite and sandstone. The lighthouse is octagonal, and the base is wider than the top. Originally an open coal fire was used, but in 1845 it was replaced by a so-called third-order lens using a colza oil lamp. In 1910 a kerosene lamp was introduced, combined with a shutter system that made it possible to produce different signals for the shipping lanes." She paused and turned to Simon and Adam. "Just imagine, boys: before they installed an elevator, the poor lighthouse keeper had to carry every single sack of coal up all those steps—now that was hard work!"

Simon gazed openmouthed at the guide. She smiled at him.

"Can you guess how many steps there are?"

Simon thought about it, then held up all his fingers. "More than this?"

"A lot more."

"Don't be silly. There must be hundreds," Adam said to Simon, looking superior. He turned to the guide. "My brother isn't very good at counting; he hasn't started school yet."

She laughed and patted him on the shoulder. "Unfortunately you're both wrong. There are ninety steps in total, and that's plenty, I can tell you. Just wait until you've climbed them all."

She carried on with her talk.

"The lighthouse was turned off in 1961, when it was replaced by the caisson lighthouse known as Revengegrundet just off Korsö. It was completely renovated in the 1990s with the help of government funding and now emits a faint green light. So there's life in the old lady yet."

She pointed to the steps.

"Feel free to go in, just a few of you at a time. There isn't a great deal of room. Be careful you don't trip—the steps are rather uneven."

Nora gripped Simon's hand when it was their turn.

In spite of the warm summer's day it was cold and damp inside the tower. It was divided into four floors, but it was still quite tricky to climb the steps. They were slightly deeper than normal stairs, so Nora and Simon had to lift their legs a little bit higher each time. At one point they almost got lost when they went down a blind passageway that didn't lead anywhere.

When they had almost reached the top, Nora came to the conclusion that a person would have to be considerably fitter than she was to avoid panting with exertion. All those walks and bike rides over the summer, not to mention the jogging, ought to have produced better results than this!

After the final landing they reached a small room where narrow white-painted wrought-iron steps led up to the lantern room. At the foot of these steps there was a green door leading out onto a small walkway that went all the way around the tower.

"Can I go outside, Mom?" Simon looked at Nora.

"Me, too!" Adam said.

Nora opened the door and looked out. The distance from the ground was dizzying. She turned and spoke to the boys. "You can, but you must promise to be really, really careful. I don't want to see anybody running around when we're this high up! Do I make myself clear?"

"Come with me, Adam, and hold my hand. At my age I could do with a young man to help me keep my balance." Signe, who was standing behind Nora, reached out and firmly gripped Adam by the hand as they went outside.

The view was fantastic. It was a clear day, and the sea lay spread out before them. The hundreds of islands and islets strewn across the water were indescribably beautiful. They could just see Almagrundet lighthouse on the horizon, even though it was many nautical miles away.

Down below were the houses once occupied by the master lighthouse keeper, the lighthouse keeper, the assistant lighthouse keeper, and their families. They had recently been carefully restored.

It must have been a harsh, desolate existence, especially for the women, Nora thought. Every household task had to be carried out with neither electricity nor running water, and the lighthouse had to be manned at all times, even during the dark days of autumn and winter, irrespective of the weather or the keeper's health.

These days it was almost impossible to imagine what it was like to live under those conditions, year after year. A life where the high point was probably a trip to Sandhamn, which in itself was no more than an isolated outpost.

"It's amazing, isn't it?" Signe turned to Nora, sighing with sheer pleasure. "I've been coming here ever since I was a little girl, and I never get tired of the view."

"Absolutely," Nora said, gazing all around.

Their guide had joined them on the walkway and rested her arms on the railing. "Did you know that the stone for the tower came from the island itself? It was taken straight from the rocks, then built up with crushed brick and Gotland chalk, among other things. That's why it looks like a beautiful mosaic from a distance. Only the middle section is built of sandstone from Roslagen."

"Why is there a belt of gray stone right at the top?" Nora asked.

"There are a number of different theories. The most likely is that the final delivery of sandstone failed to arrive, and in the end the builders just couldn't wait any longer, so they used what they could get ahold of locally—which happened to be more gray stone."

"It's incredible to think they could construct such a tall building in the middle of the archipelago without the technology we have today," Nora said.

"Even more incredible when you bear in mind that the original drawing wasn't even a proper plan; it was a beautiful watercolor."

"There were no plans?" Signe asked, looking surprised. "I've never heard that before."

"It's true. We have a master mason called C. H. Walmstedt to thank for the way the lighthouse looks. He was the one who made sure it was built using the watercolor as a guide, but there were no technical specifications to speak of when they started."

"Fantastic. Who would have thought it?" Nora was impressed.

Simon tugged at Nora's hand. "Can we go back inside now? I want to go right up to the top."

"Of course. Come on."

They went in through the green door, and Simon clambered up the narrow iron steps, which led to an ornate walkway. This took up most of the space inside the lantern room, which wasn't big—no more than two yards in diameter. There was glass from floor to ceiling, with a small air vent in the corner. There was only space for a few people at a time.

This wasn't the place for anyone with vertigo, Nora thought.

"Wow! You can see Sandhamn from here," Simon said. "Adam, look!" he shouted down.

In the middle of the lantern room was the new lamp, installed in 2000 when the lighthouse was relit.

"Simon, do you know why the lamp shines with a green glow?" Nora pointed to the prisms and the lens, which was covered with a piece of fabric.

Simon looked at her. "Because it's a nice color?"

"No, sweetheart, it's because the lighthouse is called Grönskär. *Grön* means green, so a green light is perfect. Green for Grönskär."

***

After they had finished looking around the lighthouse and eaten their picnic, Nora decided to visit the little museum, which was housed in the old paraffin store. Her mother went with her, while the boys stayed with their grandfather and Signe.

As she stood leafing through the beautifully illustrated books, she recalled the conversation with Thomas and his colleague the other evening. They had talked about the rat poison that had been used to kill Kicki Berggren. She had kept meaning to ask her mother where she had bought the liquid rat poison they used to have at home, but recent events, not least the conversation with Henrik, had made her forget all about it.

The answer she got from her mother made her grab her cell phone right away. She had to tell Thomas at once.

Chapter 66

Thomas answered. He was sitting at his desk in the police station, surrounded by papers strewn all over. There was a mug of cold tea in front of him. Caller ID told him it was Nora.

"Guess what Mom told me," she said. "The rat poison we had at home when I was little actually came from Sandhamn. She bought it in the old general store that used to be where the Divers Bar is now."

"OK. So the poison we think killed Kicki Berggren used to be available on Sandhamn."

"Exactly. The shop closed at the end of the seventies. Mom also said she still uses the same stuff if they ever get mice."

"So that means the poison is still effective after more than twenty-five years." Thomas leaned back in his chair, frowning. "Is that possible?"

"I've no idea. You should probably ask someone from Anticimex, but Mom says it works."

Thomas tried to put his thoughts into words. "So if we assume the murderer bought the poison on Sandhamn, that could mean he's had a house on the island for at least twenty-five years." He fell silent for a moment, then went on. "On the other hand, he could have gotten the poison just about anywhere. It must have been on sale everywhere."

Fahlén had owned a house on Sandhamn for about fifteen years. Before that he had rented a place in Trouville for a long time. It had to be at least twenty-five years altogether. On the other hand, he was now in the hospital, possibly due to warfarin poisoning. But it was definitely worth following up.

He slid his notebook closer and jotted down a few notes.

"Thanks for calling, Nora. I'll get someone to go through the property register again. It might be worth checking who's owned a house on Sandhamn for more than twenty-five years; we might just come up with something interesting."

He ended the call and went straight to Carina's office. It looked considerably more personal than his own. A vase of blue-and-yellow summer flowers stood on the desk, with a big photograph of the family dog beside it. A selection of funny cartoons was pinned up on the bulletin board.

A feeling of loss came over Thomas, a longing for something cozy and homey instead of his own impersonal environment, where he barely left an impression.

He quickly explained why he was there and asked her to start as soon as she could.

She looked at him and hesitated. She tucked a strand of hair behind her ear. "Could we have lunch together?"

"Lunch?"

"It's a meal people usually have in the middle of the day," she said, half-serious, half-joking. "At around twelve o'clock, which is now. I thought we could go out." She smiled. The pleading tone of voice gave her away, and she looked nervous. This wasn't just a spur-of-the-moment suggestion.

Thomas was surprised; he didn't really know what to say. He gave a slightly embarrassed laugh and looked at his watch. But then he suddenly felt almost lighthearted. Why not? It sounded like a really nice idea. "I'd like that. I just need to speak to Margit about something, then I'll come back. Shall we say fifteen minutes?"

He got a beaming smile in return. "Great! We could go to Restaurant J. I think we deserve a good meal after all our hard work. What do you think? And it is Friday after all, so we ought to do something a little special."

Thomas caught himself whistling as he walked down the hallway. He hadn't done that for a long time.

They had decided that Margit would catch the afternoon train back to the west coast so she could spend the weekend with her family. She would rejoin the team on Monday morning.

The hospital had made it clear that there was no chance of speaking to Fahlén today. He was still unconscious following a major operation during the night. He had suffered a serious brain hemorrhage, and it was currently impossible to say what might have caused it. The police were welcome to call again in the evening but would have to be patient until then.

A brief call to Fahlén's wife hadn't made things any clearer. Sylvia had found him on the kitchen floor, but by then he had been unable to talk and had soon lost consciousness. She would come to the police station for a longer conversation as soon as she was able to leave the hospital.

Thomas quickly told Margit about Nora's phone call. "If this leads anywhere, it would give us a significantly smaller circle of possible perpetrators. Someone who's had a house on Sandhamn since the seventies, in which case they must be at least middle-aged."

"Unless of course the murderer bought a house where the former owner had left some rat poison behind. Like Pieter Graaf, for example," said Margit with a certain amount of skepticism. She wasn't completely convinced by Thomas's theory.

"Philip Fahlén fits the age profile," Thomas said, "and he's been spending summers on Sandhamn for over thirty years."

"But right now he's in the hospital, possibly because he's also been poisoned."

"True," Thomas said. "But at the moment we don't actually know what caused his brain hemorrhage."

"He could have had a stroke due entirely to natural causes."

"We can't take anything for granted at this stage, but it's still an avenue worth exploring." He stretched, his joints creaking. "By the way, what happened with those teenagers from the ferry to Finland? You were going to talk to them."

"The girl isn't answering her cell phone, and there's no reply on the landline. I'll try to get a number for someone else in the family. Her boyfriend didn't know where she could be contacted. He thought she was visiting some relatives in northern Norway this week."

"And what did he have to say?"

"He said he didn't know anything. It was his girlfriend who saw the body fall. By the time she shouted out, it was too late. But he wasn't completely convinced anything had actually happened. It sounded as if he thought she might have been imagining things. They'd also had a fair amount to drink during the course of the evening, which was why she'd insisted he go with her to report the incident the following day. I've made a few notes if you want to have a look."

Thomas noticed that Margit was trying to conceal a yawn. He knew she'd sat up half the night going through material in order to compensate for the fact that she was leaving this afternoon.

"What time's your train?" he asked.

"In an hour. I'll be there around six. I'll take all my notes with me and go through them again on the train."

"Give me a call if you find anything."

"Of course. Same goes for you. What are you doing this afternoon?"

"I was thinking of going back to Krister Berggren's apartment, just to make sure we haven't missed anything, even though forensics has been there."

"Sounds like a good idea. You could take Carina with you; sometimes it's useful to have a second pair of eyes. She's worked hard over the last few weeks. She'll be a great police officer if she can just get into the academy."

Thomas agreed. Carina had been a real asset in the investigation, and he had no objections to Margit's suggestion.

"After that I'll probably go back to Harö. I need to think about something else for a few hours, if that's possible."

Chapter 67

Restaurant J was packed with suntanned customers in light summer clothes. Boats of all types and sizes were moored at its long guest jetty. The restaurant was popular both with those who worked nearby and those who wanted to show off their flashy boats.

Out toward the edge of the jetty the owner of a large Princess yacht was attempting to maneuver his vessel into a space that was far too small between two motorboats. The man was bellowing order after order to his stressed-out wife, who was scuttling back and forth with a boat hook to prevent collisions. The diners were watching the drama with ill-concealed delight.

The waitresses were dashing between tables, rushing to keep everyone happy. Carina put on her sunglasses and looked at Thomas. "I wonder if we'll be able to get a table. It looks full."

"Don't worry. I can see one over there in the corner. Follow me."

They sat down under a striped parasol, which offered some shade. At the table next to them was a family with a two-year-old in a high chair and a little girl who looked a few years older. She was clutching a big ice cream cone and running around on the jetty in spite of her mother's warnings and her father's reprimands.

"Sweet kids," Carina said.

Thomas's smile faltered. A shadow passed across his face, and he simply nodded.

Carina could have bitten her tongue. How could she say such a thing? She quickly started talking about something less personal. "I've spoken to the registration authority, and they've promised to run a check on the property register as soon as possible. If they don't have time today, they'll do it right after the weekend. I stressed how important it was."

Thomas brightened up. "Excellent. The way things are at the moment, we need to follow up on every lead." Thomas gazed out across the water, where an enormous cruise ship was passing by. "Particularly now, when there doesn't seem to be anyone else in the picture except Fahlén."

"The guy I spoke to promised to send the results across as soon as they come through. Unfortunately I didn't find anything in the passenger lists from the ferry company, but we might have better luck with the property register." Carina fell silent and started fiddling with her knife and fork. She was desperately trying to come up with a topic of conversation that wasn't too personal but would involve more than a work-related discussion of the case. She settled on Thomas's house on Harö. She knew that he went there as often as he could; his face lit up whenever he talked about the archipelago. "Tell me about your summer place. It must be really beautiful."

As Thomas described the house and life on Harö, Carina watched him from behind her dark sunglasses.

Thomas was pleasant and easy to get along with in every way, but he shut down as soon as anyone started talking about his private life. She couldn't remember any occasion on which he had volunteered information about himself since they had become colleagues. He could tirelessly discuss a case down to the last detail, but as soon as someone asked something personal, he clammed up. But the atmosphere between them was relaxed, and he had opened up much more this July than she could ever recall him doing in the past. He also seemed much happier, even though the investigation was taking its toll.

"Can you come with me?"

The question brought Carina back to the moment. She looked at him, surprised. What had she missed? She gave up and smiled at him. Busted. "Sorry, I was thinking about something."

Thomas laughed. "I said I was thinking of going back to Krister Berggren's apartment this afternoon. See if there's something we might have missed when we were there last time. I'd appreciate it if you could come along. Two pairs of eyes are better than one. If you're going to be able to concentrate, that is." He wagged a finger at her, teasing.

"Of course I'll come," Carina said. She was more than happy to spend a whole afternoon alone with Thomas.

She started on her salad, trying to spear several prawns on her fork. She was excited to be helping out with real police work; it was exactly what she needed before she put in her application to the training academy.

"When are we going?"

"Right after lunch."

CHAPTER 68

When Thomas and Carina arrived at the apartment block in Bandhagen, there wasn't a soul in sight. The only sign of life was a black cat with a white tail; it hurried across the road without looking back.

The apartment on the third floor was just as silent and deserted as the last time. The police notice made it clear that no unauthorized persons should attempt to enter. Thomas unlocked the front door and let Carina in. It smelled even more stale than before. They walked through the narrow hallway and into the living room with its scruffy wallpaper. The sparse furnishings and grubby black leather sofa were still just as depressing.

Carina looked around. "It's miserable."

"You could say that."

"Krister Berggren must have been a really lonely person." She shuddered.

A bullfinch was singing away outside the window, oblivious to whatever might be going on in the buildings around him. The desolation that was so typical of the city at the height of summer was palpable. All those who possibly could have fled the hot tarmac and suffocating air packed their bags and headed for the nearest coastline. The only people left were those who had neither the time nor the energy to get away.

Thomas pointed to the smaller room. "If I take the bedroom, can you do the living room?"

"Of course. Am I looking for anything in particular?"

"No, I just can't help feeling that we've missed something. The key to a safety deposit box where he kept the money from his underhand deals, for example, or something else that links him to Sandhamn." Thomas shrugged. "I wish I could be more specific."

Carina took out white latex gloves and passed a pair to Thomas, her expression serious. It was obvious she was trying to behave in a professional manner, but Thomas just thought she looked rather sweet.

Methodically, he began to go through the bedroom once again, tipping every drawer out onto the bed before examining and sorting the contents. Then he turned his attention to the closet, which contained nothing unusual. A few pairs of black pants, several pairs of scruffy jeans, a Windbreaker with Systemet's logo on the back. He checked the shelves inside the closet and the drawer in the bedside table.

He pulled two beer crates full of porn magazines from under the bed: an assortment of women, mostly blondes, in a variety of poses that left little to the imagination. It was somehow sad rather than titillating.

After an hour, Thomas had examined every single item in the little room. He hadn't found anything new, but what had he expected? The investigative team had already carried out a forensic search that had led nowhere.

With a sigh, he straightened up and went into the bathroom. There were no surprises in the medicine cabinet, nor in the narrow spaces behind the bathtub and the toilet. He wasn't surprised. It was very rare, apart from in movies, that secret papers were discovered taped behind a toilet tank.

He rubbed the back of his neck and stretched. Then he went to join Carina in the living room. She was sitting on the floor, systematically going through everything that had been in the bookcase. On her knee she had a photo album, one of several from the bottom shelf. She had already checked the videos, which were now piled on the table. The drawers had been removed from the desk and placed on the sofa.

Thomas carefully moved one of them, which contained piles of papers and other bits and pieces, and sat down.

"How's it going?"

"So-so."

"How were his finances?"

"I've looked at his bills going back several years, but there's nothing out of the ordinary. We've already seen his bank statements, and there are no unexplained credits or debits. If he was making money on the side, he definitely wasn't putting it into his bank account."

"Exactly. That's why there ought to be a key to a safety deposit box or something similar that we just haven't found yet. He was probably bright enough to realize you don't turn up at the bank with dirty money."

Carina pointed to a pile of magazines. "I've gone through dozens of car magazines and piles of travel brochures, but I haven't found a thing."

"So I see."

Thomas picked up a copy of *Motor Sport* from 2004 and flipped through it.

"I was thinking of going through his photo albums again, just to be on the safe side. Maybe you could take one of them? Unless you want to start on the kitchen?"

Thomas didn't answer; he simply removed one of the albums from the shelf. The pages were slightly yellowed, and some of the pictures were loose where the glue had dried. The album contained lots of photographs of the woman whose framed portrait stood on top of the chest of drawers. A neatly written caption under each one provided information about who was with her and when the picture had been taken. It must have been put together by Krister's mother; the handwriting looked like a woman's, and it was difficult to imagine Krister Berggren as the kind of person who would meticulously sort pictures into an album.

Presumably it had come to him after his mother's death.

Thomas gently turned the pages. Several photographs had begun to turn yellow. He found Krister and Kicki in an old Volvo Amazon; they were sitting in the back, proud and slightly self-conscious, both with their thumbs up.

Suddenly Thomas noticed that Carina's attention had been caught by something. She appeared to be trying to get an envelope from behind a large photograph of Krister's mother, which took up a whole page in the album. She slid it out gently and opened it. She started to read, her brow becoming more furrowed as she went along. After a couple of minutes she looked up, a big smile on her face. "Thomas, I think I've found the missing link."

She had his full attention. "What do you mean?"

She handed over the letter and the envelope. *To my son Krister,* it said on the outside. *To be read after my death.*

CHAPTER 69

Thomas held the letter in his hand, suddenly feeling that they had found the key to the mystery. He began to read.

Dear Krister, You have never known who your father was, the letter began. It was two handwritten pages. It was dated a year ago. There was no stamp on the envelope, so presumably it had been handed directly to Krister rather than being mailed.

Thomas slowly read through the text. When he had finished he sat in silence for a little while. Then he turned to Carina, who was watching him attentively.

"So now we know what linked Krister Berggren to Sandhamn."

She nodded. "And who his father was."

Thomas held up the letter. "He had every reason to go over to the island."

"Yes, especially if he found out after his mother's death," Carina said. "She died at the end of February, and he disappeared at the end of March. He must have decided to make contact soon after the funeral."

Thomas contemplated a picture of Krister; he was gazing beyond the camera, as if waiting for something or someone that never appeared.

"So he suddenly learned who his father was, and that he had more living relatives, not just Kicki."

Carina pushed her hair back. She was looking over a photograph of Cecilia Berggren, who was holding her son in her arms and looking straight down the lens with a serious expression. "It must have been such a shock," she said. "After all these years. I wonder why his mother never told him."

"Perhaps she was ashamed?"

"Or she wanted to protect the father."

"Or Krister. We don't know how the father reacted. He might not have wanted anything to do with her when she got pregnant. After all, her family had broken off all contact with her; the only one who supported her was her brother, Kicki's father."

Thomas tried to remember what Kicki had told him when they met at the police station. Cecilia had brought up her son without any help from her parents. It had been a tough struggle to survive, and she'd had to be careful with money. Cecilia had dropped out of school and started working at Systemet as soon as possible after Krister's birth.

"He must have read the letter and decided to go to Sandhamn to find his family," Thomas said.

"Who perhaps didn't even know he existed."

"True. It could be that they didn't know anything about him."

"Apart from the father."

"But something happened on the way over, or when he arrived," Thomas said.

"Something that resulted in his death."

"And subsequently the death of his cousin."

"If the deaths are related."

"Why wouldn't they be related?"

"Well, Krister Berggren's death could still have been an accidental drowning. He might have fallen overboard. What if he was just unlucky on the boat to Sandhamn?"

"And Kicki?"

"I don't know. I suppose it's not likely to be a coincidence that she was murdered so soon after Krister's death."

"Besides which, Jonny Almhult is dead and Philip Fahlén is in the hospital; we don't have a reasonable explanation for either of those events," Thomas said. A similar conversation he had recently had with Margit suddenly came to mind. He studied the letter thoughtfully. "This definitely raises a number of fresh questions. But I still find it strange that . . ." He fell silent, staring at the letter.

"What?"

"That there wasn't the slightest hint. Not the least suggestion of a family connection. After everything that's happened."

"That is odd," Carina said. "But there's no guarantee that anyone even knew about him. And if they did, they were probably embarrassed. It would have been a real scandal in those days."

"I'm sure it was. An illegitimate child was nothing to boast about in the fifties," Thomas said.

"Are you going over there this evening?"

"I'll see." He suppressed a yawn. "It doesn't really matter. Nobody's about to run off. I'm not even sure if it would be possible tonight." He got to his feet with a sigh. "I'm worn out. I think I'll probably go over to Harö; the conversation on Sandhamn can wait until tomorrow morning."

He looked at the letter one last time before carefully folding it up and slipping it back into the envelope.

Chapter 70

A whole evening all to herself. The need to be alone was physical. Her body wanted time. Nora longed to think through the situation calmly. Just to be left in peace, without having to pretend everything was OK or explain anything to anyone. After the conversation the previous evening, she had to gather her thoughts. Decide what she really wanted, deep down.

Since Henrik was taking part in the twenty-four-hour race, he wouldn't be back before midnight. That gave her plenty of time to think about what she was going to say to him.

The boys had asked if they could sleep over at their grandparents' house.

They hadn't needed to ask twice.

Nora had already taken their nighttime things across, and now she was alone. It was only eight thirty and still light outside.

Even if her mind was not at peace, she had decided to make sure her stomach was. She had bought a lovely chicken fillet, marinated it in lime and soy sauce, then grilled it in the oven. To go with it, she had made a couscous salad with avocado and a sauce of Turkish yogurt mixed with sweet chili. And to really spoil herself she had bought a bar of Belgian dark chocolate, her absolute favorite.

Of course, she was supposed to go easy on sweets because of her diabetes, but she had to indulge once in a while.

This was one of those times.

She would, however, take a little extra insulin before her meal, because she hadn't injected herself at lunchtime when they were on Grönskär. The dose would be enough to compensate for the chocolate. And they did say that dark chocolate contained a substance that made you feel better, even if you were unhappy or depressed. Just what she needed.

Even an artificially induced sense of well-being was welcome this evening.

She decided to set the table nicely even though she was alone, so she put out a crystal glass. It was silly, really, but at the moment it felt right.

She made her final preparations and opened the fridge to get her insulin pen from its usual place on the top shelf.

She twisted a needle onto the top of the pen and carefully dialed her dose. She flicked the pen with her finger and then injected it into her stomach below the navel, into the layer of fat beneath the skin. She unscrewed the needle from the pen and left it on the dish rack. She would put it into its container in the bathroom later.

Nora placed the chicken dish on the table and put on the latest Norah Jones CD, her namesake apart from the *h*.

Just as she was about to sit down, she decided to call Henrik. Even if they weren't getting along right now, she wanted to know how things were going and what time he thought he might be back.

She felt for her cell phone in the pocket of her shorts but couldn't find it. She went back into the kitchen to look, but there was no sign of it there either. Strange. Nora frowned. She went upstairs to the bedroom to see if it was there.

She picked up the landline and called her cell phone. The call went through, but she couldn't hear the cell phone ringing in the house.

Nora stopped at the top of the stairs.

When had she last had her phone? She tried to conjure up a mental picture of when she'd used it during the day. A bit like rewinding a video.

On Grönskär.

She'd called Thomas to tell him about the rat poison her mother had used. But what had she done with the phone after that? She must have put it down somewhere. Surely she couldn't have dropped the phone on Grönskär? She'd been wearing a pair of shorts with shallow pockets. Nora sighed. How stupid.

It was almost nine o'clock. If she hurried she could take the launch and make it over to Grönskär while it was still light. She'd be back in half an hour.

She looked longingly at her delicious dinner, all laid out on the table.

The cell phone was much more important. Not the phone itself, but all the stored numbers. Having to program two hundred numbers into a new phone felt like an insurmountable task.

Quickly she pulled on her life jacket and grabbed a flashlight. She took the keys of the boat out of the little blue-painted cupboard just inside the door.

The curator kept a spare key under a stone by the lighthouse; they'd talked about it during the trip when she'd asked what would happen if someone lost the key to the lighthouse.

She walked quickly down to the jetty. Signe was standing by the boathouses with her hands in her pockets, gazing at the sea. She looked unusually sad, with dark shadows under her eyes.

"Where are you off to at this time of night?" she asked as Nora drew closer.

"I need to go over to Grönskär. I think I dropped my phone when we were there today. So careless. The boys are at Mom and Dad's, so I thought I'd just pop over and look for it."

"I could come with you," said Signe.

Nora smiled. "That's kind of you. But there's no need. I'll be fine—it won't take long. I'll be back before dark."

"It's no trouble. I'm not doing anything anyway. Wait a minute, I'll just get my life jacket." She placed a hand on Nora's shoulder. "I really don't think you should go out on your own, after the state you were in last night."

"Actually, some company would be really nice," said Nora. She climbed down onto the launch, inserted the ignition key, and loosened the ropes. She checked the gas to make sure there was enough. She had no desire to run out in the middle of the sea.

Signe came back with her life jacket, climbed into the launch, and pushed off from the jetty with some force. With a practiced hand, Nora steered the boat toward Grönskär.

Chapter 71

As they passed the Sandhamn Sound, Nora glanced back over her shoulder. Behind her the lights of Sandhamn were disappearing in the wake of the launch. The familiar houses became small dots, quickly vanishing in the distance. She wondered if she should have called to let her parents know she was going to Grönskär. They might get worried if they discovered the house was empty. Then again, it was only a short trip there and back. It wouldn't take long.

The sound of the engine made it difficult to carry on a conversation, so she concentrated on steering the boat as it sliced through the calm, shining water. They had soon passed Telegrafholmen and rounded Björkö on the starboard side. After only ten minutes they could see the familiar outline of Grönskär up ahead.

There was a fresh smell of the sea and seaweed. The odd yacht, which hadn't yet found a harbor for the night, was just visible in the distance. To the south, Svängen and Revengegrundet would soon start to flash.

They were drawing close to Grönskär, and Nora decided to moor at the quay below the lighthouse rather than in the shallow harbor for small boats. Just as well to be on the safe side. She had no desire to try to maneuver the boat free in the twilight.

When they were almost at the quay, Nora cut her speed down. The swell carried the boat the last few yards.

The quay, which consisted of a rectangular block of concrete protruding from the rocks, had two iron rings attached to each side. Nora tied the boat with two sturdy knots—rolling hitches, as her grandfather had taught her when she was little. They always had spare ropes in the boat in case they needed to tie up somewhere.

She pushed back the hair that the wind had torn free of her ponytail and turned to Signe. "You can wait here if you like. I'll just run up and have a look."

Signe shook her head. "Out of the question. I'm coming with you. You're not going up that dark tower on your own at this time of night."

Nora smiled. She was really glad Signe had come with her so she didn't have to be on her own on Grönskär. "OK. Let's go."

"How are you going to get in?"

"I know where the spare key is. But I think I dropped the phone outside. I'll just have to search around. Seek and ye shall find, right?"

The flat rock above the quay was slippery with the evening dew. The damp moss had spread over the rocks like a grayish-green carpet. Nora was careful where she stepped. She could easily slip, and a sprained ankle wasn't a particularly attractive prospect.

As she walked, she thought about the old fairy tale: Rapunzel, the fair maiden with the long hair who was imprisoned in a tower. She was saved by a prince when she let down her hair so he could climb up and free her. A shudder went through Nora's body. Grönskär lighthouse wasn't a place where she'd want to get trapped, however long her hair might be.

Nora and Signe made their way up toward the lighthouse. There was no indication that Signe was almost eighty. She was agile and wiry and walked easily, despite the uneven ground. As always in the outer archipelago, the vegetation was sparse: low, windblown pine trees and the odd birch.

Nora tried hard to remember how she had moved around the lighthouse while talking on the phone. She had stopped just outside the entrance when she called Thomas. As was her usual habit, she had wandered back and forth during the conversation. The phone ought to be somewhere near the lighthouse.

She groped around in the bushes, but it was difficult to see in the gathering darkness. The flashlight wasn't much help. She walked between the lighthouse and the little hut housing the museum one more time just to check but found nothing.

Maybe she had dropped it inside, after all.

She had gone up there with Adam one last time, just before they left. They had been in a hurry, so perhaps the phone had fallen out of her pocket on the way down.

She bent down and groped for the spare key, which was indeed hidden beneath the flat stone the curator had mentioned. She undid the padlock and opened the black-barred gate.

"Can you manage all these steps again?" she asked Signe.

"I'm not completely past it yet. Come on," said Signe.

They walked slowly up the stairs and stopped on each landing to search. Nora moved the beam of the flashlight across the floor. No cell phone on either the first or the second landing. She could have done with a second cell phone to call her own number and follow the sound. But she hadn't thought of that when she'd left home.

Off the third landing was the blind passageway. Nora tried to remember whether she had stopped there. They had definitely taken a wrong turn their first time up, but not the last time. To be on the safe side, she had a good look with the flashlight anyway.

They carried on up the last stone staircase to the top landing, which was no more than a small circle, barely two yards across. It was from there that the narrow white-painted wrought-iron staircase led up to the lantern room. Next to the staircase was the green door leading out onto the walkway.

Nora turned to Signe. “Wait here. I’ll just climb up and have a look. I don’t want you to break your leg on top of everything else, just because you were kind enough to come with me.”

The view from the lantern room was incomparable. Despite the fact that she had already admired it earlier in the day, she just couldn’t tear herself away. It was like standing on a cloud and gazing out over the sea. It had been amazingly beautiful during the day, but it was even more enchanting in the twilight. The rays of the setting sun painted the whole of the archipelago in shades of pink and yellow, and on the horizon the sky melted into the dark green sea.

For a second or two she forgot her problems with Henrik. The beauty spread out before her gave her fresh courage.

It was good to be alive, after all.

Down below she could see the old lighthouse keeper’s house, which was now the home of the curator. Beside it lay several older homes owned by the Archipelago Foundation. They were silent and dark; perhaps people had been tempted by the Friday night activities on Sandhamn.

“Have you found anything?” Signe’s voice echoed up into the lantern room.

Nora looked around. When the lighthouse on Grönskär was decommissioned in 1961, they had kept the lamp with its prisms intact in the center. Above the prisms was a lens, carefully wrapped to protect it. The lamp flashed with its faint green light.

“No, nothing,” Nora shouted back. “Not a thing.”

The sun had almost disappeared beyond Harö, and the light had dimmed even more. She moved slowly, looking for the metallic gleam of the cell phone.

"Hang on. I'll pass you the flashlight," shouted Signe. She passed it up through the narrow opening. She could only just reach.

Nora swept the beam of light around the lantern room. Once to the right, once to the left. She almost felt like an old lighthouse keeper. She swung the beam around once more. Then she gave up. There was no cell phone in here. She started to climb back down. "I think we're going to have to give up. It could be anywhere. I'll have to come back tomorrow and look for it in the daylight. That's all there is to it." She cursed her own carelessness.

When she got down, she stopped in front of the door to the walkway. "It's so beautiful here. You could almost believe that God lives out there, in the space between the sea and the horizon." She turned to Signe again. "Don't the fishing rights for these waters belong to the Brand family?"

Signe nodded. "Yes, almost everything you can see out there is ours. I often go fishing, as you know. Have to put food on the table," she added with a wry smile. She shook her head as she leaned against the handrail where the steps began. "But there are an awful lot of people fishing illegally these days. There are plenty who don't pay any heed to fishing rights."

Nora looked at her in surprise. "I'm sorry to hear that. But do you think they're from Sandhamn?"

"I know exactly who they are. And which families." Signe tossed her head. "After all these years, you can be sure I know exactly who likes to stick their fingers in somebody else's pie." She went on with resentment in her voice. "Take that poor Jonny Almhult, for example. I don't wish to speak ill of the dead, but both father and son in that family fished illegally in my waters without the slightest hint of embarrassment. I caught those two many times."

"How do you know it was them? Did you ever catch them red-handed?"

"I don't need to when they're too idle to take out their needles when they've been repairing the nets. I've taken Georg Almhult's fishing nets more than once."

"Taken?"

"Didn't you know? If someone fishes in your waters without permission, you have the right to claim their nets. That's the way it's been for many years."

"Like a kind of fine?"

"Yes, exactly. You could definitely call it that."

"That's why you had nets in your boathouse that were marked with initials other than your own," Nora said.

Signe frowned. "How did you know that?"

"I saw them when I went into your boathouse yesterday to borrow your perch nets." She stood by the door to the platform, thinking. Then she looked at Signe. "Why haven't you told Thomas that you had fishing nets belonging to the Almhults? I'm sure the police would have been interested. The net that Berggren man was tangled up in was marked with the initials *GA*."

Signe opened her mouth as if to say something but closed it again.

In the distance they could hear the sound of the gulls screaming, but inside the lighthouse there was complete silence.

Suddenly, Nora understood. "It wasn't the Almhults' net that Krister Berggren was tangled up in when he died. It was yours," she said, half to herself. "It was a net you'd taken when Jonny and his father were fishing illegally."

Signe looked away. Then she nodded. "That's exactly how it was."

"But why haven't you told Thomas? It's important for the investigation. We must call him as soon as we get back and explain what happened."

Signe didn't reply.

Nora tried to tone down the seriousness in her words. "I mean, it was an accident. You had nothing to do with his death, right? Nobody can blame you for the fact that he got tangled in your net. You do understand that?"

Signe stood rigidly by the steps, not saying a word.

"Signe?" Nora said tentatively.

The question echoed around the lighthouse.

Chapter 72

The silence grew, sweeping over Nora and Signe. A terrible silence, paralyzing both of them.

In Signe's ashen face Nora saw a truth she could not accept. The shock made her back away toward the wall and sink down on the steps in front of the door leading to the walkway.

She could hardly force the words out. "But it was an accident, wasn't it, Auntie Signe?" In her confusion she used the familiar form of address from her childhood.

Signe shook her head without speaking. Her face was set in an inscrutable mask; only her thin lips moved. After a moment her expressionless voice sliced through the air like a knife. "Krister Berggren drowned because of me."

"But why? What had he done to you? You didn't even know him, did you?"

Signe's expression was implacable. "Krister Berggren was Helge's illegitimate son."

"So you were related? You killed your nephew?"

Signe nodded. "But he didn't know anything about our family connections until his mother died. Then he decided to come looking for me, demanding the Brand house as his inheritance." Signe's voice had a harshness that Nora had never heard before. It sounded as if she were talking about someone else altogether, rather than herself.

Nora had begun to shiver violently. She felt nauseous. She wished this were a nightmare and that she would wake up soon.

"I would have had to leave my home, Nora. He would have forced me to sell so I could pay him. I would never have been able to afford to buy him out." She clenched her fists in fury. "I hadn't planned to kill him. But it was the only solution. If he died, everything could just go back to normal." Signe paused for a moment, closing her eyes as if she were trying to erase something from her mind. "At least that's what I thought." She took a deep breath and carried on, her words betraying a kind of relief at being able to talk about what had happened. "Then his body washed ashore. I realized right away that it was him. I didn't know what to do."

Nora hid her face in her hands. She hardly dared ask the next question. "What happened to his cousin? That woman they found in the Mission House?"

Signe folded her arms, her hands clenching and unclenching. "That terrible woman. She just turned up out of the blue, claiming to be Krister's cousin. His only relative and heir. She demanded her share of his inheritance."

Nora was finding it difficult to breathe. "So you killed her, too?"

Signe turned away. "I couldn't let her take my home. It was their own fault. Both of them. If they'd only stayed away from Sandhamn, none of this would have been necessary." Her voice was shaking with rage. "Who did they think they were? What right did they have to come here and destroy my life?"

Nora didn't know what to say. Her tongue felt like a numb mass inside her mouth, incapable of forming anything intelligible. "And Jonny Almhult?" The words were no more than a whisper, lost syllables creeping out into the narrow tower, which by now was in near darkness.

Signe shook her head. "I had nothing to do with Jonny's death. I have no idea what happened to him. I swear."

Nora didn't know what to think. Had her Signe killed two people? Auntie Signe, whom she had known since she was a little girl? Her extra grandmother.

Signe had turned and started down the steps. "It's getting dark. I don't suppose you've got any lights on that little boat of yours?" she said.

Nora shook her head, incapable of speech. She was so cold that her teeth were chattering. After a couple of minutes she forced herself to get to her feet and cautiously began to make her way down the worn stone steps. Signe had already reached the second landing.

Nora passed the blind passageway. She was moving slowly so as not to slip. She could hardly see a thing, and the little flashlight wasn't much use.

Then she heard a door close at the bottom of the steps.

"Signe, are you there?" she called out into the darkness, increasing her speed.

Suddenly she stumbled and fell down the last few steps. She was unable to save herself in the blackness and landed headfirst on the hard stone floor with a sickening thud. She was vaguely aware of Signe's muffled voice through the door.

"I'm so sorry, Nora, but there's something I have to do. I'll make sure someone comes to find you tomorrow."

Nora sank down into the darkness. The last thing she heard was the echo of Signe's footsteps disappearing into the night.

Chapter 73

When Nora regained consciousness she was enveloped in pitch darkness. She wondered how long she had been out; she had no way of telling whether it was minutes or hours.

She sensed where the door was and made an effort to get up. She felt dizzy and nauseous. She got to her knees and managed to crawl to the door. She tried to open it, but it wouldn't move.

She was locked inside the lighthouse.

Tears came to her eyes, and she bit her lip hard.

Don't cry, she told herself. *Don't cry.* She had to think clearly. How was she going to get out of here?

The nausea made its presence felt again, but she somehow managed to suppress the urge to vomit. Her entire body was shaking, but she couldn't decide whether it was because of the fall or because her blood sugar was dropping.

The numbness in her lips and tongue suggested the latter, as did the trembling. It was a sure sign of hypoglycemia—dangerously low blood sugar. Desperately she searched her memory: when had she taken her insulin? It must have been around quarter to nine in the evening, and she had taken a higher dose. This was perfectly reasonable if the insulin was then matched by a substantial intake of food. But now the insulin could not be used to break down the sugar in a sudden influx of carbohydrates. Instead, it would consume the sugars already in the body, sugars that had already been used much more quickly than usual in climbing all those steps in the lighthouse. If she didn't take in more sugar soon, her brain would suffer from an excess of lactic acid. Without sugar, she would quickly fall into a coma.

The next stage was death.

Nora was all too well aware of what would happen. First came the trembling and a sense of weakness, then sweating, racing heart, shaking, and blurred vision. She would have difficulty concentrating. As her body's blood sugar level dropped, she would feel drowsy, then sleepy, and then she would lose consciousness. She would fall into a coma, which would lead to death. In a short time her body would give up the struggle.

It probably wouldn't be an unpleasant death, Nora thought. But she didn't want to die. Not now, not like this. Alone and locked in on Grönskär.

She forced herself not to think about the children; if she did she would just start crying.

She didn't have much time. If it was after midnight, she only had minutes before she lost consciousness. If only she had something to eat.

She usually had glucose tablets in her pocket, but she hadn't bothered to bring anything because she was only going to be away for a short time. She could have kicked herself. Had she done *anything* right this evening?

Where was the flashlight? She crawled around, trying to find it in the darkness. Perhaps she could use it to signal someone? Anyone who had spent a lot of time at sea knew the SOS signal by heart. Three short, three long, three short. With the help of the flashlight she would be able to let someone know where she was.

She ran her hands over the floor. At last. There it was. She pressed the button with trembling fingers.

Nothing happened.

She examined the flashlight as best she could in the darkness. The glass was broken, and she cut her finger. She brought the flashlight up to her ear and shook it to see if she could hear if the bulb was broken. It didn't sound like it was, but there was still no light.

Tears sprang to her eyes again. There must be a way to let the outside world know where she was. It occurred to her that if she could find her phone, she would be able to call for help. Perhaps she hadn't searched carefully enough the first time. What if it was somewhere inside the lighthouse after all?

She crawled along, feeling her way. Methodically, a few inches at a time.

Still no phone.

Breathless, she made her way up to the next level and crawled around the walls. Fumbled in the blind passageway, felt her way across every step with her fingers. No phone.

On all fours, she dragged herself up to the landing from which the narrow wrought-iron staircase led up to the lantern room. She opened the door to the walkway to let in some light, but it didn't help much. She sank down on the floor.

No one knew where she was.

She could no longer stop the tears. She was sobbing now; she couldn't help thinking about the boys, even though that made her cry even harder.

How could she have been so careless?

Why had she dropped her phone? Why had she let Signe come with her? Why hadn't she told anyone where she was going?

She curled up in the fetal position on the hard stone floor. She could hear nothing but her own terrified, irregular breathing.

She tried to use her arms and upper body to induce a sense of calm so she could think, but her thoughts simply ran away with her.

She could see herself lying dead on the floor, abandoned and forgotten.

She was so frightened.

The darkness seemed to be even more dense now. The lighthouses at Svängen and Revengegrundet had begun to flash at regular intervals.

Like a heartbeat.

Chapter 74

Nora looked at her watch. It was difficult to make out the time in the darkness; it seemed to be after midnight, but it was hard to say.

She tried to calm her breathing to prevent the panic from bubbling up. Forced herself not to give in to her shaking body. She was the only person who could do anything about this situation. She had to pull herself together; there was no other way.

She decided to go up to the lantern room—she would have the best overview from there. Perhaps someone had come back to the island and might be able to help her. She peered out into the darkness, looking for any signs of life in the houses below.

Nothing. Not a soul in sight.

Why was no one at home this evening? It was so unfair.

She tried to judge the distance from the walkway to the ground. Could she jump? It must be at least sixty feet. She would probably kill herself on the rocks if she tried.

It must be possible to signal somehow. There had to be someone out there who would pick up a signal. Nora went through her pockets again. In the first she found only a pair of gloves, in the second a wrapper, a five-kronor piece, lip balm, and a box of matches.

Matches.

Could she set fire to something, then use it as a distress signal?

Her arms and legs were beginning to feel heavy; yet another sign that there was too much insulin in her body. She tried to ignore the feeling and concentrate on the task at hand.

The light from the lamp in the lantern room was a relief. It was ghostly, but somehow it made her feel more secure. It was a reminder of life. The prisms of light shone in the green glow as Nora looked at the piece of material wrapped around the lens.

Linen would burn, and it would burn quickly. She tried to remember what she had seen in the rest of the lighthouse earlier in the day. Hadn't the doors on the landings been held open with wooden wedges? And hadn't there been piles of wood shavings next to them?

She climbed back down and felt her way along the bottom of the door. Her fingers found the wedge holding it open. Underneath the iron steps she found several bits of wood and some shavings. She gathered everything into a pile and went down to the next level, where she found another small wedge, along with more sawdust and some sticks. Cautiously, she edged over to the blind passageway opposite her treasure trove. Bingo! She discovered a whole plank about a foot long as far as she could tell in the darkness. That would burn for a decent amount of time.

But it was getting harder to fight the exhaustion, to keep her mind clear, and her limbs were getting heavier and heavier. Cold sweat was trickling down the back of her neck.

She tucked the bits of wood and shavings into her jacket and carried them up to the lantern room. Carefully she arranged them in a pile around the piece of linen, which would be best on the inside. She heaped the shavings on top. The green lamp flashed every ten seconds, giving her just enough light to see what she was doing.

She managed to get the pile in the right place on top of the light prisms. She checked that the small air vent down in the corner was open.

The fear of dying from smoke inhalation had already been superseded by the realization that she was on the point of hypoglycemic shock.

She was finding it harder to focus and had to keep blinking to see clearly. She knew she would have to make her way down from the lantern room as soon as her makeshift bonfire began to burn; she had to get as far away from the fire as possible.

With shaking fingers she struck a match. In the glow of its flame she could see her own reflection in the glass wall. Eyes wide open, terrified. Her face was tense and gray.

Was this what you looked like when you were about to die?

She brought the match to the linen, but nothing happened. She struck another match. And another. Still nothing.

In despair she struck three matches at once and held them right up against the fabric. At first it looked as if they too were going to burn out, but suddenly the fabric glowed red and burst into flames.

Nora breathed out. She couldn't suppress a sob of relief. The fire had really caught hold. One of the pieces of wood began to burn, and the orange flames spread.

Feeling dizzy, she backed away and edged down the steps. Every movement was torture. She felt as if her body were full of lead. She clutched the rail with both hands so she wouldn't lose her balance.

"Don't go to sleep," she said to herself like a mantra. "Don't go to sleep, for God's sake. Stay awake."

She crawled backward down to the last landing, where Signe had locked the door from the other side. The acrid smell of smoke followed her.

She was so tired. All she wanted was to lie down and close her eyes. For a second she thought about the air vent in the lantern room, hoping that it would let in enough oxygen so she wouldn't be suffocated by the smoke. Then she just didn't have the strength to think about it anymore.

With one final effort she crawled over to the locked door, as far away from the fire as possible.

SATURDAY, THE FOURTH WEEK

CHAPTER 75

Thomas's cell phone was ringing. It was 12:43.

"Hello," he said sleepily.

"It's Henrik."

Thomas sat up in bed. His instinct as a police officer kicked in immediately. Henrik would never call him in the middle of the night without a reason. "What's happened?"

There was a brief pause, then Henrik spoke. "I know it's late, but I just got back from the twenty-four-hour race. Nora isn't here. Her bed hasn't been slept in. There's no note in the kitchen. She's just disappeared."

"Did you have a fight?" The question was automatic, before Thomas could stop himself. He knew that the atmosphere in the Linde family hadn't been great over the last week or so. Nora hadn't gone into details, but he had realized that her job prospect in Malmö hadn't been met with enthusiasm.

"You don't understand." There was no mistaking the impatience in Henrik's voice. "We had a fight before I left for the race, but this isn't like her. Nora would never just disappear. In view of everything that's happened lately, I'm not prepared to take any risks. This is serious."

Thomas didn't push it. "Have you tried calling her?"

"Of course I've tried that, but it just goes to voice mail. It rings several times first, though, so it's not switched off."

Thomas could feel a heavy lump in his stomach. Henrik was absolutely right. This wasn't like Nora. She was a lawyer who liked to keep everything in order; she always kept in touch. "Might she have gone to the bar or the restaurant at the Yacht Club? Have you spoken to her parents?"

"Yes. They were already asleep when I got back. According to Susanne, the boys are staying over with them tonight and going out with their grandfather to lay nets first thing in the morning. Nora said she was tired and going to have an early night with her book."

"Are you absolutely certain she's not just having a glass of wine with one of the neighbors?"

"At this time of night? Nora's useless when it comes to staying up late—you know that. She's always out of it by midnight. Something must have happened." The irritation in Henrik's voice had turned into fear.

Thomas started to pull on a pair of jeans as he talked to Henrik. His entire body was tense. "Is the launch still there?"

"I've checked, and she's still moored at the jetty."

Thomas was already on his way. "I'll come right over. I'll use the Buster; it'll only take fifteen minutes. Just check the Divers Bar and the club to be on the safe side. If we're lucky, she might be sitting there with a glass of red wine."

Thomas grabbed a sweater and ran down to the jetty. He was glad he had decided to buy a decent motorboat last summer. His Buster Magnum was solid and reliable, and she could easily do thirty-five knots when necessary.

Like now.

He quickly cast off and sped away. After just a few minutes he could see the lights of Sandhamn. The gnawing fear in his belly was spreading. As a police officer he had learned to trust his instincts, and this didn't feel right.

If it had been anyone else, he might have thought it involved a little fling while Henrik was away, but in Nora's case that was out of the question. She was far too faithful, and of course she knew that Henrik would be back during the night.

The Linde family's jetty appeared in the darkness. He slowed down and pulled in. With practiced fingers he tied up the boat, then strode up toward the house.

Henrik met him at the gate. "Come in," he said. "I want to show you something."

They went into the kitchen. The table was neatly laid for one, with a plate of chicken in the middle. It looked as if it had been there for quite some time.

"Does this look as if she was planning to spend the evening somewhere else?"

Thomas shook his head.

"There's something else." Henrik pointed to a used pen needle. "This means she took her insulin. She always takes her insulin just before eating. You have to do that if you're diabetic. Otherwise, the body can't process the sugars and carbohydrates ingested during the meal."

"But she's taken her insulin." Thomas didn't understand what Henrik was getting at.

Henrik picked up the plate. "Yes, but she hasn't eaten. This hasn't been touched. And there's a bar of chocolate here, too. Nora loves dark chocolate. But she hasn't eaten it."

Thomas still didn't get it. "So what?"

Henrik glanced at him impatiently. Slowly, as if he were addressing a child, he explained, "A diabetic who has taken her insulin must also eat. Very soon. Otherwise, she's at risk of hypoglycemic shock. She could end up in a coma." He paused and swallowed hard. "If you take too much insulin without eating, you lose consciousness and die. In the best-case scenario you just end up with brain damage. Now do you understand what I'm saying?"

The color drained from Thomas's face as he realized how serious this was.

Henrik sank down onto a chair and buried his head in his hands. "Where the hell can she be?"

"How long have we got?" Thomas asked, his brain analyzing the situation.

"That depends on when she took the insulin. After a few hours there could be permanent damage, even if she's found alive."

Thomas felt the beads of sweat break out on his upper lip. "Go back to her parents'; they might have some idea where she could be. Try the neighbors, and ask if anyone has seen her."

He suddenly thought about the letter they had found in Krister Berggren's apartment.

The missing link they had been searching for all along.

He turned to Henrik. "Signe Brand might be mixed up in this. I'll go over there."

Thomas ran the short distance to the imposing house next door. The Brand residence looked desolate and lonely. The whole of Kvarnberget was deserted at this time of night. The young people who came to Sandhamn to work for the summer liked to go there on fine evenings on the weekend, but now it was silent and empty.

He banged on the door. There was no movement inside the house. The external lights were switched off. He banged again.

"Signe," he shouted. "Signe, it's me, Thomas. Open the door, please."

No response.

Thomas stared at the dark windows, unsure of what to do. Then he ran around the back of the house, which faced the sea. Sometimes the greenhouse door was open; he might be able to get in that way.

But the door was locked, the glass room in darkness.

He could see a silhouette through the window; it looked as if someone was sitting on the wicker chair. Thomas knocked again. No reaction. He thought he could see Kajsa lying on the floor beside the chair, but she didn't move.

He hesitated; breaking and entering wasn't exactly recommended within the police force. But this was an emergency.

He pulled his sleeve down over his fist and smashed a pane of glass, then pushed his hand through and opened the door.

Signe was leaning back in the chair, deeply unconscious. Her face looked peaceful, almost as if she were relieved about something. A well-used blanket lay across her knees.

Thomas had always thought of Signe as constant, timeless. It seemed to him that she looked exactly the same as she had when he was a little boy and got to know her through Nora's family. But now she seemed thin, transparent.

An old woman.

A lonely woman.

Kajsa lay by her side, her front paws crossed. Her tail had come to rest forming a semicircle. She wasn't breathing. The black coat was completely still.

Thomas bent down and felt Signe's neck. A faint pulse, almost imperceptible. Her breathing was shallow.

He grabbed his phone and quickly called Carina.

"It's Thomas. I know it's the middle of the night."

He waved an agitated hand in response to Carina's sleepy objections.

"Listen carefully. I've found Signe Brand unconscious in her house on Sandhamn. I can't determine the cause. You need to send a helicopter to pick her up and get the team over here. Nora Linde has disappeared. Put out a call right away, and call me as soon as you hear anything."

He ended the call and ran across to Nora's parents'. They were standing in the hallway with Henrik.

"Henrik, can you go over to Signe Brand's house? She's in the greenhouse, unconscious. I've sent for the air ambulance."

Nora's mother looked at him. "What's going on, Thomas?" she asked anxiously. "What's happened to Nora?"

"I don't know, Susanne," he said. "Stay with the boys. We'll keep looking for her. Don't worry. I'm sure we'll find her soon."

Thomas wished he were as confident as he sounded.

CHAPTER 76

The man in the recently purchased Arcona 36 was whistling as he adjusted the mainsail. For many years he had dreamed of having a decent yacht, and now he relished every second he spent at sea. As he leaned back in the cockpit he had to stop himself from reaching forward and patting the tiller.

He had always preferred a tiller to a wheel in a yacht. It provided a much better sense of the movement of the boat in the water. With a firm grip on the tiller he could cope with both wind and waves while holding a steady course.

Sailing was almost better than sex, he thought.

Well, not far off.

When he had suggested to his wife that they should sail overnight from Horsten to Runmarö, she had thought he was crazy. She had shaken her head at the very idea.

"You must be crazy. Why on earth would anyone want to go sailing at night? What if we hit another boat?"

But after a while she had given in; she had said she didn't have the strength to argue with him any longer. She was curled up on a cushion in the cockpit clutching a mug of tea as they sailed past skerries and islets.

"This wasn't such a bad idea, was it?" the man said with a smile.

His wife smiled back. "No. It's lovely."

The man adjusted the tiller again.

There was a gentle downwind breeze, just enough to maintain a steady speed. The Arcona was easy to sail, effortlessly cleaving through the surface of the water. The big genoa jib caught the breeze and exploited it to the full.

"Can you pass me the chart?" the man said to his wife. "We should be pretty close to Revengegrundet."

His wife put down her tea and passed the chart to her husband, who switched on his flashlight and studied the chart for a minute or so before handing it back.

"Just as I thought. We're exactly where we should be." He pointed without losing concentration or letting go of the tiller. "If you look over there, you can see the old lighthouse on Grönskär. It was built in the eighteenth century . . . or was it the nineteenth?" He frowned as he pondered.

"You mean the one that's known as the Queen of the Baltic?"

"That's it."

His wife turned her head and looked at the imposing lighthouse, stretching her neck to get a better view. "There's a very bright light. I thought it wasn't used anymore."

"It isn't. I think it was decommissioned in the sixties."

The woman left her comfortable seat and pushed back the cabin hatch. She stuck her head in and grabbed a pair of binoculars hanging from a hook just to the left of the steps. She sat down again and took them out of their case. "Actually, it looks like there's a fire in the lighthouse."

Her husband laughed. "What? You're seeing things!"

"You have a look, then!"

She handed over the binoculars. Her husband took them with one hand, keeping the other on the tiller. He brought them up to his eyes and let out a whistle.

"Holy shit, you're right. It's on fire!"

"That's what I said! You never believe anything I say."

"We need to inform the coast guard," the man said, looking through the binoculars again just to make sure.

"Can't we just call the usual emergency number?"

The man gave his wife a haughty look. "We're at sea, darling. When you're at sea, you contact the coast guard."

His wife glared at him but didn't say anything.

He waved her over. "You need to hold the tiller while I radio through."

They changed places, and the man quickly went downstairs. He switched on the VHF radio and found the correct channel. The rushing sound of radio waves immediately filled the boat. The man unhooked the microphone and held it close to his mouth.

"Stockholm Radio, Stockholm Radio, Stockholm Radio, this is S/Y *Svanen* calling."

He repeated the call a couple of times, then there was a crackling sound, and he suddenly heard a woman's voice.

"S/Y *Svanen*, S/Y *Svanen*, S/Y *Svanen*, this is Stockholm Radio responding to your call."

"We are just off Grönskär northeast of Sandhamn. I want to report a fire. It looks as if there's a fire in the lighthouse, up in the tower."

"S/Y Svanen, please repeat. I can't hear you clearly."

"I said there's a fire in Grönskär lighthouse. I repeat, there's a fire in Grönskär lighthouse."

He made an effort to speak clearly.

"S/Y *Svanen*, are you sure?" The woman sounded perplexed, as if she didn't quite know what to do with the information.

"Yes, I'm sure. We've looked through binoculars, and I can see flames up in the tower."

"Did you see any people?"

"No. The place looks deserted. The only thing I could see was the flames."

The voice on the other end fell silent for a couple of seconds as the rushing sound grew louder. Then she came over the ether once more: "S/Y *Svanen*, thank you for the information. We will investigate immediately. Thank you for your help."

The man smiled, satisfied that he had done his civic duty. "S/Y *Svanen* over and out."

He switched off the radio and replaced the microphone. He climbed back into the cockpit and looked over toward Grönskär again. The flames looked smaller now, but perhaps it was his imagination. They had sailed some distance while he was reporting the fire, and Grönskär now lay behind them.

He shrugged. There wasn't much he could do under the circumstances. Either the fire would die out, or the lighthouse would burn down. But it had stood there for almost three hundred years, so it must be pretty resilient.

Chapter 77

Henrik was sick with worry. As a doctor he knew exactly what would happen if Nora had taken her insulin and not eaten. He tried to convince himself that she must have eaten enough to be safe, wherever she was. But why wasn't she at home? And why was the food on the table untouched?

He reproached himself for the arguments of the past few days. Twenty-four hours at sea hadn't changed his opinion—he had still been angry when he came ashore—but he had decided to ignore the issue. He had already made his feelings clear, end of story. He just didn't understand why women needed to talk things through all the time. Much better to get to the point as quickly as possible, make a decision, then stick to it.

Now he bitterly regretted his uncompromising attitude.

He pictured Nora's face on the day Adam was born. She had been so proud. Completely exhausted, of course, but indescribably happy. Her hair had been plastered to her forehead with sweat, as if she'd run a marathon. Which of course she had, in a way. She held her newborn son close, beaming with joy and triumph. "Isn't he wonderful?" she had said. "Isn't he amazing? Our son."

There was a strange taste in Henrik's mouth, a mixture of acidity and something metallic. At first he couldn't identify it, but then he realized what it was. He had experienced exactly the same thing when Mats, his best friend at school, fell off his bike. Mats had been unconscious for several minutes, and during that time Henrik had been more scared than he had ever been in his twelve-year-old life.

It was the taste of deep anxiety. Pure fear.

He had been to see Signe and had concluded that there was nothing he could do for her; they were waiting for the air ambulance to take her to the hospital.

Now he was with Nora's parents. Thomas had also returned. Henrik shook his head in despair. "No one's seen Nora. It's as if she's gone up in smoke."

The shrill ringtone of Thomas's phone made them both jump. Thomas's voice was barely recognizable as he answered with a roar. "Hello!"

"It's Carina."

"What's happened?"

"I've spoken to the coast guard and Stockholm Radio. Neither of them had anything in particular to report, apart from the usual weekend drunks. But Stockholm Radio did say that a sailor called in and said there was a fire in the old lighthouse on Grönskär. They've tried to contact the curator for confirmation, but he was on another island. He's on his way over to see if anything's happened. I don't know if it's important, but you did say I should call about the least thing, and Grönskär isn't far from Sandhamn."

Thomas looked at Henrik. "There's a fire in Grönskär lighthouse. Could she be there?" He called out to Nora's parents, "There's a fire in Grönskär lighthouse. Could it have anything to do with Nora?"

Her father looked horrified. "We were there today, on an excursion with the Friends of Sandhamn."

Susanne appeared in the doorway, her arms wrapped around her body. Her face was ashen. "But what would she be doing over there? At this time of night?"

"Shit." Thomas suddenly realized he had missed something when he was in Signe's house. There had been a life jacket on the floor when he'd walked in through the greenhouse. It didn't belong there and was completely out of character for Signe Brand, who was always so tidy. But if she had just been out in a boat, that might explain it.

And the fact that Nora's boat was still moored by the jetty.

"I think she's on Grönskär," Thomas said. "We'll take the Buster."

Chapter 78

Henrik and Thomas raced down to the jetty. Henrik hardly had time to cast off before Thomas revved the engine. He blessed his years with the maritime police, where he had learned to handle boats at high speed and in difficult nighttime conditions.

But he still didn't see the rigid inflatable boat—commonly called a RIB—before it was almost upon him.

It came hurtling through the sound as if it had been fired from a cannon; it had no lights and was ignoring the speed limit of five knots. It must have been doing forty knots, maybe more.

It raced across the surface of the water, a miracle of speed that wasn't remotely under the control of its young, intoxicated driver.

Loud rock music pulsated from the speakers, but Thomas barely had time to register the noise before they were on the point of colliding. He did, however, see the driver's terrified face and could hear the sound of young girls' laughter, which quickly turned into hysterical screams. They were so close that he could smell rubber from the other boat.

Thomas gripped the wheel so hard that his fingers hurt. He tried to avoid the RIB by veering sharply to the left, as hard as possible. The sudden maneuver caused the Buster to list heavily, and water splashed in over the port side. And still it seemed as if the RIB was heading inexorably toward them. He realized in despair that there was no escape; time had run out.

With only inches to spare, they avoided a direct collision, but the other boat was so close that it touched the Buster's hull. The petrified driver, who had been trying to move to starboard, lost control. The impact made the prow jerk sideways, and the speed at which the RIB was traveling increased the effect. The engine let out a high-pitched roar, and the RIB was standing on its right-hand side above the dark water. For a moment it balanced there as the occupants desperately tried to hang on, but then gravity took over and the boat tipped over with a dull, heavy thud. The passengers were hurled into the sea as the hull came crashing down in a cascade of water.

"Where the hell did that come from?" Henrik yelled. The sudden changes of direction had thrown him down on the deck; he had managed to grab ahold of a cleat and clung on for dear life.

Thomas had great difficulty in steering the Buster, which listed heavily once again. When he had regained control he swung around and went back to the RIB, which was floating upside down surrounded by screaming teenagers.

"Are you OK?" he shouted to Henrik, who was hauling himself upright.

"Black and blue, but I'm on my feet."

Thomas tried to peer through the darkness as he headed for the capsized RIB. "Can you see anything?" he asked Henrik.

Henrik leaned over the rail. "I can see seven, no, eight or nine people in the water, I think. Could be more."

"We need help," Thomas said, painfully conscious of how vital it was to find Nora. But they couldn't just leave the teenagers to their fate. He took out his phone and called Peter Lagerlöf, one of his best friends in the maritime police. Thomas sent up a silent prayer that Peter would be on duty. And that his boat was somewhere near Sandhamn. With a limited number of boats at their disposal, there was no guarantee that the maritime police would be able to help immediately.

He was in luck.

The police launch was just off Korsö, only minutes away. Peter would inform the coast guard so Thomas could devote himself to the immediate situation.

Thomas carefully maneuvered the Buster toward the teenagers. Three hysterical girls were treading water as they tried to cling to the RIB. Several were screaming for help farther away. Thomas slowed down and let the engine tick over so he and Henrik could haul the shocked, soaking girls on board.

"How many of you were on the RIB?" Thomas asked.

"I can't remember," one of the girls sobbed as she sank down onto the seat. The other two were stunned silent.

"How many of you were in the boat?" he tried again. "This is important; you have to try to remember."

The girl looked at him, her eyes glassy. "I don't know. There were, like, lots of us. We were just messing around."

God, he thought with a shudder. *They're just kids. Teenagers playing with grown-ups' toys. They have no idea how to control the power in a boat like that.*

Henrik leaned over the side to haul up a young boy. He grabbed the boy's arms, but just as the youngster was about to climb aboard, his friend who was next to him became hysterical.

"Me first, me first," he screamed, clinging to his friend's shoulders and pushing him under the water.

Thomas didn't dare let go of the wheel in case the boat began to drift.

"Henrik," he yelled. "Stop him—he's drowning the other kid!"

Henrik bent down and seized the boy's drenched shirt with his left hand. Then he punched him hard with his right hand.

"Calm down!" he said. "Otherwise you'll be swimming home! We'll take care of both of you."

The boy stiffened, then let go. With staring, horrified eyes, he kept still as Henrik helped the two of them on board.

In his peripheral vision Thomas could see the police launch approaching. He sighed with relief. Every minute they lost before finding Nora increased the danger she was in.

The launch was picking up several teenagers out of the water.

"Sebastian," sobbed one of the girls sitting in the Buster. "Has anyone seen Sebastian?"

"What did you say?" Henrik asked.

"Sebastian was driving the boat. I asked him to drive the boat. Where is he?"

Henrik glanced at Thomas. He shook his head, and Thomas looked around. He couldn't see anyone else in the water.

"You have to find him. It's all my fault," the girl said.

"Could he be underneath the RIB?" Henrik said quietly to Thomas.

Thomas hesitated. It wasn't impossible. If Sebastian hadn't managed to swim away he could well be there, hopefully in an air bubble. "Here, take the wheel," he said to Henrik. He pulled off his jeans and sweater and dived into the water, which was surprisingly warm given that it must be at least sixty feet deep out here. With strong, rapid strokes he swam over to the capsized RIB. Resting one hand on the hull, he tried to listen for any sounds, any indication that there might be someone underneath. Then he took a deep breath and dived under the boat.

It was pitch black and virtually impossible to see anything. He fumbled around for a few seconds before he was forced to swim back out and come up for air. When he came up for the third time, the police launch was alongside. Peter was on the foredeck with a floodlight.

"Have you got an underwater flashlight?" Thomas yelled.

Peter nodded and shouted something to one of the other officers. He lay down on his stomach and handed the flashlight to Thomas, who took another deep breath and dived once more.

By the eerie glow of the flashlight he could see the boy, trapped between the wheel and the driving seat. His hair was floating outward around his head, like seaweed swaying in the current.

Thomas tried his best to free him, but he was running out of oxygen and had to swim back up to the surface to catch his breath.

"Did you see anything?" Peter asked as Thomas reappeared, gasping.

"There's a boy under the boat," Thomas panted. "But I couldn't get him out. I'll try again."

He took several deep breaths, then went back down. Now he knew where the boy was and found his way more quickly. Suddenly Peter appeared beside him. Thomas signaled to him to take ahold of one leg and pull when he counted to three.

Using their combined strength, they managed to free him, and the other crewmembers on the police launch heaved the body on board.

"Is he still alive?" Thomas asked. Deep down he was already painfully aware of what the answer would be, but the question had to be asked.

One of the police officers looked at him sympathetically. "They don't get any deader than this," he said, gazing sadly at the young boy lying on the foredeck. "There's nothing we can do. It's too late."

Chapter 79

The sky was beginning to grow light in the east. Too many minutes were ticking by. It was giving Thomas stomach cramps. He agonized over the choice between staying to help at the scene of the accident and heading out to Grönskär. But they had to keep searching for Nora, and the maritime police, who had now been joined by the coast guard, appeared to have the situation under control.

Several other passing boats had also stopped and offered their help. No one could save the unfortunate driver, who wasn't much older than sixteen.

"Henrik, which way do you think is quickest?" Thomas shouted into the headwind. "Through the harbor and out via Korsö sound, or north of Kroksö?"

"North of Kroksö," Henrik yelled above the noise of the engine. "If you go through the harbor we might meet another idiot, and we can't afford that!"

Thomas couldn't work out whether he was crying or he just had seawater on his face. They had lost at least thirty crucial minutes.

His expression was grim as he increased his speed. He didn't know he was capable of driving so fast.

After ten minutes he saw the outline of Grönskär. The trip had felt like an eternity.

He frowned, trying to spot the fire, but he couldn't see anything. The lighthouse was standing just as it had always stood. No smoke, no flames.

Carina had said that the curator was on his way, but he couldn't see any sign of life on the barren island.

They moored the boat at the concrete jetty and made their way up to the lighthouse over the slippery rocks as quickly as they could.

There were no lights in the tower. Henrik cupped his hands around his mouth and called out Nora's name.

No reply.

Thomas stopped at the foot of the tower and shouted as loud as he could.

"Shh." Henrik tugged at his arm. "I thought I heard something."

They both stood motionless, straining to pick up the sound. They heard only the waves crashing against the rocks and the cry of a lone merganser in the distance.

Thomas had an idea. "Call her phone," he said. "If she's unconscious she won't be able to answer, but we might hear it ringing."

Henrik took out his phone and called. From a bush to the left of the door came the theme from *Mission Impossible.*

"That's her phone," Henrik said. "That's Nora's ringtone. She must be nearby!" He ran toward the lighthouse and found the phone. But the door was locked, with the padlock in place. "She might be inside. We have to get in. Have you got anything in the boat that we could use to smash the lock?"

"Only an anchor and a paddle." He looked at Henrik, his face set. "But I do have something else." He reached inside his jacket and took out his service pistol, then he took a step back. "Out of the way."

"What are you going to do?"

"Out of the way!" Thomas snapped. He had no time for explanations.

He took ahold of the pistol with both hands, removed the safety, and carefully aimed at the padlock.

The shot sounded like a clap of thunder. The sound rolled across the rocks and disappeared into the sea. The padlock fell to the ground, landing among the purple heather.

"Come on, quick!"

Thomas led the way up the steps, two at a time. It was dark inside, with the acrid stench of smoke. Henrik coughed. There was no doubt that something had been burning in here.

When they reached the first level, Thomas stopped.

The door was fastened with a sturdy hasp. Through the old-fashioned bail handle someone had taken the additional precaution of barricading the door with a large black spanner made of iron, the kind that was used in times gone by to loosen nuts as big as the palm of a hand.

It was jammed.

"Nora," Henrik shouted, hammering on the door. "Nora, are you there?"

Thomas altered his grip on the spanner, tugging at it so hard that he could taste blood in his mouth. Henrik tried to help as best he could, but it was impossible to move. The spanner was held in place against the sturdy wooden door by its own weight.

Thomas let go, his hands aching. He looked at the door, wondering if it was possible to kick it down. Probably not. It had been built to last for centuries. Like everything else in the lighthouse, it had been constructed of the finest wood, using old-fashioned expertise. It would have required the strength of a giant to break it down.

He kicked it anyway, out of pure rage.

It didn't move.

"This is no good—it's completely stuck. We're going to have to chop through it." He turned to Henrik. "See if you can find an axe or something. There are houses on the island—there might be someone at home who can help us."

Once again he tried to move the heavy iron spanner, but it wouldn't budge. The feeling of hopelessness was unbearable. He saw Emily's little body in his mind's eye, lying there motionless, her lips blue; it had been so painfully obvious that she would never breathe again. He felt equally helpless now.

He couldn't lose Nora, too. There must be something he could do.

He pulled at the spanner, his knuckles white with effort, straining the muscles that had been honed over many intense handball matches. The spanner moved a fraction but dropped back as soon as he let go. He felt as if he might explode with frustration. The smoky air brought tears to his eyes. He banged on the door again, calling out Nora's name over and over, but there was no reply.

Henrik hurtled down the lighthouse steps. When he got outside, he stopped and looked around.

To the north, less than a hundred yards away, stood the old lighthouse keepers' houses. To their left, he could see a large house made of stone, in complete darkness. Behind it there was another house, and a short distance away the old master keeper's residence painted Falu red. There were no lights showing there either.

He ran to the stone house and tugged at the door. It was locked. He tried to look in through the windows, but it was difficult to see anything in the darkness.

"Hello, wake up, wake up!" he yelled as loud as he could, banging on the door, but the only response was the echo of his own voice.

He rushed over to the master keeper's house and tried the door handle, pushing and pulling at it with all his might, but to no avail. The house was silent and deserted.

Desperately he looked around for some kind of chopping tool. The outline of Sandhamn was silhouetted against the horizon in the west. He couldn't believe he had sailed into the harbor earlier, not knowing that his life was about to fall apart.

He pictured Nora trapped in the lighthouse, surrounded by flames. He bit his lip hard to push away the image. He had to stay calm. He was an experienced doctor and had seen his fair share of terrible cases.

But they hadn't involved his own wife.

What would he say to the boys if they didn't find her? How would he live with the knowledge of what his last words to her had been?

At that moment he would have sold his soul to the devil for an axe.

Down by the old small boat harbor on the northern part of the island he could just see a number of roofs. Perhaps there might be some tools in the old boathouses?

He ran with his fists clenched, panting. Suddenly he slipped on the grass, which was wet with dew, and fell over before getting back on his feet. His elbow struck a rock. He heard the sickening sound but didn't have time to think about the pain; he just kept going.

Everything was quiet down by the water.

He tried the handle of the first door. Locked.

Shit, shit, shit.

There was a small window around the side. Henrik needed a decent-size stone; down by the water's edge he found a substantial rock covered in seaweed. He picked it up and hurled it at the window with all his strength. The sound of breaking glass was like a pistol shot in the silence of the night. He quickly reached inside and unhooked the catch so he could open the window wide and climb in.

He could see the outline of various tools; in one corner, an axe was propped against the wall. He could have wept with relief. He grabbed it and climbed out of the window.

In his haste, he cut his shin badly, a nasty gash several inches long. He automatically registered that the wound would need stitching or it would leave a scar.

With blood dripping from his left leg, he raced back up the hill toward the lighthouse. He tore open the door and hurtled up the steps to the first level, where Thomas was waiting.

"Here," he panted.

He could barely speak. His lungs were aching from the exertion, and the smoky air didn't help. He had to bend down and rest his arms on his knees to stop himself from fainting.

Thomas grabbed the handle of the axe and took a swing at the door. He struck it again and again. On the fourth blow, the handle came off. The huge spanner fell to the floor, the metallic clang echoing through the lighthouse. Thomas stepped over it and tore open the door in a single movement. Henrik saw Nora lying on the floor, curled up on her side. The air was full of smoke, and it was almost pitch dark.

Henrik fell to his knees beside his wife and checked her pulse. In a second, he had transformed from a desperate husband to a physician.

"She's in hypoglycemic shock. We need to get her to the hospital immediately."

He put his arms around her shoulders and raised her gently so her head was resting on his lap. She was unconscious.

"Call the air ambulance. We need to get glucose into her at once. It's the only way to counteract hypoglycemia; we have to inject the sugar straight into the bloodstream."

Henrik looked at Thomas with terror in his eyes.

"I don't know if we're going to make it."

***

Sandhamn, July 2005

Where shall I begin? What is done cannot be undone. But I have to explain what happened.

Krister Berggren was my nephew. He came to see me on Easter; he told me that he was my nephew, Helge's son. I didn't even know he existed. His mother had kept the identity of his father secret all those years.

When my brother, Helge, was twelve years old, he was sent to a school in Vaxholm. The distance meant he could come home only on the weekends, and in winter only if the steamboat could get through the ice. Therefore he boarded with the Berggren family in Vaxholm.

The youngest daughter in the family was called Cecilia. She was two years older than Helge, and as time went by, he fell head over heels in love with her. Their love bore fruit, and Cecilia became pregnant with Helge's child when he was sixteen and she was eighteen.

Cecilia's parents contacted Father, who was furious. He brought Helge back home to Sandhamn immediately, and then he paid Cecilia's parents a significant sum of money. In return, he demanded that the matter be kept quiet, and that the child be given up for adoption as soon as it was born.

Just before he died, Father told me the whole story. Helge, on the other hand, said nothing. We never spoke of it. I don't think he had any contact with Cecilia from the day he was put on board the boat back to Sandhamn. Perhaps he didn't even know that he had a son; shortly after he returned, he went to sea following a terrible argument with Father.

Krister had only one thing on his mind when he

came to see me: he wanted his inheritance. He looked me straight in the eye and threatened to force me to sell my house unless I bought him out. As if I had that kind of money! He had spoken to a lawyer who had assured him that the law was on his side.

I was beside myself. My home means everything to me. This is where I took my first breath and where my mother fell asleep forever. My life would be destroyed if he took it from me.

I offered Krister a bed for the night, hoping that I would be able to talk some sense into him the following day. I lay awake all night, sick with worry. There had to be a solution. How could I make Krister understand that this house wasn't just a piece of property that could be sold on a whim?

The next day, I suggested that we should go out and lay nets, just as Helge and I used to do before he fell ill. Perhaps that would have some effect on Krister, help him to understand how unreasonable he was being.

It was a beautiful day. A pale winter sun hovered just above the horizon, and the sea was calm. I took him to Ådkobb, which was Helge's favorite spot for laying nets.

As soon as I had laid the first net, I felt a sharp movement and saw silvery scales shining in the water. I called Krister to come and look, but when he leaned forward to get a better view, he put his hand on the cowl of the outboard motor to support himself. I hadn't fixed the clamps properly when the motor was pushed up. As it dropped back down, Krister lost his balance and fell into the water, straight into the net.

I reached for the nearest rope and made a loop so that he could slip it around his waist, intending to try to haul him back on board. For some reason he had refused to put on a life jacket. "They're only for women and kids," he had muttered when I offered him one.

Suddenly I noticed that the rope I had used was actually the anchor rope, with the heavy grappling hook attached to the other end. The realization came in an instant. If I didn't pull him out of the water, life would go back to normal. Nobody would be able to take my home away from me. Everything would be just as it had been before.

Without really thinking, I picked up the anchor and threw it overboard. My arms carried out the movement of their own accord. The last thing I saw was his head being dragged down into the cold, dark water.

Afterward it was as if there was a kind of white winter's mist surrounding that day. It almost felt as if it had never happened. But then Krister's body washed ashore. I knew at once that it was my nephew. I didn't know what to do. Night after night I lay awake, thinking.

And then Kicki Berggren turned up. One day she was just standing there, knocking on my door. She was a greedy woman, and she claimed that she was Krister's cousin. According to her, his death meant that she would inherit in his place. If I didn't agree to give her half the house, she would force me into it.

I heard myself offering her a cup of tea before we continued our discussion. It was as if someone else was speaking.

As I was getting the tin containing my homemade tea blend out of the pantry, I spotted the bottle of rat poison. It had been on the top shelf for years. With trembling hands, I picked it up. The red label with its skull and crossbones seemed to glow in the dim light.

Then I knew what to do. When the tea was ready, I poured it into two mugs and added a significant amount of the poisonous liquid to one of them. Then I put some homemade jam tarts on a plate and took them into the other room. After Kicki had finished her tea, I asked if she could come back the following day. In an unfamiliar, hollow voice I asked for some time to think over the situation. The same unfamiliar voice promised to give her my decision within twenty-four hours. We arranged to meet the following day at twelve o'clock. But Kicki never came back.

Helge's old medication is standing here beside me on the kitchen table as I write this letter. It's morphine; I got it from the hospital when he was dying. Now it is needed one last time.

Kajsa is rubbing around my legs, whimpering uneasily. She's a clever girl; she knows that something is wrong. She is looking at me with such a pleading expression that I can hardly go on writing. But Nora is locked inside Grönskär lighthouse and must be rescued as soon as possible. We were there together this evening, and she knows what I have done. I couldn't risk her stopping me from doing what I must do, so I had to lock her in. I don't know how I managed it, but somehow I found the strength to jam the door with the big, heavy spanner I found in the corner. Then I took her boat and came back.

Tell Nora that I really am very sorry I locked her in.

A few final words: This is my own decision. No one has the right to take my home away from me. This is where I was born, and this is where I will die.

Signe Brand

With a little sigh Signe put the pen down. She folded up the letter, placed it in an envelope, and propped it up against a candlestick on the kitchen table. Then she took another piece of paper, scribbled down a few lines, and slipped it in an envelope. Slowly she got to her feet, crossed the kitchen, and got out a box of matches.

"Come along, Kajsa," she said, patting the dog on the head.

She picked up the kerosene lamp from the kitchen table, the lamp that Grandfather Alarik had bought in Stockholm, to the delight of the entire family. She had been just a little girl at the time, but she still remembered how beautiful the lamp had been when Grandfather had brought it home.

Carefully, she lit the wick and adjusted it so that the lamp spread a warm glow all around.

With the lamp in one hand and the morphine in the other, she went out into the greenhouse. With practiced movements she prepared two syringes of morphine; her experience of looking after Helge during his illness had not gone to waste.

Kajsa had settled down at her feet, on her favorite rug.

As she injected the dog, the tears poured down her wrinkled cheeks. She stroked Kajsa's soft, velvety fur and tried to hold back the sobs. Kajsa whimpered but didn't move; she made no protest as Signe injected the morphine.

Signe sat motionless with Kajsa's head resting on her knee until the dog stopped breathing.

Then she tipped out a handful of tablets and swallowed them with some water. She picked up the other syringe and emptied it into her left arm. She wrapped a blanket around herself, one that she had crocheted many years ago. She was a little bit cold, but it didn't really matter anymore. Her final action was to turn off the kerosene lamp.

She could just about make out the horizon and the familiar outline of the islands in the night. She closed her eyes and leaned back in her chair for the last time.

SUNDAY,
THE SIXTH WEEK

Chapter 80

The August moon rose behind the trees on Telegrafholmen, round and dark yellow, so close that you could almost touch it. The children had fallen asleep in their beds without too much fuss for once. Henrik and Nora were sitting down by the jetty.

There was just the hint of a chill in the air.

Nora shivered. She didn't know whether it was the coolness of the evening or the events of the past few weeks. There were a lot of things she didn't have answers for at the moment.

She kept turning her teacup around in her hands as she gazed at the sea mist where the sun had just gone down.

There was an immense distance between her and Henrik.

Nora could feel herself retreating into her shell, but she had no need for closeness. Her grief and shock over Signe's death were almost tangible. She still felt frozen and exhausted after her ordeal, but she had refused to stay in the hospital any longer than absolutely necessary. All she had wanted was to get back to Sandhamn and her children.

She had sat there with the boys on her knee for a long, long time.

The doctors at the hospital had said that her guardian angel must have been watching over her. One more hour and she probably wouldn't have survived, at least not without permanent brain damage. Thomas and Henrik had found her at the last possible minute.

Signe Brand hadn't been so lucky. She had slipped away not long after she had been admitted to the hospital.

When the police searched Signe's house, they found two letters on the kitchen table. One contained an account of what had happened. The other was Signe's will. Thomas had entered the house through the greenhouse, so he hadn't seen the letters.

Signe had assumed that someone would find Nora the following day. She'd had no idea that a night spent in the lighthouse would lead to hypoglycemia, thus endangering Nora's life.

Thomas had come by the previous day to tell them that a witness who had spoken to Jonny on the ferry to Finland had been in touch with the police.

Nora had been sitting down by the jetty, just like this evening, and Thomas had sat down opposite her. Thin clouds hid the sun, but it wasn't cold. It was almost five o'clock in the afternoon.

The witness, a man in his fifties, had started chatting with Jonny in the bar on the ferry. According to him, Jonny had been very drunk and had been sniveling about the fact that he had run away from Sandhamn because he had had a fight with some girl. He had tried to have sex with her but couldn't perform. When she made fun of him he had lost his temper and lashed out at her.

As far as the man could make out from Jonny's disjointed tale, the blow had made the woman lose her balance, and she had hit her head on something. She had rushed off after that, but when she was later found dead, Jonny had been afraid that the police would arrest him for murder.

After a while, Jonny had gone out on deck to get some air. It wasn't unreasonable to assume that he might have wanted to catch a final glimpse of Sandhamn as the ship passed the island.

One of the CCTV cameras had picked him up as he made his way unsteadily up the steps leading to the top deck. In his befuddled state he had presumably lost his balance and fallen overboard.

It seemed that his death had been a tragic accident; at least, that was what the police were assuming.

Thomas had also told Nora what had happened when Philip Fahlén eventually regained consciousness, paralyzed down his left side. He had been in no state to deny things any longer and had immediately confessed to an extensive fraud operation with Viking Strindberg as the spider at the center of the web, ably assisted by his wife. Together they had been stealing wine and spirits from Systemet for years and had earned good money by selling it illegally.

The confession, along with the lists of phone calls and the wiretap, had been more than enough to persuade both Viking Strindberg and his wife to put their cards on the table and confess.

"It was pure bad luck for Philip Fahlén and the Strindbergs," Thomas had said. "If Krister Berggren's body hadn't been washed ashore not far from Fahlén's summer place, we probably would never have caught them."

At that moment his cell phone had rung.

When he had finished the call he had looked at Nora with an embarrassed smile. "That was Carina from the station," he said, slipping the phone into his pocket. "She's coming over for dinner this evening, so I'd better go."

For the first time in ages, Thomas looked really happy. It made Nora feel warm inside; she really wanted him to find happiness again.

***

Nora gave a little sigh and pulled her jacket more tightly around her. It was getting distinctly chilly as the evening wore on.

"Do you know what's really sad?" she said quietly to Henrik.

He looked at her curiously. He was obviously making an effort to reach her, but she couldn't bring herself to meet him halfway. When he reached out and stroked her cheek, she barely reacted.

"What?"

"They died for no reason, Kicki Berggren and Signe. And Jonny, too, of course. But Signe didn't realize. Once Krister was dead, Kicki Berggren was no threat to Signe and her home." Her eyes filled with tears, and she struggled to keep her voice steady. "The law is crystal clear. Cousins cannot inherit from one another."

Nora gazed out across the sea, filled with immeasurable sorrow. Signe was dead; she would never see her again. The thought was agonizing. *Life is so fragile,* she thought. *Why don't we realize that?*

AFTERWORD

Since I first came to Sandhamn as a newborn baby, I have always loved the island; my family has had a summer home here for a hundred years.

When I decided to try my hand at fiction after writing several factual books on legal matters, the idea of a crime novel set on Sandhamn was irresistible.

However, this book would never have been written if a significant number of kind individuals had not offered their time and expertise.

I would like to begin by warmly thanking Gunilla Pettersson; she lives on the island and has answered countless questions about Sandhamn and Grönskär.

Good friends and colleagues who have taken the time to read various versions of the novel and offered valuable opinions and support are Anette Brifalk, P. H. Börjesson, Barbro Börjeson Ahlin, Helen Duphorn, Per and Helena Lyrvall, Göran Sällqvist, and my brother, Patrik Bergstedt.

My editor Matilda Lund put a huge amount of effort into the manuscript.

Sincere thanks also to Inspector Sonny Björk; Dr. Rita Kaupila, who works in the forensics department in Solna; Inspector Jim

Näström from the maritime police in Nacka; and radiologist Dr. Kattarina Bodén.

A number of points must be made. I have taken the liberty of inventing characters who bear no resemblance whatsoever to any living individuals. I have also altered some facts: The Brand house does not exist, and there is no marzipan-green house at Västerudd. The waters off Grönskär are a protected area when it comes to fishing. Systembolaget does not have a central depot in the suburbs, and the ferries to and from Finland stop passing Sandhamn by nine o'clock in the evening. The ferry *Cinderella* did not come into service until 2006.

Finally, my wonderful daughter, Camilla, has lived with this book throughout its creation and has discussed the plot during countless walks on Sandhamn. Camilla, you are fantastic.

I would also like to thank my husband, Lennart—because you are always there for me. Without you, my dream would never have come true.

Sandhamn, September 2015
Viveca Sten

About the Author

Photo credit © 2010 Anna-Lena Ahlstršm

Swedish writer Viveca Sten has sold almost three million copies of her enormously popular Sandhamn Murders series. In 2014, her seventh novel, the hugely successful *I maktens skugga (In the Shadow of Power)*, was published in Sweden and cemented her place as one of the country's most popular authors. Her Sandhamn Murders novels continue to top the bestseller charts and have been made into a successful Swedish-language TV miniseries, which has been broadcast around the world to thirty million viewers. Sten lives in Stockholm with her husband and three children, but she prefers to spend her time visiting Sandhamn to write and vacation with her family.

About the Translator

Marlaine Delargy is based in Shropshire in the United Kingdom. She studied Swedish and German at the University of Wales, Aberystwyth, and taught German in comprehensive schools for almost twenty years. She has translated novels by authors including Åsa Larsson, Kristina Ohlsson, Helene Tursten, John Ajvide Lindqvist, Therese Bohman, Ninni Holmqvist, and Johan Theorin, with whom she won the Crime Writers' Association International Dagger for *The Darkest Room* in 2010.